Becker's Farm

Becker's Farm

A Novel

WILLIAM TIMMONS

To Floyd, Lillian, and Rachel
who made this happen.

1

THE COLD IRON RAILROAD TRACKS stretched as far into the frigid Nebraska countryside to where they disappeared into the morning fog. From the east to the west, the two bars of frozen iron seemed to have no beginning or ending. Adam Becker's shiny new 1956 Ford pickup truck with a sign painted on the door; 'Becker's Garage and Custom Well Drilling, Summerfield, Nebraska' stood parked beside the rough hewn wooden platform of the St. John, Nebraska train station where it all began on a similar morning in 1944. Adam Becker got out of the warm cab and mounted the three stairs to the station platform. A pheasant from a distant cornfield announced the beginning of the new day. The air smelled of snow flavored with wisps of cow manure from the stock pens across the tracks. A sharp light shot across the dark wooden platform as the stationmaster stepped out of the warmth of the station and approached Adam Becker.

"Good morning, Mr. Becker. Sorry to have to tell you but the train will be about an hour late this morning. Looks like it had to slow down for some snow east of here. Why don't you come on in the waiting room and I'll see if I can find an extra cup of coffee" the old man said in his thick Nebraska accent.

"Thanks Luther," Becker said, "But I like the briskness of these Nebraska mornings. It gets my blood going."

"OK Mr. Becker, But I'm going back inside. Too dang cold for the likes of me out here."

Becker smiled, pulled his coat collar up around his neck and slowly walked to the opposite end of the platform. Just then a few flakes of snow began to fall. The pink glow from the eastern horizon illuminated the fragile flakes, making them look like slowly falling embers from a distant fire.

While the rest of the world had changed drastically since 1944, not much had changed in this corner of western Nebraska. Not much had changed since Adam Becker stood on this same platform eleven years earlier as a German prisoner of war. The tall, gaunt grain elevators still stood at the east end of the station, the water tower stood toward the west end of town. The only differences were the numbers painted on the water tower by the daredevils of the town's high school graduating class. The telephone lines above the tracks were still thick with black birds hoping to spot a worm looking for a bit of early morning sunshine. The cattle pens to the south of the tracks still stood empty and still piled high with prairie tumble weeds. As the flurry of snowflakes began to fall in greater numbers, Adam Becker's mind drifted back to the first time he stood on this same platform.

* * *

It was 1944and the war had fully infested Europe and the rest of the world. Adam Becker, was in those days a captured German tank driver/mechanic by the name of Corporal Helmut Sommerfield. Sommerfield had been one of the almost 300,000 German soldiers who had been captured by the Allied forces in the European and North African theaters of war. With no adequate holding facilities in Europe, these 300,000 prisoners of war were transported to the East Coast of the United States on the same troop transport ships which took US troops to fight the Germans in Europe. From the shores of the Atlantic, the POWs were put onto trains and sent inland, far inland to prisoner of war camps where they would wait out the war. Corporal

Sommerfield had been processed into one of the large POW camps in Missouri where he and several thousand other POWs were held until they could be transferred to smaller camps in the Midwest. While this process was slow and tedious, it gave the German prisoners of war a time to readjust from the rigors of war to a system of wait, wait, and wait. It also gave them an opportunity to learn English and a bit about the American system they had fought so hard to destroy. After eighteen months in a large holding camp in the State of Missouri, Sommerfield was re-assigned to a smaller camp near St. John in the southwestern corner of the State of Nebraska. The Army's Prisoner of War Command had managed to identify those POWs who had farm experience in their homeland and were willing to assist the United States in its production of farm products. With most of America's farm boys in the military, the agriculture system was seriously weakened and desperately needed help, even from enemy prisoners of war.

At almost every stopping point during captivity, U.S. or British officers would give lengthy speeches in broken high school German, telling the men that they would not be subjected to any form of torture or inhumane treatment, if they were fully cooperative. They were read portions of the international treaties time and time again, ensuring that everything would be done to make their time of incarceration as comfortable as possible. In fact, they were told, they would be given the same living conditions as any American soldier in the US military system. The emphasis on humane treatment was so great that most of the German POWs actually believed it to be a heinous trick. Amongst themselves they determined that they would eventually be tortured and killed after the pretense of the public spectacle.

It was October 12, 1944 when the train carrying Corporal Helmut Sommerfield arrived at the St. John, Nebraska train station. Sommerfield's group of 152 new POWs were given yet another speech by yet another U.S. officer, informing them again that full cooperation was vital to their being treated as fellow human beings. As Corporal Sommerfield recalled that speech given on this same platform on a similar cold Nebraska morning eleven years ago, he remembered he and his fellow POWs standing in the cattle pens across the tracks in a gentle snow penned up like cows going to market. *How funny,* he thought. *Human beings are not supposed to be in cattle pens.*

As the snow began falling on that cold October morning in 1944, a half a dozen or so old army trucks began to arrive at the cattle pens. The truck's headlights cast their eerie beams of light through the haze of fog and snow. Men were loaded, thirty to a truck. The US soldiers guarding the German POWs seemed numb to the fact that virtually all of these men had been in combat. All of these men had been front line combatants. They had all seen live bullets and dead soldiers. Many carried scars, both physical and emotional from far away battlefields. All were honestly thankful that those horrific battlefields were in fact, far away from the tranquility of these distant cornfields. While humiliated by capture, all were thankful to be alive. For the most part, the US soldiers in this POW command had seen combat only in training camps and in the movies. For some unknown reason, the captors quietly envied the captive.

As soon as the trucks had received their load of human cargo, a senior American officer mounted his jeep like some conquering hero who had just single handedly captured this band of killers and ordered the convoy triumphantly up the main street of St. John. Stores on the main street were beginning to open. Store owners, holding brooms, watched curiously as the convoy of enemy captives moved slowly past. Children's faces peeked out of windows as the trucks groaned through the thin carpet of fresh white snow. The German soldiers felt the eyes of each person glaring at him as the convoy moved triumphantly through the small town and towards the gently rolling hills of the Nebraska country side.

Within twenty minutes, the convoy reached the main gate of the camp. A large wooden sign over the gate read:

CAMP ALEXIS, NEBRASKA

UNITED STATES ARMY
PRISONER OF WAR COMMAND
WESTERN-CENTRAL COMMAND

The camp itself was an old army air base, with large metal hangers and a slightly tilting control tower. At the north end of the main runway stood a cluster of long, low buildings. These were poor excuses for supply storage units and a motor pool. The air base had been decommissioned years earlier because a large sinkhole had developed under the main run way, causing its eventual collapse. The sinkhole was also responsible for the slightly southern tilt of the concrete control tower. The entire complex was surrounded by two twelve foot high wire fences, topped with coils of rusty barbed wire. Four guard towers, each with a shivering watch guard, stood at each corner of the complex. As the trucks groaned toward the main gate, dozens of POWs clamored to the chain link fence to await the arrival "ceremonies" for the new guys. The line of trucks stopped just short of the massive doors of a huge, empty airplane hangar. The giant metal hangar doors were permanently jammed open due to the sinkhole which had partially swallowed six sections of the concrete runway. Inside the hangar was a small wooden platform, dwarfed by an enormous American flag hanging from the rafters. As the trucks stopped, US soldiers in full battle dress, grasping M-1 rifles, quick-stepped toward the rear of each vehicle. By the waving of arms and the occasional pointing of rifles, Germans prisoners of war were off loaded from the vehicles and arranged in lines six deep and twenty abreast. An overweight sergeant screamed out orders in a bad mix of German and English which made little sense to most of the POWs. They did, however, understand when the sergeant screamed out a long and exaggerated, *"Achtung."* At that point, one of the German soldiers, a sergeant, assumed authority and began to translate the situation and bark out orders in German. The POWs stiffened and resembled once again, a military unit rather than a gang of out-of-work ruffians.

From out of the adjacent airplane hangar came a jeep with three officers. The jeep pulled up in the rear of the small dais and the officers got out. This grand entry seemed to be more for a show of superiority than a necessity. The senior officer, a man of medium build and with oak clusters on his collar, walked briskly toward the podium, carrying a swagger stick under his arm. Salutes were exchanged and the officers stepped on to the dais. An officer wearing the insignia of a captain stepped to one of the microphones, tapped them both a few times and began to speak in rather decent German.

"I am Captain J.P. Thomas, United States Army. I am the official translator at this camp. I will assist you in areas where language is a concern."

For the most part, all the new POWs were more or less fluent in Basic English and American slang. In fact, some could found with a distinct British accent.

"It is my pleasure to introduce to you, the camp commander, Major Markus Reed, United States Army."

Major Reed was recognized at once as the conquering hero who led the vanquished captives through the streets of the town. Major Reed was the text book soldier. His uniform was sharp and neat and his personal mannerisms were brisk and formal. Reed was a career soldier with a single ambition, he wanted to fight. Unfortunately, for some reason his superiors preferred him in administrative positions. Reed stepped to the second microphone and began his well rehearsed welcome speech. As he read a paragraph in English, Thomas would translate into German. Most of the men clinging to the chain-link fence behind the assembly had heard the same speech several times during their stay at camp Alexis. At one point in Major Reed's speech, his voice quieted a bit as he mentioned that the camp was named after the Russian Grand Duke Alexis who, along with Buffalo Bill Cody once hunted buffalo near this very site. As Reed spoke of Buffalo Bill, his gaze turned toward the hangar's gaping doors and beyond. POWs too turned their heads as if to catch a glimpse of a passing herd of buffalo. The speech included famous statements from famous men, all related to the horrors of war and the basic goodness of mankind. The hundred or so rules of the camp and POW life were rattled off in English and German. As the snow worsened and the time between the previous night's dinner and the lack of a breakfast lengthened, the new POWs were paying less and less attention to their new commander's speech and more to the rumblings in their stomachs. At long last, the Major thanked the men for their "kind attention" and nodded to another officer on the platform. Rather than dismissing the men, the Major then introduced the third man on the dais; Chaplain Roland. J. Wolf. The old soldier with his chest covered with ribbons from a past war, moved to the microphone, removed his hat and said in perfect German, "Shall we pray."

All the POW in the line and at the fence bowed their head as the old man began his prayer.

"Father God, We have seen our brothers killed in this terrible war. We have seen the brothers of others killed as well. In fact Dear God, we ourselves have killed the sons and brothers of those in this community. Forgive us Father and give us rest in this place. Give us a new life in your Son and a desire for peace that will abolish all future wars. These things we ask in Your Son's holy name. Amen."

All of the men at the fence shouted a loud "Amen!"

Major Thomas passed a clipboard to the Sergeant who then began reading names and barracks assignments. "Each of you will be placed in barracks with some of our longer term guests. They will teach you the ropes. As soon as you have received your bunk assignments, you will fall in for breakfast."

The new POWs moved nervously toward the gates of the compound. Those POWs inside began yelling at the new guys,

"Where are you from? Which unit were you with?"

The names of towns and cities were yelled out, with occasionally a new POW smiling and raising his hand. As the new men passed through the gates, the old-timers were on them for information about the war or about old friends lost in the conflict. The event seemed to be more of a reunion than an incarceration.

Amongst the party like atmosphere, the new POWs found their assigned huts and bunks. Aside from the fact that this was a prisoner of war camp, it appeared to be quite comfortable. A scratchy bugle call from a well worn phonograph record sounded over the many loud speakers in the camp. "Breakfast!" someone shouted. The new men followed the others out of their huts and eventually found themselves being tugged into lines in front of a long narrow building. A sign over the door read;

SERGEANT AMES GOURMET RESTURANTE.

Five stars had been painted beneath the words

Row by row, the men moved in an orderly fashion into the warmth of the dining hall.

* * *

From behind him, a voice broke into his *reverie*. He was abruptly brought back to reality by the gentle touch on his arm. The stationmaster was standing next to him with a hot cup of coffee.

"Here, I though you might like this," he said handing Adam a large paper cup of steaming coffee. "If you are going to wait out here you'll need something warm."

This simple gesture brought tears to Adam's eyes and a smile to his chapped lips.

The stationmaster reported that the train had just passed through Oxford, about forty miles down the track. He suggested that the train might be arriving in an hour so, if the snow didn't get worse.

The stationmaster returned to the warmth of the station, leaving Adam to walk slowly to the west end of the platform. With the sun now clearly present in the eastern sky, he could barely see the evermore leaning control tower of the old airbase off in the distance. As he stood there looking at the old tower, his mind again drifted back to that first morning at the Camp Alexis mess hall.

* * *

Someone handed Helmut a warm metal tray as he was goaded toward a long line of boisterous men. Servers in clean white aprons and hats began filling his tray with oatmeal, a biscuit, an orange, two strips of bacon, and a fried egg. Helmut almost broke into tears as he looked down at his tray. He had not had a breakfast like this since he left home in Germany. And this was by far better food than any of the other POW camps he had seen during his eighteen months as a POW. The flow of men toward the tables took Helmut with them. He found a space and sat. A second later, a cup of hot coffee was placed in front of him by one of the kitchen staff. All around him men were eating, talking with the new POWs and laughing. It was more like a party than a prison. The man across the table from Adam asked him, "Where are you from?" "North Africa, Rommel's tank corps" Helmut replied.

"No, where in Germany do you come from?" the man asked.

"Oh, I come from a small farm community in Bavaria. It's a very small place."

"My name is Carl; Carl Baumann. I come from Leipzig." The two shook hands across the table.

"I can tell you are impressed with our little resort here." Carl said laughingly

"It's not what I expected; not at all," Helmut said as he savored the bacon.

"We are one of the best camps in the whole prisoner of war system, or so they tell us. Our work production levels are high and we have had no escape attempts—ever!" Carl emphasized the word ever by pounding the handle of his fork into the table.

"We are told that if we do have escape attempts, our food ration will be cut back to minimal standards and our privileges will be taken away from us. So, you see my friend, we have no escape attempts."

"Anyhow," Carl said in a lighter tone, "where would you go? Two thousand kilometers to the Pacific Ocean and two thousand kilometers to the Atlantic. And if you made it to the Atlantic, what would you do, swim back to Germany—where they would send you back to the front lines and you would eventually end up back here? So, my friend, enjoy your stay at Camp Alexis." Carl laughed and so did Helmut. Carl finished stuffing the last of his biscuit into his mouth and rose with his empty tray. "See you later," he said with a broad smile.

The loud speaker broke the hum of men talking and laughing. "All camp personnel will report to the general assembly area for assignment. You have five minutes."

Men began to rush toward the door at the end of the building, dunking their empty trays into a large tub of warm rinse water before stacking them in tray carts. Forks and spoons were dropped into tubs of soapy water. The new POWs followed the old-timers down a walkway, through the main gate and to the closest airplane hangar. Helmut was beginning to feel confused and disoriented from two sleepless nights on the train. As the men entered the enormous hangar, four large speakers blared out spirited polka music. Within the hangar, the men had formed two circles, one within the other. All were running in time with the music; the inner circle going clock wise while the outer circle going counter clock wise. For fifteen minutes or so, the two groups of men ran in their concentric circles appearing to enjoy this bit of silliness. While it was cold in the hangar, the running seemed to generate sufficient body heat to cause everyone to break into a mild sweat. Another small platform had been placed at one end of the huge building and again, there were two microphones standing on the dais. Behind the platform, suspended from the hangar's beams was an enormous American flag. The music stopped, a whistle blew and the two circles quickly formed a series of lines; six deep and twenty abreast. The sergeant yelled his now familiar *"Achtung!"* and there was total silence—except for the echoes still bouncing from wall to wall like ping pong balls. Captain Thomas stepped to the microphone and barked, in perfect German, *"Guten Morgen, mein herren"* (Good morning, gentlemen). The response was a jolt to Helmut and the other new men. *"Guten Morgen, mein herr"* "Good morning, Captain Thomas!" came the response, in perfect English. Helmut was astonished at the total lack of animosity between the captives and the captors. He even surprised himself when he looked at the American flag and felt no sense of hatred or fear. He was confused. Since before the war started, he was told that the Americans were the enemy; most of whom were Jews out to take over the world. Since his capture in the sands of North Africa eighteen months ago, he had not seen anything of the reported atrocities, the mass executions, and tortures supposedly carried out in American POW camps. To multiply his sense of confusion, the old chaplain stepped to one of the microphones and began to lead the assembly of men in *A Mighty Fortress is Our God*—in German! The song, magnified by the metal skin of the hangar, could often be heard for several miles around the camp. The chaplain stepped back, giving the microphone to Major Reed.

"Once again I wish to welcome our new men to Camp Alexis. You are no doubt tired from your trip and will need a day to rest and become familiar with the camp and our procedures here. Each of you has been assigned to a group leader for an orientation. Sergeant Walther will read the new men their assignments. The rest of you will report to your regular assignment."

Sergeant Walther shouted, without benefit of a microphone, "Regulars, Fall out!" Even though the order was in English, everyone seemed to know what he said. All but the new men bolted toward several dozen army and civilian trucks waiting at the side door of the hangar. Within minutes, the trucks started their engines and roared off, each with a load of men, toward the main road.

The hangar seemed twice as large now that it contained only 130 or so men. The sounds of the metal roof, expanding in the morning sun, made Helmut feel small and alone. As Walther began reading off a list of names, men would run to the front and stand at attention. Within minutes, rows of six new POWs were lined up behind their respective orientation leaders. Each leader was then given a typed list of all new men in his group, along with a listing of rules to be discussed, places in the camp to be visited, notes related to work activities, and so on.

Again salutes were exchanged and again Sergeant Walther barked out "Diiiiismissed!"

The groups of men broke up into little circles with each group leader taking his little flock to a different part of the hangar. At once, Helmut recognized Carl from breakfast as his group leader. "I see that you have decided to stay around for awhile." The two men laughed.

Carl, a man of about thirty indicated with a gesture that the men sit down on the cold concrete floor and began with introductions. The group was made up of Rommel's Africa Corps, all tank men. While none of them knew each other, they felt a strong sense of camaraderie because of being elite desert tank fighters. Carl identified himself as a radioman within one of Rommel's supply units. After the introductions, Carl smiled and in an almost joking manner asked "Are there any Nazis here?" A cold chill flashed between each of the men. All heads shook, No! *Gut,* Carl stated with an even larger smile.

While the German military was motivated and controlled by the Nazi Party, most of the troops were not members of the Party. If anything, they were fearful and untrusting of officers and men who were members.

Carl placed his small glasses on his nose and began to read the rules of the camp. The rules of war and the various conventions and treaties had been read to the men many times during their long and tedious voyage across the Atlantic in the homeward bound US troop transport ships, along with speeches about the terrors inflicted by the nasty old German war machine on the poor people of Europe. To make matters worse, POWs were told that their convoys were being watched by German submarines and that at any minute, their own military would launch torpedoes, sending them to a watery grave.

Carl finished his list of topics and asked if there were any questions. No one wanted to speak, some because of fear and some simply because they were just too tired.

"Maybe later" Carl said. "However, there is one thing I want you all to know. We operate on the honor system at this camp. If anyone messes up, he will be reported. If someone breaks the rules and the camp commander finds out, we are all punished for that someone's screwup. We will lose little things like bacon at breakfast, extra sleep time on Sunday and many other little benefits of this camp. So, if you want to fight the system here, you will find yourself fighting those who like the system. Understood?" All heads nodded in agreement. "Good."

"Now, let's get on with a tour of our little summer camp." The men rose from the cement floor and followed Carl out of the hangar toward the main gate. As they passed through the main gate, he announced, "As you will notice, this gate is open." There are guards and dogs as required, but during the day the gates remain open. As they walked toward the gate, Carl pointed in the direction of the main road. "That's the north-south highway in this area. No one goes to the highway, understood?" Over there, pointing toward a distant water tank, is the town of St. John. "No one goes there either. Understood?" The men all nodded in agreement. "Over there, as you can see, is the main control tower. In that tower are guards with binoculars who can see everything you do. If they see anyone doing anything out of line, you will hear the word 'Halt' over all loud speakers. At that instant, you will stop whatever you are doing and stand perfectly still and face the tower. If you choose not to stop, quite possibly someone will shoot you. I strongly suggest that you stop whatever you are doing and smile sweetly at the guard in the tower. Over there, on the other side of the camp is the farm; our farm." Carl said in a prideful tone. "I will take you over there later."

They passed through the gates and past the uniformed guards. In English Carl made a few comments to the guards which brought laughter to both. This seemed to give the new men a sense that friendships between captive and captor was a possible reality.

The morning was cold and crisp. Although the wind had stopped blowing, a few snowflakes seemed to fall from nowhere. In the distance, patches of snow covered the gently rolling hills around the camp. Between the need for sleep, the chill in the air, and the realization that he was a prisoner of war, Helmut's eyes began to water. Actually he was beginning to cry. He wiped his face with the sleeve of his jacket and continued to follow Carl.

"Here we have the camp infirmary. On the rare occasions when you find yourselves ill, you will request that your barracks leader issue you a pass to come to see the doctor. Sometime this next week, you will be coming here for individual physical check-ups to see what rare and exotic bugs you have brought with you from the battlefield or from your last holding camp. The Red Cross will also perform interviews to determine location of family members back in Germany and make arrangements to notify next of kin as to your well being."

As the group of men passed the dining hall Carl continued. "We are told that we have some of the best food in the POW camp system. We have bacon and ham regularly. We have honey and sometimes jam. This is because of our farm where we raise pigs, chickens, a few cows, and some rabbits. We also have large gardens which provide us with all sorts of vegetables, squash and even melons. It was obvious that Carl's interest and pride was in the farm. "We also receive farm products as payment for our boys working with farmers in this area. This leads me to a major part of our life here in this camp. The rules of war prevent our captors from forcing us to perform slave labor, however we can choose to become part of the volunteer labor system in this area. Because most of the able bodied men in this area are in the American army, fighting us Germans, we are needed to do the farmwork of those American farm boys over in Europe fighting us Germans. Doesn't make a lot of sense does it?" he said with a laugh. "Anyhow, the farmers sign up to have us come to their farms and work. The rules say that we are supposed to have guards accompany each group of POWs, but they usually only accompany groups of three or more at a single worksite. For those who work one or two to a farm, we rely on the honor system. So far, no one has broken the rules. Because of the prisoner of war rules, we have to be paid for our work. If you decide to work, you'll receive eighty cents a day and if you don't you'll get ten cents a day. Once a week, on Saturday afternoon, you'll receive your special POW cash script there next to the camp store. This money is not good outside the camp so don't get any ideas about using it to buy a train ticket home." Laughter again erupted. "You can buy all the cigarettes you want; no limit, like the Americans living around us." Again laughter. "You can buy paper, pencils, all sorts of candy and you can buy beer." The group cheered at this. American beer" Carl continued. The group moaned. Someone jokingly asked if they couldn't get German beer. Again the group laughed. "And for the truly strong of heart, there is a Saturday night 'after hours' card game. Besides the items in the store, we get regular supplies of soap, tooth paste and other goodies from the Red Cross." Then Carl continued informing the men about the work situations. "It doesn't get much better than this, although some of the larger camps even have their own bakeries where German POWs make all sorts of pastries and breads."

Some farmers will take a half a dozen men, some prefer just one. Those men you saw getting in the trucks this morning; they all work on farms. If you're lucky, you get to go north of the highway where most of the farmers are German; correction, were German. If you're not so lucky, you go south were most of the farmers are Swedes. The Swedes don't really like us. Something about us trying to take over their country." Everyone laughed. "The rules are firm. When you go to the farms, you will not come into contact with a gun of any sort, you will not take a drink of any alcoholic beverage, you will not fraternize with female civilians in your work location, and you will not leave the presence of your overseer; except to go to the toilet. As for the guards, they are usually in the kitchen talking with the Mrs. or taking a nap in the barn." Again, everyone laughed. "Seriously" Carl continued, "if anyone breaks any of the rules, the entire camp goes into a shut down. And when that happens, the offender or offenders are dealt with in the shower room. We have what is called a stocking party. Now a stocking party, for your information, is where each man places his bar of soap in a stocking and proceeds to whack the offenders on his naked back, legs and other sensitive points of his anatomy. We have only had to have two stocking parties since I have been here." Everyone seemed to get the message.

"Speaking of the shower room, over here, we take showers in the evening. Some of us come back to camp smelling like the pigs we have been working with." Unlike the showers in Africa and Europe, the Camp Alexis had the luxury of a large free standing boiler made from an old locomotive. Attached to the shower room was the camp laundry. It too enjoyed hot water from the boiler. "At the end of each work day, you will deposit your soiled clothing in the laundry baskets and take a fresh set for the next day. After your shower, it's dinner. After dinner, you'll have free time until 'lights out'. Free time means that you can go to the English class, the letter writing station, or the farm. Personally, I prefer to go to our farm," said Carl. "And speaking of the farm, let's go there."

The men continued to follow Carl out a small back gate where one guard sat in a tiny brick building. "Six, plus myself" Carl said to the guard. The guard handed Carl seven yellow cards attached to a cord. "Here put these around your necks and call out your names." One by one the six new men called out their names as the guard wrote them in his ledger. "Be sure to keep these garden passes visible at all times. If you're found out here without one or if one of the guards can't see your pass, you'll be in trouble." Carl said. The path continued through a small grove of leafless trees. On the other side of the grove, stood the "farm." There were four wooden sheds on one side, each housing some pigs. Another group of sheds contained chickens and a larger shed housed six milk cows. Each shed was attached to a small fenced area where the animals could move about. Several POWs were off to one side, loading bushel baskets of winter squash onto an old wooden hay wagon. Back behind the cow barn, was an area of about ten acres which had been cultivated. "That's our garden" Carl pointed proudly. "That's why we eat so well," he smiled. He led his small group over to where the men were loading the last of the winter squash on to the wagon. "Here are some new hands." Carl said.

The old-timers all extended hands and exchanged names with the new guys. "Just in time" one fellow said, "We'll need some help in hauling this stuff up to the kitchen. All men found a place on the wagon, either to pull or push. Together they moved the wagon back toward the camp. As they passed the pig pens, Carl yelled at one of the men standing near the pigs. "Looks like Old Suzy might be ready to come to dinner"—pointing at one of the fat pigs. "Yep, maybe next week we'll be having pig knuckles," someone replied. The men and the hay wagon continued back toward the camp.

After a week of settling in, getting physical examinations and sitting through lengthy general interviews, the new men's names were posted on a bulletin board near the shower. Although the list stated only the number of the truck in which they were to ride and the name of the farmer for whom they would be working, it caused a great sense of excitement for the new guys. When the old-timers returned back from their day out in the farm fields, the shower was alive with conversation. "What's this farmer so-and-so like?" "How's the food at his table?" and so on.

Helmut was so excited at receiving his work assignment that he had difficulty sleeping that night, especially when he was told that his truck, number seven, would be going north into the German farm community. When the 5:00 AM wake up call was sounded over the camp's loud speaker, he jumped out of bed and was the first one to the latrine and among the first to the dining hall. The conversation at breakfast was exuberant, with the new men asking all sorts of questions about their assigned farmer. After months of sitting idle in prisoner of war holding camps on both sides of the Atlantic, these POWs were finally going to be doing something which made German men, men. They were going to work; something which every good German respected.

Morning assembly in the hangar went off like the first day of school for new school boys. After Sergeant Walther barked the order to dismiss, the new men ran to their assigned trucks. The old boys sauntered to their trucks, shaking their heads and smiling at these new pups.

2

SOON THE TRUCKS WERE on the main road, some heading south and some heading north. Winter was coming on and the lush greens and golden yellows of the Nebraska landscape had given way to the bleakness of winter. The few trees along the road had lost their leaves. This was a stark contrast to Helmut's home in Germany with its abundant pine forests. It was certainly a contrast to the brutal deserts of North Africa.

About 30 miles from the camp, the truck slowed and turned west on a dirt road. A mile or so down the road, the truck pulled into a farm road and stopped in front of a neat wooden farmhouse. An old farmer, putting oil into an ancient tractor, stopped what he was doing and came over to the truck. Three POWs and a camp guard jumped down from the back. The farmer went to the driver and the two exchanged comments about the weather. The driver revved his engine, pulled back out into the main dirt road and continued westward. After stopping at six similar farms, Helmut found himself to be the last man in the back of the truck. Fifteen minutes after the last POW was dropped off, the truck turned into a small, run down farmstead. Located at the turn off was a small wooden shed with three large metal milk cans. "This is your stop" the driver shouted from the cab, "Adam Becker's farm. Unlike most of the other farms, this one was run down and cluttered with old farm implements and vehicles. The barn had a strong tilt to it from the force of the prevailing south winds. The wooden fences which served as corrals for the dozen or so cows were unpainted and shabby. The house, while nicely constructed, was also unpainted and shabby.

The door of the farmhouse opened and a man walked out to the truck. The first thing Helmut noticed was a huge wad of chewing tobacco in his cheek. Spittle had stained his teeth and the whiskers of his chin. He appeared messy, compared to the other farmers Helmut had seen on his previous stops. "Here you are Adam." said the truck driver. "He's a new one, so don't ride him too hard the first day. I'll be back at 4:00 sharp. Be sure he's ready. If I don't get these guys back to the camp by 5:15, I'm in big trouble with the Major." the driver said as he drove off down the road, leaving Corporal Helmut Sommerfield standing face-to-face with Adam Becker.

For several minutes, Helmut stood there looking at Adam Becker. Most of his face was covered with a thick brownish-gray beard. Long dirty brown hair scattered from beneath his soiled railroad engineer's cap. A broad stripe of tobacco spittle stained his beard at each corner of his mouth. His gray eyes seemed almost hidden beneath two bushy eyebrows. He wore dirty jeans, held up by black suspenders and a well worn red plaid work shirt. While not particularly tall or stout, he appeared to be somewhat frightening. Although the man's age was hidden by his appearance Helmut determined that he and Mr. Becker were about the same age.

Adam Becker seemed to take pride in looking as dirty as possible. Some folks in the neighborhood reckoned that it was his way of displaying just how hard he worked. Even the cow manure on his boots seemed to represent the many hours he spent milking his small herd of cows.

Without taking his eyes off of Helmut, Becker moved to a chair on the porch of his house and sat down, something like a judge sitting on his bench. With Helmut standing at the foot of the stairs, he began a well rehearsed speech. In almost perfect German Becker began a brief lecture on the horrors of the German Empire and the great suffering Germany had inflicted on the entire universe. It appeared that Becker was placing the blame for the entire event, including a brief mention of World War I, squarely on Helmut's Sommerfield's head. Becker continued his little tirade, suggesting that Helmut might just be exonerated for these evil deeds if he were to work twice as hard as those other lazy POW slobs who had worked for him before.

While Helmut listened to the welcome speech of this dirty little man, he noticed the truck in which he had arrived, parking at the farm across the road. The driver of the truck got out and walked slowly over to a flag pole near the front gate of a small white farmhouse. The man opened a box at the base of the pole and took out two small bundles. He clipped the bundles to the rope and raised first an American flag. Below the American flag was another flag; one with a red boarder and a gold star at its center. Helmut noticed the farmer stepping back from the base of the flag pole and lowered his head.

"Are you listening to me?" Becker yelled at Helmut.

Helmut's attention immediately returned from the farm across the road to the dirty man standing before him. Helmut noticed at once that this man had not bathed for some time, nor had he brushed his tobacco stained teeth for possibly several years.

"Pay attention when I am talking to you!" Adam Becker continued in German.

"Now, we have work to do. I have already milked my cows, probably while you were still in bed. Now we have to get the hay into the barn before the snow comes. The radio said that we had snow just south-east of here last night. If we don't get it in, I will lose it. And if I lose it my friend, it will be your fault for standing there doing nothing!" the ugly little man barked.

Helmut looked across the field and saw that the hay had been cut and was lying in long rows. He knew from his life on a farm that the hay had to be stacked or it would spoil on the ground.

"I want you to take that pitchfork over yonder and begin making piles. I'll be along with a hay wagon and a horse shortly to take the loads to the barn," Adam said in a slightly more mannerly tone.

Helmut walked briskly toward the hay field as a brightly colored pheasant sprung to flight in front of him bringing a smile to his face. For a moment, he was reminded of bird hunting as a young boy on his family's farm in Bavaria. He whispered a quiet, "Good morning" to the chirping bird. As he moved briskly toward the hay rows, he noticed an old white truck with a picture of a cow on its door, racing down the dirt road, stopping at the wooden shed where Becker's driveway intersected the dirt road. A driver in a white uniform took the three milk cans from the shed and replaced them with three others. He then took an envelope out of his pocket and placed it in a mailbox attached to the shed. Helmut picked up the pitchfork and began to form stacks of hay. It was about an hour later when Becker came into the field, riding on an old hay wagon pulled by a large gray horse. Adam noticed the many stacks of hay already piled in the field.

"Good, now let's keep going and maybe we can get this hay stacked in the barn before the end of the week."

Helmut approached Adam with a hand full of hay. "Sir," he said with utmost respect in his voice, "I believe this hay is a bit too wet to be put up in a barn. As you know, wet hay will self ignite and you will have one devil of a fire."

Becker placed his hands on his hips, leaned forward and squinted, "Just who do you think you are Mr. German Prisoner of War? I have been stacking hay in that barn for over twenty years and my father before me. It has never caught fire and it never will. Do you understand?"

"Yes sir" Helmut replied as if he had been slapped. "Now let's get this hay on the wagon!"

Helmut began foisting large pitchforks of damp hay onto the flatbed wagon. Although Becker joined him with a pitchfork, Helmut pitched two loads of hay for every one of Becker's. Soon the wagon was loaded.

"OK, let's go unload this stuff in the hayloft." Adam jumped on the wagon's seat while Helmut was satisfied to take a place on the tailgate. A few minutes later, the wagon was in the drive through space, between the two large sliding barn doors. Adam climbed the wooden ladder to the hayloft as Helmut took his place on the wagon. Helmut would pitch a load up into the loft where Becker would pitch it to the back of the hayloft. Helmut had done this job a hundred times before as a kid in Germany. He knew that tomorrow morning, he'd be sore enough that getting out of bed would be difficult. He also knew that by week's end he'd once again regain the physical stature he had lost during the past years of driving a tank in the desert and sitting in American POW camps. As he stood there pitching hay, smelling the smells of a farm, a warm smile spread over his face. For the first time in a long time, a very long time, Helmut felt truly happy.

By mid-day, the two men had loaded and off loaded four wagon loads of hay. While Helmut did not have a watch, he could tell by the position of the sun and by the growl in his stomach that it was well past lunchtime. He also knew that it was the responsibility of the farmer to provide a decent lunch for his prisoner of war workers. Helmut knew better than to suggest that they break for a mid-day meal, so he suggested that he wander over to the water pump for a quick drink of water. At that point, Becker stabbed his pitch fork into the hay pile and groaned, "Naw, let's get some lunch." With that, Becker spat a huge wad of tobacco toward the wall of the barn.

As the two men walked toward the house, Helmut wondered what he would find on the inside. Unlike all of the farmers Helmut had ever known, Adam Becker did not remove his boots before entering the shabby, run-down structure. Helmut sat on the one chair placed next to the front door and began to untie his boots. "Never mind the boots, there's no woman here to bother us about tracking dirt in."

The screen on the door had long since rusted away and the curtain on the front door window was a tangle of tattered ribbons. It took a few seconds before Helmut could see the interior of the small house.

Before he could see the piles of cardboard boxes and dirty overstuffed chairs, he could smell the stale odor of musty newspapers, smoke and garbage. As his eyes adjusted to the darkness, he could make out the images of people behind dirty glass picture frames on the walls. Becker had disappeared into the kitchen at the rear of the house. Suddenly, he reappeared in the doorway. "In here if you want something to eat."

Helmut followed the narrow path between boxes and furniture to the kitchen. A bare, battery powered light bulb hung from the ceiling and attempted to light the dingy little room. Rays of sunlight made every effort to pierce the dirty kitchen windows. An old wood burning stove stood at one wall with a sink full of dirty dishes at the other. A wooden table with two chairs sat near the back door. Becker opened the back porch door where an old kerosene refrigerator stood. He opened the door of the refrigerator and took out a cast iron pot. Returning to the kitchen, he placed the pot on the stove. He opened the fire door on the stove, tossed a few pieces of wood from a milk bottle crate into the embers and fanned the fire box with a newspaper. Soon the fire was sufficient to cause the soup in the pot to come to a boil. "Hope you like soup," Becker said as he grabbed a fist full of soda crackers from a metal can. Adam took two bowls from one of the cupboards and plunked them down along with two stained coffee mugs. He then found two large spoons and knives in a pile of dirty dishes in the sink. Wiping them off on a grease stained dish towel, he placed them on the table.

"Sit!" Adam said, pointing to a chair.

Helmut sat in stark amazement. Nowhere in his homeland had he seen such a place; such filth! Never had he seen a German in such a state of depravity. Becker proceeded to pour the contents of the soup pot into the two bowls. While Helmut sat looking into the odd concoction of potatoes, carrots and a few pieces of meat, Adam poured two cups of thick black coffee from an ancient coffee pot.

Becker took his seat and grabbed a hand full of soda crackers and crumbled them into his soup bowl.

"Well now," he smiled factitiously, "tell me about yourself. How is it that a fine man like yourself became a Nazi and tried to take over the world?" Becker laughed at his statement as if he were an interrogation officer.

Helmut slowly picked up his spoon as he pondered his response to Becker's barb. He took a spoonful of the soup and determined that it was reasonably palatable.

"You see, it's like this," Helmut began with his eyebrows raised in an attitude of defense. "Only a small percentage of the German military men are members of the Nazi party and not all Germans are in favor of this stupid war. Most of us are not angry with the French, the British or you Americans. For some reason, the higher-ups in our government want to take land that is clearly not theirs. And to make matters even worse, these higher-ups have seen fit to blame the Jews for most of the problems in our country. Any fool will tell you that the problems are caused by the greed and corruption of the power systems in our region. Just like the Russians, they are not mad at anyone. It's their leaders who want more land, more power, and more medals on their bloated chests."

Becker, who was noisily eating his soup, glanced at one of the old portraits hanging on the wall, a portrait of his grandfather who had fled Germany back when the Kaiser was doing the same thing Hitler was now doing.

Helmut continued, "I and my family were content to live our lives as farmers, but I was drafted into this madness leaving my father and his brothers to struggle with the farmwork. When this war is over, will anyone be better off than they were before it started, I don't think so."

Becker realized that his comments about Helmut's being a Nazi and being responsible for the war was offensive and stupid. He also realized that Helmut was far more intelligent than he was.

The two men sat and ate quietly for the next few minutes.

Helmut had realized that Becker was embarrassed by his comments and that the situation needed to be put aside.

31

"How is it that you are able to speak German so well and with a proper accent" Helmut said knowing that a bit of flattery would change the mood.

"Well, you see, it's like this" Adam began, looking at the portrait of his great grandfather hanging on the wall. "My people were farmers in the Village of Hoffnungstal in the Ukraine of Southern Russia when Kaiser Wilhelm began building his military machine. In fact, most of the farmers who settled in this area were from Hoffnungstal. At that time, everyone knew that the Kaiser was just looking for an excuse to start a war. My grandfather along with many of the other families in the area knew full well that if war came, they and their sons would be drafted and that their farms would become a part of the national war effort. It also meant that if the Kaiser were to lose the war, we could have very well found ourselves under the Russians or someone worse. So, my grandfather took what he could get for his farm and went to Odessa, Russia. From there, they were able to find passage on a ship to the United States. Once here, my grandfather and several other German families were able to homestead this land. In fact, most of the farmers in this county were from Germany and spoke German. My father was the first man in the family who could attend public school because he was the first one to become passable in English. Even so, my father and grandfather insisted on speaking German at home. And that, *mein herr*, is why I speak German to this very day."

Helmut smiled and nodded as Adam concluded his discourse. "So" Helmut stated, "We are all fish from the same small pond."

"Let me ask you a question" Adam said leaning forward, "If you and your family had known that Hitler was about to start a war would you have made the same choice my grandfather made? Would you have chosen to flee the country rather than be sucked up in Hitler's madness?"

"Very good question" Helmut replied "Very good!

"Patriotism is a strange thing. Your land, your people, your history is sometimes stronger than reason. All too often, the patriot tries to convince himself that that spirit of his country is really good and that if enough people simply pray for good, evil will be driven out. Unfortunately this is not the case. Evil is like a rotten tooth, it will not go away by itself. To answer your question…would we have fled our home if we had known what was going to happen? I really don't know. I guess we were satisfied to simply pray that the evil would go away."

"One more question," Adam posed. "If you knew what you know now, would you have fled before the war broke out?"

Helmut put is face in his hands. Looking up at Adam he said, "I keep praying that the evil will go away and everything will be as it was. I really don't know the answer to your question."

"So, you would still choose Germany over America," Adam countered.

"No, I didn't say that. I would choose my home, my farm, my family over any place else."

Adam shook his head as he rose from the table.

"Let's get back to work," Adam said as he drained his coffee cup. "That hay ain't going to put itself in the barn." The rest of the day, the two men worked in silence, gathering hay and stacking it in the ancient barn. All that day the question of whether Helmut would have fled Germany if he had known what he knew now, played over and over in his mind.

As the early winter's sun began to drop closer toward the horizon Helmut noticed the truck from across the road driving into Becker's farm. "Time to go home" Becker said. "You're a heck of a lot better worker than most of the Nazi boys they send me."

Helmut looked at Adam with a look of hurt and anger. He laid his pitch fork on the hay wagon bed and walked toward the waiting truck. As he started to climb in the back, but the driver yelled out that he could ride up front if he wanted to. Helmut, still very offended, shook his head and climbed into the back.

3

HELMUT AND THOSE IN HIS TRUCK talked very little on the return trip. Arriving back at camp, they went straight to the showers and lined up for dinner. While all the old-timers talked and laughed about their day, the new men were far too exhausted to speak. After the meal, most of the new men went to their beds and straight to sleep. None of them even heard the call for "lights out".

Somewhere around three in the morning Helmut awoke, crying. His dreams were of his farm and his family. A huge fire was seen off in the distance, moving closer towards his farm. Adam was there yelling, "Let's get out of here, run away before the fire gets us." Helmut's sister, mother, and father were going about their chores, choosing to ignore the oncoming flames. Adam was standing there with his pitch fork, watching the fire. Helmut ran toward Adam and then back to his family, then back to Adam. It was at this point that he woke up. He was shaking and his face was wet from tears. The dream was much too real. The question which Adam had posed the previous day revolved in his mind. Should he and his family have fled Germany when they all knew full well that Hitler was going to wage war? How could a farmer leave his farm? How could a family leave their place in a community which was well documented by the names on the tombstones in the village cemetery? How could a family leave its place in the history of the land?

On the other hand, how could a man tolerate evil and thus become a part of that evil and simply pray that it would someday go away. The question kept coming around, like a painted wooden horse on a merry-go-round. "Do you run away and become a refugee, or do you stay and become a part of that which you know to be wrong?" Somewhere just before the wake up call came over the loud speaker, Helmut resolved the issue. The dilemma which Adam had presented was flawed. Helmut did not have the opportunity to choose to stay or to run. In fact, by the time that choice would have been made, he was taken, taken by the German Army. There had been no choice, so the conflict was not real.

The lights in the dormitory came on full bright as Helmut sat up on the edge of his bed. He could see and hear the other men coming out of their sleep. Like himself, the other new men groaned with muscle pain as they moved toward the latrine. While the pain was great, it somehow felt good to revive those old "farmers' muscles" which had grown soft and flabby while in the driver's seat of a tank. Helmut dressed, put on his boots and headed for the dining hall. The smell of bacon cooking caused him to walk faster. The cold Nebraska air actually felt good; better than the hot dry air of North Africa or the heavy humid air of Georgia. The dining hall was beginning to fill with men. Helmut took a tray and moved slowly through the food line. He was still amazed at the generous portions and good quality of the food. Fried potatoes with bits of pork, hot biscuits and an orange. This was far better than anything he had had during his time in the army. He also realized that he needed to eat a bigger breakfast as long as he was working for Adam Becker.

From across the dining hall, Helmut heard someone call his name. He looked over and saw Carl beckoning him to come over and join him. It felt good to have someone invite you to sit with them. It had been a long time since he'd had a friend.

Helmut made his way through the crowded dining room to the place where Carl and some of his group were seated.

"Well, how did your day go yesterday?" Carl asked with a smile on his face.

Helmut slowly took his seat, expressing obvious discomfort in his body.

"So my friend, you seem to be moving a little slower than usual this morning. What's the matter, did your 'captor' work you a little too hard?" The men at the table all laughed.

"Never mind, by the end of the week you will be fine." Carl laughed.

As the men ate their breakfast they exchanged stories about their first day on the job. Finally, someone asked Helmut about his farmer. How was the food? Did the farmer have a good looking wife? All laughed. Helmut simply smiled and reported that his farmer had no wife and the food was not so good. Again, everyone laughed knowing full well that this guy Becker was a real bum. Carl looked toward the clock and began to count; "five, four, three, two, one." The loudspeaker clicked on, "General assembly in five minutes!"

"Well men, let's go to work." Carl stated, still smiling.

The men moved toward the dish pans and out the door. Carl caught up with Helmut and placed his arm around his shoulder as they walked toward the airplane hangar.

"Well my friend, how do you feel?"

Helmut responded, "Not so bad, not so bad at all."

They sang *A Mighty Fortress* ran their circles, and loaded up into the trucks. As the last man was dropped off at his work farm, the truck driver shouted back to Helmut, "You can come up here if you like." Yesterday Helmut preferred to be by himself in the back of the truck, but today was a new day. He jumped out of the back and ran toward the cab and climbed in.

The driver put the truck in gear and drove down the dirt road.

It had been eighteen months since his capture in North Africa and in that time Helmut had learned sufficient English, American English to communicate on an elementary level.

"My name is Helmut, Helmut Sommerfield," he said extending his hand toward the driver.

The driver nodded, choosing to ignore the opportunity for a handshake.

"I'm Henry Schmidt. My farm is directly across the road from Adam Becker's place."

"Do you live here a long time?" Helmut asked in his broken English.

"All my life" Schmidt replied.

As the truck turned the corner toward Becker's farm they passed a small, white church. Next to the church was a cemetery.

"My father and his father are buried there." Schmidt said as he pointed to the cemetery with his head. "We are three generations from the old country."

Schmidt remained silent the rest of the way to Becker's farm.

Adam was standing in the door with a cup of coffee when the truck pulled up and stopped.

For a long moment, Helmut sat there in the truck looking at the man on the porch. Then Helmut opened the door of the truck and jumped out.

"See you at 4:15" Helmut said to Schmidt, as he turned and walked toward the man on the porch.

Schmidt drove back across the road to his farm. Becker said nothing but pointed toward the hay field. Helmut moved quickly but sorely in that direction. As he walked, he again watched Schmidt walk to his flag pole, take the flags out of the box and raise them to full staff. After spending a few minutes with his head bowed, Schmidt turned and walked into the neat, red barn.

Helmut began by stacking the long rows of cut hay into piles. Within an hour, he saw the horse drawn hay wagon coming across the field toward him.

"Dang, you're a fast one. The others don't move nearly as fast as you do." Becker jumped off the wagon's seat, grabbed a pitch fork, and began to load the wagon. Even though Helmut's muscles were still sore from yesterday's work, he strove to pitch twice as much hay as Becker. The two men continued to pile hay on the wagon until it was loaded. Becker mounted the wagon and beckoned Helmut to climb aboard as well. Slowly, the laden wagon moved toward the barn.

"Tell me, Herr Becker, what is the meaning of the flag over there, the one with the star."

"That flag simply means that Schmidt lost a son, his eldest son in the war; your war."

Helmut felt as if someone had hit him in the stomach. Again he felt the terrible reality of war and the pain caused by evil men. The rest of the morning Helmut worked with a sick feeling throughout his entire body. While he tried not to look in the direction of the flag, he could not help seeing it wave in the wind. A small piece of colored cloth which represented a life, a life lost. Helmut could not help but wonder if his father back in Germany had devised some sort of symbol representing his son and displayed it as a sad reminder of personal loss. As he tried to put the thought of Schmidt's son out of his mind, he was struck by an even more horrible thought; was it possible that he was in fact the one who actually killed the boy? Helmut fell to his knees and vomited. As he heaved, tears filled his eyes and a terrible sense of remorse filled his heart. "Is it possible that I killed this man's son? Is it possible that it was my tank that caused this boy's death?" he thought.

Becker ran over to Helmut.

"What's the matter, you sick or something?" he asked.

Helmut nodded as he turned his back.

"I need to get a drink of water, that's all. I will be fine in a few minutes," he said, slowly walking toward the water jug on the seat of the hay wagon.

The two men stacked and hauled hay until around mid-day.

"Time for lunch" Adam muttered. "You un-harness the horse and I will go put lunch on the stove."

Helmut pulled the hitch which coupled the horse with the wagon and led the horse to the corral at the south end of the barn. He instinctively dipped out a bucket of oats and placed the bucket on the ground. He patted the horse as it put its muzzle into the bucket. For an instant he felt good, being back on a farm, being with animals and the earth, but the bitter thoughts of Henry Schmidt's son lying in some far away grave left him grief stricken. Once again his eyes filled with tears and he wept bitterly.

"Hey Helmut, get over here if you want any lunch!" Adam yelled from the back porch. Helmut wiped his face and headed for the house.

Lunch was on the table. Today it consisted of several pieces of boiled chicken with some string beans. Adam watched Helmut as he surveyed the plate.

"What's the matter, not good enough for you? All them other POWs complained about my food and got transfers to other farms. If it good enough for me, its dang well good enough for you!"

Helmut forced a smile, "No this looks fine. I have no problem with what is before me."

Then, for the first time since he left his home in Germany, Helmut paused for a brief second and thanked God for what he had before him. Adam noticed the pause and asked, "Are you religious?"

"I was once but this war seems to make religion a bit too confusing," Helmut said.

"What do you mean by confusing?" Adam queried.

"Our religion tells us to love one another, but for some reason we don't. We kill people we don't even know for reasons we really don't understand. We kill other peoples' sons, and for what purpose; so we can raise our little flags on our little flag poles and claim we are the masters of this place or that." At that point, Helmut shook his head in disgust and continued with his lunch. It was quiet for the next few minutes. Adam had started to realize that the man sitting in front of him was not a ruthless killer nor was he a political fanatic; he was a man just like himself. He also began to realize the he was a better man than himself; a thought which made him uncomfortable.

Adam broke the silence once again. "I suppose you are wondering why I am not in the US military? It's not that I don't want to join up; it's the fact that I had scarlet fever as a kid and it affected my heart. Whenever I work too hard, my heart takes off beating like a New York drummer. If I don't lie down, I pass out wherever I am standing. If you go up to the cemetery, you will find a dozen or so tombstones of kids who died during the same scarlet fever outbreak which almost took me. I was one of the few lucky kids in the area who didn't end up in a box that winter."

"You have much to be thankful for Mr. Becker."

"Thankful! for what? My folks left me with six hundred acres of prime farmland and God left me unable to work those six hundred acres," Adam muttered as he shook his head. "The best I can manage is eleven milk cows and the hay to feed them. This barely allows me to eat. Like I said, thankful for what?"

Helmut simply nodded and kept on eating, not wanting to get into this sensitive area.

"And Schmidt across the way, he can't go into the military because he's a farmer and farmers have to keep the food coming. Now that his son is dead, he wants to go more than ever. I guess he wants to get even with those Kraut devils for killing his boy."

Again, Helmut said nothing, but did cast a cold stare at the man across the table from him.

Adam knew that he had touched a sore spot with Helmut. He too felt the necessity for a little personal revenge.

"Well, it's about time we got back to work. There's a war going on you know and we need to do our part. Every little bit helps," Adam continued

4

WHATEVER DREAMS were being dreamt, they were abruptly shattered with the wake up call in the camp's loud speaker system. Lights came on and the morning darkness was absorbed by sharp, blinding light bulbs. Helmut tried to focus his eyes on the clock at the end of the barracks. He entered the stream of stumbling men making their way to the latrines and then on to breakfast. The routine had become second nature. It was starting to get colder in the morning and the sun was coming up later. Winter was definitely in the air.

Helmut found a place at a table with his truck crew and sat down. As he was about to finish his breakfast of oatmeal and an egg, Chaplain Wolf entered the dining hall and came over to where Helmut was sitting. "When you are finished Helmut, could I see you outside for a minute?" he said.

"Sure!" Helmut grinned.

Helmut cleaned his tray and left the warmth of the dining hall. The chaplain was sitting on a small bench under a tree.

"Have a seat." Chaplain Wolf offered.

Helmut sat down, sensing that something was wrong, very wrong.

"Helmut, we sent the notification of your capture and whereabouts to the International Red Cross. As you know, this is in accordance with the Rules of War. Your family was to be informed that you

41

were in good health and being well treated. Unfortunately, Helmut, we received a reply back from the Red Cross representatives in Germany informing us that your family, with the exception of your younger sister, has been killed in an air raid. I am sorry to have to tell you this news, very sorry." Chaplain Wolf went on to suggest that Helmut might wish to take a few days off from the farm crews and rest.

Helmut's blood seemed to turn to cold black ink. He felt like vomiting, crying, screaming, or hitting someone. He felt like running or just falling on the ground. Images of his father, mother and younger brother flashed in his mind. Images of his younger sister, crying, as she did when Helmut left to go to the army filled his mind. Sorrow and hatred competed against each other. "The Americans have killed my family!" he uttered.

He felt Chaplain Wolf put his arm around his shoulder and whisper in his ear, "I am so sorry!"

Helmut turned and looked at Chaplain Wolf directly in the face, hoping to express some sort of hatred for him but all he could see was an old man with tears running down his jagged face.

Chaplain Wolf arose, still with his hand on Helmut's shoulder. "I will tell the farm crews that you will not be going to the farm for awhile." The old man turned and walked away, leaving Helmut staring off into the distance.

In the morning announcements, Chaplain Wolf mentioned that members of Helmut Sommerfield's family had become casualties of war and asked the men to pray for consolation. To all the men assembled in group area, the organized system of killing known as war seemed so far away. News of a family being killed brought pain to all those assembled. It also brought pain knowing that one of their comrades was hurting.

After dismissal, Chaplain Wolf walked to the trucks and found Henry Schmidt. "Mr. Schmidt, could I have a minute with you? One of your crew, Helmut Sommerfield has been notified that his family has been killed in an Allied bombing raid. As you can expect, he will not be going to the farms for a few days. It is a terrible thing to lose a family member and not be able to do anything about it."

"I know, I lost my elder son in France." Schmidt whispered.

For the second time that morning Chaplain Wolf found tears running down his face.

Unable to make any consoling comments, Chaplain Wolf simply shook his head and walked back to compound. "Children's fathers killing other fathers' children." the old man uttered. "Oh God, when will it stop?"

Helmut, still in a dull, painful daze began to wander toward the prison camp's farm. He felt the need to be alone yet with something alive. He came to the garden's guard post where he took a garden pass and clipped it onto his jacket. The man sitting in the guard post had been present during the morning's assembly and had heard the news about Helmut's family.

"I am sorry to hear about your family." the American said.

Helmut simply nodded his head and kept on walking, trying to determine whether to hate this American soldier or to acknowledge his expression of sympathy and concern for another man in pain.

Helmut found himself leaning on the fence post at the corner of the pig pens. The smell and the sound of the pigs squealing caused his mind to go back to a time before the war. As he stood there, leaning against the post, he sensed another man's presence. Henry Schmidt had left his truck full of men for a few minutes to offer what words of condolence he could. The two men stood there, silently looking at the pigs nosily eating the mixture of gourds and table scraps.

Helmut cleared his throat and spoke. "You know, standing here like this, I can't help but remember my family's butcher day. It was one day each year when all the members of our family got together. My uncles would load their fat pigs into wagons and bring them to our family farm for slaughter and sausage making. It was a yearly tradition that went back as far as I could remember. All my cousins would come along with their parents. Although this was a family affair, the local church pastor and his family would be there. And for reasons un-known to anyone, the pastor would always offer a prayer before the pigs were killed. That seemed to give him a reason for being there and too, it seemed to sanctify the killing of these beasts. He also collected some of the meat for distribution to the widows and the poor in the village. After the prayer, all of the girls and young boys would run to the barn where they would bury themselves in the hay and cover their ears to avoid the death squeals of the pigs. The older boys would pre-tend to assist in the killing by holding the pigs down while their throats were cut. It was always a contest to see which cousin would run over to the bushes and vomit first. Every year, several older boys would ei-ther faint or vomit at the sight of spurting blood or at the sight of guts falling from the body of a pig hanging from its hind feet. It took a few years to get used to the sights and smells of the event."

Helmut continued telling the story as if he was narrating the event as it happened.

"After the pigs were hung from tree branches next to the barn, they were cut into hunks and chunks. Hips and shoulders were cut into hams with the rest of the carcass being cut into small pieces. While the men were cutting the meat, the intestines were cut loose and cleaned by some of the older women. On occasion, younger girls would venture over to the wash tubs where the guts were being cleaned. It was not uncommon to hear a scream and see some girl faint dead away. Other girls would then come and carry the downed female to a shady spot and administer small quantities of lemonade.

"A large tub of pig heads would always catch the attention of the younger boys who would taunt the dead pig heads with sticks. On oc-casion, one of the heads would spasm causing an ear or a nose to twitch involuntarily. The boys would run in all directions yelling, 'It's alive!'"

Helmut laughed at the recollection he had brought to mind. As he continued his story, he pointed to various locations around the pig yard and the garden as if this narrative was in progress before him and Schmidt.

"When the hams had been trimmed and wrapped in cotton wrappings, the bacon separated out, the job of sausage making would begin. There would be four huge hand crank meat grinders set up on thick wooden planks over there. My father was the sausage meister; he had the job of adding the correct amount of spices to make each kind of sausage. Beside the table, he would have a small fire, with a cooking pan. As he mixed a batch of sausage, he would take a small amount of meat and cook it. He would then taste it to see if it needed any more spice. Everyone watched as he tested each batch. After each test, my father would smack his lips and announce, 'Perfect!'"

Schmidt stood there listening as he visualized the story being told by the young man next to him.

Helmut pointed to a place under some trees and said, "Two men were operating the hand cranks as chunks of meat were fed into the wide mouth hopper. At another table, over there, two sausage stuffers would stuff the ground meat into great long lengths of gut casing. Several older boys would tie off links of sausage and string them over some rope which stretched from there to there." Helmut pointed toward two trees.

Turning his tearful face toward Schmidt, he continued, "After the sausages were finished, the pastor would take a basket and collect string sausages which were to be given to the widows and the poor. As soon as the pastor left in his wagon, some of my uncles would bring out bottles of schnapps and beer."

Helmut put his head down. "Oh God!" he moaned, "How I will miss that."

Schmidt, with tears in his eyes, placed his hand on Helmut's back. "I am sorry Helmut!"

Schmidt turned away and walked back toward his truck and the men waiting to go to the farms.

For the next week, Helmut stayed at the camp, reading the piles of American magazines, all of which had been censored or clipped of any items related to the war. He tried desperately to read aloud, lis-

45

tening to his rapidly improving English. The pain of being a captive compounded with the pain of being alone caused a strange sense of fear, hatred, and wishing to be dead. On occasion, in his reading, he would come across the words, mother, father or brother and simply break into sobs. By week's end, Helmut felt empty and drained of emotion. There were no more tears left to shed. He felt robbed that he could not at least have buried his family.

Almost like a rock hitting him in the head, he realized that his younger sister was alive—somewhere she was alive. His full attention turned to Greta, his twenty-five-year-old sister. He desperately needed to reach out and wipe away the tears she must be shedding now. He needed to contact her and assure her that he was alive and would be making every effort to find and protect her. With the realization that his little sister was alive, he felt desperate to find a way to make contact with her.

Running anywhere in the camp was forbidden, but Helmut walked just short of a run toward the camp commander's office. The man sitting at the desk outside the commander's office was shocked at the abrupt manner of the man before him.

"Sir, I must see the camp commander, now!"

"Oh, replied the man behind the desk. "And what is your name and the nature of your request?"

"Sommerfield, Helmut. My sister is alive and I must contact her, now!"

Again the man behind the desk seemed shocked at the almost insolent tone in the POW's voice.

The man arose, knocked on the commander's door and entered.

Within seconds he returned, smiling.

"Mr. Sommerfield, Major Reed will see you now."

This was the first time in many years anyone had called him, 'Mr. Sommerfield.'

Helmut entered the Commanding Officer's office and stood at attention.

"Please, Mr. Sommerfield, sit down." Major Reed offered.

"I am truly sorry about your family," he continued with a few platitudes regarding death and war.

Helmut brushed the comments aside with polite acknowledgment.

"Chaplain Wolf told me that my sister was not," he paused for a moment, 'killed'."

Major Reed pulled a brown file folder from the pile of folders on his desk. Helmut noticed his name, Sommerfield, printed on the edge of the folder.

"Yes, it says here, here, you read it." Major Reed said passing the notice of death across the desk to Helmut.

The words announcing the death of most of the Sommerfield family stabbed his eyes like a frigid winter wind causing tears to flood. Wiping his eyes, he focused on the last sentence indicating that his younger sister was alive.

"She is alive!" Helmut uttered.

Looking up at Major Reed, Helmut pleaded, "Sir, is there anyway I can get a message to her? Is there any way I can let her know that I am alive and will somehow find her?"

Major Reed eased back in this chair, folded his hands as if he were some extremely important person and said, "Mr. Sommerfield, I will do whatever I can, through the International Red Cross to locate your sister and give her the news that you are alive and in my care." Major Reed emphasized the words 'my care' as if to give the impression that he was the sole element of compassion and consolation in this terrible war.

For the first time in over a week, Helmut broke into a wide smile, jumped out of his chair and extended a hand toward the man who was his captor and his enemy.

As he shook the Major's hand profusely, he sputtered, "Thank you, *danke*, thank you, *danke*."

While it was strictly forbidden for a POW to touch any American soldier, Major Reed felt a sense of warmth in his enemy's hand.

After the German POW left his office, Major Reed's eyes filled with tears. *He's just a man, like me,* he thought to himself. *I will do what I can to help this man.*

The next morning, after a good breakfast and morning assembly, Helmut climbed into Schmidt's truck and went off to Adam Becker's farm.

5

AFTER SCHMIDT SAID, "Good morning" to Helmut Sommer-field, there was no conversation as the truck rumbled down the high-way and on to the dirt roads.

"My little sister is alive." Sommerfield finally uttered. "Major Reed is going to try to find her."

Schmidt nodded and smiled, afraid to say anything which would damage the delicacy of the comment.

"I will pray to God that you find her." Schmidt offered.

For the first time in many months, Helmut considered the thought of God. For the next few miles, he pondered his fate, the fate of his family, and the fate of his sister. *So God*, he thought to himself, *if you are there, why did you let this happen to me and my family? Why did you allow this terrible war? Why?* He stopped his thoughts, fearing that God would perceive him to be rude and offensive. After all, a good Lutheran would never shake his fist in the face of God. God would surely retaliate with some terrible punishment. On the other hand, what punishment could be worse than being captured by the enemy and having the enemy killing his family? *Perhaps,* he continued think-ing, *if I can make God angry enough, he will destroy me and my suffering will be over. On the other hand, if there is a hell, as my grandmother used to talk about, I could find myself there.* "Enough of this thinking," he said aloud.

Schmidt looked at Helmut. "What's that you say?" Schmidt asked, wondering if Sommerfield was all right.

"I said your truck sounds a little off in the engine. Sounds like your fuel pump might be clogged," Helmut offered.

"Something is not right for sure, but I don't have time to take the truck to town for repairs. Besides, both good mechanics were drafted into the army. My son Rodney is the only mechanic in the area but ever since his brother was killed, he hasn't been himself. The doctor says it's depression. He should work himself out of it someday. Rodney used to be one of the best car and tractor mechanics in the whole county." Schmidt stated, glancing sideways at Helmut.

"Back home, in Germany, I was one of the best motor mechanics in the whole area. I could fix any tractor, truck, or car, no matter what was wrong with it. That's why the army put me in the tank corps. I could fix a tank almost with my eyes closed," Helmut stated with a broad smile.

"Is that so?" Schmidt replied also with a broad smile on his face. "Tell you what, if you agree, I can ask Major Reed if you could spend a few days on my farm, and see if you could tinker with my truck and tractor. The tractor is down to about half speed these days."

"What about Mr. Becker?" Helmut replied. "Won't he object? On second thought, yes he will."

"Becker complains about everything, but I will talk with him and see if we can work a deal where you work at his place until noon and then come across the road to my place after lunch." Schmidt said.

"I have one small request," Helmut stated with a worried look on his face. "Could I come across the road before lunch? Becker's cooking is terrible, very terrible!"

Both men laughed loud enough to attract the attention of those men left riding in the back of the truck.

"Before lunch it is!" Schmidt laughed.

Becker had been informed by Schmidt that the reason for Sommerfield's absence was due to the death of his family. As the truck pulled up to Becker's dilapidated front gate, he emerged from the house, still in his long johns and holding a cup of coffee.

"Well, it's about time you got back to work. Too much time sitting around feeling sorry for yourself can be bad for a fella," he stated in German so Schmidt couldn't understand. "Sorry to hear about your people, but work goes on," Becker continued in English.

Sommerfield and Schmidt looked at each other, knowing full well that this pathetic little man in front of them was not worthy of a reply. Helmut got down from the truck and walked toward the barn. As he did, Becker shouted an order. "Take a load of hay over to the cows in the north pasture. The grass is too short to keep them happy."

Sommerfield and Schmidt looked at each other again as each man turned and went his way.

The following morning, Schmidt informed Sommerfield that he had contacted Major Reed by phone and arranged for him to work half days at his farm. Schmidt specifically mentioned that Helmut would be working on trucks, tractors, and farm equipment. Helmut's face exploded in a smile. Without thinking, the words of his grandmother erupted from his mouth, *"Gott ist gut!"* God is good!

The morning tasks seemed to last for ever. Becker was not happy that his private POW had been snatched by his neighbor. This indignation seemed to cause Becker to demand more work and demand it faster.

What really seemed to get under Becker's skin was Sommerfield's use of English. Becker would address Helmut in German and Helmut would respond in English. To Becker, this meant that his POW slave was becoming almost an equal. Helmut would even address Becker as Mr. Becker, not *Herr* Becker.

For the first time since Helmut had been working at the Becker farm, he heard the dinner bell at the Schmidt farm ring. It was obvious that Schmidt was informing Helmut that the noon meal was on the table and that he needed to come. Helmut looked over to Becker who was standing by a water tank and waved as he turned and walked toward the road. "Sorry to take you away from Mr. Becker's company, but dinner is on the table." Schmidt said jokingly.

Helmut entered the enclosed porch of the small stucco farmhouse. Schmidt pointed to a small porcelain wash basin and a clean towel on the table next to it. "Wash up and come on in."

After washing his hands and face in hot water, he brushed back his hair with his fingers and entered the house. The house was simple but beautiful. This was the first time since he had left his home in Germany that he had been in a real house. Becker's house was more like a barn. He stood there for a minute, trying to adjust to the reality of a home and its family. Through the kitchen door he could see Mrs. Schmidt taking some boiled potatoes out of a pot. She turned, smiled and said, "You are welcome here, Mr. Sommerfield. Please sit down and make yourself comfortable."

Helmut sat for a minute, looking at the many photos and pictures on the walls. Hanging over the piano were old photos of bearded men and firmly trussed women. There were other framed photos of farm buildings, wagons, and families. At the other end of the main room was a wall with one photo on it. A young man in an army officer's uniform, looking very much like Mr. Schmidt, grinned down from the wall. The frame was bordered by a black ribbon. As he stood there looking at the photo, Mrs. Schmidt came in from the kitchen. "That is, was our son Paul. He was killed 18 months ago in France," Helmut glanced toward the handsome woman with a bowl of steaming potatoes in her hands. "I am sorry," Helmut said as if he were directly responsible for her son's death.

"I was never in France," he said as if to assure the still grieving mother that it was not he that had pulled the trigger. She simply smiled and nodded.

Mr. Schmidt entered the main room from a small work room. Gesturing toward a chair, Schmidt said, "Sit here."

A young boy with thick glasses entered from the front door. He washed his hands, came directly to the table and sat down. His shyness seemed to overwhelm those in the room.

"Rodney, this is Mr. Sommerfield. He will be working for us," Mr. Schmidt paused, "for a few months."

The freckled faced boy of eighteen or so glanced up toward Helmut and extended his hand. "Pleased to meet you sir." the boy said quietly.

Rodney was a good looking boy but carried a cloud over his head, like a small black balloon on a string.

The three men sat there while Mrs. Schmidt proceeded to pour glasses of water and take her seat at the other end of the small wooden table.

Mr. Schmidt spoke. "Let us pray. Lord, bless us and our work. Protect our young men in the military, guard our President, and (there was a brief pause) please help them to find Mr. Sommerfield's sister. Amen."

Helmut was elated at the meal set before him. A plate of meat loaf, a bowl of winter peas, bread and potatoes. Not since he had left home had he seen a table set like this. Mr. and Mrs. Schmidt were both aware of Helmut's expression. They were also both aware of what sort of meal he might have been served across the road at Becker's.

"Help yourself, there is more of everything." Mrs. Schmidt offered.

Timidly Helmut filled his plate with magnificent offerings. Once again, the words of his grandmother shot through his mind, *"Gott ist gut!"*

Mrs. Schmidt was aware of the fact the Helmut's family had been killed and made every attempt to avoid the subject during the conversation. However as the meal finished, Mrs. Schmidt served a freshly baked apple pie. After tasting one bite, Helmut made a comment which brought tears to Mrs. Schmidt's eyes. "This is just like my mother used to make."

At that point, Mr. Schmidt folded his hands and lowered his head, as did Mrs. Schmidt. "Oh give thanks unto the Lord, for he is good and his mercy endures for ever. Amen."

With that Schmidt rose from his chair and moved toward the door.

"Well, let's see what's wrong with this truck of mine."

As Helmut rose to follow, he noticed a photograph on the wall next to the door. It was of a college girl, in her academic gown, receiving a diploma. She was beautiful. Helmut stood there for a minute looking at the smiling girl.

"That's our daughter Laurelie. She is a teacher over at the local school house. She graduated top in her class." Mrs. Schmidt proudly announced. As she said this, she realized that this German prisoner of war, this enemy of America was looking at a photo of her daughter. At that point, a sense of protectiveness overwhelmed her. *This man must not take an interest in my daughter,* she thought.

Helmut sensed that the warm countenance in her expression had changed to a cold shield. Mrs. Schmidt took some comfort in knowing that Laurelie left the house well before the POW would arrive in the morning and that she didn't arrive home until after he had left the area. This, she felt, would prevent any sort of contact. As Helmut followed Mr. Schmidt into the yard, she wondered if she should take the photo down and hide it from this man.

Rodney came to the door of the porch. "Dad, I finished cleaning the chicken house, can I help with the truck? I promise I won't get in the way."

"Sure, come on. Just don't interfere with Mr. Sommerfield.

Schmidt was already peering into the engine compartment of the large rust red truck. Helmut immediately focused on the fuel line, rolled up the sleeves of his blue denim work shirt and dove into the inner workings of the machine. Schmidt produced a tool box full of all sorts of greasy wrenches, screwdrivers, and hammers. The two men continued to loosen, then tighten, and loose again a number of hoses, wires, and bolts. After some time, Helmut stated with the conviction of a master mechanic, "Ah, here is the problem. This glob of hair has gotten into your fuel filter and managed to clog the fuel line. He put his mouth on the disconnected fuel line and sucked a mouth full of fuel. As he turned to spit the gasoline onto the ground, he noticed a large, bearded man walking toward him. The man was wearing a blue uniform, with gold buttons and an officer style hat. The sight of a uniformed officer jolted Helmut to the point where he almost swallowed his mouth full of gasoline. Spitting the gas on the ground, he snapped to attention, not knowing exactly what to expect. The bearded man, with huge bushy eyebrows and a large belly, stopped directly in front of Helmut. Looking him up and down, then moving to the side, looking as if he were inspecting the POW, the man spoke, or actually grunted, *"Das ist gutt! Ja?"* Not knowing what to do next, Helmut simply remained at attention. The uniformed man then turned his attention to Schmidt who seemed to be enjoying the little charade. *"Vell, Herr Postmeister, vhat do you tink?"* Schmidt asked the smiling county postmaster.

"Postmeister?" Helmut uttered, not certain whether to relax to an at ease position.

"Mr. Sommerfield, may I present His Honor, the County Postmaster, William 'Mac' McCloud." Still not knowing exactly what to do, Helmut shot his hand toward the grinning man. "Helmut Sommerfield, sir."

Still playing their little game, McCloud remarked, "I have heard about you Mr. Sommerfield."

I am pleased to make your acquaintance." the Postmaster said is his deep, strong voice. "Stand at ease."

Both Henry Schmidt and Mac McCloud seemed to totally enjoy the little ceremony being played out before them.

Turning back toward the yawning truck, Schmidt mentioned that Sommerfield had just found and corrected a serious problem in the fuel system. Holding the glob of oily hair in his fingers, Helmut acknowledged to McCloud that the problem had been solved.

Helmut dove back under the hood, re-attached the fuel line to the carburetor, ran to the cab and started the engine. The engine roared to life as Helmut pressed the accelerator. All three men grinned as the engine raced.

"*Ja, das ist gutt,*" stated McCloud in his funny German accent.

As Helmut continued to inspect all items within the engine compartment, Schmidt and McCloud walked a distance, talking quietly. It was apparent by the way they addressed each other and the way McCloud would place his hand on Schmidt's shoulder that the two men were best of friends.

They were actually closer than friends. These two men had grown up together, gone to school together and raised their families together. Schmidt's son Paul was to have married McCloud's daughter after he returned from the war. It was McCloud who delivered the tragic news of Paul's death and who had grieved with Schmidt during the months after delivering the terrible telegram.

The two men finished their brief conversation and returned to the truck and the grease covered man with the upper half of his body thrust into the engine compartment.

"Your spark plug wires are bad and the fan belt will break any minute," Helmut announced with the seriousness of a surgeon.

McCloud raised his huge bushy eyebrows and uttered, "*Das ist nicht gutt! Ja.*"

"But, do not worry," Helmut stated again with the confidence of a surgeon, "I saw that you have some old trucks and tractors," pointing toward the small red building near the west road. "If I may have permission to look into those autos and tractors, I think I may find some parts which will work."

Schmidt nodded and waved the young man toward the hog shed. "Be sure that you keep track of the time. We must leave here at exactly 4:00 and not a second later. If you mess up my truck, we, or I should say you, will be in big trouble with the Major."

Helmut grabbed a handful of tools and took off running like a school boy. After a few feet, he stopped abruptly. "Can Rodney come with me? I might need some help."

The expression on Rodney's face went from totally passive to one of delight. "Can I go with Mr. Sommerfield, dad? I promise I won't get in his way."

Schmidt nodded approvingly.

Rodney and Helmut ran toward the hog shed.

For the first time since he left his home, he felt good. For the first time since hearing about the death of his family, the sick, dark feeling was not gone but going. As he went from vehicle to vehicle, lifting rusty hoods and blowing off years of dust, he felt a warm smile move across his face. Helmut and Rodney went from one derelict truck to the next broken down tractor, finding parts like small treasures hidden away. Within a brief time, Helmut had garnered a handful of parts and wires. Running back to the truck, the two quickly replaced the worn wires and fan belt. Covered in dirt and grease, Helmut and Rodney came over to Schmidt and announced that the truck would run much better and faster now. Schmidt looked at his watch. "Almost time to go. You'd better go over to the garden hose and clean up. You will find a bar of soap and a towel next to the pump."

Helmut looked at Rodney and thanked him for helping. "Perhaps tomorrow we can work on your father's tractor. I suspect it might take a few days to get it working properly."

At this comment, Rodney beamed. Because of Rodney's general shyness and because he was always the number two son, he tended to stay in the back ground. Nothing he could do was ever as good as his brother Paul, or for that fact, his sister Laurel. Even in 4-H Rodney always managed to come in last. Rodney was the only one of the three Schmidt children who chose not to go off to college after high school graduation. Even Rodney's attempt to join the army failed because of his poor vision and thick glasses. Rodney was the runt of the family and he knew it.

Schmidt went into the house for a minute, then returned to the truck. Helmut was sitting in the front seat anxiously waiting to see the results of his work. As the truck pulled away from the barn, Helmut made a special effort to wave goodbye to Rodney. "Thanks for your help," he shouted over the noise of the engine. The truck raced down the dirt road Schmidt turned the corner dangerously fast as he grinned widely. Helmut watched Schmidt's face as he pushed the accelerator all the way to the floor. As the truck flew by the church and cemetery at the crossroad, Schmidt slammed on the brakes, sending clouds of dust in all directions.

Schmidt, still grinning widely, turned to Helmut and spoke. "My goodness, this old tank has never run like this." The accidental mention of a tank lessened the smiles on both men's faces. Sensing his poor use of words, Schmidt continued, "I can't wait to get this baby out on the highway."

The truck pulled into each farm earlier than expected. By the time they picked up the last POW worker, they were a full 15 minutes ahead of schedule. When the truck finally turned onto the highway heading back toward Camp Alexis, Schmidt shifted up through the gears and was soon cruising at 60 miles per hour. The men in the rear of the truck were all standing, cheering the driver, "Faster, faster." The excitement was good for all, especially Sommerfield. For the first time in a long time, the men of Schmidt's truck were the first to the showers.

"Good job Helmut, maybe tomorrow you can make the truck go faster." the men commented happily.

6

SCHMIDT'S TRUCK ARRIVED at Becker's farm about fifteen minutes earlier than usual. One of farmers on the route was off to Denver; consequently his usual POW would be working somewhere else for a few days. Becker emerged from the barn with a metal milk jug. Swearing profusely, he approached the truck and announced that one of his milk cows had 'made off in the night'. He yelled at Helmut, "Get the horse and go find the cursed animal." Helmut turned and smiled at Schmidt, "So, I am an American cowboy now!"

"See you at lunch Helmut." Schmidt laughed as he drove across the road.

Walking toward Becker, Helmut apologetically stated that he was not allowed to be out of sight of his farm boss. Becker laid down another lengthy barrage of profanity and indicated that if Helmut was not on the horse in three minutes, he would report him to the camp commander.

Helmut shrugged, shook his head and went to the corral at the north end of the barn, taking a bridal off the tack wall as he passed. Many times he had worked horses on his family's farm and knew how to bridle and saddle a horse. As he climbed on the horse, Becker pointed toward a break in the ancient barbed wire fence.

"Follow his tracks and bring the beast home; head first or tail first,

59

I don't care," Becker ordered as he tossed a rope to Helmut. Becker discharged a huge wad of tobacco and stomped off toward the barn.

It felt wonderful to be on a horse again. "So, this is what it is like to be an American cowboy," Helmut muttered to himself as he rode toward the breached fence. The tracks of the cow were deep and easy to see in the soft, damp Nebraska sand. Oddly enough, the tracks did not wander but seemed to follow a direct course through a fallow cornfield. From the cornfield, the cow's tracks pointed toward some small white building about a mile off in the distance. Arriving at the building Helmut discovered that this was a one room school house. In the front, there was an American flag and on the side was a playground. The playground seemed to be ankle deep in mud. In the rear were two small out building which he determined were toilets; boys and girls. Helmut was startled when a woman appeared in the door of the school house and asked what he wanted. For a few seconds, he could not speak, not knowing if she was angry at his trespassing or if she was simply inquiring about his mission. Within a few seconds, he recognized the woman as the girl in the photograph on Schmidt's wall. She must be his daughter, the school teacher.

In his broken English, he announced that he was Helmut Sommerfield and that he was looking for a missing cow. The woman was beautiful and Helmut felt as if he would fall off the horse any minute.

Shading her eyes with her hand, she descended the steps of the school house, moving briskly toward Sommerfield. By now a dozen or so students of all sizes filled the doorway and the porch of the school house, gawking to see what this stranger wanted.

Approaching the horse, the young woman extended her hand. "So, you are the Mr. Sommerfield I have been hearing about. I am Laurel Schmidt. My parents talk a great deal about you and the fine work you are doing on our farm. My dad can't say enough about how you have repaired his tractors and trucks and my brother Rodney thinks you are the greatest.

Helmut leaned over and took her hand. "I, I am pleased to meet you, very pleased to meet you." was all he could stutter.

Her blond hair, clear complexion and gentle smile completely disabled this battle hardened German soldier. He again stuttered something about a missing cow. Laurel turned toward her giggling students and asked if any of them might know the whereabouts of Mr. Becker's cow.

"No Miss Schmidt." they responded in unison, giggling at the awkward stranger on horseback.

After regaining a bit of his composure, Helmut suggested that he continue to follow the tracks past the school yard. As he turned the horse's head with the reigns, he looked back to see Miss Schmidt wave and return to her charges.

"Miss Schmidt" he uttered quietly. Passing the American flag, he nodded, as if to acknowledge it. Helmut's whole outlook on life as a POW had just changed and changed drastically. Not since before this stupid war had he felt so euphoric, so free, and so wonderful. For a few minutes Helmut floated in his reverie. Reality struck when he glanced back at the ground and noticed the cow tracks moving off the road and into a dense wooded area. Guiding his horse toward the trees, he noticed a dilapidated farmhouse, surrounded by toppled trees, fallen barns, and once upon a time chicken houses. At the side of the house were two pickup trucks and a cow. Approaching the house with caution, Helmut was not certain if the cow had been captured and was about to be slaughtered by rustlers. He had seen cowboy western movies where rustlers would steal cows and butcher them. If this were the case, there could be gun fight or even a fist fight. As Helmut approached the house, now on foot, he noticed a strange, sweet smell on the wind. The horse flared his nostrils and took a deep breath. He noticed the cow was eating something out of a large metal tub. Turning his head to look at Helmut, the cow made a few strange noises, something between a moo and a belch and returned to his meal. The smell became stronger as Helmut tied the horse to a gate post. All of the sudden, two old men, two identical old men dressed in overalls and boots, appeared in the front door of the house.

"Who are you?" demanded one of the old men.

"What do you want?" insisted the other.

It didn't take long to determine that the two men were slightly drunk and posed little or no threat.

"My name is Helmut Sommerfield; I am a German prisoner of war. I am trying to capture Mr. Becker's cow and return her to his farm."

The two old men stood, stunned at the proclamation.

"German prison of war?" one uttered.

"Are we in some kind of trouble?" the other mumbled.

"I am only trying to capture this cow," Helmut insisted as the cow continued to make strange noises as he gulped the porridge-like mess in the tub.

"Ya," said one of the men with a loud burst of laughter, "That's Molly the Milk Cow, she's been here before."

"Do I smell schnapps or perhaps, whiskey?" Helmut queried

"Whiskey!" one of the old men shouted. "We are making the best whiskey in the whole dang county, the whole country, the whole world!

Both men began to laugh, trying to remain erect.

"We are also making the best cow food in the entire universe!" one man stated as he pointed to the cow, now beginning to find her legs wobbly.

"Come in Mr. Prisoner of War." The two men invited.

"My name is Helmut Sommerfield," he said as he entered the dilapidated house.

The inside of the house had been put in order. Old chairs and a table stood in the middle of the main room. Some old pictures, possibly from a past tenant adorned the walls. Several newer pictures of women in bathing suits and less had been tacked on the wall nearest the table. On the floor of the kitchen were several dozen gallon glass jugs and Mason jars. At the back of the kitchen was an open stairway leading down to an underground cellar. From the cellar, Helmut could smell the pungent odor of whiskey and smoke. Out the kitchen window he noticed a metal smoke stack emerging from what would have been the back end of the storm cellar. This was obviously intended to carry the smoke away and into the trees.

The two old men stood there as Helmut surveyed the operation. "What do you think of our little business?" one man asked.

Helmut simply smiled and nodded.

After a few minutes of uncomfortable silence, one the old men stated boldly, "My name is Rupert and this is my twin brother Ross Rupert and Ross Ricther. We have farms over thata way," he said pointing out the window. This is our club house and our little moonshine factory," Rupert giggled. Rupert and Ross continued to giggle as Ross took an old tin cup, filled it with liquid from a glass jug and offered it to Helmut. "Here, take a little swig. It will do you good," Rupert stated, still giggling.

"Gentleman, I would very much like to taste your whiskey, but the rules for POWs are that we consume no alcohol, except at camp and when permitted. If I were caught breaking these rules, all of my comrades in the camp will lose some privileges for a week or two. I do not want to be responsible for causing that to happen," Helmut replied.

Ross, now very serious, uttered, "We won't tell a soul."

"Yes, but when I show up at Mr. and Mrs. Schmidt's table at noon, they will smell your whiskey on my breath."

"Schmidt? You are working for Henry Schmidt?" Both old men looked at each other with expressions of shock on their faces. "Harriet Schmidt is our sister," Ross blurted. No, you can not drink this!" Rupert added, pulling the cup back. Our sister is a holy terror when it comes to whiskey. If she knew about our little club house here, she would come personally and burn it down," Rupert replied in serious concern.

"And us with it," Ross added.

"Please Mr. Helmut, don't tell Harriet about this!" Rupert continued.

"Well, if you don't tell anyone that I was here, I won't tell anyone about your little secret," Helmut said.

Rupert thrust his hand toward Helmut. Helmut shook it. Then he shook Ross's hand. The pact was sealed. Both Ross and Rupert poured another cup of the clear liquid and offered a toast. "To Mr. Helmut." One drank half a cup and the other finished it.

"I must get Mr. Becker's cow back to him before he comes looking for me and we all end up in big trouble."

As Helmut started to leave, he turned back toward the two men. "By the way, that school teacher at the little school house down the road, Miss Schmidt, does she have any friends?" Helmut paused and stammered a bit, 'men friends'." The two old men looked at each other, raised their eyebrows and laughed.

"Our niece is a little too snooty, with her college education, to have an interest in any of the local farmer boys or cowboys. Story was that she had a friend at college but he turned out to be queer," Ross said, bursting into laughter. Both men doubled over in laughter, almost to the point of collapse. "That fellow came out here to the farmlands one Christmas break. Talk about a city slicker! This guy wouldn't go outside the house. He spent the whole week reading and making goo-goo eyes at Laurel. She is a good one all right, but you have to get past her mother to even say hello to that girl." The two men continued to laugh as they chided Helmut.

Helmut went back to the tethered horse and gathered the rope Becker had given him to lead the cow. By now the cow had consumed most of the contents of the metal tub and appeared to be very unstable in her movements. The sounds coming from the various parts of her body gave Helmut concern as to what he would tell Becker when he returned.

Once the cow had been tethered by the neck, it showed absolutely no interest in being led home. In fact, its only interest was to lie down on the ground and emit large quantities of foul air. The corn whiskey mash from the still had all but leveled this simple beast.

Helmut found an old broom handle and began to hit the offended cow until it began to move toward the direction of Becker's farm. The two old men disappeared back into the house as Helmut followed his tracks back to the farm.

Passing the school house, he noticed the children sitting around the muddy playground, eating an early lunch. Miss Schmidt was sitting on a bench surrounding a tree, eating hers. Helmut smiled, waved, and pointed to the captured cow. "I found Molly!" Miss Schmidt smiled in return and waved her approval.

The walk back to the farm was long and unpleasant. On occasions, Molly's intestines would explode toward the horse and rider, causing both to bolt. On other occasions, the cow insisted upon lying down in the middle of the road. This required several sever beatings with the broom handle to convince the errant bovine to proceed. Each time the cow was hit, it would issue a blast from front or rear. Helmut didn't know whether to laugh at the situation or yell further incantations to the intoxicated animal.

After much prodding, pulling, and threats of becoming roast beef, Helmut and the cow approached Becker's barn. Becker emerged from an old unused chicken house.

"So, it looks like you found her and judging by the way she is walking, she made her way down to the Richter boys still again. She smells them boys cooking the mash and makes her way to the source just like an alcoholic finds his way to a saloon. I swear, if it weren't for the fact that Rupert Richter is brother-in-law to the county sheriff, I would call the sheriff on those two. And too, I do like to buy a jug of their shine from time to time," Becker stated laughingly. "In fact," Becker snorted, "the word is that Sheriff Buckstone has been known to pick up a jug now and then, on cold winter nights."

As the cow staggered toward her stall in the barn, Becker shouted, "For Pete's sake, don't let her lie down! If she lies down, she'll bloat and kill her self. She won't be able to breathe. Fetch me two of those four-by-four timbers next to the barn."

Helmut ran and collected two four-by-four inch wooden beams and brought them to the stable. Becker was pulling the belching cow toward her stall. "Before she lies down, shove one of those beams under her belly and the other under her chest. This will force her to stand up until the mash has had a chance to pass through." Helmut shoved the two boards under the cow and blocked them in the fence of the stall. "It will take a few hours for the sour mash to pass, but we won't be able to use her milk for about a week. She's pickled and her milk is pickled," Becker stated followed by a long string of profanity.

7

ANOTHER DAY ON THE FARMS had come to an end. Men took their much needed showers and waited for the dinner call to be announced over the loud speaker system. Finally, the dinner call came and men filed into the dining hall. Helmut spotted Carl at the head of the line. Carl motioned that he wanted Helmut to sit with him at a corner table. Helmut nodded, filled his dinner plate and moved toward Carl's table.

"How's it going?" Carl asked.

"Good, very good. I like my work, especially now that I only work half a day for that Becker guy," Helmut replied.

"Helmut, after dinner, I want to talk with you. Let's take a walk down to the farm, just you and me." Carl said in a very quiet whisper.

After dinner, the two walked toward the back gate where the main compound connected with the 'farm'.

The wind began to blow as the sun had slipped below the horizon. "What is it Carl?"

"Just keep walking and I will show you something." Carl whispered.

Pointing with his eyes Carl said, "You see the place where the concrete slabs of the runway have sunk into the ground?"

Helmut nodded.

"Look beyond the runway, to that small gully in the sand."

Again Helmut nodded. "I see it."

"OK, now look at that pit where the motor pool shop dumps their used motor oil," he said gesturing with his chin toward the Quonset hut used as the motor pool.

"OK, I see it" remarked Helmut.

Carl looked around to see if anyone was watching them as he stopped to light a cigarette, "Last week, I saw a fox jump down that hole behind the motor pool and a few minutes later, I saw that same fox emerge from that gully on the other side of the runway. That means that there is a natural tunnel between the back of the motor pool and that opening outside the fence. It is most likely the same underground tunnel which caused the collapse of the runway."

Again Helmut nodded only this time with a worried expression on his face.

"Carl, why are we talking about foxes running down holes?"

"Because my friend, this little foxhole represents our passage to freedom." Carl said with a broad smile.

Helmut looked startled as he stared Carl directly in the eyes.

Carl went on. "We are supposed to escape. We are prisoners of war being held by the enemy. If we remain here, we are nothing more than cowards and traitors to our own country."

Feeling a bit sick, Helmut asked, "And just how do you plan to escape and to where? It's over a thousand miles to the Atlantic or the Pacific. If we were to reach either coast, how would we get back to Germany, swim?"

Carl reached out and took Helmut by the shoulders, "My friend, my plan is to go south into Texas."

"Texas?" Helmut questioned.

"Yes, Texas." From there, we can find a boat or ship going south to Argentina. It is well known that the German High Command and the Argentina Government are working together in providing safe havens for German military personnel." Holding a map torn from one of the camp's library books, Carl unfolded the map and pointed to Nebraska, then Texas, and then Argentina.

"Helmut, the route from here to the Gulf of Mexico is easy. Look, there are almost no towns between here and there. We can jump a train and make it to where we can steal a car or two and get to the Gulf. Down along the Gulf, there must be thousands of small boats we could steal and sail to Cuba and down to Argentina. We can do it Helmut! But I need someone like you who knows how to obtain cars and keep them running. And if we are lucky we can find a boat with an engine for the trip across the water. Just think, we will be heroes when we arrive in Argentina."

Helmut, looking for a way out began to respond. "Carl, how do you know that small hole where you saw the fox is big enough for a man? What happens if you get stuck in there and can't get out?"

With a wide smile Carl responded, "I am glad you asked that. Yesterday, I made an excuse to go to the motor pool to get some gasoline for cleaning paint off my boots. While there, I excused myself to clean my boots outside, near the spot where the oil is dumped. For fifteen minutes, I was alone and unseen. I made my way into the hole and under the runway and out the other end. It was tight in places, but the rain water has made the tunnel large enough for a man to pass. When I came back into the motor pool, my clothes were covered with motor oil. I simply told the guy there that I had slipped and fallen into the hole. No problem. No problem at all!"

Carl noticed the guard at the gate to the farm looking at them.

"Come on Helmut, let's keep going.

The two men signed the control sheet and pinned the yellow passes to their shirts. As they continued into the farm, Helmut said, "Carl, I don't like it!"

"Just what don't you like, soldier?" Carl demanded.

"Do you prefer to hide from your responsibility as a German soldier and let your country fail in its attempt to instill justice in the world? Are you a coward, like most of the men in this sheep pen? Do you ever want to see your country and family again?" Carl continued.

Not realizing it, Carl's mention of Helmut's family had terminated the conversation. Carl gave Helmut a look of total contempt, shook his head and walked back toward the gate. Helmut remained behind for another half hour until he heard the guard's whistle blow and announced that all POWs were to return to the main camp. Helmut moved slowly back toward the barracks, not knowing what sort of reception to expect when he once again encountered Carl. Helmut went directly into his barracks, and went to bed. When 'lights out' was called over the loud speakers, Helmut was already in a deep sleep.

The next morning, the camp loud speaker erupted into the morning wake up call. However, instead of the usual canned music and chitchat, the camp commander announced that all men would form up immediately at the assembly area. Assembly would be in exactly 20 minutes. As the men pulled on their clothes, they wondered out loud their concerns about the message. Some considered the possibility that something serious had happened in the war. Others offered other possible answers for this drastic change in routine.

The full complement of the camp's POWs was standing at attention when Major Reed took his place at the main podium. His aid and translator were already standing at the side podium.

Major Reed began. "I am terribly sorry to have to announce to you that one of your colleagues, Carl Bauman has made an unsuccessful attempt to escape from our camp."

The men standing at attention felt the impact of the information. Their faces became serious and pained. While there had not been an escape, or for that fact a fight, in over two years, each man knew that escape attempts or fights were considered a very serious offense and that all extraordinary privileges would be stopped for a certain period of time. This meant no more bacon for breakfast, no more free time for reading in the camp reading room, and no more farmwork. This escape meant confinement to camp and confinement to an empty routine.

Major Reed continued, "Carl Bauman managed to somehow get past the fences and make his way to the railroad tracks. He attempted to climb aboard a moving train and unfortunately, he fell under the wheels and was cut in half. As you all know, this sort of action on the part of even one POW results in a complete shut down of the camp and loss of all privileges. So, as of this date, you are under detention for seven days. You are dismissed for breakfast."

The men slowly moved toward the dining hall, some grumbling, and some reflecting on Carl. The cooks had been ordered to cut meals down to a basic of oatmeal, bread and coffee. No jam, no bacon, no sugar.

8

MAJOR REED'S SUBORDINATES had been busy all morning with issues related to dealing with Carl's body and with telephoning the truck drivers informing them not to come for a week. Unfortunately, Henry Schmidt had left his farm just five minutes before his phone rang telling him to stay home. Arriving at the camp at the usual hour, he found no one in the assembly area. Assuming something had happened, he walked over to the guard house and inquired as to why the men were not going to the farms today. The guard informed him about the escape and suggested that he talk with Major Reed. Schmidt knew the way to Major Reed's office. He thanked the young soldier and walked away.

Major Reed was sitting behind his gray metal desk, an American flag displayed behind him on the wall.

Major Reed rose from his seat and extended his hand as Henry Schmidt walked into his office.

"Sorry that you had to make the trip for nothing Mr. Schmidt, but as you may not know, we had an escape last night. Poor fellow was cut in half by the train wheels. Nice guy, but just couldn't stand confinement. I don't know where he planned to go, but he went. And in order to discourage others from making a break, or for that fact, fighting, we have a strict policy that any such behavior will cost the entire population its privileges. I hate to close everything down, but we can't be having problem behavior.

"Care for a cup of coffee Mr. Schmidt?" Major Reed asked.

"Love one." Schmidt replied.

Reed picked up his desk phone and buzzed his assistant in the outer office. "Two coffees please."

"Tell me Mr. Schmidt, what do you think of this fellow you have working for you—Sommerfield."

"I like the kid." Schmidt replied.

The corporal knocked twice and entered the office with a tray of coffee, sugar and cream. Placing it on a small coffee table, he briefly came to attention, turned and left the office. Major Reed came out from behind his desk and took a seat next to Schmidt.

Schmidt continued, "I had problems with the idea of these German prisoners of war working among us. You see, I lost a son—my eldest son—nineteen months ago in France. The thought of these Nazi pigs being given any sort of comfort bothered me. The thought of them working in our fields and eating at our tables was too much. After getting to know Sommerfield, I realize that he is no more a monster than my son. They are just boys caught up in the madness of old men's wars. The day I received news of my son's death, I could have killed all of the Helmut Sommerfields in the world and not blinked an eye. I just wonder how many Helmut Sommerfields my son killed before he was killed. I just wonder how many fathers and mothers have reason to hate my son and perhaps even me?"

Schmidt blinked back a tear beginning to form in his eye and focused on his coffee.

Major Reed sensed the pause in the conversation. "Strange, isn't it. We raise our children to believe that killing and hurting other people is wrong, yet when it comes to war, we give them medals for killing." Reed stated as he pointed to the three rows of ribbons on his chest. "I can still see the faces of some of the men I killed."

Major Reed felt comfortable exposing his soul to this farmer. Unlike military men, Schmidt seemed to understand the guilt and sorrow this man in uniform tried to hide.

"And then when we capture these boys, these enemy soldiers," gesturing toward the camp, "we treat them like criminals, which they are not." Major Reed sighed deeply. "So, what are we to do?"

Both men looked into each other's eyes. Both could feel the pain which had been inflicted on them by the God of War.

Both men sat quietly, with their coffee cups to their lips. Both men in deep thought.

"Major," stated Schmidt in a bold voice, "next Thursday is Thanksgiving. My wife and I had planned to invite Mr. Sommerfield to our table on that day. Now with the shut down, this won't happen. What would you think if I and some of my neighbors were to come here to the camp and share Thanksgiving with the German men and of course, your staff?"

Major Reed seemed shocked at the suggestion. "Mr. Schmidt, we have over 200 men at this camp. That's a lot of turkey and potatoes! You surely don't have that many neighbors!"

"Major, if you agree, I will take care of the turkey and potatoes." Schmidt responded enthusiastically.

Knowing full well that this sort of activity would violate every rule in the book, Major Reed laughed and shook his head disapprovingly.

"Mr. Schmidt, I have tried hard to maintain this small satellite camp. Many of my superiors want to bring the men back into the big camp over in the east. I truly believe this smaller camp is much better than the big ones. If I were to grant your request, we would risk being absorbed back into the central camp. I am afraid...he paused "Oh, to heck with the system! After all, what does the Good Book say, 'If your enemy is hungry, you feed him'."

Schmidt smiled broadly and continued, "It also says, "Do unto others as you would have them do unto you. If your higher ups give you any trouble on this deal, simply ask them how they would like to have their sons treated if they were POWs." They have seen the god of war, now let's show them the God of Peace."

Schmidt, still smiling, stood up and grasped Major Reed's hand. "Major, if there were more men like you, there would be fewer wars and fewer prisoners of war."

Fighting back the emotions which come on men when they stumble upon a divine truth, both the soldier and the farmer looked into each other's eyes. There were tears in both.

Breaking the tension of the moment, Major Reed turned to the calendar on the wall. "It's now Monday, zero eight hours. We are looking at Thursday, twelve hundred hours. We will have a lot to accomplish by then. Just a minute, I will need to bring my second in command and the camp chaplain into the picture." Major Reed again picked up the phone and ordered his aid to summon Captain Thomas and Chaplain Wolf.

Schmidt, still grinning spoke. "Major, I think I know a way whereby we can bring out the best in our community by bringing out their worst. As you know, most of the farmers north of this camp are of German decent and most of the farmers south of the camp are of Swedish decent. However, both groups of people are of the Lutheran faith. You have the German Lutherans and you have the Swedish Lutherans. In truth, they don't like each other. From time to time, a German girl will marry a Swedish boy and vise versa. This makes for some interesting politics. Anyhow, both the Germans and the Swedes pride themselves as being better cooks than the other. If I put the word out that the POWs prefer the Swedish cooking over the German cooking, the Germans will go wild. If I also put out the word that the POWs prefer German cooking, the Swedes will go wild. We can continue the same game with the Baptists and the Catholics as well. If we play this game right, we will have either the greatest feast in the history of the world or we will start a new world war."

Both men laughed at the thought of dozens of women working day and night to out cook their rival across the unseen lines which divide Christendom into more factions than any dictator could devise.

A knock on the door dissolved this moment of humor.

"Chaplain Wolf, Captain Thomas, come in." Major Reed requested. "I want you to meet Mr. Schmidt,"

Schmidt interrupted, "Call me Henry, that's what my friends call me." "OK Henry, this is Chaplain Wolf, this is Captain Thomas."

"We've met, thank you." Schmidt returned.

"Yes." Chaplain Wolf stated quietly, "It was regarding Helmut Sommerfield. That's right, it was when his family was killed….Terrible thing."

Major Reed opened the door to his office and asked for two more chairs. Once the chairs had been placed, Major Reed beckoned those present to be seated.

"Mr. Schmidt, Henry has made a suggestion which I feel is worth acting on. As you know, next Thursday is Thanksgiving. Many of the POWs were to have been invited 'unofficially' of course, to celebrate the day with the farmers for whom they work. As you also know, the lock down this week will prevent any POWs from leaving camp or for that fact, enjoying extraordinary privileges until next Monday. While we do have strict operational rules regarding discipline, I feel that we can and should make a selected diversion from the letter of the law.

Major Reed rose from his chair as if to make a speech to the three men assembled before him. Looking out the window of his office, he continued. "We have a situation much like Adam and Eve. As was the case with Adam's sin, one man's transgression left all men subject to punishment. Even though they themselves were not guilty of the offense, they…we must suffer."

Chaplain Wolf and Captain Thomas looked at each other, wondering quietly what the old man was getting at. Did he plan to release the whole lot of POWs simply because the war was not their fault?

Major Reed continued with the preface to his rule-breaking announcement. He even mentioned the business about the God of War and the God of Peace. Turning toward the American flag, he made a few comments about democracy and the Pilgrims having dinner with the Indians.

Then, he turned directly toward Chaplain Wolf and Captain Thomas and stated, "Gentlemen, this coming Thanksgiving we will be inviting some guests from the community to celebrate Thanksgiving with our men. We will invite all of the farm families who are kind enough to work with us in the war effort. Together we will celebrate democracy."

Again, both Chaplain Wolf and Captain Thomas looked at each other in wonderment.

Captain Thomas began to speak, "But sir, this sort of fraternization is contrary to regulations. Section…"

Major Reed held up his hand. "I know the regulations, probably better than anyone in this room, but I believe, or I should say, Henry and I believe that this gesture of Christian concern, especially in light of one of our most important national holidays, is in order. I am willing to put my leaves on the line for this one," he said, pointing to the oak clusters on his collar.

"Chaplain Wolf, I would like you to prepare a sermon, a brief sermon, for the event" he emphasized the word 'brief'. "No denominational land mines, no anecdotes which might lead to offense, and no jokes. We will be having people from a number of different church backgrounds there."

"Captain Thomas have you heard the men singing in showers?"

Captain Thomas nodded.

"Beautiful, absolutely beautiful! Could you form up some sort of choir? No German drinking songs!"

Major Reed continued as if he were setting the stage for a presidential inaugural ceremony

Captain Thomas still somewhat shocked at the events of the last few minutes, nodded that he could probably put something together.

"Perhaps something from Wagner," Major Reed said grinning. "but not Aida!"

Turning to Schmidt he explained, "Aida is all about prisoners of war. We don't want to rub it in."

77

Again Captain Thomas and Chaplain Wolf looked at each other.

"I will see what I can do, Major," Captain Thomas replied.

"I will submit my sermon text for your consideration." Chaplain Wolf stated with one eyebrow slightly raised.

"Good, wonderful!" Major Reed beamed. *If this doesn't make his superiors happy*, he thought, *it would certainly make God happy.*

As if addressing a full staff meeting, he continued. "And you Schmidt...sorry, Henry, you will take the responsibility of extending our sincere invitation to the families in the community and give me a head count by no later than zero nine hundred Wednesday."

Schmidt joined in the side glancing with Chaplain Wolf and Captain Thomas

"Yes sir." Schmidt responded almost in jest.

None of the three men in the office had seen Major Reed so buoyant or enthusiastic in the time they served at the camp.

"That will be all." Major Reed stated.

The two military men rose from their seats, saluted, turned and left the room. Schmidt remained.

Major Reed, still pondering the great event, returned to the reality of present.

Schmidt extended his hand. "There are good men and there are great men. Next Thursday, we shall see how you measure up."

A look of utmost seriousness crossed Major Reed's face. "I don't want to be great, but I do want to be remembered as a good man."

"I will contact you by nine o'clock Wednesday with a count." Schmidt said as he left the office.

Outside the major's office, the three men regrouped.

"Captain Thomas, can you get me a list of all the farmers who participate in the POW work program?"

Captain Thomas nodded and redirected the instruction to the Major's aid sitting behind the desk. The aid pulled open a file cabinet drawer and produced a three page list of names, farm locations, and telephone numbers. Captain Thomas glanced at the list and handed it to Schmidt. Schmidt ran his fingers down the list of names, occasionally stopping and nodding. "Many of the folks south of the highway are related to my mother—all Swedes. Many of these people are related to Mac McCloud. I will get him in on this deal."

"Well, Captain Thomas, Chaplain Wolf, we do have our work cut out for us, don't we?" Schmidt stated, "Let's get to it! The two officers instinctively saluted the farmer as he dismissed himself. Still looking at the list of participating farmers, he continued to smile as he walked past the guard to his truck.

9

HE STARTED THE TRUCK AND drove past the hangers toward the highway. As he drove, he noticed something he'd never seen before—a baseball field inside the camp compound. Two teams were on the field with dozens of others sitting on the ground watching. "Baseball? Germans?" he thought aloud. "Germans don't play baseball; Americans play baseball!" As he stopped for a minute to watch the game, he noticed Sommerfield with an old catcher's mitt squatting behind the home plate. Shaking his head and laughing aloud, Schmidt drove off toward the highway.

Arriving at the dirt road leading toward his farm, Schmidt slowed his truck and turned east toward town, not west toward his farm. "Better talk with McCloud face to face on this," he muttered aloud.

The dirt street which constituted the main street to the town of three hundred souls was lined with pickups, with several horse drawn wagons parked under the trees at the north end of the street.

Schmidt pulled up in front of the US flag pole which distinguished the Post Office from the rest of the buildings on the street. With the three sheets of paper in hand, Henry entered the post office, nearly bumping into the town's official greeter, Curly Brown. Curly was the town greeter, town gossip, town historian, and town drunk all rolled into one shabby little package. For the price of a beer, you could find out who was holding hands with whom. Curly seemed to have some sort of connection with Merle, the operator over at the telephone exchange. So between Curly and Merle, one could find out just about anything that was going on in the county. On occasion Curly would volunteer to assist the postmaster in sorting the mail. He especially liked to sort post cards. Within a few seconds, he could memorize every word on the three by five piece of paper, including the postmark. This was an extremely valuable source of information. As Henry passed Curly, Curly focused on the three pieces of paper. "What's going on?" Curly demanded. Knowing full well that Curly was about to become a primary player in his scheme, he stopped, propped one foot up on a bench near the front door and began. "Curly, the Major over at the POW camp is having a Thanksgiving potluck meal for the POWs. He feels they need a little cheering up, especially after that terrible accident last night. "What terrible accident?" Curly demanded.

"One of the POWs went over the hill and was killed trying to catch a train." Schmidt offered, knowing that by noon, the story would be all over the county. "Anyhow, the poor fellow went nuts and took off. Now the camp is in a lockdown. No activities for seven days."

Curly's insistence on the details of the escape and accident was intense. How many pieces was the body cut into? Was there lots of blood? Who found the body? And so on.

It was not Schmidt's intent to spark fear of another escape nor to cause alarm in the community, so he kept on repeating, "The poor fellow simply went nuts! Just plain went over the top. Poor guy."

Curly couldn't wait to dash across the street to the telephone office and inform Merle about the hottest story of the year. "But," Schmidt continued, "Major Reed feels real bad about this and wants to make things right. He and Chaplain Wolf have decided to invite some of the farm families to the camp for a Thanksgiving potluck, but there's a problem."

"Problem? asked Curley, "What problem?

"Well, some of the POWs who work on the farms tell stories of how great the cooking is on the Swede side of the highway. Those working on our side tell about how great the German farmers' wives can cook. I am truly afraid that someone could leave the potluck feeling bad. That is, if their cooking is not all that good."

Schmidt was playing with Curly.

"You mean to say that if our folks don't measure up to what the Swedes can cook, those POWs will choose to work on their farms and not ours?" Curly questioned as if he had just realized some great piece of knowledge.

"That's about the size of it. If our women don't measure up to the Swedes, we could be in trouble. All the POWs will choose to go south and we will be left short handed." Schmidt continued.

"Holy cow! That could be bad. And all the women would feel bad too." Curly added.

"Well, I need to get in and talk with McCloud before he gets too busy." Schmidt stated as he patted Curly on the back and pushed the door to the post office open.

"Well, well, well, look who has decided to come to the big city," Mac roared. "When are you going to sell that weed patch of yours and move to town?" Mac bellowed.

"As soon as you stop eating!" Henry responded "And if I sold my 'weed patch' you and most others around here would starve."

Both men laughed as they walked back toward the stove and two large wooden chairs. McCloud took two brown coffee mugs from off the shelf, filled each with coffee, and handed one to his lifelong friend.

"I see you met Curly on the way in. The way his eyes were popping out, you must have given him something really big," Mac droned.

"Yah, I told him about the escape and accident down near the POW camp last night."

Mac's huge bushy eyebrows rose like two great puffs of smoke. "Escape? Accident?"

Schmidt went on to relate the details of the event as McCloud stroked his thick, white beard.

"Before folks around here start to have bad feelings about the escape, Major Reed wants to do something positive. He and his staff feel that a potluck dinner with the POWs, the guards, and the folks in the area, might tend to make people feel better." Schmidt stated. "That would mean folks on both sides of the highway."

"What about town folks?" McCloud questioned, being a town person.

"Great idea!" Schmidt responded back as if McCloud had found the missing link. "Great idea!"

A huge smile spread across McCloud's broad Santa Claus face. Likewise, a smile grew across Schmidt's face.

Schmidt continued, "Chaplain Wolf will be giving a sermon and there will be some singing. And there will no doubt be a speech by Major Reed."

"I noticed something strange this morning, when I left the camp. The POWs were playing baseball. Baseball! Germans don't play baseball. I was thinking we might be able to pull together some of the younger men to play a game of baseball with the POWs. Now, how's that for a great idea?" Schmidt said.

"You know, you might just have something there. I wouldn't be at all surprised if your two brothers-in-law, Rupert and Ross, might just take a few bets on who wins and what the score might be."

Both men looked at each other and laughed.

Schmidt handed the three pages of farmers to McCloud. "Can you somehow talk with those people south of the highway, and I will take those on the north side?" Schmidt asked.

McCloud nodded, "I will also take those here in town. In fact, let's make a poster for the window." Like a couple of kids making a kite, the two men found paper, pencils, and a box of crayons. Soon a small poster announcing the event was taped on the glass door of the post office. As both men stood looking at their publications, Reverend Roland Steinke, the pastor of the Lutheran Church in town and several small congregations in the county, came to the door. Reverend Steinke was Schmidt's pastor at the small church across from his farm.

Steinke was most definitely not a country boy and let it be known that he preferred the city lights and seminary libraries. On occasion he would make visits to the rural members of his congregation, especially during pheasant season. 'The' Reverend Steinke, as he liked to introduce himself, was not well liked by several members of his flock, but with a war going on, you took whatever you could get from the seminary. Fortunately for Roland Steinke, he was classified 4F and not available for military service. No one seemed to know what the 4F was for but it was assumed that it was something polite people did not talk about. Perhaps one of Steinke's most objectionable qualities was that of intolerance of his fellow members of 'the cloth' as he liked to put it. If there was a common event where pastors from various community churches were in attendance, he would excuse himself, usually muttering something about 'unionism' or 'liberal theology' or simply muttering. On one occasion he walked all the way around the town cemetery to avoid coming face to face with a Catholic priest and some nuns participating in a funeral. Needless to say, his name was often times distorted, not only by the young people in his catechism class, but by men who stood outside the church after Sunday morning service. In any case, Steinke did the job; he baptized them, married them, and buried them.

Schmidt and McCloud stood there at the post office door pretending to read the poster as Steinke craned his neck to read between them. "A potluck. At the prison, on Thanksgiving Day! On Thanksgiving Day? For heaven sake, who would hold a potluck on Thanksgiving Day? That's absurd!" Steinke stated as his voice rose to almost a scream. "Who in their right minds would hold a potluck on one of our most holy festivals?"

McCloud and Schmidt looked at each as if to say, "Let's get this guy!"

"Reverend, it seems that our chaplain friend at the prison, the

POW camp, has been talking with some of his wards. It seems that they have been talking about the meals they have been receiving while working on local farms. It seems that these POWs have been giving reports to the camp officials the meals they receive from Baptist and Catholic farmers appear to be much superior to those of the Lutheran farmers. I, as a Lutheran, am somewhat concerned about this fact, if it is a fact." Schmidt said in all seriousness.

"If this continues to be the case, we could stand to lose some of our POW farm hands, not to mention the reputations of our wives. After all, our wives are some of the best cooks in the country."

Steinke's face became cold and serious. "You mean to tell me that these 'convicts' are being allowed to pick and choose the farms they are willing to work at and the tables they prefer to eat at?"

Schmidt and McCloud both nodded in unison.

"These are dark days Reverend." McCloud groaned.

"I am a Methodist and I am worried what this could do." McCloud stated in false seriousness.

"I don't know what my wife would think if she were to find out that her cooking was seen to be second rate. It scares me Pastor. We have to do something about this!" Schmidt stated trying with all his powers to keep from laughing.

Again, the two men nodded at the bewildered clergyman pondering this dilemma.

Reverend Steinke took a deep breath, cocked his head back a few notches, like he did just before beginning a sermon, raised one eyebrow and began to speak.

"Yes Mr. McCloud, these are indeed dark days; days when nation wars against nation and brother against brother. These are days when the lion roams the field, looking for lambs on which to feed. But these are days when peacemakers, men of God must arise and attempt to bring about reconciliation between the lion and the lamb in order that they may be able to lie down next to each other and live peacefully in God's good order."

McCloud and Schmidt were both ready to explode with laughter at The Reverend's little sermon.

"Yes gentlemen," he continued, "we must put aside our differences and come together in unity." Steinke was quick to correct himself, "Political unity for the purpose of taming these ruthless lions now in our captivity! We must show them mercy where there is no mercy. We must show them peace where there is no peace. We must show..."

Schmidt interrupted before another sermon could get started. "exactly Reverend. You sir, have hit the nail directly on the head. We must show them what Americans are really like. And we must show them that Lutheran wives are better cooks than Baptists or Catholics or..." Schmidt paused to glance at McCloud, "...even Methodist wives."

At that comment, McCloud's eyebrows went up as he uttered an "Oh ho! That sounds like a challenge my friend."

"You do realize that most families have already made commitments for Thanksgiving dinner at home, don't you?" Steinke noted.

"Yes, many families will choose to remain at home, but many will choose to join with community in bringing peace to these poor captured souls." McCloud continued. "Let's see what we can do. I will take responsibility for listing the names of those families wishing to share their harvest delights with those less fortunate."

Again Schmidt and McCloud glanced at each other as if they were pulling the largest piece of wool in the world over this poor man's eyes.

Steinke didn't continue into the post office but turned and walked, almost skipping toward his town church office.

Schmidt and McCloud went inside the post office where they exploded in laughter, recounting the comments of the past fifteen minutes.

"Lions and lambs!" They roared.

"Political unity!" Again they roared.

"Lutheran wives better cooks than Methodist wives!" At that they exploded to where those passing the post office were looking in the window, wondering what the two were laughing about.

By afternoon, everyone in the county and on both sides of the highway had heard about the escape and the accident. They had also heard about the challenge to their respective reputations as cooks. Germans, Swedes, Baptists, Catholics, Lutherans! The whole thing had snow-balled into a major social crisis. Reputations were at stake!

The county's telephone lines had never been so busy. Calls went out informing family members that they would not be eating at home but rather at the POW camp along the highway. Stencil's Grocery Store had never been so busy and had never had so many special orders for exotic and seldom used cooking items. Housewives dusted off old cookbooks looking for old time recipes rather than use the new, pre-mixed, hurry-up recipes. It was back to the old days. Grandmothers were called and asked for their once famous prune cake recipe or special cranberry sauce with orange peel. The tension in the community, both in town and in the country, was running high, much higher than even before fair time. This was serious!

10

CHAPLAIN WOLF SETTLED INTO his old brown leather chair where he did most of this thinking and sermon writing. His office window looked down on the front gate and most of the camp. From there he could look off to the north and see the rolling hills of the surrounding countryside for about twenty miles. He figured that his sermon had to last no longer than twenty minutes. It must not contain any offensive comments or even bits of humor which always seemed to offend someone. He realized that this might be one of the most important messages of his entire career. At that point he did something he seldom did; he fell on his knees, with his head in his chair. "Oh Father, Thy will; not my will be done." He stayed in that position for thirty minutes, deep in prayer. He arose, wiped his eyes, and took out his Bible. He opened to II Corinthians, chapter 5 verse 17. It was as if the words jumped off the page and hit him in the face. "If any man is in Christ, he is a new creature; the old things passed away; behold new things have come." He shoved a piece of paper in his ancient Smith Corona typewriter and began to plunk away with his two index fingers. After three hours, he held up twelve pages of words, smudges, and penciled in margin notes. The old man walked to the window, held up his sermon text and said, with a smile on his aging face, "Thank you, Father."

Captain Thomas left Major Reed's office is a total quandary. "A choir? A prisoner of war choir. I know absolutely nothing about organizing and directing a choir. Oh Lord! What am I going to do?" Talking to himself in an audible whisper as he walked across the camp, "I am up for promotion and I need something to make me look good." As he walked toward the kitchen, the thought occurred to him that he should talk with the sergeant in charge of the mess, Sergeant Wilber Ames. Ames seemed to know a lot about what went on within the camp's population. In fact Ames knew almost every guard and POW in the place by name.

Ames stood at attention as Thomas entered his steaming kitchen. Several other POW and staff personnel stood at attention as well. "As you were" Thomas ordered.

"Sergeant, I have a very unusual order. I must organize a German men's choir and make a formal choral presentation by next week. It seems Major Reed heard some of the men singing in the shower and believes we can make a full fledged opera chorus out of these people."

Ames smiled broadly, "No problem sir. That German sergeant, the one who weighs about three hundred pounds, he's a natural. If anyone can do it, it's him. His name is Swartz, Herman Swartz. You can find his barracks number on the roster on the wall." Ames said, pointing to the wall.

"Say, Captain, what's this choir thing for anyhow? Are we having some visiting dignitaries stopping off between the war in Europe and the war in Asia?"

"No Sergeant, we are not; but we are having about five hundred people for dinner next week."

The sergeant's face went totally blank, his mouth fell open. "You're kidding, aren't you Captain?"

"No, Major Reed has invited all the people in the area or quite possibly the state or, for that fact, the entire United States of America to have Thanksgiving dinner with us next week."

Thomas smiled sarcastically and left the mess hall leaving Sergeant Ames standing there. Ames dropped the long-handled spoon he was holding and strode toward the door.

Normally when a non-commissioned officer went to see his superior, he would at least put on a uniform shirt and tie. Ames wore neither as he approached the Major's office aid in a sweaty tee shirt and dirty whites. "Sergeant Ames requests permission to see Major Reed," he said with polite sarcasm. The young corporal at the desk realized by the expression on Ames' face that something was wrong. The corporal picked up the phone, buzzed the intercom button and spoke. "Sergeant Ames requests permission to talk with you sir."

"Please go in, Sergeant." The young corporal whispered.

Sergeant Ames stood at attention, waiting to be acknowledged. Major Reed was standing at the window, holding a riding crop, looking out at his domain.

"Ah, Sergeant Ames, I trust that you have heard the good news. We will be having some guests for Thanksgiving dinner."

Reed was so caught up in his thoughts that he left Sergeant Ames still at attention. Reed turned away from the window and invited the sergeant to be seated, more of a polite invitation than an order. Reed seemed unusually mellow and happier than usual. Ames wondered quietly if the stress of the past few days had put the 'gentleman soldier' over the top.

Reed, still standing, walked to the large calendar on his office wall. Pointing his riding crop at the red numbered date marked Thanksgiving, he spoke. "On this date Sergeant, we shall celebrate one of the most significant dates on the calendar—Thanksgiving. On this date, those of us who are assigned to this post, both German and American alike, will sit down to a meal as brothers, not captives and captors. On this date, Sergeant, we shall invite those whom we serve as guardians of freedom in this beloved country to dine with those who tried in vain to take away that freedom."

Reed's little speech had Ames worried. *The old man is way off course. It must be the thing with the dead POW,* he thought.

"Permission to speak Major" Ames almost demanded.

"Excuse me Sergeant, of course you may speak."

"Sir, I do have a number of concerns." Ames began in his strong Boston accent. "Beings that I am responsible for the food services in this camp, I feel somewhat confused as to where we will be finding food for..." Ames stopped mid-sentence, "How many people do we expect for dinner?" he asked sarcastically.

"Oh, it could be three to four hundred, plus our people here in the camp." Reed announced. "Maybe more, we will have a head count by Wednesday."

"Wednesday? That's the day before the event." Ames stated with his voice becoming quieter.

"That's right sergeant."

Ames looked dazed as he glanced toward the calendar.

"Sir, just where do we...you plan to procure the items we will need to feed eight hundred or so people?"

"From the people!" Major Reed responded matter-of-factly. "From all those coming to our little party."

"We will supply dishes, salt, pepper, and places to sit." Major Reed continued.

"Even if we should have five thousand, we would be able to make due with our 'five fishes and five loaves.'"

Major Reed rose from his chair and went to the window. "Sergeant," beckoning Ames over to the window. With his riding crop, he pointed to the hanger space. "Sergeant, I want every table and chair in the camp set up in the general assembly area. Anything flat becomes a table. Anything else becomes a chair. With a little luck, we can find places for most of our guests."

Sergeant Ames took a deep breath. "You mean, I don't have to cook anything?"

"Not a thing. And with a little more luck our guests will leave a week's worth of leftovers."

"Sergeant" Reed continued, "If we can pull this thing off, I will write you all up for some sort of medal. If I can't pull it off, I will probably be assigned to the South Pacific."

Ames left the Major's office shaking his head like the others that morning.

Halfway across the route to the mess hall, Captain Thomas called out. "Sergeant Ames!"

Ames rolled his eyes and wondered what wonderful now surprise was about to come his way. "Sergeant, I found the fellow you mentioned, Swartz, and he agreed to put together a men's choir for the Thanksgiving event. He did however ask one favor. He wants several cases of hard liquor." Actually it was not a favor it was more like a demand. "What's wrong with the beer we sell them? Isn't that good enough for their tastes?" Ames protested. "They say whiskey keeps them warm during the winter months."

"Actually some of the men have access to some moonshine a farmer is making over north of here. If you can find out how to get a couple of cases, we will have the German National Choir. If not, Major Reed will be most unhappy with us; both of us. Understood?"

"I will get right to it. By the way Captain you realize that hard liquor is completely against all military regulations, especially prisoner of war policy."

"Sergeant, if this thing goes bust, we will probably all be shipped to some prisoner of war camp for prisoner of war camp nuts."

That night and each night thereafter, the 'lights-out' order was ignored until sometime after two in the morning. Each night from one hour after dinner until two or so in the morning, voices of men could be heard throughout the countryside. The first few nights there were few voices with the numbers of singers and volume swelling late into the night. The guards at their post were totally enthralled with the beautiful sounds which came from the mess hall turned choir room. Swartz had surpassed all expectations, even his own.

After two days of making corrections and polishing his sermon text, Chaplain Wolf stapled the corners of his twelve page sermon together and marched down the hall to Major Reed's office.

"Chaplain Wolf to see Major Reed," he announced to the corporal.

Upon entering Reed's office, Reed rose and announced, "T'day, minus three, Chaplain Wolf. Three days! Three days to one of the only significant events in this chapter of my miserable military career."

11

CHAPLAIN WOLF PLACED his sermon on Reed's desk. "For your advice and consent, sir," Wolf said.

"I hope this is one of the best sermons of your entire career Roland," referring to Wolf in a rare but endearing tone. The two men spent several hours going over the detail of the Thanksgiving Day event, all the way from placing signs along the highway to the final prayer of the evening. About an hour into the planning session, the telephone on Reed's desk rang. "Sir," said the corporal on the line, "Mr. Schmidt is on the line and wishes to speak to you. He says it is important."

"Put him through."

"Henry, what can I do for you?"

"I am calling from the Postmaster's office in North Fork," Schmidt said. "We still don't have a full head count yet, but I do expect to have a firm number by tomorrow. Major, what I want to know is this, can your POWs put together a legitimate baseball team by the day of the dinner?"

Reed, somewhat shocked by the question responded, "Mr. Schmidt, I have one of the best baseball teams I have ever seen. Why do you ask?"

"Well, I thought a little game after dinner might be in order. We have some pretty good players in the community; and, well, I thought we might see what your boys can do."

"Mr. Schmidt, this sounds like an event on which one may wish to make a wager."

"I suppose if one were inclined to wager, one might wish to do so, I suppose." Schmidt replied.

"What sort of wager would you suggest, Mr. Schmidt?"

"Would five dollars be too rich for your blood Mr. Schmidt?" retorted Reed with a wry smile.

Schmidt smiled at the other end of the phone line, "Why don't we make it ten?"

"Done!" replied Reed.

This simple event seemed to weld the relationship between two men from different worlds into a friendship.

"I will call you back tomorrow with the number of people wishing to attend the event." Schmidt said, hanging up the phone.

Reed replaced his phone and smiled broadly, as did Chaplain Wolf.

"So, we have a little entertainment for the afternoon, do we?" smiled Wolf.

"Find out who among the POWs knows the most about baseball and get him in here as soon as possible." Reed ordered.

Chaplain Wolf, like Captain Thomas, made directly for the kitchen and Sergeant Ames.

Sergeant Ames was walking out from the walk-in refrigerator, where he had been checking on packages of ground beef.

"Sergeant Ames! Just the man I was looking for," Wolf said.

Ames didn't bother to come to attention. Even though Chaplain Wolf held the rank of Major, everyone considered the old man simply a preacher in uniform.

What now? Ames thought behind the stiff smile.

"I am looking for someone who can coach our camp baseball team."

"Camp baseball team! We don't have a camp baseball team." Ames replied with as much courtesy as possible. "We have a lot of guys who like to hit balls and catch balls and other guys who like to watch guys hit balls and catch balls but we really don't have a baseball team."

"Major Reed has it in his mind that we have a baseball team and that our baseball team will play and defeat the local team." Chaplain Wolf pleaded.

"So, it's Major Reed's idea, something like this grand picnic planed for Thursday."

"Yes, the game will take place after the Thanksgiving dinner." Chaplain Wolf added.

"So, we will have dinner for ten thousand farmers, a choir concert consisting of three hundred German prisoners of war, *and* a World Series baseball game. All in one day!" Ames said with the utmost sarcasm. "Chaplain, I am going to lock myself in the walk-in refrigerator until next Thursday has come and gone. After that, I will go back to cooking meals, like they promised me at the recruiting office."

"Come on Sergeant Ames, all I need is to find someone, either one of theirs or one of ours, to coach the team."

"OK, go see Branovitch in the motor pool. He knows baseball."

"Branovitch it is."

As Wolf walked away, he turned back toward Ames. "Please don't take this too seriously. Major Reed is simply trying to make life a little easier for all of us."

"Easier!" Ames began to laugh as he walked back into the freezer. "Easier!"

Wolf found Branovitch working on a broken jeep headlight. While everyone did guard duty at the camp, Branovitch spent half his time in the camp motor pool. The motor pool consisted of one Quonset hut with the end cut out and a small room for parts and supplies.

"Private Branovitch," Wolf stated as he entered the shed. Branovitch stood at attention as Wolf adjusted to the darkness of the shed.

"Stand easy. I understand that you know something about baseball."

"Yes sir!" Branovitch almost shouted.

"I played in a number of minor league teams around Chicago before I got drafted."

"I assume that you have seen the POWs playing all on the north field?" Wolf queried.

"Yes sir, I watch from a distance. As you know sir, we are not supposed to fraternize with the POWs. Playing ball or sitting with those watching would be considered as fraternizing, would it not?"

"It certainly would. But," continued Wolf, "we have a special situation. One for which we need your help. As you know, Thursday, Thanksgiving Day, we have invited the whole community to the camp. As a part of our program, we would like to have a baseball game with the local people. Major Reed feels that this would help to educate the Germans in American traditions and generate stronger support for our farm-work program."

"Chaplain, with all due respect, we have only three days until Thanksgiving. You can't build a team in that time."

"Private Branovitch, if you simply field a baseball team and keep them playing for nine innings, you will become corporal Branovitch. Let's call it a field promotion."

Branovitch reluctantly accepted the charge.

"Oh, Corporal Branovitch…excuse me, Private Branovitch, consider yourself on duty leave from this time until the game. I will contact your commanding officer."

Branovitch made a bee line for the kitchen. As he entered the kitchen, he saw Ames.

"Sergeant Ames!"

"I know, I know," Ames interrupted. Reed wants you to create a World Series baseball team by next Thursday."

"How'd you know?" Branovitch asked.

"Never mind," Ames grumbled. "Let's go over to the ball field now and see what we can find."

Within an hour, the two men had organized a team. With the help of one of the POWs who spoke fluent English, the rules were translated and written on the score board with a stub of chalk.

Branovitch noticed that they were three ball gloves short of everyone having one.

"How much money do you have on you, Sarge?" Branovitch asked as if he and Ames were equals.

"Twenty bucks, give or take."

"I have sixteen. I'll see what I can get from Chaplain Wolf. We need to go to town and buy three more mitts." I will see if I have enough for a new ball. This one's almost shot." Branovitch said.

"I am on leave till Thursday, so I can go without a pass." Branovitch said with an air of independence. "I'll be back in a few hours."

As Branovitch walked off toward the Chaplain's office, Ames realized that he was stuck with the 'team'.

"OK you guys, let's practice throwing the ball from base to base and then from the outfield to home plate."

Helmut Sommerfield squatted behind the pillow which represented home plate. He pounded his hand into the pie shaped glove as the well worn ball was tossed at less than bullet speed from player to player.

Ames set up a batting system where each man was pitched three balls. If he hit one, he got three more. Several men would go on hitting until they struck out or, as in the case of two men, hit in the head. By mid afternoon, Branovitch returned with three new leather gloves, a new ball and two new bats. The new gloves were issued out to the basemen. Branovitch then divided the players into batting groups, with one ball and one bat for each of the three groups.

Within two days, the German POWs began to look something like a baseball team.

On the other side, Schmidt had contacted the coach of the local young men's Saturday-afternoon league. They too were practicing.

12

AFTER FOUR HOURS of tracking down every table and chair in the camp and setting them up in the main hanger, the men were dismissed to lunch. The huge American flag hanging at the rear of the hanger was tightened and other flags from various offices were placed around the hanger.

"Things are starting to look good." Reed mentioned to Ames.

"With a little luck we can get the kids to move over in the corner and we can free up some table space." Ames suggested.

As Reed and his small group of officers moved toward the main platform, Sergeant Walther came running toward them.

"What's wrong Sergeant?" Reed demanded.

"General Porter is in your office and wants to see you. *Now!*"

"General Porter? Here? wants to see me now! I am a dead man." Reed uttered as his shoulders dropped and he moved toward his office.

Passing the main personnel gate, Reed noticed General Porter's jeep, complete with his one star flag on the front bumper. There were three other jeeps parked behind.

It was well known that Porter always traveled with a large staff group. It made him feel important.

It was also well known that Winston Porter was a West Point graduate who got there because his father was a congressman. It was no secret that his father was actively grooming his son to follow in his footsteps. Through 'Daddy's efforts, Winston Porter managed to land a position on Eisenhower's general staff in Europe. After getting his feet slightly dirty in France, Porter was transferred to the Pacific theater where he served safely in a regional headquarters unit. He even managed to pick up a Purple Heart when he caught a piece of shrapnel while flying over a combat area, perhaps the luckiest event of his life. This allowed Major W. Porter to return to the US as a wounded war hero of not one but two theaters of war. Porter was well on his way to a political career. Because of the dime sized fragment the doctors took from his lower leg, he was no longer considered eligible for front line duty. Assigned to a desk in the Pentagon, near Daddy, Porter quickly rose to Colonel and then to Brigadier General. While the old boys at the Pentagon went along with the politics of the deal, no one wanted Porter in a command where someone might actually get hurt or for that fact, get someone else hurt. So, they gave him responsibility for the prisoners of war in the central region of the US. Normally this was a billet for a colonel, but the powers that be wanted to keep Daddy happy and Winston out of their hair.

It was obvious that everything Porter did, every word he uttered, and every back he slapped was part of his political agenda. When the war was over, he would be familiar, very familiar, with the voters of this region.

As Reed entered his office area, he noticed the dozen or so officers which always traveled with Porter. He also noticed the enlisted man holding a press camera, also a constant traveling companion.

"Marcus, good to see you old man." said Porter, being three years younger than Reed. While Reed attempted to come to attention and offer a salute, Porter grabbed Reed around the shoulder as he posed for a photo. "You're looking good!"

Porter turned to his entourage of officers and dismissed them into the outer office. Closing the door, Porter pulled up a chair and sat down. "Marcus, could you get an old general a cup of coffee. We left headquarters at four this morning and I need a jolt."

Reed picked up his phone and ordered a pot of coffee and donuts.

"Thanks, I am beat." reiterated Porter.

"Marcus I received your report on this POW who attempted to escape and was killed. As you know, I personally investigate every escape attempt and every POW death. I want to make absolutely certain that none of us ever ends up in a post-war court marital situation where someone accuses us of atrocities, dereliction of duty, or any of that other political crap which goes on after a war is over. It's funny, we can kill these guys on a battlefield but we can't touch them after they put their hands in the air and we take them prisoner."

Major Reed's aid knocked twice on the office door and entered with a pot of coffee and four donuts. The general smiled at the aid, remembering that someday he will be old enough to vote. "Thank you son" Porter said.

Reed thought it amusing that everyone becomes 'son' when you become a general.

Reed poured two cups of coffee, taking one for himself. "So where do we begin general?"

Taking a long slow and noisy sip of coffee, General Porter said, "Let's go and look at the dearly departed's quarters. I want to make sure that his lodgings were in keeping with the Geneva Rules of War. Did he have a goose down comforter, did he have hot and cold running mineral water in his shower; did he have the finest of meals in his dining hall and so on." Porter said with a sarcastic smile. "And then, I need to see where and how the poor chap escaped and exactly how he made his way to the railroad tracks."

"General, all of those issues are clearly stated in my report, complete with signed statements from his colleagues." Reed said defensively.

"I know that Marcus, but I just want to cover my rear and yours by being able to tell someone up the line that I personally…personally, mind you, confirmed your report. That keeps you and me out of the soup, if someone should say that we chopped the guy up and dumped his body onto the railroad tracks."

"Here, have a donut Marcus; I don't want to be the only fat slob in this command."

After stuffing down the three day old donuts and another cup of coffee, General Porter rose and said, "Let's get this over with. I need to get over to Camp Walker before dinner. They have a great new head cook over there. I am told that he 'offers rewards' to local farmers for pheasants and cooks up a mean pheasant under glass."

The group of twenty or so uniformed men moved outside the office unit and toward the barracks. Halfway there, Porter noticed the dozens of tables and the hundred of chairs placed in the hangar. As Porter stopped, so did Reed's heart.

"Major Reed, what is this?" Porter asked pointing to the hangar.

Reed's mouth went absolutely dry. He knew full well that tomorrow's event was in total contradiction to Army regulations regarding fraternization between the POWs and the locals. As Reed attempted to catch a breath and respond to General Porter's question, Chaplain Wolf stepped forward and responded.

"You see general, morale is one of the most important factors in maintaining order in a prisoner of war camp. Likewise, morale is critical in our POWs interacting with the farm community. We desperately need these men working on the farms in order to maintain a balance of production and demand. If the POWs are not happy and choose not to work on the farms, everyone loses. Crops don't get planted and crops don't get harvested. After Carl Bauman's death, morale hit rock bottom. This, coupled with the regulation that the camp had to be shut down for seven days resulted in bad feelings among the men. Likewise, the farmers who knew Carl felt bad that this fellow was dead."

The color began to return to Major Reed's face as Chaplain Wolf continued with his explanation.

"So where do all these tables and chairs come into the picture,

Chaplain?" Porter interrupted.

Taking a deep breath and knowing not only his career, but Reed's was on the line, he continued.

"After seeing the effect of this man's death on the camp and the community, Major Reed formulated a plan. He consulted with one of the farmers in our POW—Farm Support Program, a Mr. Henry Schmidt and asked him if he felt that a community event might help to improve morale. Of course Mr. Schmidt agreed that it would. Because of the lock down coming over the Thanksgiving Day, Major Reed asked if he felt that a Thanksgiving meal between our POWs and the community would be appropriate—here on the base."

Reed and Wolf held their breath as the words sunk in.

"You mean to tell me that the farmers in the community are coming here, tomorrow, for a Thanksgiving meal?"

Wolf interjected one last comment, hoping to hit a soft spot. "I will prepare a banquet table in the presence of mine enemies…" quoting from the Twenty-third Psalm.

Porter gave Wolf a long a hard stare.

"Major Reed, do you realize that this constitutes a total violation of Army regulations and could get you busted back to Private?" General Porter stated.

Reed nodded pathetically.

General Porter looked skyward as if to ponder the movement of the planets.

"Marcus, this is the best idea I think I have heard since this stupid war began."

"Just how many people are you expecting for this little event?" Porter asked.

"About three hundred and sixty from the community and our three hundred POWs, and our forty-five camp staff." Captain Thomas offered.

That's three hundred potential voters, Porter thought to himself.

Porter continued to stare skyward as his staff photographer

snapped a picture.

After a long pause, Porter stated, "Major Reed, you have my full and complete permission to proceed with this operation." Porter paused, "Providing that I and my staff can participate with you."

"Of course you can participate, sir. We would be honored."

The phrase "political dynamite" was heard uttered by one of the general's staff.

Realizing the true intent of the general's interest in the Thanksgiving Day event, Captain Thomas spoke up. "General Porter sir, would it be appropriate, particularly under the circumstances for the general to make a brief speech at the dinner?"

"Captain Thomas, I would consider it an honor to address your party. A true honor!"

Major Reed winked at Thomas as the general consulted with his staff.

The phrase, "Prepare a banquet table in the presence of mine enemies…" was heard as the small group huddled around the general.

"Major Reed," General Porter gushed, could I see a copy of your program for tomorrow's activities?"

"Captain Thomas, could you arrange to get the general a copy of our program as soon as possible?" Major Reed said, knowing full well that no such schedule existed and that Thomas and Wolf would have to crank one out within the next few minutes.

As the two officers made a slow dash for the headquarters office and a typewriter, Major Reed suggested that the group resume its inspection of the barracks and the place where Carl had made his escape. Within the hour, Wolf and Thomas reappeared with a document listing the events and times for the newly named Thanksgiving Day Community Festival.

Handing the document to Major Reed for his perusal, Reed handed it on to General Porter.

Pondering the program, General Porter suggested that a brief fifteen minute speech might be appropriate right here, between the end of the choir and the baseball game.

"Baseball game? queried the general. "You are going to have a baseball game?

"Yes, sir, a game between the POWs and some of the local boys." smiled Chaplain Wolf.

"We thought a little touch of American baseball would be nice."

General Porter glanced at his group of officers. "Did you hear that, there's going to be a baseball game between the Germans and the Americans! How's that for a story?!"

One of his officers made the comment, "Yanks and Nazis slug it out on the diamond!" The general smiled widely and nodded his head. "You think of everything Reed!"

Chaplain Wolf was quick to note that there were no Nazis in this camp.

The erring officer offered a polite, "OOPS, sorry!"

Halfway to the barracks, General Porter stopped the group. "Major Reed, perhaps this investigation is not necessary. And I really need to get over to Camp Walker. I have invited the local mayor for dinner and I would hate to miss all those pheasants under glass. I will be back here by 10:00 tomorrow."

Major Reed and his staff came to attention and saluted. General Porter returned the salute, turned and walked toward his vehicles. As he walked toward the jeeps, he was heard to say, "Martin, make sure you have enough film and flash bulbs. This could be good!"

The file of jeeps lurched to life and raced off toward the highway. Major Reed and his staff exhaled, almost in unison. "That was close," said Captain Thomas.

"If it were not for the fact the General Porter is hot on the political trail, we would all be in a foxhole in the South Pacific by this time next week."

Major Reed, addressing Wolf and Thomas said "You guys really pulled this thing out of the fire. I owe you a big one."

As if they had been energized by some cosmic force, Reed's officers began to rattle off items which needed attention: rest room areas for the women, parking plans for cars, and so on. Each officer took off in a direction, barking orders to anyone standing near. The sense of enthusiasm shown by the officers soon infected all in the camp. Grounds were being swept, windows cleaned as the camp was being made ready for tomorrow's event.

13

THE NEXT MORNING, at seven, a small troop transport truck pulled up in front of the main gate. An enlisted man jumped out and announced that the general had telephoned and asked that his office flag and his "Brigadier General on Base" flag be brought over from headquarters. Major Reed, seeing the truck from his office window, ran to the gate to see what was going on. The guard at the gate handed the Major the flags, along with a leather attaché case, and relayed the message. The enlisted man saluted and returned to his truck as the driver headed back for a four hour drive to headquarters. Within minutes, word had caught up with Wolf and Thomas. Both men were standing next to Reed as the truck turned on the main road and headed north.

"The general wanted his flags." Reed said.

"I guess when you are a general running for public office, your need your flags." Thomas sighed.

"Thomas, see that this flag is placed on the platform, next to the podium. And the very second the general arrives on post, see to it that someone raises his flag on the main flag pole, but be sure that no one puts it above the US flag. He might like that, but let's try to keep things in perspective. I'll take the general's attaché case to my office." The men shook their heads and returned to their respective duties.

At eight o'clock, Schmidt and his family arrived. One of the POWs was in the parking lot to point the way to a parking space.

"Good morning Henry," Reed said, offering his hand. "Good morning Mrs. Schmidt." Reed nodded at Laurel and Rodney.

Addressing the POW in charge of parking, Major Reed instructed him to take the large baskets Mrs. Schmidt and Laurel were holding.

Her hands free, Mrs. Schmidt took the initiative and offered her hand to Major Reed. "Harriett Schmidt."

Major Reed introduced Captain Thomas who, upon seeing Laurel, had joined the group. Captain Thomas was introduced all around, shaking hands, but focusing his attention on Laurel.

Within minutes, Bill McCloud's car pulled in next to Schmidt's. Mac and his family were escorted to where Reed and the Schmidt's were standing.

"It's about time you got here McCloud; we have been here since before sun up." Schmidt chided.

Mac raised one of his eyebrows, "Henry, I was just behind you. I saw you hit that hen pheasant back there by the bridge. Sun up my foot." The POW took the McCloud's food baskets and placed them on the first table.

"You might want to have those baskets put in the refrigerator. Lot's of stuff that will spoil," Harriett stated.

"My baskets too," Ramona McCloud added. Several POWs took the baskets off toward the kitchen, one taking a peek as he went.

"I told the rest not to come until closer to noon. That way, we won't have to put everything in the refrigerators."

As Captain Thomas stood there looking at Laurel, as if he had never seen a woman before, she sensed a need to redirect his attention.

"Captain Thomas, I don't think you were introduced to my good friend, Sarah McCloud. She is in her forth year of college and plans to be a teacher."

The re-direct seemed to work. Captain Thomas was equally as taken with Sarah McCloud who didn't seem to mind the attention at all.

"Now, Major Reed, if I can see your seating plan," Harriett requested as if she were in command. "Seating plan, ugh, other than the head table, everyone will sit where they choose." Major Reed stuttered.

"Oh no, that will never work. If we do that, all the people from south of the highway will sit on one side and those from the north side will sit on the other. We must assign tables and families. Likewise, the Catholics will sit with the Catholics and the Methodists will sit with the Methodist and the Lutherans will probably sit outside. With your permission, sir, I will assign places." Taking the clip board with the three hundred or so names on it from Captain Thomas, she nodded to Ramona McCloud. Together with Laurel, the three took off toward the platform at the end of the hangar. From there, they assigned places by jotting down numbers next to names of families and individuals.

"If women were responsible for wars, we would be finished in a few days." Major Reed commented in jest. "If women were responsible for wars, we probably wouldn't have wars." Schmidt retorted.

"Henry," said Reed, "we have had a minor change in plans. Yesterday, my big boss, General Porter showed for an inspection of sorts. He likes what we are doing here and has invited himself to dinner."

Schmidt and McCloud looked surprised. "A general!"

Reed went on, "General Porter, Commanding officer for the POW camps in this region."

McCloud entered the conversation. "Is this the same General Porter whose daddy is in Congress? The same General Porter who is trying to get himself elected to almost any political position he can find once the war is over?"

"Yep, that's General Porter."

McCloud stopped for a minute. "I suppose that General Porter could help me keep my job as Postmaster, if I smile sweetly."

Schmidt and Reed nodded in agreement.

"Politics!" said Reed. "Politics."

Back on the platform, the three women were checking names and pointing to the various tables around the hangar. Harriett pointed to the last table on the outside, "Our family will sit there, at table 16 near the desert table. We will need two others to fill the space."

"Mom, let's put our POW, Mr. Sommerfield and (pausing for a minute) Uncle Rupert with us."

"Our POW?" Harriett said looking at Laurel, "So, it's our POW is it?"

"Oh Mother, we know the man and he speaks English. If we have one of these other people, who knows what we will get. Besides, Daddy likes Mr. Sommerfield."

"Daddy likes Mr. Sommerfield?" Harriett exclaimed with her eyebrows at full mast.

"So does Rodney and so do I. There, I have said it," Laurel announced with polite defiance.

"And," attempting to change the subject a bit, she continued, "I think you should place Captain Thomas with the McCloud table."

Harriett's mouth fell open.

"After all, Congress has declared him to be an officer and a gentleman," she continued.

Not knowing how to respond to her 24 year old daughter, she shrugged her shoulders and put the two names down. Noticing Laurel's pleased look, Harriett looked at her and said, "Why not, he has to sit somewhere."

Back at the group of men, McCloud lowered his voice a bit and took on a serious air. Major Reed, there will be another special guest at the event as well. A Mrs. Jorgensen will be here. Her son is a prisoner of war in Germany, and from what we understand the boy is not in the best of shape. Needless to say, under the circumstances Mrs. Jorgensen is not terribly fond of German soldiers. Her pastor did convince her to come today, as a part of a healing process. He says that if she sees that the German POWs here are not savages, she may be inclined to believe that her son is being treated humanely."

"I hope we can give her some hope that all Germans are not mad men and killers." Chaplain Wolf interjected.

At precisely ten o'clock, General Porter's jeep came roaring up to the hangar. At precisely the same second, his one star flag was raised on the flag pole next to the main gate. Getting out of his jeep, the general took notice of the flag going up. He smiled.

Everyone in the area stopped and came to attention, soldiers, POWs and civilians alike. "As you were," the general uttered.

The twenty or so in the general's entourage fanned out in various directions. His aids and his photographer stayed close as the general moved toward Major Reed, Henry, and McCloud. The general glanced toward the platform and noticed his flag and the three women at the podium.

As the general entered the group of men, he entered with is hand extended. Addressing Henry Schmidt, he said, "Pleased to meet you, I'm Winston Porter," pumping Schmidt's hand.

"Henry Schmidt." Schmidt replied, not knowing exactly how to read this introduction.

Then, addressing McCloud, "Pleased to meet you, I am Winston Porter. These guys, pointing to the officers, "have to call me general because they work for me. You guys on the other hand can call me Winston because I work for you."

Spoken like a true politician, Wolf thought to himself.

"General," Major Reed interrupted, "Chaplain Wolf has just informed me that one of the people attending today's festivities has a son who is a prisoner of war in Germany. I though you might like to meet this lady."

"Meet her? I want her sitting at my table!" Porter ordered as he shot a glance at his aid. "I want a complete run down on the boy, where he is and so on," he continued.

"Before I forget, Major, where is that briefcase I asked to have delivered?" the general asked.

"It's in my office sir. I can have someone get it for you." Reed responded.

Addressing his aid, the general ordered him to retrieve the briefcase on the double. The aid saluted and ran toward the headquarters section. Within five minutes, the panting young officer held out the briefcase while the general opened the locked case. Opening the case, he barked an order. "Major Reed, Major Wolf, Captain Thomas, stand at attention!"

The three men, completely stunned by the order responded automatically by coming to full attention not knowing what to expect.

Porter reached over to the gold oak clusters on Reed's shoulders and one at a time, removed them. From this brief case, he took out two shiny silver oak clusters and pinned them to the shoulder flaps. "This is no job for a major. I need a Lieutenant Colonel in this post." The general said matter of factly, "Lieutenant Colonel Reed, stand at ease."

Again Reed felt himself wondering if he was going to fall over or fly away.

Porter's huge hand grabbed Reed's limp hand and shook it. Porter then moved to Wolf, removed his emblems of rank and replaced them with two bright shiny silver oak clusters. He then stepped sideways immediately in front of Thomas. Removing his Captain's bars, he replaced them with the gold oak clusters of a Major. All three men saluted as Porter returned the salute.

"Now Colonel, let's get to work." Porter ordered, not knowing exactly what to do next.

Before the group could determine which way to go or what to do, Rodney came up behind his dad along with Helmut. "Dad, Uncle Rupert and Uncle Ross asked me and Helmut if we could help take some boxes of picnic items into the camp kitchen. Is it okay if we go inside the camp?" Schmidt looked toward Lt. Colonel Reed for direction. Knowing that civilians entering the camp were strictly forbidden, the new Lt. Colonel took a deep breath and tried to formulate an answer that would not get his new silver oak clusters snatched from his shoulders.

General Porter interrupted, "Of course you can go into the camp. If you do anything wrong, I will simply lock up your father!" The group exploded in laughter. Rodney and Helmut took off running toward the pickup truck parked at the far end of the hangar. As Rupert handed each man a carton, he said, "Be careful with those boxes, if you drop one, we are all dead!"

As the group of men found other things to do, General Porter asked Schmidt if this Helmut Sommerfield was working with him.

"Yes, Mr. Sommerfield came over to our farm sometime ago. He has been invaluable in keeping the truck and tractors in the area going. And I suppose with his family being killed back in Germany, we were able to keep him going in his time of need.

"Family killed? Tell me more, Mr. Schmidt." Porter placed his hand on Schmidt's shoulder as if they were long lost buddies.

Schmidt related the story, particularly the part about Sommerfield's sister still being alive somewhere in Germany.

As Henry finished the story, General Porter interrupted for a second. He turned backward and ordered his aid to get a complete file on this 'Sommerfield guy'.

Turning back to Schmidt he continued, "I will see what I can do to find the girl. If we can at least locate her, we can attempt to get her and her brother back together after the war."

14

BY ELEVEN O'CLOCK the dirt road leading into the camp was bumper-to-bumper with cars, trucks, and a church bus. Those POWs assigned to the parking lot were busy placing cars, while others were helping families carry baskets and cardboard boxes filled with food. The smell of roasted turkey almost overwhelmed the aroma of hot mincemeat and apple pies. Huge platters and bowls of food were placed on three long tables at the far end of the hangar. Sergeant Ames had devised a system whereby he would write the name of the family and place it on a small lump of moist bread dough. This would allow for each person taking a portion from a particular platter or bowl to know the identity of the woman who had spent the last 48 hours creating this masterpiece. A system had been worked out whereby some families were to bring turkeys, some salad dishes, some deserts, and so on. By noon, the tables were full almost to the point of collapse.

Little clumps of people from south of the highway began to move toward small groups of people from north of the highway. A few Methodists ventured into a group of Baptists. Before long, friends had recognized other long lost friends and strangers were introduced to strangers. Teen aged boys were focusing on teen age girls who they had seen at the store in town or sitting across the field at local football games. More than one telephone number was exchanged that morning. By noon, the roar of conversations and laughter had abolished the clouds which had for so long had covered this community.

Reverend and Mrs. Peterson from over at St. Olaf's Swedish Lutheran Church entered the hangar with Mrs. Jorgenson. Mrs. Jorgenson, dressed in a grey frock, gazed around the hangar with a frozen glare. Almost without exception, everyone in the community knew about her son being prisoner of war in Germany. As she and Reverend Peterson moved toward where General Porter and Chaplain Wolf were talking with a group of pastors, all eyes focused on the small frail woman. Chaplain Wolf extended his hand to Reverend Peterson, "Good to see you my friend. And this must be Mrs. Jorgenson."

Without expression, the woman extended her hand to Chaplain Wolf. At that point, General Porter moved toward Mrs. Jorgenson. He removed his hat and bowed his head slightly as he took her hand with both of his. Porter moved closer to the lady and began to whisper in her ear, as several camera flash bulbs went off. She whispered back as the general nodded his head. Still holding her hand, he moved her to the head table and held a chair as she sat down next to his seat.

At twelve o'clock, Colonel Reed instructed Sergeant Walther to call for general assembly. Walther went to the microphone and issued the order, "All personnel will gather at the main assembly area immediately!"

Within seconds the hangar was filled with POWs acting more like children than captive soldiers. As they entered the hangar on the way to the assembly area, they passed the long tables of food and the groups of people standing near. Shouts of "Hey, Mr. Swartz! Good to see you Gotthold" and other such greetings which only occurred between friends could be heard. Hoots and yells came from the POWs as they passed the tables of food.

The POWs and the camp staff quickly formed their lines and came to a hurried attention.

Colonel Reed rose and came to the microphone. Glancing sideways at his new silver oak clusters, he began to address the group. "On behalf of the United States Army and," looking directly at General Porter, "the Commanding Officer of the region's prisoner of war system, Brigadier General Winston Porter, I wish to thank you all for coming. I realize that those of you from the community traditionally spend your Thanksgiving Day with your families. And those of you who are residents of this camp usually spend the day in your bunks. Today is perhaps a first. We will spend the day together as friends. As one great American once said, 'A stranger is only a friend you haven't met yet.' There are many strangers here today. I pray that by the end of the day, there will be no strangers and many friends. And speaking of praying, I wish to ask Lt. Colonel Wolf to come and offer the blessing," emphasizing the Chaplain's new rank.

Chaplain Wolf mounted the platform, removed his hat, as did all present. "Heavenly father, you have commanded us to 'do unto others as we would have them do unto us.' In so doing, we would ask that our sons and loved ones be shown similar mercies from their captors. Amen."

As Chaplain Wolf returned to his place, Mrs. Jorgenson could be heard sobbing as General Porter put his arm around her and a flash bulb went off.

Turkeys were stripped to the bone and bowls of potatoes and gravy were emptied. Hot rolls and jam were devoured as if all present had not eaten in a week. The dozen or so armed guards had abandoned their weapons and found their way to a table. After all, what prisoner of war was going to escape from an event like this? By the time most participants had been back to the dwindling offerings at the tables, Colonel Reed excused himself and approached the microphone.

"If I may have your attention for just a minute. I would like to invite the members of the men's choir to please begin taking dessert."

As the men in the choir cheered, others laughingly booed and hissed playfully.

At the various tables, POWs and guest chatted amongst themselves as if they were neighbors. Conversation about "home" and "fam-

116

ily" were open and dealt with comfortably. There was no mention of war, politics, or hate. At General Porter's table, Mrs. Jorgenson was once again assured that he would launch an effort to insure her son's well being. As soon as the men's choir had taken their share (and then some) from the dessert table, Reed announced that everyone else was invited to the dessert table.

General Porter managed to place himself near the head of the dessert table, shaking hands with almost every guest in line. Each time someone would mention that he or she had a son or daughter in the service, Porter would instruct his aid to take the name and unit of the service man or woman. "I'll check on you son or daughter!" he would declare. "I'll let them know we had dinner together. Yes, siree, those Navy guys really know what they are doing. Those Air Corps guys really know how to fly them airplanes," and so on.

Reed, standing near the general, thought to himself, "This guy's good! He will make a great politician."

As the men in the choir swallowed their last bit of apple, pumpkin, or mincemeat pie, Colonel Reed instructed Sergeant Ames to assemble his choir on the platform. Several dozen men with swollen bellies waddled toward the platform and took their places. Sergeant Ames announced to the assembly that the Camp Alexis Choir would offer a brief musical program, followed by a Thanksgiving message from Chaplain Wolf.

Sergeant Swartz moved from his place in the front-line, gave a small bow toward General Porter and to the audience. Turning toward the assembled men, he raised his arms as if he were about to conduct the New York Philharmonic. Looking to his right and then to his left, his hand began to move. The audience was brought to tears when they recognized a magnificent version of "America the Beautiful" then came several German folk songs, sung in multipart harmony. Many of the older guests, those whose grandparents had come from Germany recognized some of the tunes and some of the words. There were many damp eyes up and down the tables. There were tearful smiles on the faces of those POWs sitting at the tables as well. Thoughts of home, family, and good times drifted through the minds of these captives. For the final piece, Swartz turned toward the audience and announced that the final selection was "The Battle Hymn of the Republic" and that it was dedicated to Carl Bauman.

The hymn began with the choir marching in place, their cadence setting the time for a march. The first words of the song were issued in a whisper, gradually becoming louder. By the time the choir arrived at the "Glory, Glory, Hallelujahs," General Porter rose to his feet in much the same way King George must have done when he first heard the Hallelujah Choir. Within seconds every person in the area was standing. The second verse the choir sang in German. Again, some of the old-timers were seen with damp eyes. The third verse began in a language known to those from south of the highway. Colonel Wolf had managed to obtain a copy of the hymn in Swedish from Pastor Peterson over at St. Olaf's Swedish Lutheran Church. Most of the older people from south of the highway were in tears as they heard enemy soldiers singing one of their great anthems, and in their native language. Then the final verse in full voice. About halfway through the stanza, Swartz turned and began to march down the platform stairs, followed by the men of the choir. General Porter stood at attention and saluted the group as they passed down the center aisle and to the rear of the assembly area. By this time, all those present were in full voice singing, especially the "Glory, Glory, Hallelujahs." There was not a dry eye in the place as the crowd applauded wildly as Swartz and his choir bowed.

Colonel Reed then mounted the platform. He was in a state of euphoria, marked with a sense of absolute panic. After the tremendous success of the meal and the choir, he did not know what to expect next. So far, it was just too good to be true. "General Porter, ladies and gentlemen, we have asked Chaplain Wolf to bring a Thanksgiving message."

Wolf, too, was in a state of shock. He had not been prepared for such a powerful prelude to his message. The little man moved to the side of the platform where he picked up the wooden podium and moved it to the center of the platform. While he placed his notes on the podium, his intentions were to use the podium to support his trembling body. He had never delivered a sermon, message or even prayer in front of a general before. Since graduating from seminary his congregations had consisted of soldiers with an occasional military funeral in the community. Never before had he preached or spoken before a group of civilians. He closed his eyes and bowed his head for a few seconds. "Lord" he whispered, "let these words be your words and not mine."

For a few more seconds Wolf stood at the podium, looking out over the crowd of prisoners, farmers, guards, and towns people. The brief silence was accented by the chirping of a few birds eyeing the table scraps on the serving tables. The wind blowing through the old airplane hangar caused the metal roof to creek and crackles a bit. It was silent. Everyone there was waiting for Chaplain Wolf to speak.

"All of us here today are prisoners. Not just our friends from Germany, all of us."

Many sitting at the tables changed expression when they heard these words, silently thinking, *What does he mean, we are all captives? Only those with the initials PW on the backs of their shirts are prisoners of war.*

Wolf went on, "In fact, we are actually all prisoners of war. Let me explain further. War is a state of chaos; hostile and angry conflict between people. On the other hand, peace is a state of harmony where conflict is limited to minor and unintentional infractions. Today, this nation is locked in a state of war with other nations. As a result, families are broken, lives are broken, and chaos rules. There is no harmony. There are some here today who have lost family members. Likewise, there are those here today who have been forced to inflict chaos upon others. For those, they will suffer the loss of innocents and they too will bear the scars of the chaos."

The reaction to these burning words was being felt throughout the assembly. General Porter reached across the table and took the hand of Mrs. Jorgenson whose face was awash with tears. Helmut Sommerfield looked across the table and into the eyes of Harriett Schmidt whose blue eyes seemed to have turned to a dull grey. Mrs. Schmidt returned the look, knowing that Helmut was still locked in deep pain over the death of his family. Henry Schmidt looked at Helmut, knowing that he also carried the horrendous guilt of being a part of the war machine which had killed so many, including his son. Other POWs sitting around the tables returned to the horrible reality of war for a few minutes. Some looked off in a far away direction, trying to block out the words that were being spoken. Some looked around the group of people and wondered why these people chose to share their meal with these enemy soldiers rather than to simply hate them as they deserved.

Wolf continued, "It was said that World War I was the war to end all wars. It was said to be the most horrific of all wars in human history. We will have to wait and see what the historians have to say about our current conflict, but I truly believe that each new war will be more terrible than the last. But what difference does it make whether you lose a loved one in a big war or a small war? The scar is the same. The loss is the same. What about small wars—those in communities—communities such as this one for example, communities where families and friends are divided by the smallest differences, communities where families and friends are divided because of their ancestry or interpretation of God's Word? We all know what happens when a Catholic boy from south of the highway marries a Methodist girl from north of the highway. A small war breaks out; and we attack each other with the weapons of gossip, and slander and have a good old-fashioned Christian war.

I will refrain from pointing anymore fingers at you and point a few at my side of the fence. Those of us in the military slander and ridicule our superiors and for that fact, our subordinates. Everyone is an idiot, everyone except for us. Our generals don't really know what is going on, our colonels are a bunch of dopes, and those below us are totally incompetent. This too is a war, a little war and we are prisoners of this little war. We are caught in this conflict, like a fly on fly paper. The more we struggle, the more we become entangled in the deadly snare.

Let me ask you one simple question. Who came into the world to kill, steal and destroy?"

Wolf paused and looked around the now sober audience. "Was it Christ? Well, was it?"

Thoughtfully the heads in the crowd moved slowly from side to side.

"No, it was not Christ. When someone is killed on the battlefield, was it God who took that person? Was it God who killed, stole and destroyed that person?"

Again the audience indicated that it was not.

"Well, if not God or Christ, then who?"

Wolf let this question hang for a long thirty seconds.

A small voice announced the answer from one of the tables "Satan" spoke the child.

In the loudest tones ever used in his ministry and with his eyes wide, Wolf yelled, "Yes! It is Satan, the God of War! The god who kills and causes others to kill. The god who destroys families and individuals. The god who causes hatred and fear. The god who causes chaos. To some extent, we are all his prisoners; prisoners of his war."

Wolf let the assembly savor the thought for a minute. During those few seconds countless glances were exchanged across the room. Old enemies glanced at each other. POWs looked toward their captors. Pastors looked toward priests. There was an unspoken acknowledgement of guilt in light of what Chaplain Wolf had said.

"Now," Wolf continued, "Who came into the world to bring peace?"

Another small voice shouted out, "Jesus!"

The assembly laughed, breaking the tension of the moment.

121

"Yes, Jesus came into the world to bring peace; not war, not hatred—peace.

Now, how does this affect us? If we ask Jesus to make peace happen will He do it? Probably not".

At this comment, the audience was shaken. They had always been taught to pray for peace.

"I want you to try something," Wolf went on. "When you get home, I want you to go out alone to a quiet place, somewhere no one can see or hear you. Then I want you to point your finger in the face of God and say, 'Why don't you do something about this mess!" Then listen quietly. Listen all night if you have to. I believe that God will speak to you and these will be the words he will speak. 'I am doing something through you.' I know this because I stood in my quiet place and I pointed my finger in the face of God and told Him to do something about this mess. He said, 'I am doing something Ronald, through you and through all those who are called by my Son's name.' You are the peacemakers. You are the ones who can abolish the darkness of chaos with the brilliance of peace or as we in the church call it, the Gospel. God could do it, but that's not the way He has chosen to work."

Again Wolf allowed for a pause, a time for what he had said to sink in. Around the assembly there were many expressions of conviction, concern and personal reflection.

The silence was broken as Wolf barked the words, "'If any man be in Christ, he is a new creature; the old things are passed away and new things have come.' If any one of you be in Christ, the Prince of Peace, he is a new creation. All guilt which has resulted from acts of sin, be they on the battlefield or in the wheat field, are passed away. All condemnation as a result of sin is passed away. If you are in Christ and Christ in you, you are a new creation. You are a maker of peace, whether that peace is between neighbors on the streets of town or between soldiers on the battlefield. You cannot be a servant of the God of War and the God of Peace at the same time; it simply won't work."

Again Wolf repeated that passage, "If any man be in Christ, he is a new creature; the old things are passed away and new things have come."

Then Wolf did something he had never done before—he raised his head and hands toward heaven and groaned, "Oh Father, if any one person here even dares to whisper in his or her heart that they wish to become new creations, please Father, visit them! Make them new creations. Make them peacemakers in a world of war. Amen."

Wolf seemed exhausted as he leaned against the podium. This was, without exception, the most powerful message he had ever delivered. He truly felt that he had spoken the words God had wished him to speak. The audience was still hushed as Wolf returned to his seat. No one moved. Then, Mrs. Jorgenson rose slowly from her chair and walked over to one of the POWs standing near one of the empty serving tables. She looked the confused man in the eyes and embraced him. As she held the bewildered man in her arms, Harriett Schmidt rose and went over to Helmut Sommerfield and stood looking at him. She held out her hands to him and as he stood, she embraced this former enemy soldier. As she held him, he whispered in her ear, "Is it true that I can become a new creation?" She nodded. Within minutes, small groups of people were embracing all around the hanger. The silence was accented with whispered sobs and gentle murmurings between former enemies. POWs were whispering expressions of forgiveness toward fellow POWs or guards. Even General Porter put his arm around a few folks—without flash bulbs flashing. For most of those at the Thanksgiving Day dinner, the war was over.

General Porter, seeing that things were getting a bit too emotional, jumped up on the platform and shouted, "Let's play ball!" A cheer went up from all those in attendance. It was as if the peace treaty had been signed and now it was time to get on with life again.

Members of the two baseball teams clustered together and moved noisily toward the ball field while most of the women stayed behind to help with the clean up. The men and children followed the teams.

Over clean up, there were many more hugs and embraces. Invitations to Sunday dinner were exchanged between those on both sides of the highway. The war was over, at least for this generation.

15

THE PLAYERS BEGAN to move toward the ball field at the east end of the camp. Their overstuffed bellies resulted in groans of happy discomfort. Branovitch jumped up on a table and began to chant like a cheerleader. "Come on my over stuffed wonder boys. You can beat these country boys with one hand tied behind you! Come on my 'one week wonders', you can make me a corporal!" The twenty or so German POWs moved out and began to jog around the ball field with Branovitch leading the bunch.

General Porter, still standing, grabbed Reed around the shoulders and moved him toward the ball field. It was like the two were long lost brothers. Reed, still shaken by the overwhelming affect of the meal and the sermon, seemed to move in a trance. Wolf and Thomas followed behind, also in a state of wonderment.

As the officers and guests moved toward the ball diamond, the two teams were already practicing their throws, pitches, and batting swings. The camp staff had been given an order by Sergeant Ames to gather all the chairs and set them up behind the home base area. A number of chairs were placed directly behind the home plate, intended for General Porter, Lt. Colonel Reed and Major Thomas, and Lt. Colonel Wolf. Branovitch blew a whistle and the crowd was quiet. He approached General Porter and handed him a quarter, "Sir, would you toss the coin to determine which team goes to bat first?" The general beamed at the chance of again being in front of so many people. "Private, what are the names of the two teams?" the general demanded. So far, no one had thought to give names to either side. Branovitch looked at the general with a gaze of a deer in the headlights. "Sir, these," pointing to the Germans, "are the Rhinelanders and these, pointing to the other team, are the Flatlanders." The crowd, seeing the situation, laughed and cheered at the announcement. Branovictch pulled one of his Rhinelanders in and beckoned for one the Flatlanders to come over. The four men stood while the general held the coin, ready for the toss. Addressing the German, he asked, "What will it be, heads or tails." The German looked at Branovitch wondering what was happening. Branovitch whispered, "Say heads." The POW uttered, "Heads."

The general tossed the coin high into the air, mostly for effect. It plunked down in the soft dust, obscuring the image on the coin. Branovitch dropped to his knees, blew away the dust so that the general could see the head of George Washington. "Heads it is!" shouted General Porter. Then to add to the grandeur of the moment, Branovitch handed the baseball to General Porter and asked, in a very loud voice, "Sir, would you do Colonel Reed the honor of throwing out the first ball?" Colonel Reed knowing nothing about his little gesture but smiled and nodded his agreement. General Porter took the ball, rubbed it in his hands for a few seconds and then stopped abruptly. "Hold it. We don't have an umpire for this game. You can't have a baseball game without an umpire." Looking around at the audience, now fully intent on this grand event, Porter spotted McCloud, sitting next to Schmidt. "Postmaster McCloud, front and center!" the general ordered. The crowd went wild with applause. Of course McCloud had to make the best of his procession to the home plate. Schmidt yelled out, "Hey Mac, take my glasses so you can see the batter." The crowd exploded with laughter as McCloud raised his eyebrows and pointed a finger at Schmidt.

"I can see better than you can you old coot. At least I don't run over hen pheasants." As McCloud took his place behind the home plate, General Porter tossed the ball toward the pitcher's mound. The Flatlander's pitcher had to make a definite effort to catch the indirectly thrown ball. As the pitcher caught the ball, General Porter yelled, "Play Ball!" McCloud turned, faced the general and yelled, "You sit down mister, I'll tell them when to play ball!" Again the crowd and the general exploded into laughter.

By now, most of the guests had made their way to the ball diamond. Many of the women had opted to remain behind and clean up the leftovers and help to stack the dirty dishes. Sergeant Ames and several camp staff attempted to take responsibility for the cleanup effort, but were soundly defeated by the women who preferred the opportunity to chat with some of their neighbors from across the highway.

The Rhinelanders had their first man at bat. The pitcher threw the ball past the batter, almost without his knowing that it had been thrown. Branovitch yelled an encouraging comment to the dazed batter. "Keep your eye on the ball!"

Another ball went past without the batter's being aware of its passing. And another. McCloud, standing behind the Flatlander catcher shouted "Steeeerrrike!" three successive times. The POW, not really understanding why Branovitch was beckoning him toward the sidelines, walked away from the plate. Another, and then another POW went to the home plate only to see the pitcher make a motion and then hear the ball slap into the leather glove behind him.

Finally, after three Rhinelanders left the plate, Branovitch motioned the team toward the field. "At least," he thought, "they won't get hit by a pitched ball out there."

The man Branovitch selected to be the pitcher for the Rhinelanders was able throw a fairly respectable pitch. Unfortunately, too respectable. The first batter managed to hit the ball to the right center field, where one of the POWs sort of bumped into it. Then, another Flatlander's batter hit a ball, far into the outfield, causing two runs to be scored. The inning seemed to last for a long time, with six runs being scored. At last, the Flatlanders went down and the Rhinelanders moved off the field. Balls were thrown and balls were missed. On occasion, balls were hit and balls were caught. By the sixth inning, the score was Flatlanders 27, Rhinelanders 0. At this point, General Porter stood up and declared it to be the seventh inning stretch. As fans and players alike realized the gravity of the situation, the players began to huddle. The Rhinelanders were totally discouraged and wanted Branovitch to call the game off. The Flatlanders were concerned because they did not want the Germans to lose face by such an overwhelming defeat.

"Let's give it one more try. Come guys, you can do it!" Branovitch chided, "You have to do it," he whimpered as he realized that his promotion was not even a remote possibility.

The two teams took to the field. The sun had gone down and the lights which illuminated the camp provided sufficient light to see what was going on.

The Rhinelanders were at bat. Two outs with the catcher Helmut Sommerfield, at bat. Branovitch yelled out, "Close your eyes and swing!" Sommerfield did. As he did, he felt his bat shudder in his hands as he heard a loud crack. Opening his eyes, he noticed all faces looking toward the same direction...up. Several outfielders were running backwards, holding their mitts up. All present were standing, with breaths held. Staggering backwards, the Flatlander's out fielder jumped high in the air, landing against the twelve foot high chain link fence. The ball had come to rest in a tangle of barbed wire at the top of the fence and refused to fall earthward. As the outfielder stood there looking at the ball, the entire field, fans and players alike, broke into a tumultuous roar. Branovitch ran to the plate where Sommerfield was still standing, holding his bat. "Run you fool, run the bases, you hit a home run." Without really knowing why, Sommerfield ran the bases, shaking hands with all three base men and a short stop. Upon his arrival at home plate, General Porter was waiting, almost obscuring the home plate.

"Step on the plate, step on the stupid plate!" Branovitch shouted over the shouts of the crowd. As Sommerfield stepped on the sack, McCloud shouted, "Safe!" Shaking General Porter's hand, Sommerfield asked Branovitch, "What does this mean?"

General Porter exclaimed, "You got a home run boy, we can go home now."

The Rhinelanders did not completely understanding how the opposing team could be 27 runs ahead and with a single home run, could end the game. But no one really seemed to care who won. The Rhinelanders hoisted Sommerfield to their shoulders, yelling and shouting, "Baseball! baseball!" left the field. The Flatlanders, smiling at their game also left the field feeling fairly good about themselves.

As the teams and the crowd began to move away from the ball diamond, General Porter, Colonel Reed, Colonel Wolf moved toward Henry Schmidt.

"Mr. Schmidt," said General Porter, "I am deeply grateful for what you have done here. You have helped to teach these men that America is not simply a place on the map but a way of life. After this war is over, they will return to their country knowing that Americans are good people. You have helped to win the peace. Mr. Schmidt, your son would have been very proud of you. I certainly am." Schmidt stopped for a second and reflected on what General Porter had just said. In a small way, he had become one of the peacemakers Chaplain Wolf had just spoken about. A warm feeling filled his soul.

Mac made his way over to the little group, standing at home plate. "I couldn't have done it without the help of our Postmiester here." Schmidt responded as if to take himself out of the spotlight.

"Done what?" McCloud insisted.

"My heartfelt thanks to you, Mr. McCloud, for what you contributed to this event." McCloud brushed off the comment as if to brush off a fly. I want you to know that I will be contacting the Postmaster General regarding your efforts here today. You are the kind of man we need in government service."

McCloud's eyes and cheeks reddened at these comments. He too felt a warm feeling move throughout his body.

"You know general, I was thinking. I hope we do not repeat this event next year," McCloud said.

Looking somewhat shocked, General Porter, said "Why not, it was wonderful!"

"I hope and pray that these men will all be at home, with their families and this stupid war will be over."

All agreed with McCloud's comment.

Car headlights began to turn on and move toward the highway. Hugs and handshakes were exchanged between old friends and new friends. The POWs were in the showers with strains of The Battle Hymn of the Republic reaching far beyond the chain link and barbed wire fences of the camp. As the lights out signal was given, the camp became dark, but the singing by POWs and guards alike seemed to go on well past midnight. On more than one occasion, one could hear glasses clink together and the phrases, "Here's to Rupert and Ross. Here's to Helmut, Here's to Colonel Reed," and so on.

16

THE MORNING FOLLOWING Thanksgiving was declared a holiday, just as it was outside the camp. Men were allowed to sleep an extra hour and the mess hall remained open to accommodate those who opted to sleep in. Many of the men found their way to the baseball field, tossing balls around, throwing and catching, and batting a few. Some noticed the ball caught in the barbed wire was no longer there.

At nine o'clock, the loud speakers announced a general assembly in the main hangar area. While this was not unusual, the POWs collectively wondered what was happening. Within minutes, all POWs and camp personnel were assembled. Sergeant Walther shouted his usual elongated "Attention!" order and the men stood at attention. Colonel Reed, with his new eagles prominent on his shoulders, took his stand behind the main podium.

"Gentlemen, I want to thank you all for the wonderful event which you helped to put on yesterday. Not only did we have a fine meal, some songs and a baseball game, we had a peace conference as well. Many fences were torn down, many hatchets were buried, and many of us grew to a new level of humanity." Tears began to well up in his eyes. "The lions and the lambs are getting closer."

Most of those hearing these comments did not really understand what he was talking about; especially the part about the lions and the lambs.

"I don't want to take too much of your day off for speeches, but I do wish to make a few presentations. Private Branovitch, front and center," Reed barked.

Private Branovitch immediately strode forward from his position on the side of group. He came to an abrupt halt immediately in front of Colonel Reed and saluted. "Sir, Private Branovitch reporting as ordered."

"Private Branovitch, I understand that you had a deal with Captain Thomas, excuse me, Major Thomas. As I understand it, you were to be given the rank of corporal, if you won the baseball game."

Branovitch looked like a kid who had been caught in the cookie jar. "That is correct sir."

"But, Private Branovitch, you didn't truly win the game did you?"

"No sir." Branovitch whispered.

Reed continued with a look of disappointment. "So in that case, you will not be promoted to the rank of corporal.

However, because of the way the game turned out, that is to say, the over all game, I think it can be said that you rose above and beyond the call of duty. Therefore, I am issuing a field promotion. Because I don't really need another corporal, and I do need a motor pool sergeant, I am promoting you to the rank of Sergeant."

Branovitch's face expressed total shock.

The assembled men applauded wildly.

"That will be all, Sergeant!" Reed ordered.

Branovitch returned to his place where he was pounded on the back by fellow staff personnel and POWs alike.

"Sergeant Mike Ames, front and center!" Reed barked.

Ames marched forward and stood before Colonel Reed.

"Sergeant, your contribution to yesterday's event was not without notice."

"You can say that again, Sir!" Ames retorted, causing all assembled

132

to break into laughter.

"Sergeant, I have another stripe to add to your shirt and a small token of the Army's appreciation for a job well done, very well done."

Then Reed opened a small blue box and removed an olive and blue medal. "For outstanding service performed at this post, the US Army proudly presents Sergeant Mike Ames with the Army Achievement Medal."

As Reed pinned the medal on Ames bulging chest, he whispered in his ear. "Mike, do we have any of that mincemeat pie left over from yesterday?"

Ames whispered back, "Colonel, if I don't, I will personally make you two hundred of the best mincemeat pies you have ever tasted."

As Ames saluted and rotated on his heel, his medal flashed on his chest. Again, all assembled applauded wildly.

Colonel Reed called for quiet. "Corporal Helmut Sommerfield, front and center! Now this came as a complete surprise to everyone. Sommerfield stepped out of the line of men and made his way forward. Halting in front of Colonel Reed, Sommerfield stood wondering what was going to happen to him.

"Corporal Sommerfield, while I am not able, nor authorized to issue you a medal or a promotion, I am authorized to proclaim you 'Home Run King of this camp'. Pulling a well worn baseball cap out of a sack on the podium, he placed it on Helmut's head. "Three cheers for the King!" Reed shouted.

The place went wild as Helmut stood there with his ball cap on his head. Above the cheers of his fellow POWs and the camp staff, Reed stated, "Dismissed."

With that, the entire group of men moved off toward the ball field.

17

THE COLD DECEMBER WINDS were blowing down from the north. Inside Schmidt's barn, the big John Deere tractor lay open and exposed like a patient on an operating table. Rodney had rolled in a small black table on which several dozen wrenches, pliers, and other assorted tools were laid. He had also rigged a battery powered light bulb which hung over the engine section. Helmut approached the engine head as a surgeon would approach a patient.

"First we shall crank loose the head bolts and then lift the head off and expose the broken gasket," Helmut explained to Rodney. "Here, you try to break loose the bolts," Helmut said, handing a large wrench to Rodney. Rodney smiled as he took the tool. Placing the box end over one of the head bolts, he pulled until the bolt gave. Soon, all twelve greasy bolts lay on the table next to the tractor. Carefully, Henry and Helmut took hold of the ends of the engine head and moved it upward and out of the engine well, exposing the cylinder and the pistons.

"There is the problem," Helmut stated triumphantly "a simple broken head gasket, nothing more than that."

The sense of achievement for Rodney was broken when Harriet came running toward the barn. "There's a fire over at Becker's," she yelled as she pointed to billows of black and white smoke emerging from Becker's barn.

"Call the fire department!" Schmidt yelled back to his wife, "And call all the neighbors."

Helmut, Rodney and Schmidt sprinted toward the burning barn like three men being chased by a bull.

Schmidt was the first to reach the door of burning barn. "Becker, are you in there?" he yelled.

A muffled response came from inside the now fully enveloped building. The sound of frantic cows bellowing and kicking against their confines could also be heard. While Schmidt could not see where the choking voice came from, he none the less entered the building. Falling to his knees, he crawled toward what appeared to be Becker's form. The heat and smoke became almost insurmountable. After falling flat several times, Schmidt finally reached Becker. Becker's face and hair had already taken enough heat to make him unrecognizable. His thick bush beard was all but gone. As Schmidt grabbed Becker's coveralls, most of the garment disintegrated in his hand. He then grabbed for Becker's leg. As Schmidt began to pull himself and Becker toward the door, he felt a blinding pain as one of the cows stumbled toward the barn door. The beast's rear foot planted itself directly on Schmidt's leg, snapping it like a dry twig. Schmidt knew that he and Becker were dead. Through the roar of the fire and the bellowing animals, Schmidt could hear Sommerfield calling. "Schmidt, Becker! Where are you?"

"Over here!" Schmidt groaned.

A bale of burning hay toppled on top of Sommerfield as he crawled across the floor. As his hair and clothing began to burn, he remembered the admonition of this father, "If you catch fire, lie down and roll." Rather than roll toward the safety of the open door, he rolled toward Schmidt and Becker. Reaching the two prone figures, he grabbed each by the wrist and pulled. Overcome by the smoke from burning hay and lumber, he yelled out, "Oh God, where are you? Help me!" Helmut managed to stumble to his feet, pulling the two injured men toward the door. Rodney and one other man were standing near the door with buckets of water. As the three figures broke through the smoke, they were doused with cold, painful water. All three men were badly burned. Within minutes, dozens of pickup truck arrived with farmers and neighbors running toward the burning barn with buckets. Helmut managed to rise to one knee. He shook head and moaned. "Don't bother, the barn is gone. Try to keep the other buildings from catching fire." At that point, he lost consciousness.

The ancient village fire truck, along with the ambulance arrived with sirens screaming. Men grabbed coiled hoses and attempted to start portable water pumps. Small and insignificant streams of water fell short of the burning building. Seven scorched cows huddled nervously in the corner of a corral, still bellowing frantically.

Harriet Schmidt eventually came running toward the rapidly disintegrating barn. She spotted Rodney kneeling down beside one of three bodies. Emitting a scream, she sprinted toward the lifeless form lying on the ground. The volunteer ambulance crew, led by Bill McCloud, was lifting the form she recognized as her husband onto a litter. He rolled his head and groaned. His leg has been trussed to two boards and wrapped with a long cloth strip. As they lifted Henry, Mac McCloud was kneeling over him, talking to him and holding his hand. Harriet looked at the two other charred forms lying next to her husband. Both were unrecognizable, with their hair and clothing badly burned. Other men were ministering to them, placing them on stretchers. McCloud yelled an order. "There's only room for two of these men in the ambulance. Put that one," pointing to Sommerfield," in my truck. I'll follow the ambulance to the hospital."

Harriet was now on here knees, sobbing hysterically. "Please Henry, please wake up." Then, almost as if she had been hit in the face with a bucket of cold water, she ceased her crying, stood up and began to pray aloud—very loud. All of the men and now a few women all turned toward the tall woman and bowed their head as she continued to pray.

"Heavenly Father, you have said that whatever I ask in your Son's name, you will honor. I am asking for the lives of these three men. You have also promised that you can and will bring good out of evil. This fire is evil! The Evil One came into the world to kill, steal and destroy. He is here present today. Please Holy Father, defeat him in this act of terror. Amen!"

The dozens of people standing, heads bowed, responded with a loud amen.

Harriet turned to Rodney and instructed him to go with Uncle Rupert, who had just arrived in his pickup and fetch Laurel from the school. "Please take her to the hospital and I will ride with the ambulance and meet you there." Turning to address her brother Ross, she instructed calmly but firmly. "Ross, you go and call the hospital and tell them what has happened. Ask if they can get Doc Williams to come in."

Rodney, Ross and Rupert responded to the order as if given by a general. Rupert's pickup was racing down the road toward the schoolhouse as the ambulance and McCloud's truck roared off the other direction toward town. Ross drove as fast as his old pickup would go toward the Schmidt farmhouse and the telephone.

The ride in the ambulance was made more difficult due to the fact that the front windshield had been broken out several weeks before and a new one had not yet arrived. The cold air against Harriet's face kept her alert. Usually, she found it necessary to offer instructions to whomever was driving, "slow down, be careful of this turn, and so on." Today however she said nothing. On occasion she would turn and look at the two men laid out on stretchers in the rear and intensify her prayer.

At the point where the east-west dirt road crossed the main highway, Sheriff Buckstone had parked his patrol car with lights flashing. His deputy was standing in the middle of the highway, stopping the few cars which passed. As soon as the ambulance and McCloud's pickup approached, the sheriff summoned his deputy into the car and raced to the head of the line, leading the convoy toward the small town of North Fork another nine miles down the road. As the ambulance passed the small black and white sign indicating the city limits of North Fork, and the 25 mile an hour speed limit sign behind which Sheriff Buckstone usually hid, Harriet expressed a brief laugh as she glanced at the speedometer "Sixty-three miles an hour!"

18

AS THE CONVOY APPROACHED the red brick hospital building, dozens of people had gathered next to the emergency door. This was a regular occurrence when an emergency had been telephoned in. The gathering was a combination of human curiosity and need for the small community to unite in prayer for the victim and his or her family. Because there were three stretchers, several by-standers had to be recruited to assist the hospital staff. Those gathered were collectively shocked to see the extent of burns on the three men lying on the litters. As soon as the three burned men were placed on examining tables, all those not on the medical staff were asked to wait outside.

Harriet announced that she would be staying. Mac, however, came over to her and put his arm around her shoulder moving her gently out the door. By now the news had spread all over town and into the surrounding countryside. The dozens now became well over a hundred. One of the last to arrive was Pastor Steinke and his wife. He immediately went over to Harriett Schmidt and expressed his heart-felt concern. Steinke began to whisper a brief but well rehearsed sermon on the issue of "The Lord giveth and the Lord taketh away."

"Oh shut up you, jackass! The Lord didn't burn these men, the damn Devil did!" she exhorted for all to hear. It was the first time in history anyone had heard Harriett Schmidt use a swear word. "Besides, nobody's dead yet," she went on. "All I want to hear is a whole lot of praying! Not a bunch of stupid theology." McCloud, standing next to Harriet added to her instruction as he raised his huge bushy eyebrows at the now cowering Steinke.

"Quiet praying" McCloud added, looking directly at Steinke

People moved to benches or simply sat on the grass in prayerful poses. Some went to their knees. Pastors and priests from other congregations attempted to gather members of their flocks to them for a more concerted prayer.

Within an hour, Laurel, Rupert and all of those who had stayed behind to attend to the fire, had arrived at the hospital grounds. On occasions the nurse would open the emergency entrance door and announce that all three men were in serious but stable condition. Each had sustained serious burns, smoke inhalation and that Henry Schmidt had suffered a broken femur. As soon as the report had been given, the groups would return to prayer.

Around four o'clock in the afternoon, a US Army jeep carrying Lt. Colonel Reed, Chaplain Wolf, and Major Thomas roared into the parking lot. Lt. Colonel Reed jumped out and ran toward the group assembled near the emergency door.

"Mr. McCloud, thank you for calling me. I came as fast I could. How is he, or I should say, how are they?"

McCloud responded, "As of about twenty minutes ago, the report was that all men had suffered serious burns, smoke inhalation and Mr. Schmidt had sustained a broken leg. I suppose they will tell us if anything changes."

Harriet stood and made her way to where Colonel Reed was standing. "Colonel Reed, your Helmut Sommerfield is a hero. From what I am told, it was he who entered the burning barn and pulled Mr. Becker and my husband to safety. Had Mr. Sommerfield not been there, both men would have perished in the fire."

With tears welling up in her eyes, she lifted her hands and her face toward the sky and exclaimed in a loud, firm voice, "Praise God!"

Colonel Reed and Chaplain Wolf pushed their way through the emergency door and into the small white room. The smell of burning cloth, hair, and skin was very prominent. At once, Colonel Reed noticed three men, naked, except for the white dressings. Their faces were completely covered by gauze pads with intravenous drips taped to their arms. The impulse to vomit struck both Colonel Reed and Chaplain Wolf. Both men took deep breaths and diverted their attention to the doctor standing over one man's leg.

"This will be difficult." the doctor uttered, "With the skin burned, it will be difficult to set and cast the bone. He was not burned as badly as the other two, but he will have to remain in the hospital until the leg heals."

Then addressing the two Army officers, he introduced himself. "I am Doctor Williams. I understand that one of these two men," pointing to the two burnt victims lying next to them, "is a German prisoner of war and that you are responsible for him."

"That is correct doctor. I am Lt. Colonel Marcus Reed, commanding officer of the prisoner of war compound at Camp Alexis, and this is Lt. Colonel Roland Wolf."

Colonel Reed continued, "Is Corporal Sommerfield able to be transported to our hospital at Camp Alexis?"

"Absolutely not. Colonel Mr. Sommerfield is in stable but critical condition. He could go into serious shock at any time. Besides," he continued, "I have called the regional hospital and requested two of their burn specialists to be brought in. I expect them sometime around midnight."

"Very well, Doctor, I will leave Corporal Sommerfield in your capable hands. I will also leave my aid, Major Thomas here. If you should need anything from the Army, you have only to ask."

"Now, if you will excuse me, I have to deal with this leg before it gets out of hand." Dr. Williams stated.

"Just one more thing," Chaplain Wolf added as he bowed his head and raised his hands toward the injured men. "Lord, Thy will be done."

Henry Schmidt raised his head briefly and repeated, "Thy will be done."

The sun was setting over the west rim of the valley which sheltered the small town. As soon as the sun melted behind the hill, a cold wind came through the trees from the north. Some of the townspeople began to slip away in their cars and pickups. Soon they returned with quickly made sandwiches, jugs of lemonade and thermoses of coffee. Others managed to cram fifty-five gallon burn barrels into the trunks of their cars along with small loads of wood. As fires were lit in the parking lot and sandwiches consumed, individuals would begin to sing familiar hymns. As soon as one hymn was begun, all those present would join in. From another group would come another hymn. And so it went through the early hours of the evening. At about 11:30 PM, a car with a flashing red emergency light positioned on its roof, arrived at the emergency room entrance with two doctors from the regional hospital.

Throughout the night the vigil was maintained by the group of people on the hospital lawn. Inside, the doctors worked with all their skill to maintain the delicate spark of life now flickering in each of the burned bodies. Every hour or so, the senior nurse would open the door of the emergency room and announce that the doctors were still working and that each victim was still in serious but stable condition. By first light, many of those who had kept vigil around the burning barrels had slipped home to continue their prayers in the comfort of their beds. By eight o'clock, most of the townspeople and many of the local farmers and their families had returned to the hospital. Harriett, Laurel, and Mac were still huddled in blankets on the steps of the emergency entrance. There had been many offers for them to spend the night at a neighbor's house or even inside the hospital. Major Thomas did accept the hospital's hospitality and took a fold up bed in the hall way. Harriett had insisted that she would remain outside, where she could look God directly in the face. At eight o'clock, the doors of the emergency entrance opened. The two doctors from the regional hospital, Doctor Williams and Major Thomas stepped out into the cold morning air. They were all visibly exhausted.

Doctor Williams extended his arms to Harriett and embraced her. "We have done the best we can. We believe all three men will recover. We do not know at this time how extensive their internal injuries are. Their lungs may have sustained some injury. Henry Schmidt suffered a broken leg and will require some time to mend. All of the men will carry scars for along time to come. We have done all we know how to do. They are in God's hands now."

Doc Williams spoke directly to Harriett. "You can go in and see him now. He is on morphine to ease his pain, but he is conscious. I would ask that you visit with the other two men as well. From what I understand, Mr. Becker has no relatives and Mr. Sommerfield is a prisoner of war. These men will need some support."

"Now, if you excuse us, we all need some sleep." Doc Williams announced to the crowd. The two regional doctors moved toward their car and driver and drove away. Doc Williams walked to his car and went home.

Harriett removed her blanket, straightened her hair and followed the head nurse into the hospital. All three men were in the same room, all three bandaged from head to foot. One man had a leg splint suspended from a pulley on the ceiling. That, she assumed, was her husband. As she approached the man on the bed, the smell hit her square in the head—burned flesh, and medicinal smells. She felt faint and the urge to vomit came over her. Shaking her head a bit, she continued toward the bedside of her husband.

Henry's eyes were red but alert, peaking through the facial bandages. His mouth and burned lips could be seen through a smaller opening below.

Henry's eyes focused on his wife. "How are the others?" he groaned.

"The doctors say they are in serious condition but stable. At least they don't have broken legs," Harriett replied matter of factly.

"That dang cow!" Henry mumbled.

"Are you in pain?" Harriett asked, mainly to keep the small talk going and to keep from breaking into tears.

"Oh, I hurt a little, but the doc said he had given me about two gallons of painkiller. It's probably some of that stuff your brothers make."

Harriett chose to ignore the comment about her brother's moonshine industry.

"Speaking of your brothers, could you ask them to come and see me. Someone will have to see to the farm and the fields. They owe me quite a bit of work time. And I trust them."

Harriett smiled at the compliment paid to her brothers.

"Don't worry about the farm. I will see to everything," Harriett assured him.

"I would like to see the kids before I go to sleep. Could you send them in?"

Harriett went down the hall to a window. From there she beckoned for Laurel and Rodney to come into the hospital.

"Kids, your dad is in pretty bad shape but he has asked for you."

The three walked back into the ward where the three mummy-like men were lying. Walking toward the man with his leg suspended by ropes, Rodney's legs began to buckle.

Harriett put her arm around her son and stabilized him. "Your dad's going to be okay. He looks a little rough now, but he'll be fine," Harriett reassured.

The man on the bed next to Schmidt's moved his head as the three approached. He continued to gaze up at the young lady he had seen back at the school house. Tears began to blur his vision as he tried to recall that magnificent day he went cow hunting. He tried to recall the feeling of the air and sound of the birds as he sat atop his horse and introduced himself to this beautiful woman. The three family members focused their full attention on their father and husband. At one point, Schmidt asked Laurel to come close so he could whisper something in her ear. She bent down to hear her father's words and then looked directly over to Sommerfield. She then moved from the side of her father's bed to that of Helmut's bed. Leaning close to the man's face, Laurel said, "My father told me that it was you who pulled him and Mr. Becker to safety. It was you who saved my father's life."

Inside the facial bandages, Helmut smiled painfully. Again, tears flooded his eyes.

"God bless you Mr. Sommerfield, God Bless you!" she said in a whisper.

The morphine in his blood had taken most of the pain from his charred body, but the words just expressed by the most beautiful thing he had ever seen, left him feeling completely intoxicated.

At that point, the nurse entered the room and asked that everyone leave saying, "These men needed rest."

In keeping with Doc William's request, Harriett walked over to Adam Becker's bed. He too had been given a large dose of morphine and was in a semi-conscious state.

"Adam!" Harriett whispered, "Adam, we will tend to your cows and see to your chores. Don't worry about a thing. Your neighbors will take care of everything."

Adam closed his eyes and pretended to go to sleep.

"We are praying for you Adam. Jesus loves you," she said as she backed away.

Adam felt like exploding in tears. "Jesus doesn't love me, no one loves me!"

19

THREE DAYS AFTER THE ACCIDENT, Schmidt and Sommer-
field had been downgraded to 'serious but stable' conditions. Becker
still remained critical but stable. That afternoon, Chaplain Wolf managed to find a jeep and a driver to take him to the hospital. Upon arriving, Wolf encountered McCloud going into the hospital. "So, Mr.
McCloud, I assume we are going to visit the same people."

"I visit as often as my sister Helen, the Head Nurse here at the
hospital, and the Postal Service will allow. That guy Schmidt is one of
the finest men I know," McCloud said.

"That makes two of us, my friend. That makes two of us," Wolf
repeated.

"That man of yours, Helmut, is not such a bad guy either. In fact,
I would hate to see him sent back to Germany after the war. From
what I hear on the radio, the war in Europe could end soon. That
would mean that all your POWs would have to go back. And from
what I hear, Helmut doesn't have anyone to go back to, with his family being killed and all," Mac said.

"From what we hear from Washington, we could have the victory
within the next few months and our POWs could be home by this
time next year," Wolf responded. Both men seemed to pick up on their
use of the phrase of "from what I hear" and make it into a joke.

"From what I hear, a lot of the Germans would prefer to stay here and make a new life for themselves" McCloud continued

"Tell me Chaplain, what would it take to have Helmut stay on after the war?" McCloud asked.

"I really don't know. I do know that all POWs must be returned to their home country, unless they are facing war crimes charges. Then, we will keep them for awhile and hang them," Wolf said matter-of-factly.

The two men entered the room where the three fire victims still lay, bandaged from head to foot.

Wolf walked over to Helmut's bed while McCloud walked over to Schmidt's bed. Before taking a seat, Wolf did acknowledge Becker by asking how he was feeling. There was no response.

"He sleeps a lot," Helmut replied. "He told me once that he had a bad heart."

For fifteen minutes the conversation focused on the events of the outside world. All of the news of the neighborhood and the POW camp was exchanged along with what the nurses and doctors did and said.

From the bed near the wall, Becker's bed, came a gasp of air followed by a lengthy groan. Both McCloud and Wolf moved quickly to Becker's bedside. Peering from the eye slits in the facial bandages, both Wolf and McCloud could see Becker's eyes; wide open and not moving. Chaplain Wolf put his ear next to the man's face and waited for signs of breath.

"I think he is dead!" Wolf whispered so as not to scare the other two burn victims. McCloud nodded in agreement, having seen quite a number of people pass away.

Wolf, looking shocked by the passing of this man, took several deep breaths and spoke. "I will fetch the doctor."

McCloud reached out and held him by the arm. "Wait, wait a minute," McCloud whispered.

"Chaplain, do you recall your sermon last Thanksgiving? The

business about "…if any man is in Christ, he is a new creation. All old things are passed away."

"Yes, I remember quite well. It was one of the best sermons I have ever preached," Chaplain Wolf said.

"This old creature," pointing to the lifeless body of Adam Henry Becker "has just passed away. What God does with him now is His business, but the part about "if any man is in Christ, he is a new creation" this could mean Helmut Sommerfield."

Wolf looked confused. "I don't understand what you are trying to say."

"What I am trying to say is this, plain and simple. "Here," pointing to Adam's body, "we have a man who just passed away, a man with a large farm and, most importantly, an identity—an American identity." "Here," pointing to Sommerfield, "we have a new creation, desperately needing an identity."

By this time, both Sommerfield and Schmidt were keenly aware of the conversation going on before them. Both were keenly aware of the plot Bill McCloud was presenting.

"If you mean what I think you mean Mr. McCloud, you are completely out of line. It would be a crime to do what you are suggesting. Let me get this straight. You want to pass the body of Mr. Becker off for that of Mr. Sommerfield? Is that what you are suggesting?"

McCloud simply smiled and nodded.

"That's insane!" Chaplain Wolf exclaimed emphatically.

"Why?" McCloud countered.

The small hospital ward took on the air of a court room. The prosecuting attorney insisting on the letter of the law, while the defense attorney was trying to win the case with logic, reason, and compassion.

"Look Chaplain, here we have," pointing to Adam's body, "a man who almost cost the lives of these other two men. And here," pointing to Helmut, "we have a man who almost sacrificed his life to save these two men. Doesn't the Bible state that 'Blessed is he who sacrifices his life for others?'"

Wolf nodded in partial agreement.

Didn't you yourself say that any man who accepts Christ into his life is a new man. You know Helmut has accepted Christ into his life at the Thanksgiving dinner. He did it in response to your sermon at the dinner. My wife told me after dinner Helmut whispered in her ear that he wanted to accept Christ into his life. He is a new man! Why not give him the chance to live his life as a new man?"

"This man," Mac said pointing to Becker "is the old man. He leaves behind an opportunity for Helmut to do something good with his old name. On the practical side, Becker owned a lot of land. He has, excuse me, had, no one to claim that land. Everything of his would go to the state for sale. Why? All we have to do is simply exchange the two beds and the medical charts and the world changes. It is Mr. Sommerfield who died and Mr. Becker who lived on to do God's will."

Both Schmidt and Sommerfield listened intently as the two men deliberated. Just then, Helen McCloud, the head nurse entered the door.

"Gentlemen, just a few more minutes if you don't mind. These patients need their rest."

The two men stood staring at each other.

"I like the idea," Schmidt uttered from beneath his bandages.

"What about you Helmut?" McCloud asked

Helmut's head could be seen nodding in agreement.

"We can never get away with this. If someone finds out we will all be in big trouble," Wolf responded emphatically.

"Quite possibly Chaplain, but I am willing to put my head on the block. After all, is any one getting hurt? No! Is any one cheating someone? No! Is Sommerfield a decent man and does he deserve a second chance at life?" McCloud summarized.

"Yes!" said Schmidt, "Yes he does."

Clearly beaten, Chaplain Wolf dropped his shoulders and nodded.

McCloud smiled at his beaten adversary.

"Quick, help me change the beds."

149

Then McCloud and Wolf exchanged places with the dead man's bed with that of the new Adam Henry Becker.

"Now, go fetch my sister and tell her that you think Mr. Sommerfield has expired." McCloud instructed.

The sound of the nurses shoes could be heard coming down the hall at a fast gait. Just before she arrived at the room, McCloud noticed that he had not exchanged Becker's medical chart for Sommerfield's. Both charts were still moving on their hooks as Nurse McCloud entered the room. She went immediately to the still form in the center bed.

"Helen, we were just standing here when all of the sudden Mr. Sommerfield gasped for air and stopped breathing," McCloud offered.

Nurse McCloud left the room in search of a doctor as the four living men exchanged glances. McCloud raised his eyebrows and nodded to Chaplain Wolf. "I think it's going to work."

Within seconds the doctor on duty entered the room and went directly to the dead man. Asking for scissors, he cut away some the bandages covering the chest area. Placing his stethoscope against the burned flesh, he listened for a few minutes. "This man is dead!" he announced as the nurse took the chart from its hook at the end of the bed. Looking at his watch, he continued, "Time of death 5:17 PM. Cause of death, burns over eighty percent of his body and heart failure." The nurse wrote these simple facts related to the termination of a human life on the chart. The doctor excused himself and left the nurse to wrap the body in the bed sheet and call for a gurney to take it away. "Gentleman, could you wait outside while we deal with this situation." Nurse McCloud ordered in a polite but firm tone.

After Adam Becker's body had been taken to the basement, McCloud and Wolf asked the nurse if they could have just a few minutes to talk with Schmidt and 'Becker'.

"Five minutes, and not a second more. Those poor men have had quite a jolt this afternoon. They need quiet!"

"Yes Ma'm!" McCloud said, addressing his sister in utmost subordination.

The two men almost ran back into the hospital room.

"We did it! McCloud whispered. "From here on, the body will be in a closed casket and then buried. Then it is up to us to deal with our new creation," McCloud said gleefully.

Wolf was still somewhat unhappy about the whole charade but resigned to go along with it.

Beneath their bandaged faces, both Helmut and Schmidt were smiling, mainly at the facial antics of the two men standing before them.

"OK Helmut, or I should say, Adam Henry Becker, do not say anything to anyone. Until we can work on your English a bit more and fill you in on who you were, simply respond by nodding your head or if you must, talk in a whisper. We don't want your German accent to give our little game away."

"Now, as far as the mortal remains of our dearly departed friend Mr. Helmut Sommerfield is concerned, Chaplain, you can report to Colonel Reed that Mr. Sommerfield died in service to his fellow man. He, in fact, saved the lives of two Americans, at the sacrifice of his own. And, if you like, Chaplain Wolf, I will be happy to talk with Reverend Steinke about internment in the Lutheran cemetery which ironically is located on Adam Henry Becker's land. It may further be appropriate for a delegation of Mr. Sommerfield's comrades to attend his funeral along with various members of your staff and of the community."

Wolf regarded McCloud for a minute and then broke into laughter. "You know something Mr. McCloud, you are crazy, but I like you."

All four men smiled.

The nurse stood at the door. "OK Mac, time's up. Get out of here!"

"Henry, Adam, we will see you guys tomorrow, that is if Head Nurse Helen will allow it," McCloud said on the way out of the room.

As McCloud and Wolf walked toward the parking lot McCloud spoke. "Chaplain Wolf, did you happen to notice the time of death?

5:17. It may be a coincidence, but that is the chapter and verse in II Corinthians where you find the text regarding becoming a new creation."

McCloud continued on to his car while Wolf stood silently pondering McClouds comments and the events of the afternoon. The silence was heavy. For a second, he thought he heard someone whisper, "I am doing something…through you."

20

THE NEXT MORNING, as McCloud sat at his desk in the post office, the phone rang. It was Colonel Reed calling from Camp Alexis. "Mr. McCloud, I want to thank you for all that you were able to do in providing comfort in the final hours of our departed friend, Helmut Sommerfield. I understand from Chaplain Wolf that you have generously offered to assist in making final preparations for internment. Usually, in cases like this, we try to place the body in some sort of US government cemetery. However, in the case of corporal Sommerfield, I feel it would be proper and acceptable for internment in a local cemetery, particularly under the circumstances. Actually, I understand that the cemetery you are considering is in sight of the barn in which corporal Sommerfield received his fatal injuries."

"That is correct, Colonel. The cemetery and the church are Lutheran and I believe that Mr. Sommerfield is, or I should say, was a Lutheran."

"I want you to know that the US Army will take care of all expenses involved with corporal Sommerfield's medical treatment and internment. I can allow one hundred dollars for a proper headstone, and, shall we say, five hundred for a casket and burial," Colonel Reed suggested.

"I would be happy to make the arrangements and let you know

the exact costs," McCloud replied.

Reed went on, "Chaplain Wolf suggested that he deliver the message and that we transport twenty or so of Sommerfield's comrades from the camp to the cemetery."

"Colonel, I think corporal Sommerfield would have been very pleased with your concern," McCloud commented.

McCloud looked at his wall calendar for a second. "How do you feel about Wednesday of next week? I will clear all this with the local funeral director and the pastor of the church and confirm the date and the time."

"Excellent Mr. McCloud, I will await your call."

McCloud pressed the receiver button on his telephone and waited for a dial tone. He telephoned Walter Peoples at the funeral parlor across the street. "Walter, could you come over for a few minutes. We have some business to take care of."

On Tuesday morning, eight members from the little country church gathered at the cemetery. Each had been here before; many times before. It was the custom for a few of the older men in the community to "invite" some younger men to set the gravesite and dig the grave. The older men set the site and the younger men did the digging. It was a time when the older men could reflect upon their own mortality and suggest where they might wish to be "planted" when their time came. It was a time when the younger men could once again hear the stories of those who were already "planted." Each of the older men knew that someday a small group of men would spend time telling stories about them the day before they had been "planted." It seemed to be a way to keep the dead among the living. While the digging of the grave took two to three hours, the ritual of remembering took five to six hours. Each living old timer would recall an event or story associated with one of the dead old-timers. There were a lot of funny stories, some of which had been enhanced over the years. "There was old Walter Plunket over there, in the corner. Run over by his tractor. Now if he had been run over by his plow horse, they would have shot the critter between the eyes. But rather than shoot his tractor, his widow kept the dang thing and drove it to town when the roads got snowed in." Everyone laughed.

"Over yonder, lays Oscar Brush, froze to death when his pickup ran off the road in a blizzard. Because he rolled up like a cat, it took the undertaker three days to thaw him out and get him straight so they could put him in a box." Again everyone laughed at the story of poor Oscar.

"And right here, we have our old friends Henry and Annie Becker. Poor old Henry was a good old feller, but his wife drove him nuts. He owned all this land, including this cemetery and the church property. He told the pastor back in his time that he wanted to deed the church land and the cemetery to the church. But he never got around to it. One day, as the story goes, Annie tossed Henry out of the house for something or another. Henry went to hide out in the barn over yonder." The story teller paused as he pointed to the still smoldering barn a half mile down the road. "As the story goes, he put a shot gun to his head and pulled the trigger. Annie told everyone that Henry had planned to go pheasant hunting that afternoon and that the shot gun went off by accident. The sheriff wrote the report out as an accident but told everyone round about that it was a self inflicted gun wound. And because of that, the new pastor of the church refused to give Henry a full Christian funeral. Even though Henry owned the cemetery land, that pastor required he be planted way back here in the back corner. Annie was pretty mad about the whole thing. In fact, she constantly threatened to evict the church and the cemetery from her property. What a woman." Once again, everyone laughed.

"Just imagine, digging up all these folks and planting them somewhere else!" someone added.

"Anyhow, this German boy, Helmut what's-his-name will be in good company. Old Henry liked to speak his German and listen to German Victrola records. He was fresh off the boat from the old country. He and this Sommerfield feller should get along just fine." The stories and jokes went on until almost dark. At last, a tidy hole in the Nebraska soil awaited its new occupant. As each man left the gravesite, they stopped to pay a silent visit with one of their people lying beneath the Nebraska ground.

The following Wednesday morning, Walt Peoples' old black hearse lumbered the 14 miles to the small country Lutheran Church and Cemetery. Sheriff Buckstone's black and white patrol car, with its red lights flashing, led the way. Two military transport trucks and two jeeps were already parked along side the dirt road leading to the ancient cemetery. Twenty German prisoners of war lined the walk way into the cemetery while Colonel Reed, Chaplain Wolf, and Major Thomas approached the hearse. Walt Peoples and Mac McCloud got out of the front and came toward the back. As the door of the hearse was opened, Major Thomas called out an order. "Honor guard, to the front!" Six German soldiers, dressed in clean and proper POW uniforms, fell into two lines at the rear of the hearse. Mr. Peoples and Mac pulled the casket from its place as the six POWs took hold of the cold, metal hand rails. The group of soldiers and civilians walked up the hill toward the open grave. Off to one side thirty or so members of the community, including Harriett Schmidt, Laurel Schmidt, and Rodney Schmidt stood silently. Sheriff Buckstone and Reverend Steinke stood toward the back of the group as if to oversee the events in the back section of the cemetery. The POW pallbearers placed the casket on the board which constituted the final gate between the living and the dead.

Chaplain Wolf removed several pieces of paper from his uniform and began to read. "If any man be in Christ, he is a new creation. All old things are passed away...."

At the conclusion of the sermon, a German bugler sounded the lonesome notes of a warrior's tribute to a fallen comrade. The six men took the ropes running under the casket, lifted the little wooden box and lowered it into the Nebraska ground. As the group of people moved toward the gate of the cemetery, several of the men remained behind and began to fill the hole. It was a day of mixed emotions. The deceased had no family to mourn him. Therefore no one seemed to know what to do or how to express their sense of loss. Sommerfield was a good man and a good worker, but there were no real emotional ties. As the POWs climbed back into their trucks and headed back toward the camp, a few of the men began to gather near the front gate. Rupert and Ross, who attended almost every funeral in the area, were talking with some of the men. Quietly the two brothers were suggesting that an after-funeral wake be held over at the 'club house'. The first drinks were on the house—as was the case with most local funerals.

Harriett passed her brother as she exited the gate for the one mile walk to her house. As she passed the two, she said in a loud, clear voice, "Drink one for me boys."

The two old men stood amazed that their blue nosed sister would even suggest such a thing.

As Harriett and her two children walked down the dirt road toward their house and toward the still smoldering ashes of Adam Becker's barn, she said, "Actually, I liked Mr. Sommerfield. Granted, he was an enemy soldier but he meant no harm to any of us."

Rodney added that he too liked Mr. Sommerfield and wished that he were still alive. "Mr. Sommerfield" he said, "was one of the few people who made me feel like I was an adult."

"I didn't get the chance to really get to know him but I would have liked to," Laurel said raising an eyebrow as she looked toward her mother.

Her mother said nothing.

The three stood at the point where the road turned east into their farmstead and west into the farm of Adam Becker.

"Poor Mr. Becker, what will it take to turn him around?" Harriett wondered aloud.

"When he gets out of the hospital, what will he do? He has only seven cows left and no barn. How can he get enough milk to make a living with only seven cows?" Rodney asked.

"Perhaps we need to keep Mr. Becker in our prayers and trust that God will help him to find an answer to that question. God's will be done!" Harriett exclaimed as she did so often.

21

THE DAY FOLLOWING THE FUNERAL, Laurel returned to her classes at the little country school. Rodney had been asked by Colonel Reed to fill in for his dad delivering the POWs to the various farms in the area. Because of the money involved Rodney could not refuse. With his dad in the hospital, Rodney was now the bread winner of the family. Ross and Rupert went over to Becker's to try to assemble some sort of structure to keep the cows out of the cold and to drain their swollen udders. Since the fire, their milk was not fit to drink and had to be poured on the ground. Slowly, the men of the neighborhood managed to extend the roof over the unused chicken house. The seven cows could, if they wanted to, squeeze into the close quarters.

Harriett gassed up the old pickup and pointed it toward town. While she had driven the road many times before, she hated driving with a passion. Those who encountered her would pull to the side of the road and let her have her half, right out the center of the road. Upon arriving at the point where the dirt road crossed the north-south highway, she would come to a complete stop, look both ways between ten and twelve times, utter a brief prayer and then cross.

As she passed the city limits sign, she looked in among the bushes and saw Sheriff Buckstone's black and white patrol car. Bucky, as usual, was waiting for someone to exceed the twenty-five mile an hour speed limit. Arriving at the hospital, Harriett parked in the parking lot and entered the red brick building where all three of her kids had been born. "Good morning Helen," she said as she passed the nurses desk. "Good morning, Harriett," Helen McCloud replied. "Your husband is doing much better. Last night, he chased me around the room before I jumped out the window."

Both women laughed a well needed laugh.

The room seemed much larger without the third bed. There were several vases of flowers and hundreds of cards taped to the wall. Even Mr. Becker had get well cards and a vase of flowers.

"So, you chased Helen around the room last night!?" she stated with her hands on her hips.

Laughter came from both bandaged bodies lying there.

"I saw the whole thing Mrs. Schmidt." The one body whispered.

There was something strange about the voice and the way he spoke.

Realizing that he had broken his silence, he began to cough in attempt to cover up his comments.

"Harriett, sit down," Henry directed as he pointed with his bandaged hand toward a chair next to the bed. "Please, before you sit, close the door."

Harriett, sensing something odd, did as she was told.

Henry placed his bandaged hand on her lap.

"Harriett, there is something very important, I…we need to tell you. You must give me your word that you will never tell another soul."

Harriett frowned and cocked her head. Slowly, she agreed, "I will give you my word. What is going on here?"

"The man lying next to you," Henry whispered, pointing toward the next bed "is not Adam Henry Becker. Adam Becker was the man they buried. This man is Helmut Sommerfield."

Harriett turned and looked at the man next to her and then back to Henry. Her mouth was half open and the expression on her face was one of total shock.

"What do you mean this is Helmut Sommerfield, I attended Helmut's Sommerfield's funeral. All the POWs were there. Colonel Reed and Chaplain Wolf were there. How could this be Helmut Sommerfield? she continued.

"Harriett, the man in the casket was Adam Becker. Now, believe me, it was Adam. He died right here. I saw him go. That man in that bed is Helmut Sommerfield!"

Harriett continued to express confusion. She took deep breaths and pulled on her earlobe which she did when she was out of sorts.

"Perhaps, Henry Schmidt, you can tell me what is going on here and why!" she eventually insisted.

"In a few months, maybe six at the most, the war in Europe should be over. The Germans are in full retreat. It is only a matter of time until they give up. At that time, all German POWs held in the US will be sent back to Germany. For most of them there will be unemployment and hard times. Most will have a family to go home to. Helmut will have no one and nothing. He has still had no word as to where his sister might be."

A small sigh could be heard coming from Helmut's face.

"Adam, on the other hand, had six hundred acres of prime farmland, a house of sorts and a few possessions. Adam had no heirs of any sort. When he died, the state would have gotten all of his properties. When Adam passed, we…Mac, Chaplain Wolf and I…felt that it would not be right for Adams estate to go up for auction and it was not right for a good man like Helmut to be made to return to Germany. And too, it was Helmut who pulled us from the burning barn. Let's not forget that little piece of business. He saved our lives! So, when Adam breathed his last, we simply changed the places of the beds and the medical charts. The doctor came in and officially declared Helmut Sommerfield to be dead and that was that."

Harriett said nothing but continued to tug on her earlobe and breathe heavily through her nose.

After what seemed like hours she spoke. "You think you can get away with this Henry Schmidt? What will happen if someone finds out? What will happen when this man," pointing to Helmut "has his bandages removed? What will happen when he speaks?"

"Harriett, pick up the Bible and read to me, II Corinthians 5:17; go ahead, read it!" Henry insisted.

She picked up the black Bible on the bedside stand and opened to the place. "If any man be in Christ, he is a new creation; all old things are passed away, behold, new things have come.'" She exhaled loudly. "So, you think this passage gives you permission to change places with a dead man?"

"Yes! I, we, do!" Henry stated, emphasizing the word we.

"After all, it was Chaplain Wolf's Thanksgiving sermon that moved Helmut to commit his life to Christ."

A mutter of agreement came from Helmut.

"Would you want to see Helmut returned to Germany without a home or family? Would you want to see Adam's place go on the auction block, with all the money going to the government?"

"Honestly, you men!" She uttered, beaten by his argument.

"I suppose you're right," she retorted, "But what happens if you get caught?"

"I prefer to think of what might happen if we don't get caught. This fine young man will have a chance to become "a new creation." Henry said, knowing full well that any reference to scripture stifled her arguments. "And if we do get caught, it will be for a noble cause. Just think, "A greater love hath no man than that he lay down his life for a friend," he said, tossing on another little piece of scripture for good measure.

Harriett stood up and turned toward Helmut. Looking directly into his eyes she said, "I hope to God that this new creation of Adam Becker is better than the last one. God bless you Mr. Becker."

"God has blessed me Mrs. Schmidt," Helmut uttered in a loud whisper.

Tears came to her eyes as he smiled. "Yes Mr. Becker, I guess He has."

162

Helen opened the door, breaking the tension in the room.

Entering the room with a rolling cart, Helen said, "I will have to change the bandages twice a day from now on. It could be a little uncomfortable."

"Helen, I would be happy to help," Harriett offered with a smile.

"Well, you might be able to work on Henry but I think I should work on Mr. Becker," she said with a smirk on her face.

"You know what I mean. Of course I would work on Henry," Harriett responded.

The mood in the room changed drastically.

An hour later, after the fresh bandages had been applied and a brief meal had been sucked down through a glass straw, the two women left the ward and walked toward the main door.

Looking around to see if anyone was near, Helen whispered, "Harriett, do you know what's going on here?"

Harriett gave Helen a curious look and said, "whatever do you mean Helen?"

Harriett, you realize that the man in the bed next to your husband is not Adam Becker. He is actually Helmut Sommerfield!"

"Helen, what gives you that wild idea?" Harriett stated, trying to fain ignorance.

"Harriett, I tended Adam Becker when he had his ruptured appendix some years back. Doc Williams left a nine inch scar on that man's belly. When I removed the bandages from the man who died the other night, there was a nine inch scar on his belly. After changing the bandages on this other fella, the one we are calling Adam Becker, I find that there is no nine inch scar on his belly. It appears to me that your husband and my brother and possibly those two fellas from the POW camp did a switch! I want to know why!"

Harriett looked as if she had been cornered. "Helen, let's take a walk outside."

The two women walked out the front door of the hospital and toward a small bench under a Chinese elm tree. Sitting down, Harriett let out a long sigh. "Helen, it's been a rough few years. My Paul is killed and I don't know why, my younger son dries up emotionally and now, my husband is nearly killed. I don't know what God has in mind for us, but I know He loves me. I also know that all things work for good to them that love Him."

As Harriett took another deep breath, Helen took Harriett's hand. "Harriett, I respect you more than any woman I know. I also respect Henry and know that if he is involved in something, it must be honorable."

"Helen, you are right, that man in Henry's room is Helmut Sommerfield. It was Adam Becker we buried yesterday."

Almost like two giggly girls finding out a deep dark secret, both women smiled and laughed a small laugh.

"OK Helen, I gave my word to Henry that I would not tell another living person, but you figured out our little secret by your self."

For the next hour, Harriett gave the details of the great conspiracy. Helen was fascinated. Now, she was a part of the great conspiracy. As soon as all the facts were given and whole story was between the two women, Harriett again sighed.

There was a long pause as the two women watched the two or three cars that passed the hospital.

"Helen, my daughter seems quite fond of that man in there."

Helen looked shocked as she looked her friend straight in the eyes.

Harriett continued, almost at the point of tears, "Mr. Sommerfield or is it Adam Becker, I don't know anymore. He is an enemy soldier. He is a foreigner. And now he is an imposter. What am I to do?"

Helen knowing that any answer at this point would be fruitless simply shook her head.

Harriett continued, "You know that Laurel is strong willed and always gets what she wants. If she finds out that Becker is really Sommerfield or is it Sommerfield is now really Becker, she will..." At that point Harriett broke off her sentence.

Harriett wanted to cry, but she never cried. She had to remain in control.

It was Helen who began the tears. "Oh Harriett, I believe that God has placed you at the center of a series of events which seem so strange and confusing. To tell you the truth, I have often wondered if you were being punished for some horrible sin with Paul's death and all. But in all honesty, Harriett, you and your family are beacons of light in this place. You and Henry are respected above all in the community. I just can't bring myself to believe that God is punishing you. But I do believe that you are being used in some strange and wonderful way. This business between Laurel and Helmut; perhaps it a part of God's plan too. I don't know."

The two women sat silently as the sky filled with stars.

"Finally Harriett spoke. "Well, at least he's no longer an enemy soldier." Both women laughed.

One of the other floor nurses interrupted the two women sitting on the bench.

"Sorry to interrupt, Nurse McCloud, but Doctor Van Patten is on the phone. Something about a surgery tomorrow morning."

"I have to run now, say good night to your husband now and go home," Helen said as she walked back to the hospital.

"I will also say good night to Mr. Becker," Harriett whispered.

The drive back to the Schmidt farm was long and slow. At night, Harriett cut her speed from the usual twenty miles per hour to ten. She claimed that she didn't want to hit deer along the road. During the long drive home, Harriett pondered all the events of the last few days, months, and years. Was Helen right? Was God using her family for some specific cause? Were the events of the past few months, the Thanksgiving Dinner and the fire a part of some sort of divine plan? Was this business with Becker and Sommerfield a part of God's plan? Several times during her conversation, she would shake her head, exhale, and say aloud, "Thy will be done!"

Several miles from home, she came to the realization that she would have to tell Laurel and Rodney what was happening. At one point, she stopped the car in the middle of the road. "They will realize the charade at once. We, I, have got to tell them. No, I promised Henry that I wouldn't tell another soul." She pondered this issue for several minutes. "I will make Henry tell them!" She stated aloud as she began to move down the road toward the church and home.

22

THE NEXT MORNING Harriett dialed Rupert's telephone number. She knew full well that Merle, the operator over at the telephone exchange would more than likely be listening on the line. Sarah, Rupert's wife answered. For the next few minutes Harriett and Sarah reflected on all the events of the past few days. Harriett was careful to give only the most positive information about "poor Mr. Becker," knowing that Merle would be reporting every thing which the two women had said. "Poor Mr. Becker has come face-to-face with the angel of death and from what I can see, repented of his sins," Harriett stated. "Poor Mr. Becker seems to be a changed man, now that he has had his sins burned away." "Poor Mr. Becker has whispered to me that he wants to make thing right with all his neighbors when he gets out of the hospital." On and on she went about 'Poor Mr. Becker'. Finally, Harriett asked if Rupert was about. He was. Rupert did not like to talk on the phone. "Too many ears for my pleasure," he would say.

"Hello Hattie. What can I do for you?" Rupert shouted into the receiver.

"Rupert, I would consider it a great favor if you and Ross could see about Adam's farm. The poor man is going to be laid up for some time and things need tending to."

"Hattie," as Rupert liked to call her, "me and Ross have been over there every day since the fire. We have milked them stupit cows, we have tried to keep the place from completely falling down, and we even brought over a dozen bales of our own hay to keep them dang bovines of his from starving to death. I also have his horse over here with mine."

"God will bless you, Rupert," she stated.

With that, Rupert hung up.

As she stood by the telephone, Harriett looked out the window to where she could see Rodney hitching a hay wagon on the back of the old John Deere. It had been a long time since she had seen Rodney working with the field equipment. He seemed to have come out of his shell. As he mounted the tractor and drove off toward the south corn-field, she realized that Helmut Sommerfield had been the one who brought him to this point. "Thy will be done," she uttered.

With Henry in the hospital, neighbors by the dozens were stopping by to see what they could do to help and to pick up on news of the two men's recovery. Without exception, every one of them brought a jar of fruit, a loaf of home made bread, or a pie. It got to the point where Harriett would keep a full pot of coffee on the stove all day long, knowing that five or six people would be stopping by. And too, Mac had the mail delivered directly to the house, not the mailbox a mile away.

It had been a week since the fire. The farm was running, thanks to Rodney. Becker's cows were being cared for and milked regularly and the two men in the hospital were on the mend. The doctor's reports indicated that the burn injuries had not become infected and that with a little luck there should be very little scarring. Schmidt's broken leg appeared to be knitting nicely.

Doc Williams indicated that Adam Becker apparently suffered some sort of minor brain injury which has resulted in a minor speech problem

"OK," Harriett thought aloud, "it's time to take the bull by the horns. Those two men will be coming home in a week or two. It's time

Henry told Rodney and Laurel exactly what happened." Harriett had told Rodney to find someone who could take his afternoon POW run back to the camp. She told Laurel to let the students go home a little early today. They all needed to go and visit their dad. Laurel came home about three o'clock. Rodney came in and washed the grease and dirt off his hands and face. He filled the gas tank on the pickup, checked the oil and water as his dad had instructed him to do every day that he used a vehicle. Rodney drove and Harriett supervised the driving. As they neared the city limit sign, Harriett issued a warning, "Sheriff Buckstone will be behind that city limits sign. Slow down!

As the three entered the hospital's main desk Harriett spotted Helen talking to a junior nurse. "Helen, I am going to need your help this afternoon. Please come on in with me," Harriett ordered.

Laurel and Rodney looked at each other, wondering what their mother meant.

"Rodney, Laurel, you two wait here. I will call for you when I want you to come in," Harriett continued to order.

The two sat down, and their mother and Head Nurse McCloud walked off toward their father's room.

As Harriett entered the room, she asked, "How are you two fellas doing today?"

Henry answered, "Doc Williams tells us we are doing fine. So, I suppose we are doing fine."

"Henry, I have asked Rodney and Laurel to come today. I think it's time that you told them about this little game. After all, this new Mr. Becker is now our closest neighbor. Over time, Laurel and Rodney will most surely figure this thing out anyway. I believe that it would be much better if you were to tell them yourself or maybe I should say, yourselves."

Henry attempted to raise his body up a bit and prop a pillow behind his back. "Here, let me do that," Helen insisted.

"As usual Harriett, you are right. I do need to tell the kids. I wouldn't want to think of this as a lie or a trick. They need to understand that it is a simple exchange of identities."

"Simple exchange of identities?" Harriett replied with an expression of shock.

Henry responded, "Let's not get bogged down with what to call it, let's just learn to live with it."

"Henry," his wife whispered, "What do you plan to tell them?"

"Harriett, go and get the kids and I will show you what I plan to tell them, by telling them."

Helen left the room, returning shortly with Rodney and Laurel.

"Hey Dad, you look better than the last time I saw you," Rodney said.

"I feel much better, especially where that stupid cow stepped on my leg. That hurt like blazes. From now on, every time I eat roast beef I will think of that cow," Henry replied.

Laurel stepped forward, "Daddy, is Helen treating you okay?"

Henry made a few humorous comments about Helen, the food, and the bed bugs.

"Now Mr. Schmidt," Harriett stated, "we have some explaining to do. These kids have to know the truth."

Rodney was standing at the side of the bed, next to the wall. Harriett and Helen were standing at the foot of the bed and Laurel was standing with her back to Becker's bed. Schmidt was surrounded.

"OK, here goes," Henry began. "Rodney, Laurel, the man in that bed," gesturing toward Sommerfield, with his bandaged hand, is not Adam Becker. Adam Becker died and was buried. This man is Helmut Sommerfield."

Both Rodney and Laurel looked toward the man in the second bed. Both stood there with their mouths open and expressions of total disbelief on their faces.

Laurel was the first to speak. "Daddy, do you mean to tell me that there was a mix up?"

"Well, sort of a mix up Laurel," Henry said.

At that point, Helen entered the conversation and explained the entire situation. As the reality of the situation began to sink in, Rodney began to laugh. Laurel began to cry. Both Henry and Helmut, hearing the story again wondered if the whole thing was for real or if this was a dream that went hand-in-hand with the painkiller.

After a few minutes of emotional turmoil, Laurel slowly walked the few feet over to Helmut's bed and looked him in his still bandaged face.

"Helmut, is it really you?" Laurel queried cautiously.

Helmut whispered a firm "Yes, I am Helmut Sommerfield, but no one must ever call me that name again. I am now to be called Adam Henry Becker."

Laurel turned and smiled at her mother. "God's will be done," she whispered aloud.

Her mother repeated the phrase, "God's will be done."

Helen broke the euphoria of the moment by informing Harriett and Laurel that it was time to change the bandages and that she needed help. She opened a small drawer on a dressing table and removed two pairs of scissors.

"One for you Harriett, and one for you Laurel. Now, you two work on this old man and I will work on this young buck. Rodney, why don't you help me with Mr. Becker here?" Rodney looked slightly aghast. His mother gave him a look that suggested that he needed to rise to the occasion…and fast.

Slowly, the two teams cut the gauze wrappings, exposing tender, pink skin below. The few blisters and serious areas of burned skin on the arms and legs had begun to heal over nicely. As the facial bandages were carefully cut away, Harriett and Laurel held their breaths, not knowing what to expect. For Henry, his face was pink with much of his hair and eyebrows gone. There appeared to be no significant scarring. Helmut was less fortunate. He no longer resembled Helmut Sommerfield nor did he resemble Adam Becker. Laurel stood looking at his new face for several minutes as the man on the bed looked back at the most beautiful face he had ever seen. For the next hour, with Helen's careful supervision, the two burned men were cleaned, medicated, and re-wrapped like mummies in a horror movie.

"There," stated Nurse Helen. "Wasn't that fun!"

Helen then reached over and took the small electric call button next to Schmidt's bed. Within seconds a duty nurse entered the room. "Nurse Reiner, will you please bring dinner for these two patients."

Five minutes later the young nurse re-entered the room with two trays of food. Placing one tray on each bedside stand, she smiled at Rodney and left. Rodney noticed the smile. So did his mother.

Again, it was Helen who broke the silence. "Harriett, Rodney, you feed Henry. Laurel and I will see what we can do with Mr. Becker here."

Helen looked directly at Harriett. Harriett reluctantly nodded her approval.

Becker was propped up with pillows so that he could take food. His hands were still bandaged so that he could not hold a fork or a knife. The bandage opening around his mouth was larger now so that he could open wider.

Laurel pulled up a chair and sat down. She took the knife and fork and began to cut the pork cutlet on the plate. Slowly she placed the morsel of food up to Becker's mouth. Suddenly, he said, "Wait, we have not asked the blessing on this food." Becker went on, "Lord, you have given us a new day, let us begin. Thy will be done."

All in the room acknowledged with a firm "Amen!"

Helen busied herself by pretending to write on Becker's chart. Harriett and Rodney chatted about issues of the farm. Gossip picked up from the numerous visitors and, of course, the weather. There was no verbal conversation between Laurel and Becker. No words could have possibly defined the expressions exchanged between the two. As Laurel would dab away bits of gravy or apple sauce from the corners of Becker's mouth, he would tingle. On occasion, Helen would interrupt the meal with a comment or two, just to keep things from becoming too much for Harriett.

As Rodney continued to feed his dad, Harriett stood back and assessed what was happening. Rodney was no longer the baby of the family or the younger brother. Since the fire, he had become a man. Harriett felt good. Glancing over at her daughter, feeding a strange man, she felt strange—but a good strange.

It was well past hospital visiting hours when Helen suggested that visiting hours were over and her patients needed their rest. As the visitors moved toward the door, Harriett spoke. "We will keep you both in our prayers, especially you Mr. Becker."

Becker responded, "And I will pray for you, and your family."

Harriett smiled as did Laurel. As the small group of visitors passed the nurses station, Rodney glanced over at the young nurse at the desk and smiled. Harriett thought to herself, "Oh Lord, what is happening to my family?"

The ride home was filled with questions. "Mom," Rodney asked, how will Mr. Sommerfield...oops, I mean, Mr. Becker, be making a living?"

"I don't really know," she responded. "He is now the owner of six hundred acres of prime farmland and seven cows.

"But," Rodney continued, "He has no tractor, no farm equipment. He will need all those things if he is going to be a farmer."

As she looked out the window of the pickup at the millions of stars in the ink black sky, she responded. "I really don't know what Mr. Becker will do. But," she continued, "God will provide. He always has and he always will."

As the truck turned right at the church and passed the cemetery, Laurel whispered, "Good night Mr. Sommerfield."

It had been almost a month since the fire. Almost every other day Harriett would gas up the pickup and drive the fourteen miles into town to see Henry. Laurel had worked out a deal whereby she could arrange to meet the mail carrier's truck toward the end of the mail route. Although it was not totally legal to hitch a ride with the US mail carrier, McCloud justified the action because Laurel would sort the mail which had been posted back to the post office. She would get dropped off a block from the hospital and ride home with her mother in the pickup. Several times a week Rodney would take the long way home from his POW route and go by way of North Fork to visit with his dad and Mr. Becker.

Several times each week, Mac McCloud would bring his brown paper bag lunch over to the hospital and eat with Henry and Becker. Most of McCloud's time was spent bringing the two men all the current news of the community and the world. Daily reports on the progress of the war were a significant part of the briefings. On one occasion, McCloud brought a small package for Becker. It contained a get well card and a black, leather-bound Bible. On the inscription page was a brief note. "If any man be in Christ, he is a new creation." It was signed, Chaplain R.J Wolf, Mid-wife in Christ.

As reports of the two injured men's conditions were circulated throughout the area, more and more of Schmidt's relatives, friends and neighbors would make visits to the hospital. While they would acknowledge Adam Becker and make idle chitchat, they would focus their attention on Henry Schmidt. Both Adam and Henry found it amusing when a visitor would relate certain items of information that Harriett had discussed over the phone with Sarah. Merle! The two men particularly enjoyed visits from Rupert and Ross. They always seemed be in their own little worlds. They usually had some bit of off color gossip or a funny story about someone in the neighborhood. And they always had to make fun of the fact that Becker's cows were now their personal pets and no longer interested in Becker.

After each visitor would leave the hospital room, Becker would ask Schmidt to give him a complete history of the person and his family. He wanted to know things about their farms or businesses. When that particular person would make a return visit Becker would try to engage them in conversation regarding some of the facts about their lives.

During one of Mac's lunchtime visits, Becker asked Mac for a favor. "Mac, could you get me a copy of the maps of Becker's farm?"

Mac replied that he would stop by the county court house and pick up a map. "I should be able to get it this afternoon and drop it by tonight on my way home."

"Thanks."

That evening, just after Harriett and Laurel arrived at the hospital, Mac delivered the map. "Sorry I can't stay; we have a special church meeting tonight. We have to pray for you Lutherans," Mac said with mock seriousness as he handed the brown envelope to Becker.

"Here you are Mr. Becker," Mac said as he turned and left for home.

Laurel went over to Adam's bedside as Harriett took a seat by Henry's.

"What's this?" she inquired.

Opening the envelope and removing the map, Adam muttered, "Oh, I just want to see what I inherited when I became a new creation. Adam unfolded the four pieces of paper which had been taped together to make up a single map of the area around German Ville District. Laurel pointed to Adam's land which McCloud had outlined with a colored pencil. "Your barn is or I should say was, right here," she said pointing to a spot on the map.

"This is our farm," she said pointing to some lines on the paper. "We have four hundred acres," she noted. "You have six hundred."

Becker studied the map, trying to make out physical landmarks.

"Where are the church and the cemetery?" Adam asked.

Laurel opened her purse and took out a pencil. Drawing some lines on the map and writing the words "church" and "cemetery," she handed the map back to Adam.

Pointing to the map with the point of her pencil, she said, "And here, Mr. Sommerfield, is where you are buried."

While this was intended to be a joke, Adam felt a strange twinge in his chest.

Going along with her little "joke" he replied, "This is where the old creation is buried."

"And this," pointing to the location on the map where the house was located, "is where the new creation will soon take up residence."

"Laurel," Adam said pointing to the lines indicating the church and cemetery, "I want to give this land to the church. I want to give them the papers for the property."

"You mean you want to give them the deeds?" she questioned.

"Yes, whatever you call the papers, I want to give these two pieces of land to the church. Could you tell me how to do this?" he asked.

Laurel smiled and replied, "I will contact Lester Hammer, a local attorney and see if he can handle the process. Lester is a good man and I believe he will do a good job."

"Laurel, I have been doing a lot of thinking about this land. I am not a real farmer and I don't truly want to be one. I am a mechanic and a good one. I now have all this farmland and I don't need it. Is it possible for me to sell it somehow?" Adam questioned.

Laurel looked at the map and considered the question.

"I suppose you could sell most of the pastureland. It is supposed to be some of the best farm ground in the county. After all, it has never been planted and only used to graze yours and your father's cows. It should be worth more than most other farmland," Laurel explained.

Laurel continued to look at the map, pondering its potential.

"You know Laurel," Adam continued, "my land sits on a major crossroad for this area. With the church and the cemetery being located here," pointing to the penciled box on the map, "we might want to think about using this land for something else. For example we might want to use this small strip, next to the main road, for a school."

"A school?" Laurel responded with a surprised smile.

"Why not? That little school of yours is much too small and sits in a giant mud puddle."

Laurel was speechless.

"How will we afford to build the school buildings?" she asked.

Seeing that Laurel was becoming more and more excited about

the idea of a new school, Adam went on thinking out loud.

"Laurel, if I donate the land, perhaps the farmers in the area will take care of building the buildings."

"It is certainly worth a try," she responded.

Looking at her face, Adam could see that she was already planning the layout of the classrooms.

"I have only two conditions to this donation. First, the school must be called the *Paul Schmidt Memorial Elementary School.*"

At this comment, Laurel's smile left her face and was replaced with an expression of pain.

"Yes that would be good, the *Paul Schmidt Memorial School,*" she responded trying to hold back her feelings of sorrow and pride.

"My second condition is that this piece of land next to the school," he said pointing to a spot on the map, "this will become a baseball field—a real baseball field."

Laurel's face broke into a tearful smile. For the first time, Laurel took Becker's hand and held it tightly.

From the other side of the hospital room, Harriett noticed that the conversation had become emotional and physical.

"What's going on over there?" Harriett asked in a stern but friendly voice.

"Mom, come over here, we want to show you something," Laurel ordered with tears running down her face.

Harriett left Henry's side and moved toward the bed on the opposite side of the room. Not knowing exactly what to expect, she approached Becker's bed with a sense of caution. *Why is Laurel crying and smiling at the same time? What has happened?* she thought.

"Mom," she said holding up the map, "Adam is going to donate the church land and the cemetery to the congregation. He wants to issue a deed."

Because of the friction between the Beckers and the rest of the community over this problem, the issue was like a nagging sore. With Annie Becker frequently suggesting that she was going to have the church evicted off her land, the community was never sure what would happen next. Likewise, the cemetery was on her land and that too was a bone of contention.

"Well," Harriett responded, "It's about time Adam Becker did something good for the community. From beneath his face bandages, Henry smiled broadly and uttered, "It is about time."

Laurel continued as she again held up the map. "That's not all Mommy." It was the first time in years she had called her mother Mommy. "Adam wants to donate this piece of land for a school, the *Paul Schmidt Memorial Elementary School.*"

Harriett's face broke. She took a deep breath and began to weep.

By now both women's eyes were filled with tears.

"That's not all," Laurel continued excitedly, "Adam wants to donate this piece of land to a baseball field; a real baseball field.

Harriett laughed aloud, "Well, Mr. Adam Becker you certainly know how to become a new creation! And tell me, Mr. Becker, how do you propose to make a living if you sell off or give away all your land?" Harriett queried with a wry smile.

Becker was quick to respond, "*Vell.*"

Laurel interrupted, "It's well, not *vell.*"

"OK, well, I think a person can rent his land to other farmers. Is that not correct?" Becker asked.

"Yes, of course you can rent your land," Harriett answered.

Becker continued, "*Vell*…oops. Well, I will offer to rent my pastureland to who ever wants to farm it. I will keep this little bit of land here," he said pointing to a blank space on the map next to his farmhouse near the cemetery. "Here I would like to build a small building were I can fix cars, trucks and tractors. It could be my business. After all, I am a very good mechanic."

From the other side of the room Henry agreed, "Yes, I can attest to that, he is an excellent mechanic and Lord knows we could use one in the neighborhood. And Adam, while you are at it, why don't you put in a gas pump."

As the enthusiasm for the idea began to grow, Laurel added another idea to the now boiling pot. "Adam, why don't you try to find someone who might want to open a small store or small café? With the school, church and a garage, more and more people will be coming this way."

Harriett stood there with her arms folded, her face still wet from tears. "You know something Mr. Becker," she announced, "I am beginning to like the Lord's new creation better and better each day."

Laurel, still holding Adams hand smiled at her mother and then at Adam.

Laurel stated that she would get Attorney Hammer to drop by the hospital tomorrow and arrange for papers to be drawn up.

"Daddy," Laurel asked, not having called her father Daddy for some years as well, "do you think Adam could find renters for his land?"

"Laurel, that is the best land in the county. We could find a dozen farmers to rent that land and for a premium price," Henry added,

"And what about your cows? Do you want to keep them?"

"No!" responded Adam, "I hate those stupid cows. I would like to sell them as soon as possible."

Harriett still standing with her arms folded in the middle of the room interjected, "In that case, I will ask Ross and Rupert to haul them off to the sale barn as soon as they can load them up."

"You do that Mrs. Schmidt and the sooner the better," Adam said.

He continued, "I will need some money to pay for my hospital bills or they won't let me out of here. Nurse Helen will keep me here to clean the floors and wash dishes for the next twenty years if I don't pay."

Henry spoke up, "That is not a problem Adam. McCloud tells me that the military gave him money for your, or I should say, for Sommerfield's casket and burial. Actually, they gave a little too much money. It seems that my good friend McCloud sort of exaggerated the bill just a bit and we find that we have some money left over to cover your hospital bills. So, you can use the money from your cows toward your garage."

Just as Henry was finishing his sentence regarding the garage, Rodney entered the room.

"Though I would drop by and see how things were going," Rodney said in a casual way.

"And what's this about a garage?" he asked.

Harriett, taking the floor, with her arms still folded answered, "Well, Rod, it's like this." Rodney jolted as his mother addressed him as Rod. "Rod, Mr. Becker here has decided to deed the church land and the cemetery to the church."

Rodney smiled and nodded his agreement toward Becker, whose hand was still being held by Laurel.

"Furthermore," she continued, "Mr. Becker will be renting out his land to his neighbors. And," she continued, "Mr. Becker will be opening a garage for automobiles, trucks and tractors."

Henry interjected, "Let's not forget the gas pump!"

"And a gasoline pump" continued Harriett.

Then it was Laurel's turn to add to the story.

"Rod, you know that land west of the church?" Laurel asked excitedly.

Rodney nodded.

"Well, Adam is going to donate that for a new school and…and a baseball field!" she squealed.

She continued, "And do you know what he wants to name the school?"

Rodney shook his head. "No, I don't."

"He wants to name it the *Paul Schmidt Memorial Elementary School*. Isn't that wonderful?"

Laurel continued as she squeezed Becker's hand to the point of pain.

Rodney, somewhat overwhelmed by the news stood there smiling.

Rodney became serious for a minute, "Tell me more about his

garage you want to start. How do you plan to make it work?"

"*Vell*…oops again. Well I believe that, with a few basic mechanics tools and a place to work, I can get started. I have also thought about going around the county offering to buy old cars, trucks and tractors. If I can get a supply of broken down vehicles, I can use parts of these rather than pay the price for new ones, just like I did with your trucks and tractors. If business gets slow at the garage, I can offer to load up Adams, oops, my old truck and make visits to farms and do repair work at people's farms. Just like the doctors making house visits."

"Fantastic idea!" Rodney blurted out.

Becker, seeing that a major opportunity was standing in front of him, thought for a minute.

"Rod, what would you think about throwing in with me? I can't do it alone."

Rodney stood there totally amazed by what he was hearing. Both Henry and Harriett looked at Rodney anticipating an answer.

Rodney looked at his father as if to ask permission and then at his mother. Both smiled and nodded slightly. For the first time in his life, Rodney felt like a man.

"Answer the man," Laurel demanded.

"Yes, of course," Rodney stammered.

"Then it is settled. We shall begin as soon as I get out of this bed and get to my home," Becker stated emphatically. "Rod," he continued, "I want you to make a drawing for a building about twenty meters by forty meters."

Harriett interrupted, "Mr. Becker, we don't use meters here! You need to get that straight."

"OK, OK, whatever twenty by forty comes out in your measurements. Get me a plan with a cost. I would like the building to be red brick so it won't burn. I want a small room at one end for an office."

"Don't forget the gas pump and a soda pop machine," Henry added jokingly.

As visions of the new projects began to grow amongst the five people in the hospital room, Nurse Helen entered.

"Time for you to get out of here and let these poor over-worked men get their rest," she said referring to charges. "Why are you all looking like five cats that just ate a cage full of canaries?"

Everyone in the room began to talk at once trying to explain what was happening. Harriett, holding up her hands for silence, said, "Helen, let's you and me go outside and I will tell you what's going on."

Like so many times in recent weeks, the two women went outside to what they were now calling 'their bench'. Pulling their sweaters tight against the evening wind, they sat down. Harriett began relating what Adam had just announced. Helen was overjoyed at the developments. Harriett became very serious. "Helen, my daughter is in love with that man. What shall I do?"

Helen smiled and replied, "Of course she is in love with that man, you ninny. Do you think I am blind? And to make matters even worse, he is in love with her. So, Harriett, my dear friend, what shall you do? Well, you can act like a complete idiot and oppose what will certainly happen next or my dear friend, you can try to control the world and make it happen."

Harriett began tugging on her earlobe. "But, he is German," she uttered.

Helen responded, "As I understand it my dear, so was your grandfather and Henry's grandfather.

"Oh, you know what I mean Helen," Harriett moaned.

"Harriett," Helen began in a very serious tone, "your daughter needs to be married; she is much too independent. Likewise, our Mr. Becker will need someone to take care of him. Laurel could do better, but she could also do worse. Just think back a few years to that goof ball she brought home from college. My goodness, folks are still talking about 'Mr. Twinkle Toes'. "And too," Helen continued, "our new Mr. Becker is now a man of means."

"Oh, I suppose you are right Helen."

"Of course I am right. I, of all people should know. I missed all the chances I had to snag a husband simply because I was too smart, too smug and too stupid," Helen said sorrowfully.

"In fact," Helen continued, "If Laurel doesn't land this guy, I will!"

At that, both women laughed and returned to the hospital room.

Plans for the school, garage, baseball field, and other buildings had taken on the scope of building a city. Lists of tools were being considered, desks being found, and teams of men who would build the ball field.

"I want this ward cleared in thirty seconds!" ordered Nurse Helen. "If it is not cleared in exactly thirty seconds, I will get Sheriff Buckstone out of his warm little bed and have you all tossed in the local pokey."

Kisses on the foreheads of both bandaged men were given and goodbyes whispered. Harriett and her kids walked with their arms around each other to the parking lot. Helen watched from the window near the nurses' station, wishing that she had had a family like this. "Go get him Laurel!" Helen whispered to herself. "Get that little Kraut!"

23

THE PHONE RANG in McCloud's office. It was Chaplain Wolf.

"Mr. McCloud, I was wondering if you would have time for lunch today. I am at the headquarters, up here in Arlington and will be passing by North Fork about noon. I also have a little surprise for you folks."

McCloud replied, "I would be delighted to clear my schedule for lunch. I was supposed to have lunch with the President today at the White House, but I am sure he will understand." Both men laughed.

Wolf continued, "I recall a small café on Main Street. What do you say to meeting at around noon?"

"I'll be there Colonel, and if I can't get rid of the President, I will have to bring him along."

"You do that Mr. McCloud. In any case, I will see you at noon," Wolf said ringing off.

Millie's café was just down the street from the post office and from his side window McCloud could see all the cars coming down Main Street. At about 12:05 a brown military car came down the street. Behind it was an almost new ambulance. The car pulled into the parking space in front of Millie's while the ambulance remained in the center of the street. The streets were made wide so that grain trucks could park in the middle while their drivers went to the café or to the small tavern. McCloud was at the café by the time Chaplain Wolf exited his car.

The two men greeted each other with a warm handshake and wide smiles.

"Why the ambulance? someone sick?" McCloud asked.

"No, this is my little surprise. General Porter received this almost new ambulance; and with the war looking like it is almost over, he thought you folks might need it more than he does."

McCloud's face went blank. "You mean this thing is for us?"

Wolf nodded and continued to smile.

Wolf continued, "Now, here's what I want you to do. I would like you to telephone Nurse McCloud over at the hospital…"

Mac interrupted, "You mean my sister, that Nurse McCloud?"

Wolf continued, "Yes, Mr. McCloud, your sister. After all, she gave enormous assistance to one of our boys, you know," he whispered, "our Helmut Sommerfield. I want to present the ambulance to her for the hospital." McCloud couldn't help but notice as Wolf talked about his sister that Wolf's face was bright red. I want my driver to go over and pick her up and bring her here. I will give her the papers and she can take the ambulance for a drive around town."

The driver of the car and the driver of the ambulance were both standing outside of their respective vehicles.

Wolf addressed the driver of the ambulance, "Corporal Milford, I want you to go over to the hospital and find a Nurse McCloud and ask her to accompany you here. If she asks if it is an emergency tell her no, but it is important."

The ambulance by now had attracted a great deal of attention.

The two men went into the café and took a table by the front window where they could see the street.

After ordering two cups of coffee, McCloud leaned forward and asked, "Roland, what' this all about? What's with the ambulance and what's this with my sister?"

"Mac," Wolf began in a whisper, "General Porter has just asked

185

me to join his campaign staff when the war is over. Please don't tell a soul. General Porter is planning to run for the Congress as soon as the war is over and he officially retires. He believes that General Eisenhower or General Doug Mc Arthur will enter the Presidential arena and that other generals will find their way into senior government positions. Porter believes that, with his father's connections and his war record, he can get elected. This thing with the ambulance, it is intended to win a few votes. After all, the Army plans to scrap most of its surplus items when the war is over. He is using his clout to see that a number of local towns get a few items before they go into the surplus lists. As for your sister."

Just as he was about to respond to this most delicate issue, the ambulance pulled up in front of the café. Nurse McCloud got out of the passenger side of the vehicle and entered the café. Mac remained seated as he greeted Helen. Wolf however rose from his seat, stood at attention and shook her hand.

"Take a seat," Mac said.

"Please be seated," Chaplain Wolf requested as he held the lady's chair. Once again, his face became bright red.

"Could someone please tell me what this is all about?" Helen asked. "I am in the middle of some fairly serious business back at the hospital."

Mac began to open his mouth when Wolf held up his hand.

"On behalf of General Porter, Commanding General of the Central Region's Prisoner of War Units, I wish to present this ambulance to the North Fork Memorial Hospital. It is given in light of the extremely professional level of services rendered to the United States Army and its charges in time of war. General Porter wishes me to convey his heartfelt gratitude to the people of North Fork for their support of the men and women in his command."

As Nurse McCloud sat there with her mouth open, the dozen or so people in the cafe applauded. Nurse McCloud finally rose from her seat and went out on the street to examine the vehicle. Mac, Wolf, and *one word* /

the people in the café followed. Within minutes about thirty people had surrounded the ambulance.

Wolf came over to where Nurse McCloud was standing looking in the rear window.

Seeing that the rear of the ambulance was filled with boxes and cartons, Wolf opened the rear door and explained that these were some items he tossed in for good measure.

"These are some medical items I thought you might need. They were just sitting around the ware house and I thought you could use them."

Nurse McCloud turned to Wolf, "I could just kiss you!" she exclaimed.

Mac, standing a few feet away, responded, "Why don't you, I don't think he would mind."

She did, and he didn't.

The small crowd around the ambulance went wild as Nurse McCloud kissed Chaplain Wolf full on the mouth.

As soon as Wolf regained his composure, he addressed the small crowd with the same speech he had given in the café.

"Let's take this baby for a ride!" Mac yelled. Helen you drive! Roland, get in. The three got in, with Wolf sitting in the middle. The ambulance began a twenty minute drive around the town. At times, Wolf would hit the siren button on the dash board or the flashing lights. Helen was laughing hysterically as she turned corners and squealed the tires. "I haven't had this much fun since I was in high school." Halfway into their joyride, Sheriff Buckstone caught up with them. Rolling down his side window, he yelled, "What's going on?"

"Bucky, we are just trying out our new ambulance," Helen yelled. With that, she rammed the gas pedal all the way to the floor and left Buckstone in a cloud of dust.

Buckstone continued to follow at a distance as the three eventually made their way back to the café. As the three returned to Millie's, a much larger crowd had formed to see the city's newest emergency vehicle.

"Let's get something to eat," Wolf said. "I am famished."

The lunch specials came and were consumed over friendly conversation between the three. Over the brief lunch, it became obvious to Mac that Chaplain Roland J. Wolf had taken an interest in Helen R. McCloud. Mac smiled.

After an hour of conversation, Helen looked at her watch and said, "I have to get back to work. If anyone finds that they can get along without me, maybe they will decide that they can. And then where will I be? Out on the street?"

Chaplain Wolf responded, "I don't think we would let that happen, dear lady."

Helen smiled.

"Oh, by the way Helen, the documents for the ambulance are in the glove compartment. So, just take the keys and it's yours," Wolf added.

Helen got into the ambulance and drove off toward the hospital.

The two men remained in the café for a third cup of coffee.

"She's a wonderful gal," Mac said as he watched Wolf's face.

"That she is my friend; that she is," Wolf responded with a grin.

Moving closer to the table Mac said, "Roland, tell me more about this business with General Porter. How serious do you think his chances are of getting elected?"

Wolf, also moving closer replied, "Very serious! According to his father's political machine, General Porter has done all the right things. He even managed to get himself shot. That alone will result in a lot of votes. A wounded soldier is always a hero."

Wolf continued in a whisper, "My role in this will be to help dissemble the POW camps under Porter's command. This will mean getting rid of all sorts of items, like your new ambulance. Without appearing too obvious, I must see that Porter's name is attached to every paper clip that is given away. It's all perfectly legal, providing the US Army gets the public credit."

Mac responded, "I see nothing wrong with that, providing Porter's name isn't painted on the side of our ambulance."

Taking a deep breath, Wolf continued, "As for you Postmaster McCloud, General Porter was deeply impressed with you."

McCloud looked shocked, "With me?"

"It must have been the way you umpired that world famous baseball game last Thanksgiving."

Both men laughed.

Wolf continued in an even quieter whisper, "General Porter wants to appoint you as his campaign manager for this county. If the general wins the congressional seat, and I believe he will, you will be on his team. How does that sound?"

Mac's eyes were big, his face was red and he was speechless. He simply sat there nodding. "But my friend," Wolf continued, "if he doesn't win, you could lose your job. Nothing is for certain."

Still nodding, he began to smile. The two shook hands.

"Now," Wolf continued, "tell me about our Mr. Becker. Is he going to be able to make the transition once he is released from the hospital?"

McCloud responded, "Our Mr. Becker is a true miracle. Between Henry, Harriett, their two kids, and my sister working with him, he knows how to be Adam Becker better than the old Adam Becker."

Wolf interrupted, "You mean your sister knows about the switch."

McCloud nodded, "Yes, she figured it out. She's no dummy, Roland."

"Who else knows besides those you mentioned," Wolf queried

McCloud responded, "No one. In fact, everyone in the community truly believes that Adam Becker had some sort of miraculous transformation in the fire and that he is a changed man. Harriett has seen to creating the legend. I honestly don't think anyone will ever catch on to what really happened."

Looking at his watch, Wolf announced that he needed to get back to camp. He and McCloud again shook hands and left the café.

24

IT WAS A COLD TUESDAY afternoon when Laurel entered the hospital room with a huge smile on her face. "Daddy, Adam, Nurse Helen told me that you guys will be allowed to go home by this Friday."

"Yep," Henry said, "If I can walk on this busted leg, Doc Williams will let me go home. I was just getting used to all this laying around with no work and being fed by some good looking gal."

"Well Daddy, if you really like it, I am sure we could arrange for you to say a few more months. But Adam here is going home," Laurel said looking directly at Adam. "He has a garage to build."

"Adam," Laurel continued, "may we have permission to go into your house and do a bit of cleaning?"

Adam laughed. "First of all, you have to get into the house, and that might not be easy. Adam was not the best of housekeepers you might say. I only saw a few rooms of his house, but what I saw is difficult to describe."

"Never mind. We will take care of everything. You can't live like a hermit. After all, you are a new creation," Laurel chided. "Mom and I will fix things up so that you can get started."

That evening, after returning to the farm, the two women gathered several kerosene lanterns and walked across the road to Adam's house. It was dark and the old owl which used to roost in the barn had taken up residence in the new cowshed. As the two women approached the owl flew low over their heads as if to chase them away. For whatever reason Harriett yelled out, "Hello, anybody home?" No answer came from the dark and foreboding house. Carefully, the two climbed the two cement steps to the front porch. Both fully expected to see the ghost of Adam Becker standing at the front door. Harriett pulled open the tattered screen door and turned the door knob. The smell hit both women in the face like a January blizzard. Something inside was dead. Harriett quickly closed the door.

"Maybe we should wait until tomorrow," Laurel suggested.

"No, we need to get a good look inside to determine what we need to get the place in living condition," Harriett ordered.

Taking a handkerchief out of her dress pocket, Harriett pushed open the door, extended her lantern into the cave-like room and entered. On one other occasion, when Adam had been sick, the two women had seen the inside of the house. They had however entered the house from the back porch and seen only the kitchen and the back bedroom.

The small wooden house had a main room, with a small fireplace, a bedroom off the main room, a kitchen at the rear of the house and a small bedroom off the kitchen. An outhouse was located about fifty feet to the rear of the house.

As the two women stood surveying the main room, Laurel pushed on the partially closed bedroom door. With her lantern going ahead of her, she entered the room.

"Mom, come and look at this," she whispered.

Inside the room, there were bundles of newspapers piled high against the walls. An old bed was piled high with scrapbooks. Laurel picked up a scrapbook and opened it. Pasted on yellowed pages were clippings and articles about local high school students involved in basketball, baseball, and other athletic events. Other articles related to neighborhood kids involved in 4H programs. Photo clippings of county boys who went off to join the Army or Navy filled several pages. As the two women went through the various scrapbooks Harriett found one which brought tears to her eyes. Laurel noticed at once that this particular scrapbook was significant. Moving over to where her mom had taken a seat on a dusty chair, she saw news clippings of her high school graduation photo and her college graduation photo. There were dozens of articles related to winning 4H awards at the county fair. There were articles about "Local girl graduates top in her class" and "Laurel Schmidt to Become Teacher at Her Former School." Turning the pages, they found a dozen or so clippings on Paul. There were many photos and related stories about Paul's athletic achievements, then came several about his enlisting in the Army. Another page consisted of photos and headlines; "Local Boy Killed in France!" In all, there were two dozen pages of clippings on the Schmidt family. There were well over a hundred scrapbooks covering births, deaths, and most events in between. All were articles about Becker's former classmates, his neighbors, and those whom he knew in the county.

About two hours into their looking, Laurel and Harriett sat on the bed and wondered out loud, "Have you ever seen such a thing?"

"Mom," Laurel asked, "Why would a person collect all these articles?"

"I suppose it was because the poor man had no family and no part in the community. This was his way of being involved with folks."

"It is so sad. Adam never came to any neighborhood functions or community events. The only time anyone ever saw him was at the grocery store and the gas station, poor man," Laurel offered.

"Mom," Laurel began, "why do you suppose that God made such a poor, miserable man?"

Harriett replied, "Laurel do you remember when you and Paul were just little kids and we went to town and saw that little child with the terrible cleft palate and split-open face?"

Laurel replied, "Yes, I think I will never forget that child."

"At that time, you asked the same question, 'Why did God make that child that way?' If you recall, it was Paul that gave us the answer. Paul said, "To see if anyone would love her," Harriett said with her voice beginning to break.

"I really don't know if God made Adam Becker to be such a mean, ugly man to see if anyone would love him, but I really can't think of another good answer," Harriett replied.

Laurel continued, "If that was the case, we all failed. Adam died without ever having been loved. And we, his closest neighbors are the most guilty of failing to meet God's intention for this poor man."

Harriett nodded, almost in tears.

Laurel spoke in a solemn whisper, "We must never let this sort of thing happen again."

Again Harriett nodded.

Looking at her watch, Laurel noticed that it was twelve-thirty. "Laurel, you have to get up for school in a few hours. We need to be getting home. We can finish with this mess tomorrow. I will come over in the early morning; and you can come after school, that is, if you don't have to go and see Adam."

Laurel laughed, "No Mama, I think Adam can do without me for at least one day."

The two women stacked the scrapbooks on the bed, took the lanterns and walked home.

The next day, after Laurel left for school, Harriett put on her cleaning apron, tossed a cleaning bucket and mop in the pickup and headed over to Becker's farm. She knew that she would be needing the pickup truck for hauling newspapers and other junk to the burn pile.

Harriett spent three hours hauling bundles of old newspapers to the burn barrel. Then she dug out old clothes from the closets, most belonged to Annie Becker, and quite possibly to her dearly departed husband. It appeared that Adam never bothered or had the heart to get rid of his parent's things. He just left them there. Adams items amounted to a dozen or so shirts, several pants, and a cardboard box of assorted jeans and bib overalls. Other cardboard boxes contained ragged underwear, long johns, and socks—all with holes. In a closet she found several pairs of old boots, most with holes in the soles. It was a sad thing to see such poverty when the man owned some of the richest farmland in the county. In the top shelf of the closet in Adam's bedroom, Harriett found a small cardboard box containing bundles of papers and an old leather-bound Bible. The Bible had a leather latch and a small brass lock. The gold letters on the cover indicated that the Bible was in the German language. Harriett made an attempt to open the latch but the lock would not move. She removed a hairpin from her hair, bent it open and used the end to stick into the key hole. Within a few minutes, the latch gave and she opened the Bible. The printing and illustrations were beautiful. In the margins were penciled notes, again in German. Flipping through the large book, she found several envelopes with German words written on the fronts. One at a time, as if opening someone else's mail, Harriett examined the contents of each of the six envelopes. The first contained three photos of a bride and groom. On the reverse was written, Annie Borg and Henry Becker. "This was their wedding photo!" Harriett exclaimed aloud. The other two photos were of Annie and Henry holding an infant. One was marked 'Adam' and the other was marked 'Baby Mary, died at one month.'

Other envelopes contained the deed to the farm and other documents related to the property. One envelope contained six very official looking documents, complete with gold seals. They were something to do with shares in the Burlington Northern railroad. The ten certificates contained several paragraphs of very complicated language. "I had better take these and let Attorney Hammer have a look at them," Harriett uttered to herself, "They could be important." Harriett placed all of the envelopes in the glove box of the pickup.

With the huge piles of newspapers out of the house and the clothes out of the closets, Harriett turned her attention to the kitchen. Without exception, every box of rancid food, can of spoiled tomatoes, everything was tossed into a metal barrel. Small mountains of mouse droppings were scooped out of cabinets with a shovel. Mousetraps with long dead mice were found everywhere. Pots and pans in the various cabinets were placed in a wash tub to soak years of layered grease away. On occasion Harriett would find herself uttering aloud the words, "Oh Adam, Adam, Adam!" In one closet she found a large glass jug half full of a clear liquid. Carefully she took off the top and sniffed the contents. She snorted and moved the bottle away. "Rupert and Ross!" she exclaimed. "Them and their moonshine."

Just then, Laurel entered the door. "Wow Mom, looks like you have been working."

"Laurel, there is thirty years of dirt, mouse droppings, and just plain junk in this place. I don't know if we can ever get it clean."

"Mom, we have no choice. Adam will be coming here to live tomorrow. We can't let our closest neighbor live like a hermit, now can we?" Laurel said smiling.

"No my dear daughter, we can't let this dear man live like a hermit. We shall see that he has everything he needs," Harriett said with one eyebrow raised. Shaking her head, Harriett returned to cleaning the area under the sink.

By the time Rodney returned from taking the POWs back to the camp, it was dark. Seeing the lights in the Becker house, Rod drove in to the yard.

"Anybody home?" he yelled.

"It's about time you got here. We have some heavy work to be done." Rodney came into the house. Not since he was a little kid had he been inside the Becker house. Shaking his head he said, "This place is a mess!"

Harriett, covered with dirt and dust from head to foot came out from the kitchen. "Rod, I just finished hauling six pickup loads of junk out of this place to the burn barrel, before, it was a mess, this is good."

"Laurel," Harriett said, "why don't you and Rod go over to our place and get that bed of grandma's out of the hayloft. Last time I checked, it was still in mint condition. If you two could get it over here, our poor Mr. Becker will at least have a decent place to sleep.

"Rodney broke in, "Mom that was Grandma's bed."

"Rod, I think under the circumstances Grandma would approve. Besides…," she said without finishing her sentence. She smiled at Laurel and Laurel smiled back. It was that look and that smile that gave Laurel permission to pursue her man.

"Also, bring some of Grandma's chairs and other things you can toss in the pickup," Harriett called out as the two climbed into the pickup.

"I just don't understand how Mom can give away all of Grandma's stuff," Rodney said as they drove off.

"I do," Laurel whispered to herself.

The following morning, after Laurel had left for school, Harriett took a writing tablet and pencil and sat down at her kitchen table. Looking out the kitchen window she could see Becker's house. She began writing; large box of soap powder, can of coffee, box of salt and so on. Within an hour, she had a full page of items Adam would need in order to survive. With the list in hand, she went to the telephone and dialed Stencil's Grocery Store in town. Herman Stencil answered. For the next ten minutes, Harriett listed off all the items on her list. "Herman, could you find someone coming this way and have them bring this stuff along. They can put the things in Adam's house. He will need them as soon as possible. It looks like Adam will be coming home today and he will need something to eat."

When she mentioned that Adam would be released today, she clearly heard a noise on the line—a human noise. She knew that within the next few minutes Merle would have the news all over town. She also knew that volunteers would be solicited to bring the groceries out so someone could get a first hand look inside Adam's place. "And, Herman, put the groceries on our ticket. We will settle up with Adam later. Thanks"

As Harriett hung up the phone, Rodney drove into the yard after delivering the POWs to their respective farms. He came to the house rather than spending ten or so minutes tossing a stick for Jack.

"Mom, what's the matter with Laurel? Last night when we were up in the hayloft, she kept going through Grandma's things like they were hers. She would hold up curtains and quilts; why, she even got into Grandma's dishes. And she smiled all the time. What's got into the girl Mom?"

"I don't really know Rod. It must be that she's happy that her dad is coming home," Harriett lied.

25

SINCE THEIR BANDAGES HAD been removed both men looked
like men with bad sunburns. Adam had a few scars on his face but
nothing serious. Both men were well on their way to a full head of
hair. Eyebrows had now re-grown, along with facial hair. Shaving was
a bit painful but necessary every morning. Henry had a few scars on
his forearms but Doc Williams said they would go away within a year
or so. Both men felt extremely lucky that no permanent damage had
resulted from the fire. Adam however did resort to a hoarse whisper
when ever a visitor came to call. He felt that some sort of injury to his
lungs or throat would explain away his accent and use of the English
language. It was suggested by Harriett over the telephone that Adam
had taken a slight bump on the head during the fire and that this was
the primary reason for his speech problems. Thanks to Merle, everyone in the community now understood that Adam Becker's speech
problems and occasional laps of memory were due to a bump on the
head. In her many telephone conversations with Sarah Richter, Harriett would suggest that Adam's appearance had been changed by God.
"Adam no longer looks like an old hermit, with a thick beard and long
hair. He looks like a new man. Thanks be to God!" she would say.
"Why, Adam even reads his Bible every day. He is a changed man,
since the fire."

On Tuesdays and Thursdays of each week, there were women's Bible studies and prayer meetings over at Millie's Café. Both groups were made up mostly of townspeople with several ladies coming in from the country. Because of the impact the fire had made on the community, Merle felt it her God given duty to take an hour off from her telephone service and provide updates on Adam and Henry. While everyone in the area knew that Merle had gotten her information by listening in on Harriett's conversations with Sarah, they overlooked the slight infraction of telephone confidentiality.

The word was out. Adam had been miraculously transformed by God into a kind, benevolent, and loving man. Most of those who had known Adam did not like him and had difficulty seeing him in a new light. When Merle was asked when Adam and Henry would be leaving the hospital, she whispered, "I will let you know as soon as I find out and we can all gather at the hospital to welcome Adam and, of course, Henry back."

The excitement was contagious. Pastors in the town continued to pray for the two men in the hospital and would ask from the pulpit if anyone knew of their release date. Rumors were passed at the grocery store that the two men had already gone home. One rumor suggested that the two men may have seen an angel in the fire because someone saw them while visiting the hospital. Their facial bandages had just been removed and they both seemed to glow, like someone who had seen an angel. The fact that they were basking in a sunlamp may have had something to do with the glowing.

While it was not unusual for Merle to received calls from curious housewives regarding a particular event in the community, her switchboard was now being flooded with calls wanting to know when the two men were to be discharged. Hospital nurses and general staff were being singled out at the grocery store and probed about the miraculous healing of Becker and Schmidt. The event began to take on the stature of the three Hebrew boys in the fiery furnace; only one of the boys got cooked.

26

ON THE PREVIOUS MONDAY, Harriett had talked with Helen about bringing both men home to their respective farms. Harriett had offered to have one of her brothers drive Becker's old pickup truck in to town and bring him home. Helen however insisted upon delivering her patient in the hospital's new ambulance. Henry was free to ride with his wife and son. It was Helen's way leading the parade, and getting a chance to see where Adam was going to begin his new life.

On the Friday morning on which both men were to be released, Harriett called Helen at the hospital.

"Is everything still on for the big jail break?" Harriett queried.

"Yep, the coast is clear and Doc Williams has given his okay for the boys to leave," Helen said, knowing full well that Merle was listening on the line.

"OK, I will be there in about an hour. Get our boys dressed and shaved."

By the time Harriett had driven the pickup truck to the gas pump and filled the tank, most of the people in North Fork had been informed that the two men would be leaving the hospital. Mac, who had been informed by his sister a few days back, had planned to take the afternoon off and drive out to the farm with the two men, just in case someone needed something. Wilt Chalmers, who had volunteered to bring Adam's grocery delivery to his farm had already left town and planned to be at Adam's farm when he arrived. This would give them an exclusive vantage point when it came to a gossip session back at Millie's.

By the time Harriett and Rod arrived at the hospital, there were dozens of towns people gathered around the front door. It was as if Hollywood celebrities were about to appear from the hospital. As Harriett and Rodney approached the front steps, the crowd parted. "Thank you all for coming," Harriett uttered to the crowd. "And thank you for your prayers."

Henry and Adam were sitting on the edges of their beds, dressed in heavy, warm clothes and shaved as ordered. Helen was filling out the final lines on their charts. As she scrawled out the last word, she said, "Dismissed."

Harriett and Helen picked up two shopping bags of get well cards and flower vases and moved toward the front doors. Henry braced himself on his crutch and moved down the hall. Before exiting the hospital, expressions of gratitude were exchanged between the two men and the hospital staff. Just as the group moved toward the main door, Mac entered from the back door. "Helen," he said, "your ambulance is waiting."

The group opened the doors to tumultuous applause from the dozens of people standing on the front lawn. Henry took one hand off agree his crutch and attempted to wave at those applauding. Almost falling, Harriett grabbed hold of his arm and crutch. While most of those at the hospital were friends or relatives of Schmidt, the majority of the attention was focused toward Adam. Some were interested to see if he was still glowing. Most had never seen Adam, at least since he was a boy, without his thick shaggy beard or long hair. Most looked closely to see if there were horrible scars on his face. With the exception of a few scabs, he looked almost normal. Nurse McCloud had found him a pair of sunglasses and a red, plaid hunter's cap to protect his eyes and skin from the sun and the cold. It was like some movie star exiting the hospital. Someone in the crowd yelled out, "How are you two fellas getting along?"

Henry made several comments about feeling wonderful and wanting to get back to his farm. Becker simply said in a loud clear voice, "God is good!" Everyone there shouted "Amen!"

Henry was helped into the passenger's side of his pickup as Adam got into the front seat of the ambulance. Sheriff Buckstone was waiting in the street with his patrol car's red lights flashing. As the pickup and the ambulance exited the parking lot, they fell into a procession with Bucky's police car leading the way toward the highway. Mac and a half dozen other people followed in their own cars as the small procession drove toward the farm country.

The convoy of vehicles arrived at the crossroad where the white church stood and stopped by the cemetery gate. Adam had asked Nurse McCloud if she could stop for a minute so he could visit the grave of Helmut Sommerfield. The dozen or so cars stopped while Adam slowly wandered toward where Sheriff Buckstone had pointed out Helmut's grave. As Adam moved toward the grave, with its new headstone, he removed his hat and bowed his head.

"Thank you friend for giving me a new chance. Thank you Lord for making me a new creation. Use me Lord!" Adam whispered.

He walked slowly back toward the group waiting at the gate of the cemetery. Entering the ambulance, he said to Nurse McCloud, "Just wanted to say hello to an old friend."

A few hundred yards down the dirt road, Schmidt's pickup turned right into his farm as the ambulance turned left into Becker's farm.

About half of the cars in the caravan turned into Adams place, including Sheriff Buckstone. While Buck had been out to Adam's farm several time since the fire, he again wandered over to the ruins of the barn. Several of the townspeople likewise wandered with Bucky, kicking over old plow shares and other items amongst the ashes.

"I figure it was some wet hay that combusted and caught fire." Buckstone said. Most of those gathered around agreed. "Yep, must have been the green hay."

Inside the house, Adam wandered from room to room looking at his new world. In the kitchen he found Mr. and Mrs. Wilt Chalmers putting the items from the grocery store into the kitchen cabinets.

"I fired up your stove, Mr. Becker," Mr. Chalmers said. And I put a pot of coffee water on if you don't mind?"

Becker smiled a broad smile. "I like that just fine. If I can find some cups, we can all have a cup of coffee."

Mrs. Chalmers offered to make the coffee if Adam just wanted to rest awhile.

While the house and the items in the house were old, the place was now clean and tidy. The smell of dead mice and musty paper had given way to the smell of Clorox and soap. Adam noticed that the small bedroom off the kitchen had been completely cleaned out, including the bed. The room now stood empty. Wandering into the front room, he found that all the furniture, which had been covered by sheets and piled high with junk, was now reasonably neat and clean. The carpet through the front room, with its single worn path down the middle was for the first time in many years, cleaned and proper. In the bedroom he found a neat bed, complete with comforter and down pillows. Opening the closet door, he found several pairs of jeans, work pants, shirts and other items of used clothing. On the floor, were several pairs of work boots and a pair of dress shoes. Adam smiled. "Mrs. Schmidt," he thought aloud.

As Adam stood there, in his new house, he heard a slight commotion outside in the yard. Looking out the window he saw Ross and Rupert both on horseback and leading another horse—Adam's horse. Adam came out to the front porch where all those present assembled. Adam smiled and said in a low hoarse voice, "God is good! Thank you all for helping me in my time of trouble."

Rupert mentioned that he was donating an old saddle because Adam's had gone up in the fire. Adam walked over to the old horse and took him by the muzzle. The horse sniffed the man several times and seemed to recognize him.

Ross informed Adam that he would unsaddle the horse and put him in the newly converted hog shed where the cows had been.

Within an hour, all those at Becker's farm had seen what they came to see and left. All were totally convinced that Adam Becker was indeed a new man, a good man. Like the fabled phoenix bird, which had risen out of the ashes, Adam too had risen.

It was late afternoon when Adam began to realize that this was his new home and this was his new life. After cooking and eating a can of chicken noodle soup, he lighted a kerosene lamp and went into the bedroom. He sat on his new bed and pondered his fate. Looking to his right, on a bedside table, he noticed the old German Bible. Opening the book, he began to read. It was well past three o'clock in the morning when he closed his eyes and drifted into a dreamful sleep.

Early the next morning, Adam awoke from his brief but satisfying sleep to the sound of the horse snorting. As he walked out through the kitchen, he noticed a small basket of on the table with a note. The note read, "We will expect you for lunch, as usual." In the basket were several freshly baked biscuits and a small jar of blackberry jam.

Adam spread jam on two of the biscuits stuffed them into his mouth and went out back to tend to his horse and to visit the outhouse. All morning long, Adam moved around his farmstead, examining each of the buildings and each piece of farm equipment. They were his now and they looked different than they did before the fire. With each building or piece of equipment, he would ask himself how it could be fixed or gotten rid of. Ross and Rupert had apparently mowed down all the high grass around the farmstead to where it looked neat and well cared for.

27

THERE WAS A LOW FOG COVERING the farmlands that morning. Adam still felt as if he were wandering in some sort of a dream. Standing on his porch with a cup of hot coffee, looking out over his front forty acres, he noticed a dim light moving down the road, and turning toward his house. The single light became two beams as the black Buick came to a full stop in front of his front gate.

"I am looking for Adam Henry Becker's farm." Yelled a short, fat man.

"I am Adam Henry Becker," Adam replied.

"I have been driving around these parts for hours looking for this place. The fog is so thick you can cut it with a knife," the man continued.

The man mounted the three steps to the porch and stuck his hand out. "My name is Samuel Hammer. I am a lawyer from North Fork. A Mr. Bill McCloud asked me to drop by and see what we can do about changing some land titles. I also have some very good news regarding those documents of yours; you know the ones from the railroad."

"Please come in Mr. Hammer," Adam offered.

"Care for a cup of coffee Mr. Hammer?" Adam asked.

"Love one," Hammer responded.

Adam handed the fat man a cup of steaming coffee and offered him a chair at the kitchen table.

After some preliminary chitchat about the weather and about Adam's farm, the lawyer reached for his leather briefcase and unzipped it. Pulling two files from the case, he asked, "Which file do you want to start with, the church business or the railroad business?"

Adam knew nothing about any railroad business, so he suggested they get on with the church and the cemetery issues. Opening the manila folder the lawyer produced a copy of the original deed and related papers.

"A Mrs. Schmidt managed to locate your original documents. I also have copies from the courthouse," Hammer said. He continued, "Now as I understand it, you want to donate a part of your land to the local church. And subsequent to that, you want to donate other portions of your property for a local school and a baseball field. Is that right?"

Becker looked at the papers and nodded.

Hammer retrieved a large folded map from his brief case and unfolded it to where it covered most of the kitchen table. "According to our mutual acquaintance, Mr. McCloud, these are the areas you wish to donate," Hammer said pointing to four rectangles outlined on the map.

Again, Becker nodded his agreement.

"Very well Mr. Becker, I have taken the liberty of drawing up several quit claim deeds for each of the respective parcels you wish to donate."

Placing the first set of documents in front of Becker, Hammer said, "This one is giving the church the land on which the church is located. If you will sign right here, the land becomes the property of the church. Adam took the fountain pen from the lawyer and signed his name as best he could remember from seeing Becker's signature on his weekly pay slips from the milk carrier. Adam prayed quietly that the officials at the courthouse, seeing this signature would understand that he had suffered a serious injury.

Likewise, sign here, and the cemetery as well becomes the property of the church," Hammer instructed.

On the second set of documents, Hammer said, "Sign here and the property for the school will be vested in the hands of the local county school district. And because there is no one to own the baseball field, I have taken the liberty of putting title to that parcel in the hands of the school board as well. It seems to me that the two go hand-in-hand."

Again Becker nodded and signed his name at the bottom of the page.

Mr. Hammer then signed his name and placed a notary stamp in its proper place.

"If you will simply sign this power of attorney, I shall record these documents as soon as possible," Hammer said with all the efficiency he could muster. "You should have the new deeds for these parcels within the next few days. At that point, I suggest that you give them to the pastor and to the school board officials."

"Now," Hammer continued, "There is the matter of the railroad bonds. Hammer placed the six stock certificates on the table, like a royal flush. Each certificate was decorated with ornate lettering and a large gold seal at the bottom. As you know, these were purchased by your father some time ago. Being that they are negotiable, and in your possession, they are yours to do with as you please."

Becker didn't have any idea of what the lawyer was talking about. He knew nothing about railroads, bonds, or anything else related to this business. A cloud of confusion began to sweep over him. He was ready to ask the lawyer come back another day, but chose to remain silent.

"I took the liberty, Mr. Becker of contacting a colleague in Chicago regarding the net worth of your bonds. It appears, Mr. Becker that your railroad bonds have a current market value of approximately three hundred and ninety eight thousand, one hundred and twelve dollars."

Becker's eyes locked in on the man sitting across from him. The lawyer seemed to delight in watching the expression on the man's face. Hammer then took his fat fountain pen and wrote the numbers $498,112.00 on a piece of paper. Becker's eyes fixed on the numbers as they emerged from the pen on to the paper.

"Does this surprise you Mr. Becker?" Hammer asked smiling.

"Yes" was all the Adam could say. "Yes."

"Now, Mr. Becker, I have taken the liberty of drawing up sales instructions on each bond, in the event you choose to sell these bonds and take their cash value."

"Tell me, Mr. Hammer what does all this mean?" Adam whispered in a state of confusion.

"'Well, Mr. Becker, as you know, your father purchased these shares of a railroad company back a few years. Since that time the railroad company has grown a great deal and so has the money your father put into the company. At today's price these certificates are worth $498,112. So, Mr. Becker, you can choose to sell these certificates back to the railroad and take your money or you can choose to leave your money where it is and sell them some other time. If I were you sir," continued Hammer, "I would sell."

Becker was more taken with the fact that Mr. Hammer had addressed his as 'sir' than by the facts regarding the money.

"Sir!" Adam thought to himself. "Never have I been called 'sir' before.

Adam's mind was turning over like a windmill in a storm.

The attorney sat looking at Adam's face.

"Well Mr. Becker? Perhaps you would like some time to think about this decision," the lawyer asked.

"No, I wish to sell these pieces of paper," Adam said, his voice shaking a bit.

Hammer continued, "I would be happy to handle the sale and the paperwork for you, for a small fee."

"Yes," Adam uttered.

Hammer smiled and placed six more pieces of paper before Adam. "Simply sign here and I will notarize document and we will be on our way. As soon as the funds arrive, I will contact you and we can deposit them in your bank account."

After all the paper signing had been completed and a few more pleasantries exchanged, Mr. Hammer excused himself and drove off toward the highway.

For the next few hours, Adam walked around the farmstead in a state of confusion. Two months ago he was a German prisoner of war, with nothing. Today he is the owner of a six hundred acre farm and four hundred and ninety-eight thousand dollars. "How could this be happening to me?" he wondered aloud. "What sort of game is God playing with me?" Eventually Adam wandered back into his house and to his bedroom. Picking up the old German Bible he found the passage Chaplain Wolf had talked about; II Corinthians 5:17. "Therefore if any man is in Christ, he is a new creature; the old things passed away; behold, new things have come. Now all these things are from God, who reconciled us to Himself through Christ and gave us the ministry of reconciliation, namely, that God was in Christ reconciling the world to Himself, not counting their trespasses against them, and He was committed to us the word of reconciliation."

While this passage seemed to be somewhat confusing, Adam began to ponder its content. "I am the new creation. I was Helmut Sommerfield and because of a fire, I am now Adam Becker," he muttered aloud.

"Now it says, '…all these things are from God.'" While Adam had difficulty understanding the part about reconciliation, he did realize that this new situation directed him to become an instrument of peace, not only between men but between men and God. He further realized that his newly acquired resources were to be directed toward that end. Adam placed the open Bible back on the lamp table and lay down on his bed. He lay back against his pillow, folded his hands and began to pray. The words did not come. At first he tried to pray in English but it was difficult. He then continued his prayer in German. Finally the words came and so did the tears. For more than an hour Adam lay on his bed talking with his God in the most intimate and passionate of terms. At long last, Adam got up from his bed, washed his face, went outside and saddled his horse. For the next few hours, he rode for miles in all direction. For the first time in his life, he felt free and powerful. He also felt a new love for these people who had treated him with such respect and dignity rather than as an enemy.

28

IN THE WEEKS THAT FOLLOWED his release from the hospital, Becker spent much of this time between his farm and Schmidt's. One by one, he and Rod hauled each ancient tractor, truck and plow they could find into the barn where they were totally dismantled and reassembled. Old implements were cannibalized and new systems created. Spare parts were separated out and placed in bins or on nails for easy access. Within a few weeks, all the farm equipment on Schmidt's farm was put into working order or broken down into spare parts.

While Becker's intentions were honorable in his efforts to repay Schmidt for all he had done, one small part of his efforts were selfish, actually two parts of his efforts were selfish. He enjoyed the noon meal with the Schmidt's, and he wanted to be around when Laurel returned from school. This seemed perfectly natural as Henry was still on crutches and needed help with his farmwork.

At about 4:15 each afternoon, Laurel's green Studebaker could be seen turning off the main road and coming toward the Schmidt farm. She would park her car in the old storage shed and walk to the house. After a few minutes, she would come out to the barn where her father, Rod and Adam were working. When the breeze was coming from the direction of the house, Adam could tell when Laurel was coming from the scent of her perfume. Usually after a few minutes, Henry and Rod would drift off to some other part of the barn or the farmyard, leaving Adam and Laurel to talk about their day. At about five o'clock, Adam would respectfully excuse himself and return to his farm across the road. On several occasions, Laurel would walk to the end of road with Adam as Harriett watched them approvingly from her kitchen window.

According to the calendar on Adam's kitchen wall, it was Saturday. It had been three weeks since he had been released from the hospital and three weeks since he had begun a new life. Sitting at his kitchen table, eating a muffin and drinking his second cup of breakfast coffee, he began to ponder his new life. What should he do about his farm? How should he go about making a decent living? And what should he do about Laurel? His thoughts were interrupted by the sound of a car driving up his driveway. By the time he reached the front door, he could see Mr. Hammer climbing the steps. "Good morning Mr. Hammer," Adam said with a broad smile.

"Good morning, Mr. Becker. This time I found your farm without getting lost."

"Please Mr. Hammer, come in and have a cup of coffee."

Hammer took off his hat and coat and laid them on the living room couch. As he entered the warmth of the kitchen, Becker handed him a cup of hot coffee.

"I will get right to the business at hand Mr. Becker," Hammer stated.

"I have all the quit claim deeds completed and filed with the County Clerk's Office. All you need to do now is to give these new deeds to the pastor over at the church and to officials of the local school district. As of yesterday, the land is theirs."

Becker nodded, not completely understanding all that Hammer had said. He did however understand that the church land, the cemetery, and the ball field had been officially given away. At this, he felt good, very good.

"Now, on to the business of your railroad stocks. As I mentioned,

212

those certificates were valued at $498,120. Upon your request, I sold those certificates."

Hammer reached into his brief case and pulled out an envelope. From the envelope, he produced a fancy looking piece of paper with numbers on it.

"This, my friend," Hammer said with a huge grin, "Is all yours. I did however subtract my legal fees for processing your deeds and a small fee for the transaction."

Becker took the piece of paper with both hands and simply stared at it. The enormity of the numbers caused his heart to pound and his breathing to become fast and deep. Before he knew what was happening, he was lying on the floor, looking up at the light. Hammer was hovering over him, still grinning.

"I suppose I would be flat on my back too if someone gave me a check like that," Hammer grinned.

Becker tried to set up, still holding his check. Finally, with some help from Hammer, he found his way to a kitchen chair.

"Mr. Becker, I strongly suggest that you deposit this check into your local bank. I would hate to lose that little piece of paper if I were you."

Still feeling somewhat dizzy, Becker shook his head in agreement. "First thing Monday, I will put this in the bank."

"Well, Mr. Becker, if I can be of further assistance, please do not hesitate to contact me."

With that, Mr. Hammer retrieved his hat and coat and left the house.

Becker was still sitting at the kitchen table as he looked out the window to see Hammer's car bounce down the country road. He sat there for what seemed like hours looking at the check and then at the deeds.

"My God, what has happened to me? A few months ago, I was a prisoner of war. Now I am a wealthy landowner." Again the words of his grandmother sputtered from his mouth, *"Gott ist gut! Gott ist gut!"*

Eventually, Becker began to realize what had happened. God had worked a miracle in his life, a miracle which was a part of a larger plan. Becker moved to his bedroom where he put on his boots and flannel jacket. He picked up the large German Bible on the night stand, opened it and placed the check and the deeds inside. Clutching the Bible to his chest, he left the house and walked toward the road. Reaching the road, he turned toward the small white church and cemetery. It was less than a mile walk and took only a few minutes to reach the churchyard. He stopped at the cemetery gate and gave it a shove. He walked the distance to the top of the hill where the tombstone marked "HELMUT SOMMERFIELD" stood. "Thank you Mr. Becker, I hope you will now rest in peace."

Leaving the cemetery, Becker found his way to the back door of the church. Turning the handle, he found the church to be open. Once inside, he was startled to see just how similar this church was to the one in his village. Even the smell of the building was similar to his church at home. Except for the light passing through the two stained glass windows, the small room was dark and somber. Becker walked slowly down the wooden center aisle as the wood creaked beneath his feet. He moved toward the back pews and in the corner, next to one of stained glass windows, he sat down. He bowed his head and began to pray, in German. His prayer was not a high and lofty prayer with the fancy language of a pastor but rather the simple language of one person to another. He spoke to God as if he were really standing there, in the front of the church. He spoke to God as if God were really listening and really cared what he was saying. Becker spoke to God from his heart, not his mind. It seemed like hours that he sat there, in direct conversation with a loving and personal friend. The mood of the event ended abruptly when the rear door opened and a light came on. Becker's first impulse was to run or hide. After all, he was trespassing. As the door closed, he recognized Harriett Schmidt taking off her coat and moving toward the church organ.

Becker sat up straight and cleared his throat in order to alert Harriett that someone was in the room. Harriett was startled at finding someone in the church on a Saturday afternoon.

"Good afternoon, Mrs. Schmidt," Becker uttered.

"Good afternoon to you, Mr. Becker," she said, not knowing exactly what to do or say next.

"Amongst my many other jobs in life, I am also the church organist. I come every Saturday afternoon to practice the hymn for the next day's worship service. I will try not to disturb you."

"You won't disturb me, Mrs. Schmidt. I was just thinking about things, many things."

"Mr. Becker, you seem disturbed about something. Is there something bothering you?"

"Bothering me? Why should there be anything bothering me? Becker said in an almost sarcastic way. "I have a new life, a new identity, and now, a new fortune," he moaned.

"Fortune?" Harriett asked, "What do you mean by fortune?"

"I was told that you found some documents in my, I mean Becker's old family Bible."

"That's right, they were something to do with some railroad or another as I recall."

"Well Mrs. Schmidt," he said holding up the check, "I sold those papers and this is what they gave me."

Harriett took her glasses from her skirt pocket and looked at the check. She said nothing. Her eyes widened and her mouth fell open.

"You mean to tell me that Adam Becker lived all those years like a hermit when he had all that money. What was wrong with the man? Why didn't he cash those certificates in and use the money to buy a house in town or take a vacation?" she thought out loud.

A second later, she broke into laughter. For several minutes she continued to laugh. "I know why that old coot never cashed them in; he never knew they existed. Adam never opened his family Bible! If he had simply sought after the Word of God, even once, he would have been a wealthy man." For the next few minutes, they both continued to laugh.

"Mrs. Schmidt, there's more. You know the problem with the church land and the cemetery?"

"Yes, I know the problem quite well," she retorted.

"Well, the problem is over," Becker said.

"What do you mean the problem is over, Mr. Becker?

Smiling broadly, he held up the three documents dealing with the land donation.

Harriett cautiously reached for the documents and sat down in the next pew. One by one she opened and read each document. Tears filled her eyes and she began to cry.

Not knowing exactly what to do, Adam moved closer to Harriett and took each document and began to read it aloud. When he read the deed dealing with the school, he added that the school would be called the *Paul Schmidt Memorial School*. With that, Mrs. Schmidt began to cry louder. It seemed that all the grief related to her son's death began to flow into one enormous wave of emotion. It was the first time she had totally lost control since her son's death. For the better part of a half an hour, she cried, blowing her nose time and time again. Just like a summer rain, she stopped. Blowing her nose and brushing her hair back, she said, "Thank you Mr. Becker, now I have to get on with my practice."

As Becker turned to leave, Mrs. Schmidt cleared her throat, "You have my permission to court my daughter, if you wish."

A huge smile spread across his face. "Thank you Mrs. Schmidt, I shall consider that."

The sun was setting as Becker walked toward his home. He was absolutely euphoric with the events of the afternoon. Time and time again, he shouted, *"Gott ist gut! Gott ist gut!"*

As he stood at the road where his farm and the Schmidt farm faced each other he thought of the beautiful young woman inside that house. His heart pounded as he visualized that young woman coming across the road to his house some day. Slowly he turned toward his farmhouse and walked home. All that night he did not sleep nor was he in need of sleep. He planned how he would arrange to meet with Laurel and how he would go places with her and how he would eventually propose. All of this seemed quite confusing to him. On occasion he would begin to panic. What would happen if something happened? What would happen if she did not truly like him? What would happen if, if, if?

Morning came abruptly. While he had not slept the entire night, he seemed to be locked in some sort of waking dream. *Church! Church! It's Sunday and I must go to church!* He flew out of bed, made directly for the out house and then his shaving bowl. Within minutes he was shaven, dressed, combed and out the door. While he didn't like to use Adam's old pickup, he none the less started it up and raced down the road toward the church. This was his first time to actually attend a service here. He arrived just as Pastor Steinke arrived from town. Greeting the pastor and those standing on the front steps, Becker moved inside the small crowded church. All those in attendance were shocked to see Becker in church. Not since the funeral of his mother had he been back. Not knowing where to sit, he noticed the Schmidt family sitting on the right side, up toward the front. Henry Schmidt had taken his place at the aisle end of the pew with his wife Laurel and Rodney sitting next to him. Schmidt turned in time to see Becker looking for a place to sit. Schmidt raised his hand, "Come, sit with us Mr. Becker."

Becker smiled and moved toward the pew. Shaking hands with Henry, he acknowledged each member of the family as he cautiously moved down the pew toward the wall. Sitting next to Rod, he bowed his head, not knowing what to do. Harriett rose from her place and moved toward the organ. She began to play as the pastor entered the sanctuary adorned in his black robe. Laurel handed Adam a hymnal, which she had opened to the correct page. As she handed him the book, her hand intentionally touched his. Becker felt as if he would melt. He only wished that Rodney were not sitting between them.

217

The service was over in an hour. Becker was amazed that the liturgy was almost word for word the same as his small church in Germany. Even the hymns were the same, except for the English. The service ended with the usual benediction. As the pastor concluded the service, he asked if there were any announcements from the congregation. Harriett Schmidt rose to her feet and said, "I think Mr. Becker has an announcement which may be of interest to the congregation." Looking at Becker and smiling, Mrs. Schmidt asked Becker if he would prefer that she make the announcement. Becker didn't know what announcement she was talking about. Did she mean that she wanted him to announce that he would be courting her daughter? Mr. Becker nodded and gestured with his hand indicating that she should make the announcement. Becker took a deep breath, not knowing exactly what Mrs. Schmidt was about to say.

"As you all know," Harriett Schmidt began, "for many years now there has been some confusion over the ownership of this property and the property on which the cemetery is located. Well, it seems that Mr. Becker has seen fit to clarify this situation by granting the deed for the church property and the cemetery to our congregation. The deeds are fully recorded."

The congregation broke into a loud acknowledgement. Comments regarding Becker's being a new man could be heard whispered through out the small congregation.

Harriett Schmidt held up her hands to quiet the group. "There's more. Mr. Becker has also seen fit to donate the six acres west of the church property to the school district for a new school site. The school is to be named in honor of our son, the *Paul H. Schmidt Memorial School*. We will have to come up with the buildings and whatnot, but we need to expand our school anyhow." Again the congregation broke into loud applause. Even the pastor was openly exuberant.

Harriett held up her hands again. "Let's keep it down, she said, this is a church after all. And I am not finished. Mr. Becker has also seen fit to donate the five acres north of the new school land for a baseball field."

With that, Harriett sat down and tears of joy began to flow. Becker just sat there, not knowing what to do next. The pastor, seeing that the excitement needed to be moved outside, spread his arms and motioned the congregation out the door. Becker sat there, next to the wall and smiled. As he stood and began to move down the pew, Rod grabbed hold of his hand and shook it wildly. As Rod moved out, he came face to face with Laurel. She smiled and embraced him, giving him a small peck on the neck. Henry too grabbed his hand and shook it wildly. For the next half hour, people he never knew shook his hand, slapped his back, and talked about the wonderful deed. As the members of the community stood on the front lawn of the small church, they could be seen gesturing toward the school land building school buildings in the air. A group of young boys ran down the road to where they thought the baseball field might be located. They too began to see a vision of the baseball diamond there in the pastureland. It was a wonderful day for all those present. But roasts were roasting in ovens and Sunday dinners were in need of fixing. One by one the members of the small church moved off in all directions to their homes. It was good. God was good!

Becker began to walk toward his truck. Harriett Schmidt saw him and called out, "Adam, we are expecting you for Sunday dinner. Come on over as soon as you can," Adam smiled. "So now she calls me Adam not Mr. Becker."

Adam went home and fed his horse and changed shirt. As he looked in the mirror, he noticed a small red mark on his neck where Laurel had kissed him in church. He wiped the lipstick off with his hand and touched his reddened fingers to his lips. He was filled with a feeling he had not known before. Love. He debated whether to drive his pickup or to walk the half mile from his door to Laurel's door. He walked.

The roast beef and cabbage, along with the apple pie and coffee seemed to make Adam's dream a little more unreal. How did he get here? How did he find his way into these people's lives? The answer came back to him; "If any man be in Christ, he is a new creation."

With Sunday dinner over, Laurel and her mother moved to the kitchen to take care of the dishes and leftovers. The three men took their coffee cups and moved to the porch. Henry, still on one of his crutches, hobbled to the wooden rocking chair. Rod, as he was now called by everyone, took a stool and Adam took a folding chair. From the porch they could see the church and much of Adam's land.

Henry was the first to speak, "Adam, any idea of what you might want to do with the rest of your land? With all your cows gone, you won't be in the milk business anymore. Selling hay certainly won't bring in any money."

"Well, you know I've been thinking Mr. Schmidt," Adam began.

"Adam, my name is Henry. My friends call me Henry and my enemies call me Henry. So, why don't you call me Henry?"

"OK Mr. Schmidt…I mean Henry," he stammered with a smile.

Adam looked out across the road and rose from his chair. "You see that flat area over by the big cottonwood?"

Henry and Rod rose and moved to where they could see the cottonwood better.

"I've been thinking. Even though I was born and raised on a farm, I really don't know that much about how you farm here in this country. I don't think I would be good at it. Mr. McCloud told me that I could rent my farmland and let someone else use it. That would bring in enough money to buy bread," Becker paused, sighed and said, "but, like I told you while we were in the hospital, what I am good at is fixing cars and tractors."

Both Henry and Rod nodded in agreement.

"I was thinking about that idea we talked about in the hospital; you know, the business about a garage and a gas station. I was thinking, if I were to build a repair garage over there by that cottonwood tree and a gas station along with it, I could fix cars and tractors and sell gas. Seems to me that there are plenty of people in this neighborhood who could use a good mechanic. And when we get the school and the baseball field up and going, there will be plenty of folks who would need to buy gas. Like you said Henry, I could even put in a soda machine."

Henry and Rod looked at each other in amazement. "A garage and gas station? You really mean that?" Rod uttered.

Adam simply smiled and nodded his head.

"With a soda machine!" Becker added.

The three men stood transfixed on the cottonwood tree across the way and smiled.

Harriett and Laurel entered the porch, wondering what the three men were looking at.

"What are you looking at?" Harriett asked.

"We are looking at Adam's garage and gas station," Henry stated.

"And soda machine," Rod added.

Harriett and Laurel looked at each other with puzzled looks on their faces.

"Harriett, do you remember that little chat we had while Adam and I were in the hospital, the business about a garage and gas station? Well, Adam is seriously thinking about setting up a garage and gas station over there by the cottonwood tree," Henry said.

All five people stood at the window, looking at the cottonwood tree.

Rod broke the silence. "How would you pay for a building and tools and a Coke machine?"

Adam focused back on Harriett. "It seems that your mother found some old railroad stock over at the house. It seems that they were worth quite a bit of money, more than enough to build a garage and get started. Along with money from renting out my land, I should be able to buy bread and jam for my table."

Harriett smiled at Adam.

"Adam continued, "I do see one rather large problem however. I will have to find someone who can work with me as a mechanic. I can't

221

possibly make this work by myself. I will need a working partner."

Adam turned his head slightly toward Rod. "Rod, do you know anyone who might like to go into business with me?"

Rod stood there with his mouth agape. "Yes, yes, I would like to work for you!" he exploded.

"Rod," Adam continued, "I did not say work for me. I said, 'Go into business with me.' Your experience is worth a great deal to me. If you will agree, we can be partners in this business. I will put up the building and you and I will operate the garage and gas station together. Who knows, we might even buy a tow truck and really get fancy."

Rod was elated, as were the others on the porch. Adam stuck out his hand toward Rod. "Shake on it!"

Rod thrust his hand toward Adam's.

"Partners!" Adam said. "Tomorrow, I would like you to meet me at the cottonwood tree at eight o'clock so we can begin the plans. Perhaps by the end of the week, we can start digging the hole for the gas tanks. Then, we can start on the building. In the afternoon, I have to go to Rockford Center to set up a bank account and I can get some prices on building supplies. I will also see what we have to do in order to get a soda machine."

Still grinning from ear to ear, Rod asked, "Adam, do you mind if I go over to the site now and get a feel for the place?"

"Go right ahead, partner," Adam said smiling.

With that, Rod shot out the screen door and into the pickup. Within seconds, he was drawing plans in the soil with a stick.

Laurel looked at Adam and smiled. "That was absolutely wonderful. You are absolutely wonderful."

"Mom," Laurel said, "Adam and I are going to take a walk up to the blowout peak. I want to show him something."

"Watch out for cactus stickers up there," Harriett warned as the two left the porch.

The afternoon sun had warmed the Nebraska air to where a jacket was not necessary. Laurel led the way toward the barn and through the gate which separated the fields from the farmyard. A small path let up the side of a steep hill about two hundred feet behind the barn. At the base of the hill was a deep depression. Becker was out of breath by the time he and Laurel had reached the top of the hill.

"This," she began to explain, "is what we call a blowout. Years ago, the wind would blow in such a way as to dig out a hole and deposit the dirt from the hole off to one side. Some of these blowouts as we call them are hundreds of feet deep and hundreds of feet high. Ours is one of the highest in this area. She loosed the ribbon which held her long blond hair in a single pony tail. The slight wind began to tassel her hair like golden thread. Laurel took Adam's arm and turned him toward the north. "Over there," she pointed, "is my grandfather's farm. That's where my mother was born. "Over there," pointing to the right of her grandfather's farm "is where I went to school and where I now teach. Both of my parents also went to that school." Turning toward the west, she continued, "That is your place. Beyond that hill, behind your house is where my father was born." Turning toward the south, she came very close to Adam and pointed to a small barn several miles in the distance. "That is where my great grandfather lived. And," pointing to the church and the cemetery, "that is where all of my people are buried." Laurel looked directly at Adam. "This is my world. This is where my people are and this is where I want to remain. I love this place."

Adam was totally overwhelmed, not only by the beauty of the country but by the deep feelings Laurel had for this land. He thought for a minute. These were the same feelings he had for his homeland and for the family he had left behind. He realized the deep, unexplainable love that a person can have for his land, his people, and his world. He also realized that he could never again return to his land, his people and his world. The events of the past few months had changed that and he knew it. He was a new man in a new land. He knew that God had brought all this to pass for a reason.

Laurel, still holding Adam's arm moved closer and leaned her head on his shoulder. Not knowing exactly what to do, he moved his arm around her shoulder. She turned slowly toward him and embraced him. For the next few minutes, Adam and Laurel stood on the top of the blowout while Laurel's parents peeked from behind the living room curtains. As they watched the couple on the hill, they both nodded and smiled.

Adam and Laurel stood in each other's arms for what seemed like hours. Finally, Adam turned away toward his land and said, "I would like to build a new house—a big brick house, with many bedrooms— over there, near my new garage and filling station. Over there, will be your new school and the baseball field. From our new house, we can walk to our work, our church, our school, and our baseball field." Adam's heart exploded as he realized that he had used the words "our house, our school, and our baseball field." He had realized that in so doing, he had asked Laurel to be his wife. Laurel too realized what had just happened. The kiss was the first and most wonderful. "Adam," Laurel whispered, "can our house have a fireplace?"

"I will build you a house with one hundred fireplaces if you like," Adam said.

"I think one or possibly two will do. I just love fireplaces," she smiled.

"What about children?" Laurel asked.

"I will make you a hundred children if you like," Adam boasted.

She laughed, "No, I think two or three would be just fine."

The breeze began to suggest that evening was approaching. The sun moved closer to the edge of the world and the two moved down the path with their arms around each other. As they entered the yard, Laurel whispered, "Should we tell Mom and Dad?"

Adam smiled broadly and said, "Do you really think we have to tell anyone? I think they can see it on your face."

Laurel beamed. "Let's tell them."

Adam and Laurel entered the small white farmhouse.

"Mom, Dad, we have something to tell you. Oh my gosh," she said,

"I mean we have something we want to ask you. Go ahead Adam."

Adam took a deep breath, realizing that he was totally unprepared for this event.

"Mr. Schmidt," he sputtered, "I would like your permission to ask your daughter to be my wife."

Harriett covered her mouth with her hands and gasped as if she were totally shocked by this question.

Henry folded his newspaper and gestured to Adam to take a seat. Laurel moved toward her mother and watched the two men.

"Well, Adam," Henry said in a quiet tone, "you seem to have become one of the family simply through the events of the past few months. I don't see why you shouldn't marry my daughter, if you think you can handle here."

Adam looked at Laurel and grinned. "Sir, I think I can handle her. And, sir," Adam continued, "I have sufficient money to make a good life for your daughter."

"I know, my wife told me about your good fortune."

Harriett, now awash in tears hugged Laurel who was also beginning to cry. Henry stood and offered Adam his hand. Laurel broke away from her mother and rushed to Adam's side. Cautiously, the two embraced. At that moment, Rod came bounding into the room. Seeing Adam and Laurel embracing and his mother and father with moist eyes, he asked, "What's going on?"

Harriett blurted out, "Adam and Laurel are getting married."

"That will make you my brother-in-law," Adam whooped.

"Brother-in-law and business partner" Adam added.

"Wonderful," Rod shouted

Rod asked, "When's the wedding?"

Adam shrugged his shoulders and shook his head. "Tonight, if you wish."

Harriett shook her head, "No, no, these things take time to plan. We need to put things together. We need to do this right. Let's not tell anyone until we have everything planned. And whatever you do, do not mention anything about this on the telephone. It would be all over the country in a heartbeat. It is important to do things right."

29

ADAM SAT AT HIS KITCHEN TABLE with a cup of coffee and
his Bible in front of him. He had taken to reading a chapter or two
each morning before going out the door. He heard a knock on the
front door and rose to answer it. It was Schmidt, standing there with
his one crutch.

"Come on in, I have a pot of coffee on the stove," Adam said.

Henry followed Adam to the kitchen and took a seat. Adam poured
a large mug of coffee and handed it to his father-in-law to be.

You know Adam, I've been thinking. Since this stupid war those of
us whose families came from Germany have had to hide their German heritage and pretend that they have no connections with the old
country. It would be unwise for us to celebrate our heritage in fear of
being branded as Nazi lovers. It is a real tragedy that we have had to
bury the good along with the bad. Anyhow," he continued, "I was
thinking about something the other night—something you told me
about the day you received word that you family was killed."

"I remember that day well," Adam said.

"Do you remember telling me about the pig butchering and how
the whole community came together once a year to slaughter their fat
pigs and make sausage?" Schmidt asked.

"Yes" Adam said with a far away look, "I remember."

"You know, Adam, we used to do the same thing, back when I was a boy. It was a community thing among us old country Germans. I remember some wonderful times when all the German families would get together. I remember that my father had a large smokehouse where everyone in the community would hang their bacon and hams until they were cured and smoked. I can also remember the sausages that were made during those times. We had one old Polish fellow who lived over north who knew how to make all sorts of Polish sausages. Wonderful! Now, because of the anti-German feelings we don't do that anymore. Looking directly at Adam, with the most sincere expression on his face, Henry said, "Adam, do you think we could bring back that old tradition?"

A smile broke out across Adam's face. "I would love to see that more than anything I can think of."

Henry continued, "We can use my farm. I have one good corral where we could put the pigs and we could use the old smokehouse over at Ross's farm." "I can put the word out next Sunday at church that we will be having a ham and sausage party at my farm the following Saturday. Is that okay with you Adam?"

Adam had tears in his eyes. "Yes Henry, that would be fine with me."

Henry continued, "Ross and Rupert will need to come up with several days supply of good firewood for the smoking. We will also need some meat grinders with sausage stuffers. I can use one of my hay wagons for a work table and you have two hay wagons that weren't burned in the fire. That should about do it."

Adam wiped his nose with his red handkerchief and said, "I would appreciate it if we could invite Chaplain Wolf. I really miss the old guy."

"Done!" said Henry. "I would like that too. I will also invite our pastor and his family. And let's not forget Mac and his tribe."

Adam smiled.

It had been over twenty years since the last ham and sausage party and when the word went out about there being another one, the response was overwhelming. Even before the announcement was made in church, Henry and Harriett were receiving calls from long lost family members and old-timers in the community asking if they too could come. Some would be bringing a pig or two, some would not.

The day of the sausage and ham party arrived just as it did in the old days. People began to arrive early in the morning, with pickup trucks and family cars pulling trailers. The pigs were marked with a piece of black chalk identifying their owner. By nine o'clock over a dozen pigs were squealing in the holding pen next to the Schmidt barn. The hay wagons were in place and a fire had been built in an old stock tank. Several large cast iron kettles, filled with water to wash the intestines, were set to boil. Four cast iron skillets had been placed on a plank table next to the fire pit. In these skillets, small bits of sausage would be tried and tested. Over on the hay wagons, assorted butcher knives and metal bowls were made ready for the cutting, carving, and grinding. Firmly attached to the corners of two of the hay wagons were large meat grinders with buckets standing below. Ross and Rupert had attached two pulleys and ropes to trees near the barn where the pigs would be hoisted, gutted, and cut into manageable pieces.

"Let's get this show on the road," Henry yelled out.

"Ross, Rupert, if you guys can chase one pig at a time into the chute, I will pop him between the eyes with my pistol and we can load him into the wheel barrow, haul him over to the trees and string him up," Henry ordered.

One at a time, pigs were chased into a loading chute, shot between the eyes and strung up in the trees. It was almost exactly like Becker's description of the event back in Germany. The children ran to the barn and squealed as each pig was shot. As heads were cut off, small boys poked the lifeless heads with sticks and ran away when one of the heads would move. Girls would peek out from inside the barn or from inside the Schmidt's house and faint when a carcass was hung and gutted. Two pigs at a time were strung up, gutted and cut into hams, bacon, and sausage meat. As each set of intestines were emptied out into a pit and washed, they would be taken over to one of the kettles of boiling water for cleaning. Hams were trimmed and sewn into old cotton flour sacks, tied with string, and would be taken to the smokehouse later on that day for smoking. By ten o'clock the whole operation was in full production. Mac McCloud and his wife arrived, and he was immediately appointed *Sausage Meister.* Bedecked with a large red apron, several bags of dried spice and several skillets, McCloud went to work. It was up to him to season each batch of sausage, fry a sample in one of the cast iron frying pans, and make the official tasting. Sausage grinders were getting loads of meat ready for spicing and stuffing.

From the porch came the sounds of the latest hit parade records being played on Rodney's record player. Many of the younger children were playing in the tree swing near the house while their mothers and grandmothers relived a tradition almost forgotten in this community.

By mid-morning a dozen or so lifeless pig heads filled an old oil barrel. In another old oil barrel, thick chunks of pig fat was being boiled down into lard. Carcasses had been completely stripped of meat, bones stacked in a pile, leaving dozens of hams to be wrapped, piles of ground meat to be crammed into long, white gut casings, and slabs of bacon to be smoked. As Becker, Schmidt, and the Richter brothers finished dismembering the last pig, a brown military car could be seen driving past the church and toward the farm. By the time the car pulled into the Schmidt drive, the three men had gone over to the hand pump at the base of the windmill and cleaned the blood which covered them from head to foot. As the car passed the cottonwood tree, it could be seen that Colonel Wolf was driving. It could also be seen that Nurse McCloud was sitting in the seat next to him—in fact, very close to him. As Wolf exited the car, he stopped for a second, came to attention, and saluted the flag which was fluttering on the wind. He then moved to the passenger side of the car and opened the door for Nurse McCloud. She wore a pretty black and yellow dress, a wide brimmed hat, and a wide smile. As the two were greeted by those gathered around the car, expressions of surprise and whispers were exchanged by those still at the tables. The electricity of anticipation infected all those in the farmyard as the soldier and the nurse moved toward the sausage table. Mac, still covered with his red apron and still frying small bits of sausage, stood wondering what was happening. Wolf and Nurse McCloud, along with Schmidt, Becker, and Rupert moved toward the *Sausage Meister.* Helen wore a smile seldom seen. Wolf removed his hat, tucked it under his arm, and extended his hand to Mac. Mac wiped his greasy hand on his apron and received the out stretched hand. Wolf cleared his throat, stood as erect as possible, looked at Helen and back at Mac.

"Mr. McCloud," Wolf began in a firm voice, "As you well know, I have devoted my life to my country and my God. As you also know, I will soon retire from the Army and begin a new life as a civilian. Likewise, your sister Helen has devoted her life to the welfare of those in this community. She too will soon retire."

The anticipation of what was being said and what was to come next hung in the air as each person strained to hear and guess Wolf's next words.

"Sir," Wolf continued, "over the past few months, your sister and I have come to know each other and appreciate each other in a way we have never known before. We have also decided, sir, with your permission, to be married and to dedicate the rest of our lives to each other."

All eyes were focused on Mac who stood there with his mouth open and his eyebrows raised to the top of his reddened face. As clumps of sausage began to burn beyond recognition, Schmidt broke the silence, "Well, do you approve or not. For Pete sake, give the poor man an answer!"

As tears filled his eyes, Mac removed his meat stained apron and moved toward his sister, embracing her in his huge arms. He then turned toward Wolf and embraced him. "Of course you can marry my sister. I would be honored to call you my brother-in-law." The two men shook hands as everyone in the farmyard clapped, cheered and whistled.

Within minutes, Chaplain Wolf was surrounded by men shaking his hand and slapping him on the back and Helen was surrounded by the women hugging and asking the details of the wedding.

Amidst all of the hugging and back slapping Harriett noticed that it was coming up on eleven thirty. Marching over toward the house she slammed the iron rod against the triangular dinner bell. All attention focused on her. "OK, it's almost time for dinner. Let's get this mess cleaned up and have something to eat."

She began barking orders regarding the clean up. Everyone was given an assignment; and within a reasonably short time, the farmyard returned to its normal state of propriety. Tables were washed and moved to the shade of the small grove of Russian olive trees on the west side of the house. Women began to bring casseroles and large bowls of potatoes from the kitchen. Several large glass jugs of lemonade were placed on kitchen stools along with paper cups. The line of men waiting to wash up at the hand pump had dwindled to a few boys. Once again, Harriett sounded the dinner bell. All of those in the farmyard and the house began to converge on the tables in the grove. Sixty or so folks took places on the wooden benches, with children sitting on blankets under the nearby trees. Harriett rose and clapped her hands.

"OK everybody, I will ask Reverend Wolf to ask the blessing."

Wolf rose from his seat and began to speak.

"Today I want to ask you to do something different. Rather than bow your heads I want you to raise your faces toward heaven, and lift your hands as well. I want you to look God straight in the face and say 'Thank you!'"

As he took hold of Helen's hand and raised it toward heaven, the rest of the group did likewise.

Wolf began to pray, "Almighty God, who has allowed us to call ourselves your children, we come to you with hands, hearts, and faces lifted toward your throne. We thank you Father, as a child would thank his earthly father for the wonderful and unmerited gifts provided without end. Father we thank you for our traditions which make us a unique people and which connect us with our past. Father we thank you for new relationships which cause our simple lives to extend beyond ourselves and into the lives of others. And Father, I wish to thank you for the new relationships which will come to pass as a result of this community. And let us not forget; thank you Father for this food and the hands which prepared it. In your son's name we pray. Amen."

With that plates began to be filled with potato salad and baked beans. Children soon began to return to the tables asking for more. As plates were emptied and gathered up, several women went to the house, returning with pies. Orders for apple, cherry, or rhubarb were shouted as the women cut slices of pies and placed then on clean white plates.

Laurel rose from her place between her dad and Adam and beckoned to her mother over to the chicken house. The two women whispered together for a few minutes. Harriett moved back to the tables to where Colonel Wolf and Helen were sitting. She asked if they could join her over by the chicken house for just a minute. She then beckoned Henry and Adam who looked at each other, somewhat surprised. Few noticed the six people standing in a small circle next to the chicken house. Few noticed broad smiles which erupted on the faces of those in the small circle. Almost no one noticed the handshakes and the hugs amongst the six people standing near the chicken house. Almost no one except Ross and Rupert. Rupert had looked up from his double helping of cherry pie and wondered aloud, "What are they up to?" Within seconds, all eyes were focused on the six people standing near the chicken house. As the six returned to the tables, Harriett remained standing. With tears in her eyes, she said, "Folks, Henry and I have an announcement to make. Henry, you tell 'em."

233

Henry made several attempts to open his mouth. Each time no words came. Finally, in a cracking voice, he said, "Harriett and I don't want to stand in the way of Colonel Wolf and Helen's announcement, but we have an announcement of our own. "Adam here has asked our permission to marry Laurel."

There was silence. After a long pause to clear his cracking voice and wipe his nose, he continued.

"We have given our permission."

With that everyone in the group went wild.

There was yet another round of handshaking, back slapping, hugging, and endless questions regarding wedding dates, colors of the bridesmaids' dresses, and so on. For over an hour the jubilation for both brides-to-be and grooms-to-be continued. As always occurs, when farm folks gather, the men moved to one place and the women moved to another. The children found themselves playing tag and hide-and-go-seek in the back pasture. The older kids found themselves in pairs—taking long walks, talking vicariously about the recently announced weddings and all that goes with them. On this afternoon, the men found themselves up at the barn, talking about the crops, the war, and the events of the day. As was so often the case, someone in the group, in this case Ross brought along a jug of his finest white lightening and a sack of paper cups. Within minutes several toasts had been offered to the two new grooms-to-be. Even the grooms-to-be consumed their share of the fiery libation. Then someone asked Adam when the big day would be. Adam smiled and moved toward the west side of the barn. The group of men followed him. Pointing toward the huge cottonwood tree which stood next to the road between his place and the cemetery, he said, "As soon as I finish my new brick house there by the big tree…I can't take my new wife into that old junk pile," he said, pointing to the house directly across the road. "My wife will have a new brick house with twenty or thirty bedrooms, one for each of our children," he laughed. The entire group of men laughed wildly at this. It was the first bit of humor anyone had ever heard from Adam

Becker or for that fact, the first time he had ever seemed so totally happy.

Rupert spoke up with a slur to his speech, "If we start work tonight, we can have your house finished by morning." Again, everyone laughed.

"Speaking of work," Ross muttered, "who is going to help me watch the fire over at my smokehouse tonight?" Several neighbors offered to stay for a few hours or simply stop by for a minute. They all knew full well that a smokehouse vigil involved a nip of white lightening from time to time to keep the chill off. Smokehouse vigils, like setting graves, were for the most part, a good time to catch up on recent jokes, gossip, and old stories.

Chaplain Wolf then spoke up, "I would hang around and help you fellas but I have to get Mac's little sister back home before dark. I wouldn't want to cause a scandal." Again laughter exploded.

Back in the house, the conversation was all about dresses, cakes, and flowers. Harriett looked at Laurel and noticed that she had never seemed so totally happy.

As the afternoon melted into evening, families began to leave the Schmidt farm for their own homes.

Harriett quietly invited the McClouds, Chaplain Wolf, and Becker to remain behind for a small supper of leftovers. As each of the cars drove off with their hearts filled with the joy of community and tradition, the small group of people re-entered the house. Rod, feeling the effects of the three paper cups of Uncle Rupert's whiskey asked to be excused and went to bed. After their brief supper, the group of friends moved outside onto the small bush lined front yard. It was a warm but not hot night. The sound of crickets and frogs created a symphony from over by the stock tank. Fire flies filled the bushes with their dim blue-white lights. Henry and Harriett sat in the swing while Wolf and his bride-to-be held hands while they sat on the door of the storm cellar. Mac and Ramona sat on lawn chairs. Adam lay on the cool grass while Laurel teased his face with a sprig of plucked grass. No one spoke for the longest time. Finally Adam spoke, "Colonel Wolf, Laurel and I would be honored if you would perform our wedding. After all, you are apart of this mysterious plan of God."

"I would be honored," Wolf replied.

"I too have a small request," Wolf whispered. "I would be most honored, Henry if you were to be my best man. And you Adam and Mac I would consider it an honor if you were to also stand beside me."

Helen interrupted, "Walter, you forget, Mac has to walk me down the aisle."

A gentle laugh went through the group. "I guess you are already spoken for Mac."

The beauty of the night sky was brutally cut in half by a distant sound. A squadron of bombers recently borne in a California airplane factory roared across the sky flying toward its destiny over some city in Germany. The tranquility of the moment, the beauty of life was interrupted be the distant roar of the infernal engines. For a brief minute, everyone in the small circle once again realized that the man lying on the grass was, in fact, an enemy soldier. Fortunately, the tension of the moment was broken by the sounds of Rod vomiting in the bathroom. The focus of the group abruptly turned away from the machines of war toward gastric torment of a young man with his head in the toilet.

At that point, the guests determined that it was time to go. Mac pointed a joking finger toward Chaplain Wolf, "Now don't you two go parking down by the creek. If Sheriff Bucky were to find you two making out down there, it would be all over town by morning." The group laughed as they entered their cars and drove off into the night. Harriett and Laurel went into the house to see if they could help Rod with his problem. Henry asked Adam to wait a minute and he would be right back. Henry went into the porch, grabbed two jackets and a flashlight, and informed Harriett and Laurel that he would be back soon. He wanted to walk Adam home. Laurel gave a look of disappointment as she had planned to walk Adam as far as the road. Harriett and Laurel were in fact needed to clean up the bathroom floor and get Rod into bed.

Henry tossed Adam a red plaid jacket. "Here, let's go for a little walk."

The two men walked toward the roads which lead to Adam's farm. At the crossing, Henry turned south, toward the church. The two men walked quietly down the dusty road without saying a word. The old owl that lived in Adam's barn flew a few feet over their heads off toward the west. They passed the old cottonwood tree and neared the cemetery. Henry walked toward the cemetery gate and opened it.

"I want you to meet my people, and for that fact, some of yours," Henry said in a quiet voice. The moon and the stars allowed sufficient light to make out most of the tombstones. From inside his jacket pocket, Henry took a small flash light. "Let's get started with your people," Henry said as he led the way to the upper level of the small cemetery. Henry stopped abruptly, shining his light on a raised portion of ground. "By the way, this is the grave of a German soldier, a German soldier who gave his life to save the lives of myself and one other man. This German soldier's name was Helmut Sommerfield, an honorable man and to be remembered as such. The blood in Adam's veins froze. This was the first time he had realized that his past was buried under this rock. "Don't ever forget him and what he did," Henry instructed.

Henry continued up the hill a bit further. Adam realizing that he had been left behind, moved quickly in the direction of Schmidt. Schmidt pointed his flashlight toward a large headstone. Here lies your grandfather and grandmother. They came over from Germany after most of the farms had been settled in this area. Because he had a lot of money from the sale of his dairy farm in Germany, he was able to buy some of the best land in the area. My father told me that he was a fine man. "Your grandmother here," redirecting his light beam to her name, "was a fine woman as well. I can remember her when I was a child. She could heave a bale of hay as high as any man."

Moving farther up the hill toward another set of headstones,

Schmidt played his light on the two names carved in marble. "These here are your mother and father. Your father was a reasonably good man, all things considered. Your mother was one of the meanest, stingiest human beings on the planet. She would yell at your father to the point where the cows would run off. If your father got a little drunk, for which no one blamed him, your mother would lock him out of the house and he would end up sleeping in the barn for days at a time. The poor man used to walk across the road about lunchtime to borrow a tool or something just hoping my folks would invite him for dinner. I can remember your father going to church and having your mother glare at him if he put too much money in the collection plate. She was a mean one. You may notice that your parent's graves are up here at the far end of the cemetery, not next to your grand parents. The reason for that is that your father's death was thought to be a suicide. Your mother insisted that he shot himself in the head while he was getting ready to go pheasant hunting. Well, Adam Becker, I can tell you for certain that it was not an accident. My father was the first man on the scene. Minnie was ranting and raving, insisting that he had not shot himself but that he was about to go hunting. Adam, a man does not go hunting in mid-afternoon when its time for the evening milking. He simply could not take another minute with that woman, so he blew his brains out. Sadly, the pastor at that time refused to perform a proper burial and insisted that your father be placed at the outer edge of the cemetery. Actually, he wanted your father to be buried in another cemetery several miles away. But since your father actually owned the land where the cemetery is located, they couldn't keep him out. Your mother finally gave up the ghost after years of living in seclusion and depression. You went to school and lived your life in her shadow and under her thumb. You had no friends nor did you attend church. When your mother finally died, you continued to live pretty much as a hermit, making a living off the few dozen milk cows left from your dad's herd. You stayed to yourself, shopping over at Cloverdale, twenty miles west of here so you wouldn't have to socialize with any of your neighbors. You seldom went to any community events except for a farm auction now and then. You were thought to be a bit teched in the head by most. Now Adam, I am telling you all this so you will know who you were. However, you are a new man, and will soon be my daughter's husband. From that I would expect that you will have children and grandchildren. Adam, it is entirely up to you to redeem your family name. The past, present, and future of your family is in your hands. The old Adam Becker is dead. He's right there under that headstone. The new Adam Becker is alive."

There was a long silence as the two men stood looking at the gravestones.

At long last, Adam spoke. "You have my word, before God that I will bring honor to my house and to yours."

The two men turned toward the cemetery gate and proceeded toward the road. Stopping at the gate, Henry pointed toward the old church. "That's where all my people were baptized, married and buried."

"I will consider it a great honor to be married in that church as well," Adam said with a smile.

As the moon rose higher in the sky, the two men walked back toward their respective farms. At their respective drive ways, they shook hands and each went to his home.

one word

30

ADAM DID NOT SLEEP THAT NIGHT. He brewed a pot of coffee, poured a cup, and went to the front porch. Taking a seat on the small wooden bench, he held the warm cup between his hands and smiled. Raising his face toward the night sky, he muttered, "God is good." Across the road he could see the last light go out in the house of his bride-to-be. Turning his head slightly to the south, he could see the church where he would soon be married. And he could see the cottonwood where his new house and garage would be built. He began to laugh, "Why me God? What wonderful thing have I done to deserve this new life? What have I done to deserve this land and this man Adam's money? What have I done to deserve this wonderful woman and her loving family?"

A thought whispered in his mind, perhaps God breathed, perhaps just a thought. "It's not for what you have done Adam, but rather what you are expected to do."

Adam again smiled broadly and took a sip of coffee. In the distance, a coyote cried followed by yelps from her pups.

As Adam sat staring at the sky and the stars, his mind slipped back to his boy-hood farm in Germany. In the blackness of sky he could visualize the house, the barn and the woods to the north of the barn. He could visualize his father walking in from the barn and his mother on the porch cleaning vegetables in a basin. He could visualize his sister playing on the ground near the front steps. As his future lay before his eyes, so did his past. Tears began to flow down his face. He began to sob at the vision of his past and his future.

Somewhere between conscious thought and vague dreams, Adam managed to find his way to his bed. The dreams continued, both good ones and not-so-good ones.

The sky had become a pale pink as Adam awoke. Thinking that he would like to stay within the warm comfort of his bed until at least he could see the sun rise over the horizon, he fixed his attention on the calendar on the bedroom wall. The calendar bore a photograph of Jim Sellers and his grocery store staff, inviting one and all to come to his store for the freshest and best of fruits, vegetables and meats. For a few minutes Adam tried to determine whether it was Thursday or Friday. At last he fixed on Friday. Groping for the terry cloth housecoat Harriet Schmidt had given him, he went from the warmth of his bed to the cold of the kitchen. Adam tossed some pieces of wood into the fire box of his stove, wadded up a piece of newspaper, and struck a match. Within minutes, the warmth of the stove melted the cold of the morning. Before making a quick trip to the outhouse in the rear of the house, he filled the coffee pot with water and dumped three spoons full of coffee grounds into the filter. After a huge bowl of corn grits and butter along with some sausages, he felt ready to seize the day.

It had taken him four days to repair the old pickup truck to where it could be trusted to travel more than twenty miles from home. Spark plugs had been fouled, the carburetor was coated with carbon, fuel lines were cracked and prone to leak. The pickup was a mess.

A new well to provide water to his new garage and home were at the top of Adam's to-do list. With this in mind, Adam's plan was to drive the sixty-five miles over to Farmington to talk with the only well drilling company in several counties. He planned to stop for an hour or so at North Fork for a new set of tires.

It was early afternoon by the time Adam arrived at Farmington and found the Scribner Well Digging & Pump Company. It was an ancient building on the edge of the small farm town. Pipes, ladders, and junk of all sorts surrounded the structure making it look like a junk collectors' dream. Adam spotted what appeared to be an office to one side of the house. Approaching the office he was interrupted by a shrill, "Hey, what do you want?" From behind an old fuel tank a huge woman wearing bib overalls emerged. "If you're looking for Walt, he ain't here. He and the boys are down the road drillin' a well." Adam slowly moved toward the huge woman.

"Where might I find Mr. Scribner?" Adam asked.

The woman laughed. You can find *Mister* Scribner, emphasizing the mister, down that road about ten miles and one mile to the south. He is at the Harris farm punching a hole in the ground."

"And if you find *Mister* Scribner, you can tell him that he had better order up some more gas for this tank or he will be walking for a few days." Again the woman laughed.

"Thank you. I shall tell Mr. Scribner of your request," Adam said as politely as possible.

Twenty minutes later, he found the drilling rig near a small, neat farmstead. Getting out of his pickup Adam could hear Mr. Scribner yelling and cursing at the four young men involved in drilling a well. Walt Scribner was a thin, gray-haired man, about sixty with a short black pipe clinched between his brown, tobacco-stained teeth. He was perched on the top of the cab of a drilling truck. The truck consisted of a thirty foot tower, with pulleys and cables running in all directions. From his seat, he controlled a number of levers and switches which turned drills, hoisted pipes, and dragged dirt. It was obvious this vehicle had been made from the assortment of junk at his building.

It was about ten minutes before Scribner acknowledged Adam and climbed down from his seat on the drilling rig.

Scribner's hands were covered with grease and dirt to where Adam put his hands in his pocket hoping to dispense with shaking hands. Scribner made no attempt to extend his hands but rather took the pipe out of his mouth and barked, "S'pose you want a well dug!?"

Before Adam could answer one of the twenty foot pipes stacked against the truck's tower crashed to the ground. Scribner turned toward the four men near the rig and let loose a string of profanity, most of which Adam did not understand. Then, with a broad, sarcastic smile on his dirty face Scribner again asked, but in a nicer tone of voice, "I s'pose you want a well dug. Otherwise, you wouldn't be here, right?"

"Yes, Mr. Scribner, I would like to talk to you about having a well dug on my property...and a big one at that."

Scribner threw his head back and laughed. "The only reason anyone wants to see me is when they needs water. And at that, people want me and my boys to come a-runnin' as soon as they can. They all wants to pay as little money as possible and they all wants the biggest, deepest well as possible." Another string of profanity blasted from his mouth.

"Well, Mr. what did you say your name was?"

Adam said respectfully, "My name is Adam Becker and my farm is over near North Fork."

Scribner continued his little speech about people needing water. Reaching into his shirt pocket, he pulled out a small, soiled note book, flipped through a few pages and said, "Looks like I might get to you in about four months."

Holding up the small note book, Scribner said. "There's no other well-diggers in three counties. I am not only the best well digger; I am the only well digger in three counties. And if you want me and my boys, you have to wait; and you have to pay my price."

Scribner smiled again, took out a pencil, and with a broad smile asked, "Well, do you want water or don't you?"

Adam paused a few minutes, looking over the rig, the four young men, and the pile of mud on the ground.

"I would like some time to think about this matter," Adam said quietly. "Do you mind if I watch you drill," Adam asked.

"Take all the time you want but remember, I am the only well digger in three counties; and if you want water, you will have to deal with me. So, Mr. Becker, take your time. Take all the time you want."

Scribner poked his pipe back in his mouth, pulled out a blue tipped match, struck it and sucked the flame into the bowl of the pipe. He turned and returned to his seat on the top of the drilling rig. Adam moved back into the shade of his pickup truck and watched the process. After an hour and a half, Adam climbed into the cab of his pickup, waved at the man on the top of the rig and drove off.

For the next few hours, Adam reflected on the drilling rig—the pulleys, the wenches, the drilling bits, and the power supply. He reflected on the harsh, arrogant words about being the only driller in three counties and about paying whatever price Scribner wanted to charge. It was dark by the time Adam drove into his farm. He had stopped at Millie's in North Fork for dinner so he did not need to cook that evening. As he waited for his dinner to be served, Adam pulled some sheets of blank paper from a cabinet drawer and began to make sketches of a drilling rig. On another piece of paper he noted down some prices and specific items he would need to purchase. As he ate his plate of blackberry pie, he looked at the many pieces of paper on the table. He leaned back in his chair and smiled. "Mr. Scribner," Adam whispered aloud, "You may not always be the only well driller in three counties."

The following morning, Adam woke with a start. He had been dreaming about the well drilling rig when one of the casing pipes in his dream fell toward him. After showering, shaving, and a quick breakfast, Adam drove down the road to where the building crew had begun to lay the top row of red brick on his new garage and gas station. Rod had been there for at least an hour before Adam arrived.

"Rod, I want to show you something," Adam said as he pulled the stack of drawings from out of a brown paper bag.

"I went over and talked with the well driller, Walt Scribner yesterday and talked with him about putting in a well for us. Mr. Scribner was not an easy man to talk with. Anyhow, I figured out a way we can drill our own well and drill wells for other people in this area. As soon as we get the garage finished and get some tools in here, we can put this thing together," Adam said pointing to the drawings.

Rod looked through the twenty or so drawings and notes and laughed. "We can put this thing together! No problem," Rod exclaimed.

"The one problem we will have is finding a drilling crew. You and I can't be here at the garage and out drilling at the same time, and it does take at least four good men. We will have to come up with help," Adam explained.

"Let's go talk to my dad about where to come up with some help. Between him and Mac, they know everyone who has ever poked a hole in the ground," Rod added.

The two men found Henry in his shop working on a plow bearing. After a few comments about the weather and the state of the crops, Adam opened his paper sack and took out the drawings.

"Henry, Rod and I have come up with a scheme to drill some wells. I went over to talk with Walt Scribner and truly believe that we can build a well drilling rig as good as his if not better and dig wells cheaper than he is charging. Rod here thinks we can build this thing as soon as the garage is finished, but we need some men to run the thing. He and I can't run the well drilling and work the garage at the same time. We will need to find some men to work with us," Adam said.

Henry looked through the clutch of drawings and nodded. "Looks like it might just work," Henry added.

"Men, should not be a problem, especially in the slow season. Lots of young farmers or their sons are looking for extra money between planting and harvest. And there are two young fellas just home from the army who might be interested. Let me make a few calls."

"Before you make any calls, there is something else. I've been thinking about this thing. I don't want men who will work *for* me; I want men who will work *with* me. I want men who will become partners with Rod and I in this business. I believe if a fella owns a part of the business and gets a part of the profit, he will work harder and better than if he works for someone else and gets a salary. If it is okay with you Rod, let's make these men a part of our drilling business. You and I will provide the drilling rig and an office and they will provide the labor. We will split the profits equally. What do you say about that?"

Rod looked at his dad for a few seconds not knowing what to say.

"Sounds good to me," Henry said.

"Sounds good to me too," Rod responded.

"The first job will be a big well on the top of the hill behind the church and cemetery," Adam added. "That one will be paid for by me. I want it to serve my new house, our garage, the church, the school, and any new buildings we might want to build," Adam continued.

Henry interrupted, "You know Adam, for a system that size you might want to consider putting up a large water tower and tank."

Adam looked at Henry for several seconds.

"You know Henry, that's a good idea, a water tank."

"I suppose we could make one when the garage is finished. It would be hard, but we could do it."

Rod broke in, "Wait a minute, there is an old steel water tower and tank over near the old packing house at the Wellman rail crossing. old man Wellman died and his widow had let the packing house go to ruin. I'll bet she would sell that tower and the pump for any price you would offer."

Smiles broke out on all three faces.

Henry reached for his cane, and said, "If you are serious about this thing, why don't you two guys take a run over to widow Wellman's place and talk to her about this and I will make some calls.

From the doorway of the shop, Laurel spoke, "Why don't we make that 'us three guys' ride over to widow Wellman's place? I haven't been out for a ride since yesterday."

"OK, Rod said, "You can come along."

246

Adam smiled and put his arm around Laurel.

"I will tell you what this is all about on the way," Adam said smiling at Laurel.

Henry walked off toward the house at a faster than normal place while Adam, Rod, and Laurel drove off in Adam's pickup.

By the time they reached widow Wellman's small dilapidated house next to what use to be one of the largest packing houses in the area, Laurel knew all the details of the new project and gave her total support to the idea.

Mrs. Wellman was a frail old woman sitting in an even older rocking chair on the porch of her house, drifting in and out of the past and the present. A large black cat covered most of her apron and looked up with one eye to see the three approaching. The old woman raised her head and covered her face with a smile. "Howdy do. What can I do for you folks?" the old lady chirped.

Laurel was the first to speak. "Mrs. Wellman, I am Henry Schmidt's daughter Laurel. This is my brother, Rod. And this is my friend, Adam Becker."

The old woman looked directly at Adam for several seconds. "Adam Becker, folks say that you seen an angel in a fiery furnace and got cured of all your evil ways."

Adam smiled and responded, "Mrs. Wellman, I don't know about an angel but thanks to Miss Schmidt and her daddy, all of my evil ways are a thing of the past."

"Well, I hope so. Folks say that you were pretty twisted in the head," the old lady stated.

"Thanks to God, my head is untwisted," Adam offered.

"Sit, sit," the old lady offered. "If I weren't so dang old and infirm, I would get you all a glass of lemonade."

"No thank you Mrs. Wellman, we just came to visit," Laurel said with a smile.

"Well, actually, that's not totally correct. Laurel countered. "We actually came to talk with you about that water tank over there. Adam

247

here is looking for a water tank for his new project and we thought that you might not need yours any longer."

The old lady stared at the water tank, with the faded words, "Wellman's Packing House" painted across rounded sides. "I suppose I could let it go. After all, since my husband passed we ain't killed no live stock here at the packing house. Soon as I am gone, my daughter will take the place and she will sell it off before I am cold in my grave. How much do you suppose its worth?" the old lady asked, knowing that she had barely enough money to provide her with two meals a day.

Laurel looked to Adam.

Adam spoke, "Let's see, scrap metal would bring in five cents a pound over at the scrap depot. I figure it weighs…"

"Never mind how much it weighs, how much do you want to pay for the dang thing?" the old woman insisted.

"Tell you what. I will give you two hundred dollars for the tank, the tower, and the pump."

"Sold!" the old woman blurted, waking the cat from its nap. "You can take all the pipes that go with it and anything else you want to take. Lord knows, I don't need any of that stuff anymore. And it's just one more thing my daughter won't get to sell off."

"Adam," the old woman inquired, looking him straight in the eye. "tell me true, did you see an angel? I want to know what one really looks like."

"Mrs. Wellman, the only angel I have ever seen is this one right here," pointing to Laurel.

The old woman began to laugh hysterically. "Well if that be the case, I suggest that you don't let her get away. Put your brand on her backside and make her yours."

"That's exactly what I plan to do Mrs. Wellman," Adam said as the four continued to laugh.

"Adam," Mrs. Wellman continued, "there's a bunch of machines and old trucks over back of the main building. I would be much obliged if you were to cart all that stuff off as well. That is, if you want it."

From where he sat, Adam could see at least two old large-box hauling trucks used for hauling live cattle to the packing plant. The tires were flat and weeds covered most of the machinery.

"I will be delighted to take whatever I can. I am sure most of it can be used," Adam said as he passed a check for five hundred dollars to the lady. She fixed her gray eyes on the amount and spoke. "We agreed on two hundred dollars, Mr. Becker."

Adam retorted, "The extra three hundred is for cat food for your cat."

Again the old woman laughed hysterically.

Looking directly at Laurel, the old lady spoke. "He is a good one. Don't let him get too far from home."

Laurel smiled as the three rose and shook the old lady's hand.

"If you don't mind, we will go over and take a look at the tower and the machinery," Adam said.

"You go ahead; me and Casper will wait here," replied Mrs. Wellman.

The three examined the tower, the pump, all four of the trucks, and general machinery. They also examined a rattlesnake that had made her nest under one of the trucks.

"From what I see," Adam said, "We have enough parts to build at least one drilling truck and possibly two more trucks for support. With those pipes over there, we can build a derrick tower; and if I can get that engine to work, we can use it as a wench. Almost everything we need is right here. We will have to get at least two trucks running before we can lower the tower and the tank. If the engines were drained of water, they should be workable. Let's get back home and get this thing planned out.

All the way back to the farm, all three jabbered in three directions—about what they saw, what they needed to do, and how they should do it. As they pulled into the Schmidt's farmyard, they noticed three other pickup trucks near the barn. Upon hearing Adam's pickup pull to a stop, Henry came out of the work shop with three other men.

Adam, Rod, and Laurel hurried over the workshop.

"Adam," Henry chimed, "These are the fellas I told you about. They all live near here and all are farmers or sons of farmers. One other fella will be coming as soon as he gets back from town. He is just back from the army. Anyhow Adam, these guys like to work and Eric Grubber here has even worked on oil drilling. He says he can work a water rig as easy as an oil rig."

Adam extended his hand to each of the men standing in the shop. The strong farmers' handshake gave a sense of confidence that each man was a hard man, capable of hard work.

"Henry, did you tell these fellas all the details of the deal? Adam asked.

"No, I thought I would let you do that," Henry said.

"Come outside for a minute," Adam ordered the men and Laurel.

"You see that hill, the one behind the church?" Adam pointed out. "Well, I want to drill a deep well there and place a water tank, a big one on that hill. I want that well to serve my house, the garage over there, the church, and the school. Now, if I wait for the only well driller in the area to get around to it, it could be sometime next year and be very expensive. If on the other hand, I or I should say, we, can build a drilling truck and poke the hole ourselves, I will save a lot of money and have water within a few months. And if we build a drilling truck, there is no reason we can't go into business drilling wells for other folks."

The men stood in a broad circle looking at Adam and then at each other.

"Take this a little further Adam," John Collins stated. "I'm not sure I totally understand what you are saying here. Exactly what do you mean by 'we'?"

Adam smiled. "We mean that you John, and you Jason, and you Sy and you Eric, go into a partnership with Rod and me in a well drilling business. There is more than enough work to keep a team busy in this area alone. And if we keep our prices down, we can get more business than the driller over in Farmington. To be sure, we will have to limit our drilling to what we can do between planting and harvest time. I figure we can drill five wells each year in our off time. The other thing I meant about we is this, you won't be working *for* Rod and me. You will be working *with* Rod and me. We will share in the profits. I will supply and maintain the rig, Rod will contract the business and make orders and you guys will do the digging."

For several seconds, the group stood looking at the hill in the distance.

Finally Jason Rash spoke up. "When do we start Adam?"

The group turned inward and began shaking hands. "Sounds like a good deal to me," Jason stated.

"My dad has been wanting a new well over on his west section but couldn't afford it," Eric said.

After a round of handshakes, Adam spoke, "The first thing we need to do is to get over to Waterman Crossing and fix some of the equipment I and Rod bought from widow Waterman. We have four hauling trucks, three of which might work if we pray real hard. Once we get the trucks running, we can dismantle the tower and pull the pump."

At that point, Laurel entered the conversation. "Speaking of praying, why don't we just stop for a minute and do just that. You men are beginning what could be a real fine business, one that is sorely needed in this area. Psalm 37 says if we commit our way unto the Lord, he will give us the desires of our hearts. Rod, why don't you lead us in a prayer?"

Rod looked at Laurel totally exasperated as if to say, "Why do you always do this to me?"

Rod cleared his throat as the others removed their hats and bowed their heads. "Lord," Rod began, "You know the desires of our heart and you know that we need water to do our work. Lord, make this project successful and bring a blessing to your people in this place." After a few words Rod began to pray more fervently and with greater ease. Soon he was calling for blessings on each of the men in the circle and their families. He went on to ask for prosperity and good health for his brother-in-law to be. Shortly after he finished, Jason began to pray. He too went on, asking the Lord to bless all those who brought water to this area and asked for blessings on Adam and his wife to be. The little prayer meeting soon attracted the attention of Harriet who came running from the house thinking something was wrong. As soon as she realized what was happening, she too joined in the prayer circle with a lengthy prayer. All in all, the little prayer session lasted well over an hour. At its conclusion, Laurel nodded an affirmation toward Rod and said, "Thank you Rod."

The following morning, all the men, including Sy Breach and the sergeants just returned from the army gathered at widow Waterman's old packing house. Harriett and Laurel had packed a large picnic basked and filled several glass jars of lemonade. After clearing away the clumps of thistle and grass, and the rattlesnake, the men began to tear into the engines of the four trucks. With batteries brought from their respective farms and fifty gallon barrels of gasoline and oil, they cranked and cranked the truck engines until one by one all started, except one. One by one, flat tires were filled by old hand pumps. By mid-afternoon, three trucks were lined up on the dirt road with their engines running. The fourth truck was tethered by two heavy hemp ropes behind one of the working trucks. Piles of pipes, iron beams, steam engines and all sorts of machinery were piled on the beds of the three trucks. Belching great clouds of black smoke, the convoy of trucks, followed by several pickups, began to move toward the main road and west toward Becker's new garage and gas station. Twice the ropes parted and had to be re-tied. By early evening, the large trucks were standing in a line behind the five-foot brick walls of the unfinished garage and gas station.

A few neighbors and family members of the new well drilling company had gathered at the gas station-garage. They carefully examined the trucks and assorted machinery. One of the younger children of

John Collins asked, "Where are the water tower and the pump?"

Rod answered for the information of all present, "As soon as we build us a derrick truck with a tower and some winches, we can go back for the tower and the pump."

Another child asked, "Where do you plan on digging the well and placing the tower?"

"Come on," Adam beckoned, as he moved away from the trucks. "Come with me, and I will show you."

The dozen or so people followed single file as Adam and Laurel walked toward the ridge of the hill above the church and behind the cemetery. Because this had been posted as private property, Adam's private property, few people had ever been up on this hill. Adam and Laurel stopped at the crest of the ridge. Pointing to the ground beneath his feet, Adam said, "Here I shall dig Adam's well. Or I should say, Adam and Laurel's well."

The small group of people stood on the top of the hill and looked in all directions. From this point, they could see all of the farms in all directions. Adam pointed off to the west, "See there, there is Cloverdale's water tower. And over there is the water tower for North Fork. And if you look real hard, you can see the big water tower at St. John." Near the distant water tower of the town of St. John he noticed but did not mention the control tower of Camp Alexis.

As the small group of people was standing on the top of the hill, Ross and Rupert drove passed the church on their way home from a farm sale. Seeing the group, they stopped, climbed through the barbed wire fence, and rushed up the hill. "What's the matter?" Ross insisted.

Collins replied with a bit of sarcasm, "We are looking at Adam's new town down there."

Just below the group of people was the cemetery and to the south of it, the small, white, wooden church.

"Over there, is where we will build the new school," Adam continued. He drew Laurel close and whispered in her ear, "Laurel's new school."

Laurel smiled and put her arm around his waist. "And over there," he continued, "Will be the baseball diamond."

"The water from this well will be enough to meet the needs of all of these things. In fact, I might just build some more buildings over there and maybe one over there," Adam said as if he could actually see the buildings standing before him. Some of those standing with Adam began to look at one another with questioning looks.

Just then, the six brick masons who had been working on the gas station garage and the new house began to move toward their trucks. From a distance they waved at the group on the hill and drove off to their homes.

Ross broke the silence. "What about a café somewhere down there?"

Adam turned and looked directly into Ross's eyes. "The café will be over there, between the school and the ball diamond. The café will also provide hot lunches for the school and hot dogs for the ball games."

"What about beer?" Rupert chimed in.

"No beer, no wine, no whiskey!" Adam said, looking directly at Ross and then over to Harriett.

Harriett broached a gentle smile and nodded while Ross and Rupert shook their heads in mock disgust.

"What about the super-duper market?" someone else called out in a humorous but almost sarcastic tone.

"Let's not get too far ahead of ourselves," Adam replied with the same level humor. "But, I have given it some thought," he continued.

Adam again whispered to Laurel, "I did talk with Scribner in town about him setting up a small grocery store out here. He said he would give it some thought and get back to me."

Laurel looked shocked. "Adam, you are talking about building a whole town, right here."

Adam smiled and looked Laurel directly in the eyes. "Why not?" he whispered.

"Do you see that last electric pole over by Wagner's farm?" Adam asked the group. "Well, Mac tells me that the electric company will be extending the electric lines all the way from Wagner's to the oil road over east. That means that within a few months the electric lines will be planted all the way along this road. Within a few months, each farm along the road will have electricity. That goes for the new buildings and the new school and, I would add, our new well. The mention of electricity within a few months shocked everyone standing on the hill. While there had been talk of the electrical lines being placed for sometime, most people figured that it would take several more years.

Adam continued, "I talked to a fella from the electric company the other day and he tells me the lines are coming soon, very soon."

The little group of people remained on the top of the hill as the sun came closer and closer to the western horizon. A cock pheasant called out announcing the end of another day and the group moved toward their trucks and homes.

Adam called out, "Monday morning! We can get started on building the derrick. See you fellas then."

As Henry and Harriett climbed into their pickup Adam called out. "Do you mind if I borrow your daughter for a little while longer? We have some things to talk about."

"Don't be too late. Tomorrow is church," Harriett called back.

"Come with me," Adam said, bursting with enthusiasm. "I want to show you my town…excuse, me, our town."

Together, hand in hand, the two climbed back up the hill and stood at the well site.

As the brilliant orange Nebraska sun pushed its way below the horizon, Adam reached out his arms taking Laurel by her shoulders. "Laurel" he said in a strong but quiet voice. "God has given me a new life, he has given me a small fortune, and he will soon give me a wife and I hope children, many children. It's like that fellow in the Bible named Job. At first he had everything taken away. At long last, he had everything returned, even better than before. I had my family taken

255

away; even my identity is buried over there in the graveyard. Then God gave me you and this land and your family. I have so much! But I know that I must use these gifts for others and not myself. And this business about a town. Why not a town? Why not a school? Why not a café and a store? If I can use my new wealth to make this a better place, I want to do it and I want you to do it with me. I want your family to be proud of you and of me. I want to leave this place a better place than I found it."

Tears were cascading down Laurel's cheeks just as they were on Adam's face.

Laurel embraced Adam as the two stood silhouetted on the hill. After an hour of just holding each other, the two walked to Adam's pickup and drove off to the Schmidt farm. Seeing all the lights out except the porch light, Laurel kissed Adam goodnight and went into the house.

It was another night when no one on the Becker farm or the Schmidt farm slept. Thoughts of new building, new wells, new everything raced through half dreams and played out on bedroom ceilings.

31

THE FOLLOWING SUNDAY MORNING, the church was filled. Some folding chairs had to be brought up from the basement and placed in the aisle. While most of the hymns were written in the sixteen hundreds and meant to be sung in slow, lugubrious tones, Harriett cranked up the tempo and the volume of the ancient organ. At the end of the service, Pastor Steinke removed one of the many layers of clerical attire and announced that he had an announcement to make. After some clearing of the throat and wringing of the hands, he announced that he and his wife had accepted a Divine Call to another congregation in Chicago. There was collective gasp from all members of the congregation. Steinke was terrified at the thought of the congregation breaking into a wild applause at the suggestion of his departure. One young boy was heard to whisper, "Hot dog!"

Herman Wittenberg, the elder member of the congregation and the chairman of the congregation rose from his seat and addressed the pastor. "Well, Pastor, this comes as a bit of a surprise; but we all know that God moves people from one place to another for good reasons. While we all hate to see you and your wife leave our community, we know that he has something good in store for you and for us. We will begin our prayers for a new pastor. We thank you for all that you have done for us. God bless you and your new ministry."

Once again, the people of the congregation did not know whether to applaud or sit quietly. Before the people could do anything, Pastor Steinke announced that the people were dismissed. For the first time in the church's history, the ushers did not dismiss the congregation row by row. Everyone rose and moved toward the exit. Some even left the sanctuary by way of the basement door. Outside the conversation was unanimous. Quiet elation carefully couched in respectful tones was expressed by almost everyone. For years the congregation had wanted to find a tactful way of getting rid of Pastor Steinke. His sermons never once contained anything controversial enough for which he might be given the boot. In fact, his sermons seldom, if ever contained anything worthy of controversy at any level.

Herman Wittenberg managed to pull together the elders of the congregation over in the parking lot.

In hushed tones Herman announced that Steinke would be gone after next Sunday's service. The relief was almost visible. Wittenberg indicated that Steinke had told him of his departure in the small vestry closet just before the service. With several weddings coming up, Herman suggested that they move quickly to find a new pastor. Milford Bonner the congregational secretary, was asked to write a letter to the district office and get the ball moving. It was Bonner who then suggested that a picnic be held after next Sunday's service. Bonner went on to suggest that an invitation be sent out to all the churches in the area, as was the custom when a pastor left the area or when a new one arrived. It was agreed. A full blown community picnic, next Sunday at one o'clock. The small group of elders moved from the parking lot back to the church steps. "If I may have your attention for just a moment," Wittenberg pleaded. "It is only fitting and proper that we honor our dear pastor and his wife by holding a neighborhood picnic on these grounds one week from today. We shall make all efforts to give a fitting farewell to our beloved pastor within the company of the entire community. I will ask the head of the alter guild to make the proper arrangements for the meal. Thank you all."

With that the congregation began to move off toward their cars, trucks and homes.

Laurel managed to get Adam's attention from across the small church. She was visibly upset. "Adam, we will have to wait until we have a new pastor before we can get married."

"You forget my little bride-to-be that we have already asked Pastor Wolf to perform our wedding. Remember?" Adam said.

She smiled. "I forgot."

As usual, Adam was invited to Sunday dinner at Schmidt's home and as usual, Adam accepted. And as usual, after pie and coffee, everyone moved to the front yard to enjoy the rest of the Lord's Day of rest. In the midst of some idle conversation about something or another, Laurel stood up and said, "Adam, let's go and look at our new house."

Even though they had visited the construction site every day and sometimes more that once a day, Laurel wanted to go and dream aloud with Adam.

The two got in the pickup and drove toward the construction. The walls were now finished up to the second story. The stairs were in place as were most of the window frames on the lower level. The sub-flooring was finished on the lower level and partially finished on the second floor. For the thousandth time, Laurel went from room to room discussing what kind of curtains they would hang and what kind of painting would hang on this wall or that wall. The massive brick fireplace, the only fireplace in the whole area dominated the front room. The kitchen and bathrooms were plumbed for running water, not from hand pumped water. Every ceiling was wired for an electric light and every wall had at least one electric plug. This was to be the finest house in the neighborhood. Not ostentatious or elegant but truly a fine house. Laurel would waltz from room to room, pretending how her new castle would look and how she would feel in her palace. She would stand at the doors of the two upstairs bedrooms and imagine children—her children in their beds or playing blocks on the floor. Her joy was immense, occasionally being expressed by exploding into tears. Adam understood. Adam on the other hand would simply utter the words, "God is good."

After a final inspection of the house, Adam and Laurel would walk hand in hand back to their respective houses. At the turning roads, they would embrace, take long looks at each other and walk dreamily to their homes.

32

THE WEEK THAT FOLLOWED was filled with Adam making dozens of trips to lumberyards, brick factories, hardware stores and the bank. Using a small black leather-bound book, he would maintain exact figures on bank balances, bills owed, and money coming in from the rental of his land. Every penny was accounted for.

Laurel remained totally occupied with her classes and, of course, a wedding dress.

By Saturday evening, progress on the garage and the house had gone from a few red bricks piled one upon another to all the walls finished, window and door frames in place and the fireplace chimneys jutting into the sky. All that was left was the roof and the interior. As Adam and Laurel stood in the road watching the workmen pack their tools, one of the brick layers shouted, "You will be sleeping here this time next month." The impact of that comment hit Adam like a rock. Laurel smiled broadly and said, "Maybe we had better get serious about a wedding, Mr. Becker." Adam simply smiled and nodded. Adam and Laurel took one more trip through the house examining recent work. Laurel uttered dozens of comments regarding what needed to be done while Adam simply nodded and smiled. As the sun disappeared in a cloudy west, the two walked back toward there respective farmhouses. At the crossroads, they embraced and moved off toward their separate homes. "Don't forget the picnic after church tomorrow," Laurel called out.

It was the horse that woke Adam. He managed to see the alarm clock next to his bed. It showed 4:35 in the morning. Then he heard what sounded like a train somewhere outside his window. He bolted from his bed, grabbing his pants and shirt; and within seconds, Adam was standing on his back porch watching tree branches and an old milk can fly by. The wind was pushing against the walls of his house causing the back porch to actually move. The roar of the wind became louder and louder as dirt was scooped up and smashed against the house. Adam grabbed his plaid wool jacket from off a hook and made a dash out the back door toward where he remembered the storm cellar to be. Halfway to the cellar, Adam stopped as he heard the horse yell from somewhere in the darkness. Thinking for one second that he must find the animal, he realized that the horse's life was not worth risking his own. Finding the door handle of the storm cellar, Adam fought against the weight of the wind to lift the door and fell inside the dark, dank cellar. The door slammed shut with the weight of the wind pushing it closed. Adam remembered the kerosene lantern and the box of blue tip matches that he had seen on a shelf next to the door. Groping in the darkness, he found the matches and lit one. Seeing the lamp, he gained a flame from its wick. The cellar reminded him of an ancient tomb. For what seemed like hours, the wind roared against the door of the storm cellar. On several occasions, Adam thought seriously of trying to run across the road to the Schmidt farm to see if Laurel and her family were safe. After making several attempts to raise the cellar door, he realized that even if he could get the door open running across the road would be stupid and possibly fatal. The roar began to lessen. Slowly Adam was able to press his back against the wooden door and push it open. With considerable effort, he managed to open it to gain access to the world. Holding his lantern, he could see that a large tree branch had fallen on the cellar door. He could also see that his temporary barn was gone as was his out house. The main house seemed to be unharmed. Moving toward the north side of the house Adam saw a sheet of dirt and grass caked against the outside wall. It was then that he noticed a light coming from across the road. He could see people holding a lantern, standing in the yard. With his lantern in hand, Adam ran as fast as he was able toward the light across the road.

Most of the leaves which covered the trees and bushes around the Schmidt house were gone. Tree branches covered the driveway and front lawn. As Adam arrived at the group of people, he found Laurel and embraced her. "I was so worried," Adam coughed.

"Tornado." Stated Harriet in a matter of fact sort of way. "Nebraska tornado."

Adam, panting from his run, was unable to talk.

"You wait in the house," Henry ordered. "Me and Rod will see if there is any serious damage to the house."

Within a few minutes it was determined the Schmidt house had withstood another Nebraska tornado without damage. Harriett had fired up the kitchen stove and made a pot of coffee. Because Adam had never experienced a tornado, in fact, did not really know what a tornado was, the Schmidts spent over an hour telling stories of tornados which had lifted up cows and deposited them in the next county, driven two-by-fours through trees, and so on. The stories became more and more unbelievable as they were told. Adam sat there, wondering if they were serious or simply playing with him. The stories ended abruptly as Harriett went to the kitchen window. The sky had become pink with promise of a sunrise there somewhere. She gasped and covered her mouth. The others in the small farmhouse kitchen all came to the window. With tears streaming down her face she whispered, "The church, it's gone!" One by one, each person searched the southern horizon where the small wooden church had stood as a beacon for well over one hundred years. The five people stood around the kitchen window, saying nothing. Finally Rod spoke, "I will get the truck." With Rod, his mother and Laurel in the cab and Adam and Henry standing in the pickup bed, the truck moved around tree branches and occasional boards toward the church. The one mile drive went without a word. Arriving at the church site, the group simply stood and looked. The roof, almost intact had come off and been tossed on to the front lawn. Most of the walls were shattered and lying in huge pieces. Church pews were strewn about, with a few actually blocking the main road. The altar, oddly enough, remained where it had stood for over a hundred years. Harriett spied the organ lying in the road side ditch. She ran over to it and began trying to move it upright. Almost like some wounded animal, she tried to comfort the ancient instrument and set it straight. The sun was looking over the eastern rim of the world by now. Another pickup truck could be seen coming down the dusty road. "Looks like Wacker's pickup," Henry stated. Within minutes Arnold Wacker and his family were standing among the rubble. "God moves in mysterious ways," Arnold stated as tears stained his face. Harriett shot back, "Arnold, God didn't do this. He doesn't go around smashing people's churches. You can chalk this one up to someone else."

As the Schmidts and Adam moved through the rubble, Laurel dashed over to Adam. "Adam, let's go and see about our house."

"We will be right back," Adam announced to the Schmidts. "We need to look about our house." The two ran down the dirt road to where they could get a good look at the two brick buildings. Not a brick had moved. Both the garage and the house were undamaged. "God is good!" Adam uttered. Standing there, looking at their new home and business, Laurel began to sob. "What is the matter with you young lady. Our house is in good order," Adam whispered. "Yes, but now we don't have a church where we can be married," Adam held Laurel tight. "I promise you, we will have your church."

Together they walked back toward the churchyard.

Within an hour, the parking lot was filled with dozens of vehicles with people picking through the wreckage of what had been their church. By nine o'clock the full congregation had arrived. At last, Reverend Steinke and his wife pulled up in their grey Plymouth. The only words Reverend Steinke could utter were, "Oh no! How could this happen? And on my last day!"

Because this was to be the last day for the pastor, everyone was there. All of the old shut-ins managed to dress themselves and drive the many miles to the small church. The elders, along with the pastor assembled on the cement steps which led up to the church door. The elders talked among themselves as to what they should do next. As they pondered the situation, the sound of an organ rose from the ditch next to the road. "If you men will help me get this thing on to flat ground, we can at least sing a hymn," Harriett shouted. With that a dozen or so young men began to lift the ancient instrument onto the lawn next to the stairs. Someone found a folding chair and placed it at the organ. "Rod, you man the air bellows," Harriett commanded. Rod began to pump as Harriett began to play. *A Mighty Fortress* filled the churchyard. After an introduction, the congregation began to sing. Each of the four verses, which were memorized by each person there, became louder with each verse. The hymn concluded as it had never concluded before. Someone in the crowd yelled out, "Pastor, do we get a sermon this morning?"

Reverend Steinke moved up a step and began to take some papers from his inside coat pocket. As he began to sort through the papers, one of the Wacker boys came running up to where the pastor and the elders were standing. "There is a metal box, over there in the corner of the busted up church building. I think there's something in it," the boy panted. The elders moved over to the corner of the church. "Here, here it is," the boy said as he pointed to the metal box hidden inside the cornerstone of the building. The granite slab which had carried the phrase, *Ein Festiberg—A Mighty Fortress—1842 A.D.* remained in place. Using pieces of broken lumber, they quickly extricated the metal box from the rubble and placed it on the steps of the church. The box measured about two feet by one foot by one foot. Its lid was held fast by a leather thong and a wax seal. All eyes were fixed on the metal box sitting on the topmost step of the church. Herman Wittenberg, the chairman of the congregation looked at the pastor. "Should we open it?" he asked. Pastor Steinke looked at the box, not knowing exactly what to do. "Of course we should open it," stated Laurel. Rod took a pocketknife from his trousers, opened blade and began to slice through the thin leather thong. Slowly he lifted the lid. Those on the steps could see in the box while others stood on their tip toes trying to get a peek into the black metal box. From inside the box, Wittenberg removed two smaller wooden boxes. Opening the first, he found a bundle of what appeared to be letters tied with a red ribbon. Placing these on the steps, he took the second box. These contained large paper envelopes. Opening one of the envelopes, Wittenberg pulled out photographs mounted on heavy paper frames. One by one, the other envelopes were opened; and the photographs were held up. As Wittenberg revealed each photo, he would hand the item to Henry Schmidt who read the name of the person or persons who appeared in the photo. For the next twenty minutes, the names and photos of the families and individuals who had built this church in 1842 were revealed to those standing in the rubble of the church. Almost without exception, every photo was claimed by one of the decedents of those in the photos. After the last photo was given out, attention was turned to the bundles of letters. Cautiously, with utmost reverence, the ribbon was untied and the letters were taken from their envelopes. These were letters written by those who had not only built this church, these were the people who had established the first farmsteads in the area. These were the people who had fled Russia and Germany and found their way to a new life in America. These were the great, great-grandfathers and mothers of those standing in the churchyard. These were the people who lay beneath the granite headstones in the cemetery behind the church. One by one the letters were passed out to the families. Some of the original names had been changed, but everyone knew which letter belonged to which family. For the next few minutes small groups of people stood soberly while some quietly read the letters. Simon Kline made his way to the steps. "Pastor, it looks like my letter is in German. I never did learn to read German. Could you read it for me?" Simon asked. Pastor Steinke took the letter, placed his glasses on his nose and attempted to use his seminary German. Seeing that this would be a slow process, Adam approached Pastor Steinke. Taking the letter from Steinke Adam said, "Let me read this, my parents always insisted that we speak German at home." Adam began:

To my children's children,

God's blessings on you all. By now, I trust that there are many who carry our family name. I trust that you are all honorable men and virtuous women. I pray to God that you have all found happiness in this great and wonderful land. I also pray that you will always remember where you came from and how you got here.

This past year has been difficult. This past winter was especially hard. Most of us farmers are just getting our farms and fields in order. Crops were planted, but harvests were poor. Some of us have managed to buy a few cows and a pig or two. Unfortunately, either the coyotes or the local red Indians have made off with some of our animals; but God is good and we have had food on our tables, and our children are healthy. I and Mama wish you all God's continued blessings in this wonderful land.

Most sincerely,

Gotthold Kline

Another member of the group of people held up a letter. "Mine is also written in German." Two others, holding up letters also indicated that their letter was in the German language. One by one Adam took the sacred items and proceeded to read them aloud. One letter indicated that several children had died of the croup that year. Another mentioned letters they had received from relatives back in their homeland. Without exception, each letter extolled the blessings of this new land and the goodness they found in its people. Each letter seemed to be the sermon of a simple man, giving thanks to God for a new life in a new country. For more than an hour letters were read aloud, both in German and in English. For more than an hour those in the church-yard felt the gravity and the power of the messages from those who now rested beneath the Nebraska soil. One final letter was handed to Adam. On its envelope was the name, Gottlieb Becker. Adam opened the envelope and removed the ivory sheet from within. Quietly Adam read the letter. Laurel, standing next to him asked if he would like to read it aloud. Clearly moved by its content, he began:

My children,

My wife and I have recently arrived by sailing ship from Odessa Russia. Unlike some of our kin in Germany, we were able to sell our farm and escape the Kaiser and his gang of murderers. The pain and death we left behind in our homeland is something I wish to forget but cannot. Since arriving in this new and wonderful land, Momma and I have been blessed with a new child, a new farm, and a new life. We no longer have to fear those who wish to take our farms, our money, or our lives. America is a place where we are all new creations.

At this point in reading the letter, Adam began to weep. The mention of being new creations seemed to hit him square in the heart. Was Gottlieb Becker talking to him from the grave? This message would not have meant anything to the real Adam Becker. Was God using this event to restate what he had stated so many times during the past year? Adam cleared his throat and wiped his nose with a handkerchief. He continued to read:

For the one who reads this letter,

I have but one request. I challenge you to leave this land a better place than you found it. And I ask that you pass this obligation on to your children and their children's children. I pray that God will bless all that you do in this land.

In Christ's Holy Name,

Gottlieb Becker, American Farmer

A sense of holy reverence fell upon all those standing in the churchyard. A feeling of enormous humility permeated every man, woman, and child in the congregation. Letters continued to be read and re-read as photographs were reverently passed from group to group. Several families walked back toward the cemetery north of the church and found the tombstones of those who had written the letters. Small, quiet groups stood in the churchyard and cemetery sharing the contents of their letters and showing never before seen photographs of those who had stood on this land one hundred year ago.

As some groups continued to talk about their letters and those who wrote them, others chose to pick through the rubble of the fallen building. A few had taken it upon themselves to collect all of the hymnals while others attempted to collect pieces of the four shattered stained glass windows.

As noon approached cars and pickup trucks began arriving from all directions. Members of other churches and other communities began to arrive for the going-away picnic for Pastor Steinke. As they approached the shattered church, and those standing around in the rubble, their faces expressed the shock they felt when seeing their neighbors picking through what had been a physical and spiritual landmark for over one hundred years. Within a relatively short time, there were over a hundred people standing either in the cemetery or in the churchyard. Herman Wittenberg mounted the cement steps of the church and gave a loud whistle. Using his hands as a megaphone, he yelled out. "Folks, we came here to have a picnic, so let's have a picnic. Reverend, if you will offer a blessing we can eat and get on with the task at hand." Reverend Steinke mounted the steps, bowed his head and began a short prayer. Wittenberg once again mounted the steps and instructed folks to find a grassy spot and some friends and begin eating. Dozens of people moved toward their cars and trucks, returning with picnic baskets and lawn blankets. As soon as the baskets were opened and dishes were filled with fried chicken and potato salad, the mood changed from somber to festive. Nothing, absolutely nothing brought a community together more than a disaster and a meal. In this case, there were both.

Father James Patrick, the priest from St. Mary's Catholic Church, over near North Fork began to move from group to group, singling out pastors from the dozen or so churches in the area. Reverend Steinke did not like this man in the least and let it be known even from the pulpit. Steinke's frequent reference to Martin Luther's disdain for the Pope and his band of infidels often times found its way into sermons and public comments. Steinke watched with a suspicious eye as Patrick assembled the assorted collection of Baptist, Nazarene, Brethren, and so on, in a group. Reverend Steinke almost panicked as he noticed the group of clergymen heading toward Herman Wittenberg, his congregational chairman. Jumping to his feet, Steinke hurried over to where the group of clergymen had assembled. "What's going on here?" Steinke demanded in a shrill voice. "Come with us, " Father Patrick responded. Patrick led the group over to the steps of the church where he mounted to the top step. "If you could all gather around, we have something to discuss," Patrick shouted.

"This is still my church, and I demand to know what is going on here!" Steinke insisted.

"Oh shut up!" Wittenberg said looking Steinke in the eye.

Father Patrick held up his hands for quiet. "The members of this community have come together to celebrate. Unfortunately, things have changed in the past few hours. Rather than coming together to honor this brother (pointing to Reverend Steinke) for his many years of service to our community, we are faced with mourning the destruction of your house of worship. While we all call ourselves by different names, some Baptist, some Methodist, and some Lutheran, we are part of the same faith. We are all Christians brothers and all members of a community. When our brothers rejoice, we rejoice with them.

270

When our brothers grieve, we grieve with them. Today, we do both. I have briefly discussed the situation here with my fellow shepherds and we all agree. We would consider it a great honor to help you rebuild your house of worship. Within the next few days, each congregation will determine what it can contribute in terms of money, materials, and manpower. I would suggest that we hold a meeting next Wednesday evening at my church to develop a building plan for your new building. Seven o'clock at St. Mary's. Let's do it!" Meanwhile, Pastor Foster of the United Brethren Church, just south of here, has offered his church for your Sunday morning worship services." Father Patrick looked directly at Reverend Steinke and offered his hand. "I don't know what to say," Steinke uttered. "Then don't say anything!" Wittenberg interjected as the crowd laughed. Herman began to speak. "On behalf of our congregation, I would like to accept the loving offer to help us rebuild. This time," Wittenberg continued, "Let's build our church out of brick and mortar like Adam's new house and garage over there. At least they are still standing. And by the way, in case you haven't heard, Adam here has given us that land over there for a new school building. He also has plans for some other buildings and a baseball field over there." Herman continued. For the next hour, people milled about looking in the direction of the new school and baseball field. Some even walked down the road toward the new red brick garage and house. There was a great deal of excitement that day. Grief had given way to hope as the afternoon gave way to evening. People began leaving for their homes. Reverend Steinke and his wife were among the last to leave. They came over to where the Schmidts and Adam were standing. Steinke extended his hand. "I am so sorry." Were the only words Steinke could utter. His wife too extended her hand to all. They turned and left.

"Well, that's that!" Henry stated "Gone but never to be forgotten."

"Henry!" Harriett scolded.

It was at this point that Adam and the Schmidts realized that they were all wearing work clothes and not their Sunday clothes. They began to laugh. "Let's go home. I am pooped," Henry laughed. "Adam, how about some supper?"

After a light supper, Adam walked home. Standing at his front porch was his horse seeming to wonder where it would spend the night. Adam moved toward the back of the house to where the makeshift barn had tilted over at an angle. Taking a two-by-four, he pushed the building almost upright and propped the building up to where he felt the horse would be safe. "Enough for one day" he whispered to the horse. Before going to bed, Adam took the letter from Gottlieb Becker and the photograph of Becker and his wife and placed them in the old German Bible where they belonged.

33

THE MORNING FOLLOWING THE TORNADO, Adam rose from the warmth of his bed, dressed, and made breakfast. Sitting at his kitchen table, he reached for a pencil and pad of paper. After two cups of coffee and a bowl of oatmeal, Adam had filled a dozen or so pages with sketches and numbers. He then began making lists of materials and places where these items would be found. He began making lists of people he needed to see. Adam had a house and a service station to finish and a church to build.

As the sun rose, he saw the kitchen light come on in the Schmidt farm. He bundled his papers into a small cardboard box and left the house. Before leaving, he drove around to the back of the house and fed his horse.

Adam knocked on Schmidt's door. "Morning Adam," Harriett greeted. "Care for a cup of coffee?"

"No thank you. I have too much work to do this week," Adam stated. "I can't get married because the church is broken. I cannot repair cars and tractors because my garage is not finished, and I can't move into my new house because it does not yet have a roof. If I sleep in my new house without a roof, I will get wet. If I get wet, I will catch a cold and die. And if I die, well, everything goes poof," Adam stated jokingly.

"We can't have you go poof, now can we?" Harriett replied with a smile.

Just then, Henry came out of the bedroom.

"Henry," Adam said with slight degree of discomfort at being so familiar, "I thought that I would go over to Westhaven and talk with that guy the contractor who is building my house and garage told me about. Perhaps this Westhaven contractor can give us some help on rebuilding the church. My father always told me, 'Do it right or don't do it all.' With this church, I truly believe that we must do it right."

Henry, taking a cup of coffee from Harriett, agreed, "Do it right or don't do it all!"

At that point, Laurel came from the bedroom still brushing her long blond hair. Adam melted as she came over and gave him a hug.

"I am going over to Westhaven for possibly a few days. I wonder if Rod could feed my horse until I return?" Adam continued.

Rod was out on the POW delivery run.

"No problem, we will see to your horse," Laurel replied. "Why will you need to be gone so long?" she said plaintively. "I will miss you."

"I want to talk with my contractor and I need to order some tools for my new garage. "And," he continued, "I want to order a Coke machine. Now, while I am gone, I have a job for you two," Adam said pointing to Laurel and Harriett. "I want you to make a complete list of all the furniture, stoves, and whatchamacallits we will need for our new house. Then, next Saturday, we can go to town and order the things. OK?" Both Laurel and Harriett were overjoyed at the thought of going big-time shopping. "And, remember one thing," Adam interjected, "we will have electricity in our new house so we will need lots of electrical stuff." As Adam started to leave the house he stopped and turned around. "Harriett, I want you to order up one of those electric organs for your house."

"You will have electrical wires here very soon," Harriett beamed.

"And Laurel, let's get one for our house too," Adam ordered. "I

274

want my kids to learn to play the organ as well as play baseball."

Laurel beamed.

Adam arrived at the garage site just as Rod drove up. "Rod, I am going over to Westhaven for a few days. If you can keep the brick masons going, they should be able to finish by Friday. If I can work a deal with our builder, maybe I can get his help in rebuilding the church and possibly some of the other buildings we are dreaming about. Anyhow, I will be back for the meeting on Wednesday evening."

"I will keep things moving here boss," Rod said.

"Not Boss, it's *partner*. Remember, partner!" Adam shot back.

"OK, I will keep things moving here, partner," Rod replied with a huge grin.

Adam wanted to pass by North Fork before going the 98 miles to Westhaven. While it was out of his way, he needed to talk with Herman Stencil about putting in a grocery store somewhere near his new garage. Herman had the only grocery store in a fifty mile radius and he knew it. While several other stores had tried to come into the area, Stencil offered the one thing none of the others could—thirty days credit on all accounts.

It took two hours and three cups of coffee to convince Herman Stencil to throw in with Adam and open a store somewhere near the school. Adam offered a rent-lease deal that would insure Stencil couldn't lose. Adam figured if the people came to Stencil's store, they might also buy gas at his station. Stencil figured that those going to church or to the ball games would be likely to stop in the store. While it was not his place to do so, Adam suggested that the new school and the café might just make all of their purchases through Stencil. The two men shook on the deal which would be committed to paper at a later date.

Driving down the thin ribbon of black pavement, Adam thought to himself, *Well, we will have a new grocery store, a new garage, a new well drilling service, a new church, a new baseball field, and my new house. Now all that's left is to get Rupert and Ross to figure out how they can make a café work.*

About five miles outside of North Fork, he slowed his pickup and made a U-turn. The thought occurred to him that the electricity lines were critical to the whole project. He found the local electric service office, just off the main street, and was lucky enough to find the area supervisor at his desk. Adam introduced himself and was invited to have a seat and another cup of coffee. After thirty minutes of conversation, Adam and the area supervisor agreed that the lines running past the new project needed to be up and running as soon as humanly possible. "Give me sixty days," the supervisor assured, "and you will have your electricity."

The two men shook hands and Adam moved toward his pickup. Stopping just short of the office door he turned and asked, "What would it take to get a line over to the Schmidt farm?"

The supervisor looked at a large wall map of the county, paused for a few seconds and said, "Consider it done!"

Adam smiled and left the office.

By noon Adam had arrived in Westhaven, one of the larger towns in Western Nebraska. After a quick lunch at the local café, Adam found the office of Calvin R. Block, Architect & General Contractor. Although Adam had no appointment, he was invited into Block's palatial office. On the walls were dozens of certificates and framed documents of all sizes. Where there were no certificate, there were photographs of buildings with Block standing somewhere in the photo.

Block offered Adam a chair and yet another cup of coffee.

"So," Block began, "What can I do for you Mr. Becker?"

"Well," Adam began, "I want to build a town."

"I see," Block retorted, as if he had been splashed in the face with a cold glass of water, "A town?"

"I suppose you would call it a village, but someday it could become a town," Becker replied. Adam went on to explain about the need for a new school and now the need for a new church. He added the strong desire for several buildings to house a café and a store. "And who knows what after that?" Calvin Block sat quietly as he tried to visualize Adam's dream. As Adam talked about the rolling hills and the wheat fields, Block began to see his vision.

Adam continued, "I want this town or village or whatever it is to become to be a beautiful place, with beautiful buildings from the very beginning. And something else I want for this town: I want to see the culture and traditions of those living near this town to be felt. In other words, I would like to see a bit of old Europe in the style of the buildings."

"Old Europe?" queried Block with a smile emerging across his face.

"Yes, most of the families in the area are descendants from Europe." Adam stopped short of saying *Germany*. If we could build our American buildings with a European flavor, I think our families and our children would have a lasting attachment to their home town."

Block rose from his enormous desk and went to a bookcase which covered one entire wall. Pulling a large book from the shelf, he opened it and placed it on the coffee table in front of Becker. "You mean something like this?" Block asked.

"Yes, exactly like this, pointing to a photograph of a red brick church and similar buildings," Adam stated enthusiastically. "They are more than just ugly little boxes which keep people out of the rain. They are things of beauty, works of art."

Block sat down across the coffee table from Becker. "You know Mr. Becker, most of the people who come into my office want these little boxes you mentioned. You are the first person in a long time who wants to give your buildings personalities and souls."

"I especially want the church to be a monument of faith, a lighthouse in the land. I want people who see this church to stop their cars and go inside. I want the children of those living in the area to look forward to being in this building," Adam whispered in almost poetic tones.

"I will tell you very honestly, Mr. Becker. It has always been my dream to build a town, a town with a soul," Block replied. "Tell you what…your church has been destroyed. If you and your congregation are in agreement, I will provide the building plans at no cost. You will, of course, have to pay for the materials yourself, but I will give you the plans, something like this," Block stated pointing to the church in the photograph in the book. "The other buildings you have mentioned, I will design at minimal cost. Your current builder can do the actual construction, under my supervision, of course. Now, the one thing you will have to agree to is this: Somewhere in your land title documents, I want you to include a covenant stating that from this day forward all buildings in your town will conform to this European style of architecture."

Adam thought for a minute, "I agree; but first, I must discuss the style of the church building with those in the congregation. After all, it is their church. There is a meeting planned for this coming Wednesday night where we will determine where we will go from this point. But I think they will agree with what you have offered."

For the next three hours, Adam and Block searched picture books, made sketches, and counted costs. It was apparent that both men were creating a thing of beauty, a work of art, a community with a soul. Both men left Block's office with a feeling of great anticipation. With a large folder of sketches and papers under his arm, Adam walked toward his pickup. Once again, a feeling of euphoria overcame him. "God is good!" He uttered aloud.

Adam found a small motel with a café attached. After a dinner of fried chicken and mashed potatoes, Adam spent most of the evening going over the sketches and the numbers. Even while he slept, he was laying bricks and mortar. At one point in his dreams, he found Laurel standing in the road wearing a wedding dress, waiting for him to finish building the church. At another point in his dreams, a large tornado came near the buildings but retreated without a brick being damaged.

The following day was spent going from one hardware store to another. Adam visited auto repair shops, tractor repair shops, and tool stores. By evening, the back of his pickup truck was filled with welding tanks, boxes of tools, steel cable, and parts of all sorts. It was too late and Adam was too tired to drive back to his farm that day. Another fried chicken dinner and another night in a motel and another night of dreams.

Wednesday morning, Adam filled his pickup with gas for the trip home. There in the parking lot of the gas station was a Coke truck. It was then that he remembered his promise to order a Coke machine for his service station. Adam went over to the delivery truck driver and asked how he could get a Coke machine for his service station. The driver took his name and address and assured Adam that someone would be contacting him within the next few weeks.

Driving back home, Adam calculated mentally the costs of his buildings and amount of rent money projected from each. He tried to determine the amount of money which would come in from his land rental, the well drilling, and the profits from his garage and gas station. Adam felt confident that all the numbers balanced.

As Adam passed the church, he noticed several people stacking pieces of broken lumber and attempting to salvage usable items. He smiled as he visualized a new brick church, with a bell tower standing on this spot. He also visualized a wedding party standing on the steps of the red brick church. "I had better hurry he muttered aloud." Passing the garage and the house, he noticed that almost all of the walls had been completed and the roof rafters were being finished. "Another two weeks for the garage," he thought aloud, possibly a month for the house." Adam pulled into the garage where he found Rod talking with one of the builders. "Rod, can you give me a hand with these things?" Adam called. Together Rod and Adam unloaded the welding tanks, boxes, and crates of tools and put them on a corner of the almost finished building.

Just as the two men finished unloading the pickup, Laurel pulled into the gas station. "Fill it up!" she ordered. "And check the oil and water." She ran over to Adam and embraced him. "How was your trip?" she inquired.

"You won't believe what has happened," Adam whispered

"Tell me, tell me!" Laurel insisted.

"Let's do it like this," Adam said, "I will pick you up at 6:30 this evening and we can drive to the meeting at St. Mary's together. Your parents can come in their car. On the way, I will tell you about my discussions with this Mr. Block. I think you will be pleased."

In the thirty minute drive to St. Mary's Catholic Church, Adam tried to relate the conversation he had had with Calvin Block. Unfortunately, the words did not come. Words simply could not describe the vision Adam and Block had developed during their time together. The parking lot and road in front of St. Mary's church was filled with cars and trucks. Small groups of people gathered around the church talking and laughing. Usually when there was an interdenominational gathering like this it was for a funeral.

At exactly seven o'clock, Father Patrick mounted the small platform in the church parish hall. Calling the meeting to order, Father Patrick did something which shocked many of those present. He invited Reverend Arnold Miller, pastor of the Holiness in Christ Pentecostal Church, to give a brief prayer. Everyone held their breath as Miller came to the platform. "Lord, we invite you into our presence. Give us wisdom and direction in our task. In your son's name we pray, amen." No fire, no brimstone, just a simple prayer.

Father Patrick then invited Herman Wittenberg to the podium. Herman gave a few remarks about the storm and the destruction of the church. "Where do we go from here?" Herman asked in a plaintive tone. At that point, Father Patrick interrupted. Brother Wittenberg, wherever you decide to go with this situation, those of us here are going with you. While we do not always agree on our understanding of the Holy Scriptures, we are none the less brothers and sisters in Christ. As we said last Sunday, while standing in the ruins of your church building, we will help in any way we can to rebuild your church." Those in the audience all nodded in agreement along with a few amens thrown in for good measure.

The meeting began to move in many directions with people making suggestions as to the style of the building, the type of flooring, the color of the water pipes and so on. After about twenty minutes of nondirected chatter, Adam raised his hand and was recognized. Adam uttered a silent prayer as he rose to his feet. Laurel reached over and gave his hand a gentle squeeze. Adam cleared his throat and began to speak, "As most of you know, the Lord has recently come into my life. As you also know, I was given life. I have also been given a new dream. And that dream is to build a place where my family, friends, and neighbors can prosper in this wonderful land. I have suggested that we build a new school, a school where our kids can be taught all things good and be well pleasing to God. I have suggested that we build a baseball field where our families can come and enjoy times of recreation. I now plan to build several more buildings which will house a grocery store and a café and who knows what else?" The mention of these new enterprises sent a wave of excitement and anticipation through the audience. Ross and Rupert looked at each other from across the room and smiled. Adam continued, "Now we have a problem. Our church was destroyed; so we need to build a new one. And rather than build a church building which serves only to keep the wind and the rain off our heads, I would like to suggest that we build a church that will stand as an example of this communities love toward its fellow members. I would suggest that this church reflect our personalities and our cultures. I would suggest that this church represent something which cannot be knocked down by a mere wind." Adam directed his attention toward Rod who was holding the large cardboard folder from Calvin Block's office. "Rod, could you take those drawings and pass them around the room." As people saw the sketches of the church and buildings they were awestruck. The sketches of the church attracted the most attention. One man holding a sketch of the church directed a question to Adam. "Won't this be terribly expensive?" Adam replied, "It will be about twenty-five percent more expensive than a wooden church, but a brick church will not have to be painted every few years;

we won't have to worry about dry rot or termites. Also the risk of fire and being knocked down by wind are less. One other thing I wish to mention, if we use this plan and I build all of my building using this plan, the architect will not charge the church for the plans. This alone will save a lot of money."

Another man raised his hand. "How much money will this building cost and how will we pay for it.?"

Block tells me that we should be able to get a loan from a bank, providing we supply most of the labor. The actual cost for a building like this is twenty thousand dollars," Adam stated. While the audience gasped at this figure, Adam responded, "If twenty-five percent of the cost is labor, we can bring the price down to twenty thousand. And if we can get some help from our neighbors, we can bring the cost down even further." The room became very quiet. Adam spoke up, "I will pledge one thousand dollars!" Harriett shouted out, "And an organ." Henry Schmidt, then spoke up, "I will pledge one thousand dollars to be paid over five years. Another man spoke out, "I will donate the proceeds from the sale of one head of cattle." Soon individuals were offering all sorts of items and amounts. Then the pastors got into things. As they caucused with members of their respective flocks, they made commitments for specific amounts of money. By nine o'clock most of the twenty thousand dollars had been committed in one form or another. With the enthusiasm high, Wittenberg took to the platform. "Adam, what would you say if we were to ask you to take responsibility for overseeing the building of the church? After all, you seem to know what you are doing." Adam blushed as he looked directly at Laurel. She smiled proudly and gave him a nod. "Of course he says *yes*," shouted Harriett. "He can't get married until the church gets built." With that comment, the audience exploded in laughter. "OK," Adam replied, "I will take on the job on one condition. Each church will have to form a baseball team and play at our new baseball field." Again the audience went wild with laughter. The meeting was adjourned while the women moved off to the parish hall kitchen and the men gathered around a large table with sketches and sheets of numbers. For the next hour or so volunteer work schedules were made and a calendar of sorts was set up. If all went well, the church would be finished in ninety days. Looking at the calendar on the wall, Adam figured that was about the same time as Laurel's school let out for the summer. A good time for a wedding he thought.

The following morning, Adam was awake early. He saw the lights come on across the road at the Schmidt farm. Anticipating that Rod had already gone and that Laurel would be ready to leave for school in fifteen minutes, Adam drove across the road.

"Henry," Adam asked, "can I make two phone calls from your phone?" First of all, I want to order me a phone over at the station and secondly, I want to commit to Mr. Block. If he starts with the drawings today, and we begin the clean up today, we should be ready to actually lay a foundation in a week. From there on, it is simply the matter of one brick on top of another until we reach the top."

Laurel looked at the clock and dashed to the door. Just before she closed the door, Adam called to her, "Laurel, don't forget. This Saturday, we are going shopping for our furniture and curtains," she beamed as she blew him a kiss. "Hey, what about me?" Henry chided. Harriett came over to Henry and kissed him on the mouth. "There, that should take care of you for awhile."

After a cup of coffee and a biscuit and some conversation with Henry, Adam picked up the phone and dialed Mac McCloud at the North Fork post office. Mac was on the local telephone committee. "Good morning, Mr. McCloud. This is Mr. Becker. I am calling from Mr. Schmidt's office regarding having a new telephone installed in my new office," Adam laughed as did Henry and Mac. "I don't know if you heard yet, but we are going to begin a rebuilding project over here at the church, or I should say, what was the church," Adam continued. "It really would make things easier if we had a telephone handy."

"Adam, you know that there are ten thousand forms to fill out in order to get a telephone. We simply don't go around giving out telephones to just anyone you know," Mac chided. "But I will personally fill out all ten thousand forms myself," Mac continued. "You will have your telephone as soon as I can get one of linemen free. You should be connected by the week end." Adam hung up and smiled.

"We are on the way," Adam stated with a broad smile. "I figure, if all goes well, we can have the garage finished in three weeks. My...oops...our house finished in four weeks, and the church finished in ninety days."

"Adam, what about the water? When do you plan to begin the well?" Henry queried.

"I almost forgot about that little detail. I had better get working on the drilling equipment."

Adam left Henry and drove the brief mile to the almost finished garage and gas station. The workmen had arrived and were in the process of getting the day started with coffee and conversation. Adam approached the six workmen and inquired about the progress on the building. From the brick house some three hundred feet away, the sound of saws and hammers could be heard. Adam was satisfied that that project too was on schedule. He was told that interior woodwork would take another week. And that after that, it would be a matter of minor details. The one major factor was the electrical wires which were now less than a half mile away. With the service station and the house almost finished, Adam could turn his attention to working on the drilling rig. Before going over to the drilling equipment, several pickup trucks pulled up to the church. Within minutes, there were ten or so men with hammers and crow bars. Adam jumped into his pickup truck and drove over to where the men had gathered. Once again, Adam surveyed the rubble and determined that much of the lumber could be saved. "If we sort out all of the beam lumber and stack it over there," Adam said, pointing toward the barbed wire fence, "and all the flat lumber over there, we use most of it in the new building. Some of the pieces we can use for form lumber when we pour the cement foundation. All of the broken lumber, stack over there, pointing to the grader ditch. And we can burn it," Adam continued, "I talked with Mr. Block, the architect this morning. He says that he can have the plans ready by next week. He also said that he would drive over himself and discuss the plans with us and with my contractor." The men in the group all seemed satisfied that Adam knew what he was doing and agreed with the plan. Within minutes, nails were being yanked from broken boards; and broken boards were being sawed into usable stock.

As Adam was walking toward his pickup truck, Rod, returning from his POW delivery turned into the churchyard. "Morning!" Rod chimed. Adam came over to the large truck. "Good morning, partner," Adam said with an exaggerated Nebraska accent. "Rod, I would like to have all the guys in our well drilling project over here at the garage as soon as possible. We need to get the well in and the water pipes set sometime very soon."

Rod agreed and acknowledged that he would go home and call all the men. Within an hour all of the well drilling team had gathered at the garage. Adam removed the plans for the well drilling truck and placed them on the floor of the unfinished garage. By noon, steel pipes were being welded into derricks and iron cable reels were being attached to frames. From time to time, one of the men would dash off in a pickup truck and return with a part from someone's old tractor or a piece of steel from an old truck. An engine mount had been constructed on the bed of the truck selected to become the drill rig. The engine from the broken truck was detached from its mounts and readied for removal. In order to lift and move the engine, the team constructed a large tripod frame on a set of old truck wheels. This would allow for the engine to be hoisted, removed, and transferred to the bed of the derrick truck. The sense of team work gave the men confidence that the project would work. By the end of the day, much of the derrick had been put in place. For the next three days, the group of men worked on derrick and all its many wenches, drive chains, and hydraulic hoses. A number of pieces of equipment which could not be constructed were ordered on the garage's newly installed telephone.

285

Drill shafts and drilling bits were ordered from Houston. Steel cables were ordered from Denver, and hundreds of feet of new metal well casing were ordered from Lincoln. After eight days of work, the first derrick truck was ready to poke holes in the ground. A three hundred gallon water tank from the packing plant had been mounted on a second truck, complete with salvaged water pumps. The third truck had been fitted with a simple hoist for lifting pipe and drill shafts.

The truck from Denver had unloaded its giant stack of well casing on the hill near the well site. Everything was ready to drill.

The garage and the service station were at last complete. Rod made the call to the Mobil Oil Company in St. John and requested a delivery of gasoline and oil products. Rod also called the local Coca Cola distributor and requested a Coke machine and a supply of soft drinks.

Work on the church had progressed far ahead of schedule. Block had brought the plans for the new church. And the church members as well as all those in the community were absolutely delighted with what they saw. Two weeks after the storm which destroyed the old church, the foundation for the new building was ready. In the Sunday morning service, Wittenberg announced that a new cornerstone would be laid the following Sunday. He asked that all member families and those from the community, who wished to do so, to write letters and place them, along with photos, in the cornerstone of the new church. The following week, the workers from the now finished service station and from Adam's almost finished house turned to the church project. At the same time, the derrick truck had begun screwing its drill into the hill above the church. The section of land near Adam Becker's farm had become a beehive of building and digging activities. Farmers and townspeople would drive for miles to help lay bricks or to simply watch the drilling derrick bore its monotonous hole in the soft Nebraska ground. It was good!

34

THE RADIO IN BECKER'S PICKUP truck had predicted thunder showers with an eighty percent chance of rain across the area. This usually meant that it either would rain or it wouldn't. Most farmers didn't put much stock in the radio weather report. If a person went outside and it was wet, rain was the prediction. If a person went outside and it was dry, no rain was the prediction. Because of the possibility of rain, Adam scheduled a work day where he would be inside his new garage and filling station. There were hundreds of small jobs which needed to be completed before the business officially opened. Just as Adam arrived at the station, Arnold Wacker's pickup screeched to a stop in front of the station door.

Arnold was out of breath as he tried to speak. "Adam, some fella's car has gone over the side of the road down near Alex Miller's farm. Looks like the rain slicked up the road and he spun off."

"Is anyone hurt?" Adam asked.

"I don't know, but the fella in the car is screaming bloody murder. I was thinking. Your big truck, the one with the derrick on the back, would be just the thing to lift the car back on the road. It's terribly muddy over there and I don't think a tractor could do the job."

Adam unlocked the door of his garage and picked up the recently connected telephone, he thought for a minute and dialed. "Harriett, I

have a large favor to ask. Could you call all the guys on the well digging crew and ask them to meet me at Alex Miller's farm. It seems
someone has gone over the side of the road and we will have to use my
derrick truck to pull the car back to the road."

Harriet asked, "whose car is it, Adam? Is anyone hurt?"

"I don't know. Arnold Wacker tells me that someone in the car is
screaming so that means someone is alive," Adam said quietly. "Also
Harriett if you could call the last farm on Rod's POW route and tell
him to get over to the Miller's farm, it would save him from coming
all the way back to your farm and out again."

Before hanging up, Harriett asked, "Adam, should I call Bucky and
the ambulance?" "Yes" Adam replied and hung up.

Adam raced to the top of the hill to where the derrick truck was
parked. Grinding the starter for a few minutes, the truck roared to life.
Adam drove the truck as fast as it would go. Arriving at Alex Miller's
farm, he found several other pickups and cars along the side of the
road. A half dozen men were standing at the edge of the road looking
over the side of a steep embankment. Adam jumped from his truck
and ran to the group of men. There was a black Ford coupe leaning
against a small cottonwood tree about thirty feet down. Another thirty
feet below was a muddy water hole Alex Miller used to water his cattle. The road and the embankment were sticky with mud from one of
the passing rain showers. Within minutes of Adam's arrival, Sheriff
Buckstone and the ambulance arrived from town. The man in the car
continued to scream. Occasionally one of the men along side the road
would call down to the trapped man, "We are going to get you out,
don't worry, everything is under control." Actually, nothing was under
control. Miller had brought his tractor up earlier, but he felt that the
embankment was too steep and the car might end up sliding all the
way down the embankment and into the pond. Three of Adam's
drilling crew arrived almost at the same time.

"Let's get the derrick truck turned around. Someone get the cable
and the hook wenched out. Mr. Miller, if you will move your tractor

in front of my truck, and hook it onto the front. This will help keep me from sliding or tipping over," Adam ordered. Just as the derrick was lowered over the side of the road, Rod arrived. Looking at the car over the side and the angle of the derrick Rod said, "We can't drag the car up without possibly flipping over and sliding further. I say we, I, go down on the derrick cable and get the guy out and then we can worry about the car later."

Adam and all those standing there nodded in agreement. Aside from getting the driver out of the car, it would give Rod the opportunity to become an instant hero. Rod grabbed a length of heavy rope and hurriedly fashioned a harness around his waist. Adam had lowered the derrick boom over the side of the embankment. Rod placed the rope harness into the large metal hook. Looking back at Adam, he gave a thumbs up sign and swung out over the embankment, directly above the car below. Rod swung, mid air for several seconds before Adam moved the control level allowing Rod to move slowly toward the car. "Stop!" Rod yelled as his feet touched the side of the car. Adam stopped the wench. The man in the car again began to yell, "Get me out of here, I am hurt." Rod moved to where he could see the man, a soldier in an Army uniform. Seeing the car slip slightly in the mud, Rod yelled up, "Send me another cable to tie off the car. The darn thing is starting to slip."

A second cable was tossed down. Rod slowly opened the driver's side door and placed the cable around the steering wheel. The driver, who's head was slightly bloody barked, "Never mind the car you moron, get me out of here!"

"Mister, if I don't secure the car, you and the car are apt to end up in that puddle at the bottom of this slope. So I suggest that you shut up and cooperate with me."

Rod finished tying off the steering wheel. "Take up a little slack!" Rod yelled to the men at the top of the embankment. As soon as the steel cable went taught, Rod turned his attention to the driver. "Now listen. I want you to put your arms around my neck and hold on as

289

tight as you can. As soon as we clear the car, put your legs around me. Understand?"

The driver nodded and moved his arms slowly toward Rod's neck. Rod yelled, "Take me up by a foot." The steel cable moved slowly. The driver now clung to Rod like a long lost friend. Foot by foot, the driver was freed from the car. "Take her up!" Rod yelled at last. The two men dangled high in the air just as the car began to move toward the pond below. The cable holding the steering wheel went taut then slack as the steering column was yanked out of the car like a bad tooth. The car rolled a dozen times before it came to rest in the muddy pond below. The two men continued to dangle in mid air as the crowd on the road watched the car sink even deeper in the mud. Adam returned his attention back to the two men attached to the swinging cable. Pulling the wench level and the lift lever, the two men were lowered to the side of the road. Sheriff Buckstone, assuming all authority, yelled for the ambulance crew to bring the stretcher. Within minutes, the soldier was strapped to a stretcher and moving toward the rear of the ambulance. Sheriff Buckstone asked the soldier his name and asked why he was out here on country roads. The soldier responded, "You'll have to speak up, I lost my right eardrum in the war. See, here is my Purple Heart. And here this is a Bronze Star for bravery under fire." Sheriff Buckstone repeated his question. "My name is William Case, and I am on my way to see my old girlfriend, Laurel Schmidt. I have decided I want to marry her," the soldier responded.

Adam froze as did most of the people in the ever growing crowd. Rod spoke up. "You were the guy from Laurel's college who came to visit several years back. You were the art student who wanted to stay in the house and draw all the time. I remember you."

Case said, "Yeah, that was the old me, I am different now—new and improved." Case continued, "By the way, thanks for dumping my car."

As the ambulance crew moved Case into the ambulance, he called "Someone tell Laurel that I want to see her. I guess I will be at the hospital for a few days."

Laurel arrived from school. Harriett met her at the front door. "Laurel, we have a problem....William Case is back and is telling everyone that he is going to marry you." Laurel didn't know whether to laugh or cry. "William Case, I dumped him years ago. He called farmers hicks and hay seeds. He told me that when I became a teacher, I would rise up out of the haystack and become an intellectual, like him." Laurel stormed off to her room emerging a few minutes later with a smile on her face. "And just where is Mr. Case that I might respond to his proposal of marriage?"

Harriett spent the next few minutes filling in the details of the accident. She placed great emphasis on the part where Rod dangled dangerously over the edge of the cliff in order to save the life of a soldier in distress and the part about Case's comments about dumping his car.

"So," Laurel said, "Mr. Case is in the hospital for a few days, after which he will come to claim his bride. I don't think so." Laurel looked at the clock on the wall—three o'clock.

"Mother, would you like to accompany me to the hospital to chat with Mr. Case?"

"Laurel, I would consider it an honor."

Laurel drove well above the legal and illegal speed limits. Arriving at the city limits she burned passed Bucky's black and white partially hidden in the bushes. Bucky knew exactly where Miss Schmidt was headed and why. He rammed his car into gear and headed for the hospital. Laurel parked in front of the hospital, in the No Parking zone. She and her mother marched across the lawn toward the entrance, followed by Sheriff Buckstone. Helen was at the nurses station. "Helen, where is he?" Helen crooked her finger and led the small parade toward one of the wards. In a mock bow, Helen pulled back a curtain revealing William Case, his head wound with a white bandage. Laurel smiled a broad sinister smile as did her mother. Bucky stood in the corner of the room, smiling as he watched the show about to begin.

"Laurel darling!" Case mumbled. "I would get up out of this bed and sweep you off your feet if it weren't for my most recent injuries."

Helen added, "Mr. Case, your injuries consist of a possible minor skull fracture and a small cut on your forehead. I think you will live."

"Come here my love, let me look at you. Back in college I always knew that you would become someone someday. The guys in the ambulance told me that you are a school teacher. That's a great start."

Again Laurel and all those in the room smiled knowing full well that the conquering hero was about to be slammed against the wall.

Case pointed to the chair in the corner of the room, on which his army uniform hung. "You see those medals, Laurel? I won those for you. The Purple Heart can't replace my ruptured eardrum and the pain of war. The Bronze Star you see hanging next to it comes from killing dozens of filthy Krauts. They say I killed over a dozen of those Nazi devils before I fell. Laurel, I killed those savages for you."

The smiles around the room continued to widen as Cases story went on.

"Laurel, when I was laying in the hospital, wounded and frightened to death, I saw a vision of you. Actually, a vision of you and I standing on that blowout thing at your family farm. That was when I realized that, if I survived my wounds, I would return to the good old United States of America and make you my wife. Well, what do you say? Would you like to have a war hero for a husband?"

All those present in the room, except poor William Case, were about to explode. It was now time for Laurel to speak. As she opened her coin purse, she took out a twenty dollar bill. Handing it to the wounded soldier, she said, "Dear William, dear heroic William, here is twenty dollars. This is enough to get you a bus ticket to Denver and a hamburger. That's the least I can do for a war hero. There is a bus passing though town at three o'clock every afternoon. I suggest that as soon as you have recovered from your injuries, you take one of those buses." Still smiling, she continued. "By the way, I have chosen my man and he too is a Kraut." Realizing what she had said, she quickly amended her statement ,"Just as my family and I are—descendants of

German farmers. Goodbye, William."

The little group left the hospital room. Within twenty-four hours, Mr. William Case had left town and every man, woman and child in the county had heard the entire story, including Adam Becker.

35

FOR WHATEVER REASON, Father Patrick spent a good part of every day at the building site. Upon arriving, he would remove his clerical collar and shirt in favor of his tee-shirt. On one occasion, he brought a large four by eight piece of plywood and two buckets of black and red paint. With the help of several onlookers, Father Patrick turned the wooden panel into a sign indicating the progress of the various projects. At the top of the sign were the words: *Becker's House—Completed!* Then, *Becker's Service Station—Completed!* Next came: *The Well, St. John's Lutheran Church, The Paul Schmidt Memorial School, The Baseball Field,* and *Other Buildings.* Next to each of the unfinished projects was a number indicating the level of progress in terms of a percent number. The sign was erected along side the dirt road for all those passing to see. Every few days, Father Patrick would take a brush and some paint and change the numbers.

Rupert and Ross had managed to take an old trailer house once used for summer vacations, and turn it into a reasonably decent cook shack. They pulled the trailer over near the church site where most of the workers seemed to congregate each morning and each lunchtime. A large canvas porch held up by poles and a few fold-up chairs constituted the dining area. While most of those working on the project would bring their morning coffee and lunches in a sack, eventually, almost all became regular customers at Rupert and Ross's. The brothers relished in the satisfaction of each new stew or soup recipe. Eventually they graduated to hamburger sandwiches, with onion and lettuce.

The sign next to the road showed that the well was now one hundred and twenty feet deep. Adam expected to hit the first water at about two hundred down, but planned to go at least three hundred feet into the main body of the water bearing sand. This would insure a long term water supply and a large volume at that. At the rate the drill was moving, first water would be reached within ten days. It was time to mount the water tank.

Adam and Laurel made several trips over to Mrs. Wellman's to assess the process for dismantling and transporting the water tower. As Adam would climb the legs of the tower and dangle a tape measure, Laurel would read and record the numbers. Finally, Adam disappeared inside the empty tank at the top of the tower. After a few minutes inside the tank, Adam immerged filthy but smiling. "No holes!" he yelled to Laurel. "It looks good!"

The following day, Adam, along with the derrick truck and a flat bed loaded with tools and welding tanks, descended upon Mrs. Wellman's property. Mrs. Wellman and her cat sat in her rocking chair and watched the onlookers from town and the crew of men who attached wire cables and ropes to the tower. Bolts which could be removed with a wrench and oil were removed; those which could not were cut with a welding torch. After several hours, the main tank was released from the legs of the tower and ready to be lifted. The derrick truck moved within feet of the tower while two men attached cables to the tank. An hour later, the large tank sat secure on the back of the flat bed truck. Section by section, the legs of the tower were disassembled and loaded for the fourteen mile trip to their new location. As the trucks passed farmhouses and fields, people would stop and watch the giant steel cylinder creep down the country road. At the church, all work stopped as the tank and its iron legs approached, with the realization that an event, far beyond the building of a simple country church was taking place. With this tower, the Nebraska landscape would no longer be the same. Change was taking place. Many of those watching the tower approach its destination had feelings of exhilaration while others saw the past fading away. The derrick truck moved to the top of the hill where it waited for the flatbed truck carrying the tank. A set of four large concrete pedestals had been made ready for each leg of the tower. It was Adam's plan to erect the tank and the tower after the well was completed. In the mean time, the tower and the tank were off loaded where they could be sanded and repainted with shiny silver paint.

As the numbers on Father Patrick's sign changed, so did the personality of the crossroads in the county. The County School Board had met and arranged for financing to begin the new school buildings and baseball field. Adam had signed a contract with Stencil to open a small grocery store and an "agreement" with Ross and Rupert to operate a café but no beer or hard liquor. Because most of the county school board members lived in the area, it was felt that the use of the county bulldozer and road scraper was justified in grading the land for Adam's buildings as well as the school. Each Monday, Calvin Block, the architect, would drive over from Westhaven to bring new plans or simply check on the progress of "his new town." Each day brought more and more spectators to watch the small brick town rise up on the Nebraska horizon. Many of the spectators would find some small task, like carrying a load of bricks or mixing a batch of mortar simply so they could feel a part of the new town.

The service station soon became the focal point of all activities. Rod had his hands full pumping gas, checking oil, and making minor repairs on cars and trucks. In the afternoon, Laurel would come to the station to record all business transactions for both the station and the construction work going on. There was almost always a waiting line at the telephone, with construction men needing to order more bricks or more nails. Over at Ross and Rupert's trailer, hamburgers and egg salad sandwiches were being made from morning until late afternoon.

At the end of each day, Father Patrick, followed by a trail of onlookers would go to the sign and paint over the old numbers with new numbers. Not only was a town being built but a community.

36

THE SOUND OF THE NEW TOWN being born was briefly interrupted by the honking of Simon Gump's ancient pickup truck as
he raced toward the new church. As he came to a stop, the great cloud
of dust, which had been chasing him, caught up with and passed him.
Most of the volunteer workers stopped what they were doing and
moved toward the truck. Simon, a man in his late sixties was much too
excited to talk. It was as if he, not his pickup had been racing down the
country road. As the dust settled, Simon pointed to a person, tied and
bound, lying in the back of his pickup. Father Patrick moved to the
edge of the pickup and looked at the dust covered person. The person
was wearing a dress. After a second glance, it was painfully obvious
that the person was not a woman. Father Patrick asked Simon, "What's
going on here? Where did you find this person?"

Simon, still gasping for air and pointing his double-barreled shotgun at the person in the back of the pickup, replied, "Father, I found
this guy asleep under the old railroad bridge. He was sound asleep. I
thought it was kinda funny, a fellow dressed in a lady's dress. You know,
there are people who like to do this sort of thing. So, I snuck up on him
and bound him with some hay twine."

The man in the dress and bound hand and foot with hay twine attempted to sit up. Someone opened the tailgate of the Simon's truck

and allowed the man to scoot out and stand upright. Within minutes the entire work crew had assembled around the truck. Mac McCloud who was one of the volunteers that afternoon stepped into the group along side Father Patrick. Someone in the crowd yelled out, "Someone needs to call Sheriff Bucky!"

Mac held up his hand, "Just hold on a minute. Don't anyone call anyone until we get this fella's story.

"Just exactly who are you sir? Mac asked the man dressed in the black and white dress.

The man remained silent. Looking around the group of men, his dusty eyes fixed on Adam Becker. Adam felt a bolt of frozen lightening pass through his body. The man continued to stare directly at Adam.

At last, in broken English the bound man spoke. "I run away from POW camp. I go to San Francisco."

Still looking at Adam, Mac spoke up before the man could speak another word and barked an order, "I want everyone to go back to work. This poor fella seems to have a bit of a mental problem. Let's not make him feel like we are going to hurt him."

The cluster of volunteers moved back toward their respective projects, leaving Mac, Father Patrick, Adam and the man in the black and white dress.

Simon still stood by his truck, holding his shotgun.

"Simon, there's a jug of Kool-Aid over on my truck. Get yourself over there and have cool drink," Mac said in a polite but commanding voice.

The man in the dress never let his eyes move from Adam. The three men closed the circle around the bound man. Adam reached into his trousers and took out his pocketknife. The bound man took a deep breath as he watched Adam open the knife and move to toward the twine. As the hay twine fell off, the man, still fixed on Adam's face, whispered, "I know you."

Father Patrick looked at Mac, wondering what was going on.

299

Then, in whispered tones, the man in the dress began to speak in German. For several minutes the man spoke passionately in his native tongue. Neither Father Patrick nor Mac understood a word of what was being said, but they both realize that this man was a problem, and not a small problem at that.

After a few more minutes of conversation between Adam and the man, Adam extended his hand toward the man in the dress. Addressing Mac and Father Patrick, Adam spoke, "This is Private Klaus Wickler, German prisoner of war. He tells me that all POWs are being transferred back to the east coast for transport back to Europe, several train loads of POWs from Camp Alexis this week. Private Klaus managed to "get lost" somewhere between Camp Alexis and the train station. He found this dress hanging on a clothes line and borrowed it so that he wouldn't be recognized as a POW. It seems that Private Klaus wished to go to San Francisco where he says that he has a cousin."

Father Patrick spoke up, "Adam, we just can't allow this man to go running off to San Francisco, that's a crime."

Adam's face was dripping with sweat and not from his labors. Looking directly at Mac, Adam continued, "He also knows who I am and threatens to tell if we take him back to Camp Alexis."

Father Patrick spoke. "What do you mean, he knows who you are. You're Adam Becker."

Adam looked over at Mac whose face had filled with wrinkles. Adam nodded, "Father Patrick, we must talk"

Mac was quick to respond, "Father Patrick, what we are going to tell you comes in the form of a confession. And by the book, anything you hear in a confession must be kept between us." Father Patrick nodded.

For the next fifteen minutes Mac and Adam told the abbreviated story of Adam Becker's new life to Father Patrick. As the story concluded, Father Patrick looked at Adam Becker and at Mac McCloud with the most serious of expressions then broke out in hysterical laughter. Those pounding nails and sawing boards noticed the holy man as he hugged the necks of Adam Becker and William McCloud. "I have never in my life heard such a wild story," Father laughed. "And this little man here in the dress could blow it all away like the little church over there."

Adam and Mac looked at each other as Father Patrick continued to laugh. Private Klaus was content to sit on the tailgate and drink the paper cup of Kool-Aid someone had brought him.

"What do we do now?" Adam whispered, "If we take him back, he will tell Colonel Reed about me. I will be arrested and sent back to Germany with Private Klaus."

Father Patrick looked at Mac. "Mr. McCloud, you are an official of the United States Government, what do you think we should do with this poor unfortunate?"

Bill McCloud took a deep breath. "Well, if he has a cousin in San Francisco, I say we send this problem to his cousin for a solution."

Father Patrick reached into his pocket and pulled out his wallet. "I have thirty-three dollars, Mac how much do you have?"

Mac pulled out twenty-four and Adam came up with fifty-five.

Father Patrick spoke, "One hundred and twelve dollars should get him to San Francisco on the Greyhound. Once he gets there, it is up to him to find his kin. If he gets caught, I don't think he will spill the beans on Adam. He seems like a decent sort."

Father Patrick looked at the man in the dress. "Adam, he is about your size, why don't you run home and get him some clothes. Even the Greyhound people wouldn't let someone dressed like this on their bus." Turning to Mac, Father Patrick continued, "Mac, what do you say you and I take a ride over to Wellman Crossing and see if we can get him on the afternoon bus and out of our hair."

Within minutes Adam had returned with his best Sunday suit, socks, shoes, and a hat.

"This should give Mr. Klaus Wickler a better chance of getting on the bus," Adam said.

The three men formed a small circle around Private Klaus as he changed into his new clothes. Adam tied the red and purple tie and placed the hat on the man's head. The little man smiled as Adam placed a small bundle of US dollars in his hand. *"Gott ist gut!"* Adam said.

Klaus repeated, *"Gott ist gut!"* and shook Adam's hand.

Mac brought his car over to where Adam and Father Patrick were standing. Adam was giving Klaus some instructions, in whispered German. "Do not talk!" Point to your ears and shake your head. Make people think you're deaf and dumb. And if you are caught, make them think that you are crazy. A nut house for a couple of months is a lot better than being shipped back to Germany."

Adam opened the back door for Klaus and Father Patrick took the front seat, next to Mac.

Adam returned to the workers and began to explain that the poor man had an unfortunate accident and he didn't seem to know who he was. Father Patrick and Mac are taking him to help find a relative somewhere over in the west. Everyone seemed to accept the explanation. Simon Gump went off down the road happy that he had preformed a good deed for a man in need. Adam smiled to himself, knowing that here was another man given a second chance at a new beginning.

37

IT WAS A FRIDAY AFTERNOON as Father Patrick approached the sign with his brushes and jars of paint. As he began to paint over the number of bricks which had been laid, Sy from the well site on top of the hill yelled out, "Water! Water!" Everyone knew that the drillers were within a few feet of hitting the water level but as it happened, there was total jubilation. It was as if someone had yelled out "Gold! Gold! Everyone at all the worksites dropped what they were doing and ran toward the drilling rig on the top of the hill. Adam was one of the first to get to the site. Again, he knew that they would be hitting water any time; he too was elated as he stared down at the pile of mud which the drill had brought to the surface. There were hundred of wells in this area but for some reason, the bringing in of this particular well on the top of this particular hill was different. Adam ordered the drillers to drop the drill once more and bring the well a few inches closer to reality. Once again, the drill dumped a load of dark, wet mud on the ground. Smiles spread over every face in the crowd. Several people ran down to the station to send the news over the telephone lines.

Harriett and Laurel arrived at the well site minutes after seeing the group of people moving toward the hill. Parking their car next to the cemetery, Harriett and Laurel ran up the hill to where Adam and the others were gathered. Adam reached down and scooped up a hand full of mud. "Water," he said as if water had never been seen in these parts before. Laurel threw her arms around Adam who stood with his muddy hands at his side. "What's the matter with you people? Haven't you ever seen water before?" Harriett barked. "Yes, but not on this exact spot," Adam laughingly retorted.

Twice more the drill was lowered into the gaping hole and twice more, dark wet mud was deposited on the ground.

The sun had set and those on the hill began to move toward their cars. Father Patrick went to his sign and completed his assessment of the day's work. On the line marked *well*, he painted in *hit water*. Adam and Laurel were the last to leave the well site. Arm in arm, they walked past the top end of the cemetery toward the church.

"Adam," Laurel said, "this project of yours is beginning to scare me. This is not just a little country house with a little country gas station next to a little country church. It is a small town! You don't just go around building towns!"

"Why not?" Adam smiled.

"Well, you just don't, that's all," she replied.

"Towns have city halls and mayors and streets and all sorts of things. Towns have names," she continued.

Just as they passed the small gravestone which read, "Helmut Sommerfield" Adam whispered, "This town will have a name. I will give it a name"

"What name will you give it?" Laurel queried.

Adam smiled and replied, "For now, I shall keep that a secret.

Adam continued to smile as Laurel tried to poke and prod the name from Adam. "No," continued Adam, "I will announce the name at the right time."

Defeated, Laurel pretended to pout.

Adam suggested that they pass by their new house which needed only a few minor details before it was complete. The electricity was in and turned on, and a telephone sat by the kitchen sink. The only major item lacking was water. As soon as the well on the top of the hill was completed, the house would be ready to move in. But before moving in, the church had to be finished so there could be a wedding.

As Adam and Laurel stood in the living room of their new house, Laurel embraced Adam. "Adam, is there any way you can finish the church any sooner? I want to be your wife," Laurel smiled up at Adam with a look that caused Adam's heart to pound.

"I will see what I can do," Adam replied with a broad smile. "I will see what I can do."

By the end of the next week, all of the brick work on the church had been completed. The floors and interior woodwork were all that were left, with the exception of the windows and a bell for the bell tower. The small country church was now twice the size of the former church.

Calvin Block was now spending two days each week at the church site as well as supervising the construction at the school and store-café. He became almost a bother as he attended to details un-noticed by everyone else. Early one morning, Calvin Block arrived at the head of a small convoy of three flatbed trucks. The first two trucks were laden with large loads covered by canvas tarps and held tight by thick ropes. The third truck carried a small, single object also covered by a canvas tarp. Father Patrick was the first to greet Block and together the two whispered in private. Adam and several other men came over to where the trucks stopped. Father Patrick spoke. "Adam, friends, I would like to ask your patience on this matter. I want to hold off re-moving the covers on these trucks until noon."

Everyone standing around the trucks looked at each other won-dering what was going on. Adam scratched his head and nodded. "Noon it is!" At about eleven, word had spread by phone that some-thing was happening at the church. By eleven thirty, dozens of cars and pickups clogged the main road and parking lot of the almost fin-ished church. Henry and Harriett Schmidt left their chores and drove the short mile to the church. By eleven forty-five pastors from more than a dozen local churches, including several Swedish Lutheran churches from south of the highway arrived at the building site. Calvin Block nodded to Father Patrick who jumped on the back of one of the flat bed trucks. Holding up his hands and asking for everyone's attention, he requested that all the pastors in the group join him and Calvin on the back of the trucks. "We have a little surprise for you all. If you will look at your new church, you will notice that it has no windows. The drawings show four very simple, colored glass windows. You simply can't have a church without stained glass windows!" Father Patrick stated. "That simply wouldn't do, not even for Lutherans." At that, everyone laughed. Father Patrick continued, "Seeing your dilemma, your brothers and sisters in Christ felt it necessary to do something about your church with its dull, colored glass windows. Each congregation in this area has passed the hat, several times I might add, and ordered these magnificent windows," pointing to four arched, framed stained glass windows. Calvin Block had pulled the canvas off just as Father Patrick made his announcement. Two eight foot tall stained glass windows stood upright, held fast by ropes on the bed of each truck. All of those standing in the crowd, without exception, gasped with delight as the sun reflected off and through the brilliant stained glass. Calvin Block beamed as he stood watching the expressions on each face. Block, with a broad grin pointed to one of the windows and spoke. "If you will notice this window, it is the only one we were able to salvage and rebuild from the original church. All of the others were designed so as to fit with the design of the original." Again the crowd expressed amazement and joy. "We will begin mounting these windows tomorrow morning," Block continued.

Father Patrick jumped down from the flat bed truck and moved to the last truck and climbed upon its bed. Taking hold of one of the ropes holding the canvas covering, he yanked the shroud with a bit of theatrical emphasis. "Voila!" he shouted. It was a bell, a large bell mounted in an iron bell carriage. On the side of the bell was engraved a single word, *PEACE*. This is a gift from our good friend and distant neighbor, Mr. Calvin Block." Block, rather sheepishly but wanting to be recognized, waved at the crowd and accepted their applause. Father Patrick, still standing on the last flat bed held up his hands for quiet. "Some of you are wondering what's going on here. Why do we have Baptists and Methodists and Pentecostals and Catholics building a Lutheran church? Why are we working and giving our money to build this building which houses a religious congregation in which we do not participate? Why are Catholics, the arch enemies of Lutherans for over four hundred years, working to build this building? The answer to that question can be found in a Thanksgiving Day event in which many of you participated. We came together, we prayed together, we ate together, and we played together. When your church blew down, we mourned together. And now, we are building together. We are building more than just a church and a few other buildings, we are building a community—a community where we can all be different while at the same time being the same. The time for war is over and now is the time for peace." With that, Father Patrick ended his little sermon. Block jumped up on the flat bed and barked, "Let's get these windows unloaded!" Like a small army of ants, those around the trucks began to untie ropes and carefully move the windows to the building. Likewise, the bell was lifted from the truck and carried to the base of the belfry. Calvin Block looked something like a pharaoh, directing the construction of a pyramid, barking orders to those lifting the windows and the bell. Block was in his glory. He had taken off his suit jacket and rolled up his shirtsleeves. He felt good! Likewise, all of the pastors had removed their jackets and ties and joined the ranks of sweaty men. Within an hour, all four windows were standing beneath their respective niches. The bell sat on the ground beneath the belfry. Block announced that tomorrow, they would construct scaffoldings and pulley systems to mount the windows and the bell. At that point, Adam stepped forward. "Calvin, give me a few minutes and we can mount the windows and your bell today."

Adam took off running toward the well site at the top of the hill.

Within minutes, the drill shafts had been disconnected and the truck, with its derrick headed toward the church. Adam backed the truck toward the first window and lowered a steel cable from the top of the derrick. Several men attached the iron hook to the rope harness which held the window. With the pull of a lever on the truck, the window rose toward its place in the building. Gently, the window was eased into place and secured by several rough nails. Then the second, third, and fourth windows were placed. As the afternoon turned to evening, Adam hoisted the bell carriage into its place in the belfry. The large iron clapper remained tied with twine and cloth so as to prevent it from ringing. Smiles were on every face. Henry Schmidt, raised his cane and spoke, "Adam, why are you in such a hurry to get this church finished?" Adam responded in a loud voice, "Because I can't marry your daughter until it is finished." The whole group of people exploded in laughter. Adam then said, "If I could get these people to work all night, maybe we could have the wedding tomorrow." Again, laughter. The sun was at the horizon and people began moving off toward their cars and homes.

Calvin Block, Henry and Harriett Schmidt, Father Patrick and Adam Becker remained behind. "Mr. Block," Harriett said, "You have a very long drive back to Westhaven. Why don't you spend the night? Adam here has an extra bedroom. I can fix some dinner and we can all get an early start tomorrow." Block smiled and nodded. "Reverend Patrick, we would be honored to have you join us for dinner," Harriett continued. (Harriett could not bring herself to address him as *Father* Patrick.)

While the meal was simple, the conversation ran deep. There was no mention of the recently ended war or things outside, only talk of dreams and building a better world. Calvin Block spoke of his dream to reunite the beauty of the past in the buildings of the present. Father Patrick talked about building people and communities. Adam talked about building a town. Laurel talked about building a school. Henry talked about restoring traditions. And Harriett simply sat and listened, reflecting on the events since the fire. The though occurred to her that this was the first time a Catholic, not to mention a priest, had been in her house. She smiled at the thought.

Somewhere around eleven o'clock Father Patrick looked at his watch. "I have a busy day tomorrow. We have a church to finish you know."

This was the first time for Adam to have anyone overnight in his house. This was also the first time Calvin had spent the night in a house without electricity or indoor plumbing. The following morning Adam found Calvin sitting at his kitchen table with a note pad and some work schedules. "Adam, we are fully ten days ahead of schedule. I figure we can have the furniture in, the carpet laid, the organ placed and be finished in three weeks."

Adam's mouth dropped open, "Three weeks!" The realization that the church would be ready for a wedding in a mere three weeks hit him like a bullet. The reality of his service station and his house being finished left him euphoric but the reality of a wedding however found him in a state of absolute panic. Adam walked over to the Stencil Grocery Store calendar hanging on the wall and began to count. "Mr. Block, can you excuse me for a few minutes? I have to talk with Laurel before she leaves for school." Block nodded and suggested that he drive himself up to the church site and Adam could take his time.

Adam ran, ran as fast as he could down his road and into the lane leading to the Schmidt farm. Harriett saw him through the kitchen window and panicked. "Something is wrong!" she blurted. "Adam is headed this way at full tilt." Laurel dashed out of her bedroom almost fully dressed, meeting Adam as he arrived breathless at the door. "What in the world is wrong Adam?" Laurel pleaded. Trying to catch his breath, Adam sat down on the steps. "Laurel," he panted, "the church is almost finished. Block says that we are ten days ahead of schedule. He says that we will be finished in three weeks! That means our wedding day is almost here. What shall we do?" Adam panted.

Harriett and Laurel laughed aloud. Laurel went inside the kitchen

309

for a brief minute and returned with a calendar, oddly enough, the same Stencil Grocery Store calendar that Adam had on his kitchen wall. "Here," Laurel said quietly pointing to a circled date on the calendar. "this is our wedding day. My school will be finished here," she said pointing to another circled date on the calendar. Mom and I plan to send out the invitations next week and everything else has been taken care of. And you, my fine man simply need to make certain that our house and our church will be ready for the great event. Oh, one more thing, we will need to go to St. John and get you a new suit and a new pair of shoes. I understand that you gave your Sunday suit away to someone wearing a dress." Adam grimaced at the mention of shopping for new clothes and the realization that Laurel knew about the run-away POW. Laurel gave him a hug and stood up. "I have to finish getting dressed and get off to school. I will stop by the church on my way home. See you later." Adam remained on the cement steps, trying to absorb what had just been laid before him. Harriett laid her hand on Adam's shoulder, "Too late to run now. Your days are numbered," she said with a wry smile. Adam, still somewhat dazed by the realization that his wedding day was a mere twenty three days away rose and slowly walked back to his farm. The rest of the day, that one single though kept going through his mind. "Only twenty three more days and she is mine."

38

ADAM ARRIVED AT THE GARAGE and found Rod talking with the well drilling team. "'Morning, boss," Rod said as Adam entered the office. "Good morning, partner," Adam replied. Rod continued, "The guys tell me that the well casing has been completed down to three hundred and twenty five feet. It looks real good and wet. They figure that we can raise the water tank and connect the pump by tomorrow, if not this afternoon. So, where do we go from here?"

Adam thought for a few minutes. Let's plan on setting the tower this afternoon and tank tomorrow. Today, I would like to have the tank section set upright so I can get a good look at it."

The rest of the day, work seemed to go at twice its normal pace. With the end of the project in sight, everyone was painting faster, nailing faster, even talking faster. About four o'clock in the afternoon, Laurel arrived. Adam took her by the arm and moved her inside the empty church. The four stained glass windows were magnificently illuminated by the afternoon sun. It felt strange to be in a church with no pews, no carpet, no alter, and no people. Adam moved Laurel over to where the alter would be. Looking directly into her eyes, he said, "Only twenty three more days." They both smiled and embraced. Adam whispered, "Laurel, I would like your help tonight. If you could come up to the well site after nightfall, I want to give our town a

311

name."

Laurel looked at Adam in a questioning way. "What do you mean, give our town a name?"

Adam replied, "Like I said the other night, I want our town to have a name. I want it to have proper name."

"And just what might that name be?" she queried.

"I will tell you tonight," Adam whispered.

Later that evening, Laurel found Adam at the well site. He had set up a series of wooden saw horses and two inch by twelve inch planks around the metal water tank. Four kerosene lamps had been lit and hung on two-by-fours stuck into the ground. The tank itself had been scraped several days before of all rust and painted with a shiny silver exterior. Adam had a carpenter's pencil in his hand and was making lines with a wooden yard stick as Laurel approached. "Are you going to tell me the name of our new town or do I have to wait?" she asked.

"Laurel, who is the one person who made this whole thing possible?"

"You are Adam. You made it possible for us to build this church and school and ball field. It was your dream to add the service station, the store and the café. Are you saying that you will name the town after you?"

"Not exactly, Laurel."

"You're not thinking of naming it after my father?!" Laurel asked.

"No. The man who caused this whole wonderful thing to happen lies in a grave down there," Adam said pointing to the cemetery several hundred feet from where they were standing.

"You're going to name the town after Adam Becker?!" she asked with a touch of sarcasm.

"No, I am going to name the town after Helmut Sommerfield," Adam whispered.

Laurel looked toward the cemetery. "Sommerfield! That does have a nice feel to it. Sommerfield! Yes, I like it," she said as she put her arms around Adams neck and gave him a kiss. "Sommerfield it is!"

"I am glad you like it," Adam said with a broad smile. "Now, help me paint the name of our new town on the sides of the water tank. I want this to be a surprise when we lift the tank onto the tower tomorrow morning."

For the next four hours Adam and Laurel painted the name of their new town on the tank. It was about midnight when they took two of the lanterns and stood back at a distance examining their work. It seemed a very solemn event to be giving a name to a town, especially the name of a dead man and an enemy soldier at that. Perhaps people would think the name of the town was simply something like Winterfield or Springfield. Or, perhaps they wouldn't care at all. As Adam and Laurel stood there on the top of the small hill, they both felt as if something wonderful was being born.

Laurel broke the silence. "Adam, let's make this more interesting. What do you say if we cover the name until the tank is in place and have a little ceremony?"

Adam smiled and nodded. "How shall we do this?" Adam asked.

"Well, we can't do anything until the paint dries and that could take all night." Laurel thought for a minute. "My dad has a large roll of light canvas that he uses to cover his grain wagons. We could tie some of the canvas around the tank, with a slip knot and a pull string. Then, when everyone is present, we could pull the cover off. You could make a little speech or something."

Adam simply smiled. Laurel was excited. She was happy.

"Wait here, I will be back in a few minutes.

Laurel, still holding the kerosene lantern, moved toward her car. Within minutes, she was back carrying a roll of green canvas and a ball of bailing twine. "We can't put this on until morning. The paint is still wet. Adam, could you come over before it gets light and tie the canvas?" Laurel said in a way that Adam could not refuse, even if he wanted to.

"I will be here before anyone sees our tank," Adam said ardently.

The alarm rang at 4:30 AM only to find Adam awake, trying to take in all the events of the past few months and those yet to come. A thick ground fog covered the land as Adam wrapped the canvas around the outside of the water tank. After several attempts, he managed to tie the canvas on to the tower in a way that would allow for him to unveil the tank in a grand manner. By nine o'clock, most of the workers and many volunteer and spectators had arrived and were sipping coffee at Ross and Rupert's trailer café. As the fog began to lift, Adam, Rod and the drilling crew moved up the hill toward the tower. Sy fired up the truck engine while Rod began to attach the steel cable to the lift hooks on the sides of the tank. Someone in the small crowd yelled out, "Why do you have a covering on the tank?"

Adam smiled and said, "I don't want to get my new tank dirty."

Within an hour, the tank was bolted to the top section of the tower. The canvas covering remained around the tank after the cables had been disconnected. Again someone asked aloud, "Adam, why don't you take the cover off. Your tank isn't going to get dirty."

Adam replied with a broad smile. "At four o'clock this afternoon, I will show you all what is under the cover."

This comment gave rise to much speculation. Again lines began to form at the pay phone in the service station. The rest of the day work on the various projects continued at full tilt. Calvin Block dashed from one project to the next with his new found friend, Father Patrick in tow. Hundreds of details from door knobs to curtain rods were tended to. By 3:30 that afternoon dozens more cars and truck had arrived to see what was under the canvas covering on the water tower. Laurel arrived at 3:45 just as Adam and all those on site began to move toward the shrouded tower on the hill. Laurel ran to where Adam stood, at the base of the tower. "You are just in time," he said to Laurel.

Slowly, Adam began to climb the metal ladder attached to one of the tower legs. Carefully he found his way on to the small platform which ran around the base of the tank. He took a folding pocketknife from his pocket and reached for the twine which held the canvas. A single stroke sent the canvas flying from the tank. Those on the ground responded with a single, "Ah!," as they read the words painted on the sides of the tank. *SOMMERFIELD*. Some wondered aloud, "Shouldn't that be Summerfield?" Others commented that this was something similar to Springfield or Winterfield. From his place at the top of the tower, Adam announced that the town was named after an honorable man who had given his life while saving others—Helmut Sommerfield. By the time Adam had reached the ground, the name seemed to have caught on. It was like naming a new baby. The name seemed to fit. Laurel was delighted and expressed her joy as she embraced Adam. Block came over to where Adam and Laurel were standing. "Adam" he said, "This could be the beginning of something big, very big."

By month's end, all the projects with the exception of the school, the cafe and store were completed. The store and café would require another month. Several baseball games had been played on the new baseball field. The Baptist team, the Big Dippers were ahead in wins. A new pastor had been selected for the new church and would be arriving within a month or so. The county board of supervisors had made dozens of visits to the new "village" as they called it and plans for a hard surfaced road was discussed, as were a stop sign and other symbols of progress. Even though Adam had not planned to move into his new house until the day of his wedding, Laurel strongly suggested that he leave his old house because of its rapidly deteriorating state. And too, the tornado left the outhouse with only three sides standing. That coupled with the fact that Calvin Block was beginning to spend more and more nights at Adams house so he wouldn't have to drive back and forth to Westhaven. That simply wouldn't do.

Adam's

39

THE WEDDING WAS ONLY four days away. Adam and Block were sitting at the kitchen table, well into their second cup of coffee when the phone rang. It was Laurel. She was in a state of panic. "Adam, Rod has come down with chicken pox. He won't be able to be your best man. What will we do? We can't postpone the wedding."

Adam turned to Block and asked, "Cal, could you possibly be my best man on Saturday, Rod is out of the picture."

"Love to," Block replied. "And that was that."

Adam, in a matter-of-fact tone stated that Calvin Block would be standing as his best man. "No problem!"

Laurel seemed more exasperated at the matter-of-fact way Adam dealt with the crisis than the crisis itself. "Men!" she muttered to herself as she hung up the new telephone.

The Friday before the wedding, Roland Wolf knocked on the front door of Adam's new house. Wolf, now happily married and semi-retired appeared twenty years younger and full of life. The stiff military posture had been replaced by a warm, casual countenance.

"Adam, you are a miracle! Your house is fantastic! All of these buildings! I assume you had something to do with these. They are fantastic! God had indeed touched you!"

At that point, Calvin Block entered the room, still in his pajamas and robe.

The presence of Block seemed to move Wolf back into a more guarded stance. After all, this man was not privy to the secret of Adam Becker. Introductions were made; and within a few minutes, eggs and bacon and more coffee were served up. Adam informed Wolf that Cal Block had been his house guest for the past few days, to keep him from running away and that he would be his best man. This brought a round of laughter to the three men. Roland Wolf would also be staying the night in order that he would not have to drive the distance for the rehearsal and for the wedding itself. The new Mrs. Wolf would be coming with Mac and his family the following day for the wedding.

Breakfast took over two hours, interspersed with talk about the unfinished buildings, new drainage problems, and so on. Nothing was said about the wedding a mere twenty-four hours away. While the subject of electrical wiring to the new café was being discussed, the telephone rang. Adam answered. Looking at the black and white cat clock on the kitchen wall, he repeated, "Eleven o'clock. We will be there," and hung up.

Turning to the two men at the table he said, "Laurel wants us at the church in thirty minutes for a rehearsal or something like that."

"Oh yeah, you are getting married tomorrow...or something like that," Calvin chuckled.

"Yeah, something like that," Adam replied grinning from ear to ear.

Calvin hurried upstairs to shave and dress for the day.

"Adam," Wolf said as he put his arm around him, "This is a true miracle. God has created not only a new person but a new generation in this place. I noticed the name on the water tower—Sommerfield— the name of a dead man who is now living as a new man. The name of a man whose former self lies beneath the ground while his name has been lifted up on high. Adam, this is a mighty act of God and not to be taken lightly. This town of yours is a crossroad in God's history."

The weight of Wolf's comments brought tears to Adams eyes.

Adams only comment was, "God is good!"

At that point, Calvin came bounding down the stairs dressed and shaved. "If we leave now, we will have time to stop by the café and take a look at that electrical junction box, and then we can take care of this wedding stuff," Calvin ordered.

Adam combed his hair and put on his shoes. The three men hurried down the dirt road, passed the cemetery and the church to the building site. At exactly eleven o'clock, the Schmidt family, except for Rod, arrived at the new church.

The rehearsal went as rehearsals do—lots of fidgeting on the part of the bride and, of course, the bride's mother. There was much eyeball rolling on the part of the men in the party. After five carefully orchestrated marches down the aisle and several other details, the rehearsal was completed. It was slightly past noon when the wedding party decided to call it complete.

Laurel then announced that she and Harriett had made a picnic lunch and they would be eating in the shade of the water tower on the hill behind the church. Laurel and Harriett drove their pickup from the church to the water tower while the rest of the group walked. After a leisurely lunch of fried chicken, potato salad and lemonade, Calvin asked Adam if he, Adam, could climb to the top of the water tower. Adam agreed. The two men held cautiously to the hand rail which accompanied the foot ramp around the tank. From sixty feet above the ground, the two men could see fifty miles in all directions. A gentle breeze brought a smile to both men's faces. Below them was a wonderful sight—a town in the making. "Adam, tell me where your land lies." Moving toward the north side of the tower, Adam pointed out his property lines. "Who owns the other pieces of land adjacent to yours?" Calvin asked. Adam listed off the three other landowners, including Henry Schmidt. Calvin smiled broadly. Adam asked the reason for the smile. Calvin responded, "Adam, you have enough to worry about now, I will discuss my thoughts with you later."

Adam responded, "Cal, the only thing I am worried about is you falling down. Both men laughed and carefully descended the thin metal ladder.

That evening, Wolf, Calvin, and Adam lounged nervously in Adam's front room. Even though the weather was warm, Adam wanted a fire in his new fireplace. After a meal of canned beans and weenies, the men fell into conversation about the new town. Somewhere around ten o'clock Calvin made a statement. "Adam, I have an idea. I am on the governor's commission for higher education. Now that the war is over, we will have thousands of men returning to our communities. Many of them left when they were mere boys and as a result have no real job skills. The governor is planning to build several state vocational schools for the purpose of training some of these guys in the skills necessary to farm—welding, machinery, and so on. We have been looking for sites near small towns in order to lessen the burden of larger cities and to help smaller towns to grow. Now, here's my idea." The three men focused their eyes on the fire in the fireplace while their attention was locked to Block's every word. "I see a school made up of six or eight buildings, brick buildings, with classrooms, shops, and dormitories. This campus would be situated on that land you pointed out, the land to the north of the water tower. A road would come off the main road, past the school and baseball field. As Block went on to describe the campus and its amenities, Adam and Wolf envisioned the details of each building, walkway, and flower garden. By two o'clock in the morning, the entire plan, complete with pencil sketches had been discussed. At one point in the conversation, Wolf asked with a wry smile on his face, "Cal, would you mind if I were to discuss your plan with Senator Porter? The Senator just may have an interest in something like this." Calvin beamed. "Of course you can mention it to your boss. The more the merrier.

"Speaking of merrier," Wolf bellowed, "young man, you need to get to bed. You're getting married in a few more hours and you will need your sleep."

Block chimed in, "You probably won't be getting much sleep tomorrow night."

The three men laughed a they scorted Adam up the stairs.

Down the road at the Schmidt fa m, the electric lights burned into the night as small strings of seed pearls were being sewn on the already beautiful wedding dress.

The only one who slept that night was Rod. Visions of what was to be filled the happy minds of all those in the Schmidt house and in the Becker house. God was good!

The wedding went as most weddings go. Only, this wedding was different. It was the first event in the new church. Almost without exception, every person who laid a brick or hammered a nail was there. All the pastors from the churches in the area were there to inaugurate the new church. It was packed, with people standing against the back wall and in the aisles. Chaplain Wolf's brief sermon was based on Genesis 2:26, "Therefore, a man shall leave his father and his mother and cleave to his wife and the two shall become one flesh." His theme included reference to II Corinthians 5:17, *if any man be in Christ, he is a new creation.* "The two persons before us becoming yet another new creation, a husband and a wife." Immediately after Chaplain Wolf declared Adam and Laurel to be man and wife, he did something totally different from traditional weddings. He called all of the pastors from the congregation to gather around the bride and groom at the altar. He then asked each of them to pronounce a special blessing on this new family. Father Patrick was the first. The deed was done. Sealed by God and approved by the community. As Adam and Laurel Becker locked arms and strode happily down the aisle, Calvin Block, who had slipped around to the narthex, began pulling on the bell rope. This was the first time the new bell had rung, announcing a milestone in the life of the community. From then on, it would ring to announce the birth, marriage, and passing of all members of the community.

40

THE TOWN HAD GROWN, as had the Becker family. A boy and a girl now filled the extra bedrooms of the Becker house. Laurel arranged to teach in the new school for half a day so she could stay at home with her kids as much as possible. Harriett taught piano in the church basement to dozens of kids from the school and the community. The service station had become a tremendous success, with three full time employees. Rod had built up the well drilling business to where at least one well was being dug at any given time. He and Adam had put together several more drilling rigs for when things got really busy. The school was fully filled out, with some kids from town being bussed in because of overcrowding. Ross and Rupert had developed a full menu of hamburgers, French fries, milkshakes and the like for those wishing to have lunch "in town" or after a ball game. Stencil had his store full of all sorts of new and wonderful items. Mac had even arranged for a small post office to be placed in the front of the store, complete with a drop box and American flag. Each day, the mail truck and the milk truck would drive down the newly paved oil road which ran between North Fork and Barton Center and deliver mail and ice cream for the café. Several other new buildings had been added along the main road—one housing a small hardware store and the other, a twice a week medical clinic. The biggest change of all was the new vocational /agricultural training school located up the hill, behind the water tank. Its ten brick buildings, all in the European style, housed and taught 150 students from all over western Nebraska.

Across the road (now a paved street) was Calvin Blocks's two story brick house. Calvin, now retired from his "city job" was a part time instructor at the Sommerfield Vocational Training School. He and a dozen other "professors" had managed to purchase half acre parcels from Henry Schmidt. The small community became jokingly known as "Lofty Heights." Just to the south of town, Roland and Helen Wolf had a brick house, next to a new Methodist Church. Wolf served as an assistant pastor to a young seminary graduate interested in youth ministries.

Rod married the nurse from the North Fork hospital and built his house across from the service station.

41

THE COMMUNITY OF SOMMERFIELD had grown to somewhere around three hundred souls, including vocational students. The baseball field had become the center of the world for all those who lived within thirty miles. There were baseball games even when it wasn't baseball season. Many times, games were played in the rain or snow. Why not?

It was a cold Monday when Roland Wolf found Adam sitting in the small office of his service station. Wolf entered and closed the office door. "Adam," I have some good news. "Senator Porter is running for election again and would like an excuse to come out here next month. As you know, he loves to grand stand. Do you think we could get up a baseball game between the college kids (as they were called) and some of the local boys?"

"I will get Rod on it right away. Just give me a date and a time and we will plan a real Sommerfield blowout for the Senator," Adam said.

Wolf then placed a large brown manila envelop on the desk between them. "Adam, we found your sister," Wolf whispered.

Adams eyes filled with tear as he looked Wolf straight in the eyes. Without saying a word, Wolf opened the envelope and removed an eight-inch by ten-inch photograph of a young woman and placed it in front of Adam. Adam began to sob. "That's her, that's Greta." The questions began to pour out of Adams mouth between sobs. "Where did you find her? Where is she now? How can I get to her?"

Wolf, overtaken with emotions himself, began to read the notes on another piece of paper from the envelope.

Greta was found in the rubble of your family's farm by the Communist forces in 1945. Because she had no family, she was taken to an orphanage in East Germany. The Soviets found her to be extremely bright and sent her to one of the better schools in the area. From there she was sent to university where she eventually received her doctorate in mechanical engineering. Upon completion of her doctorate, she was sent to a project in Hungary where she met Uri Provit. Uri was a Ph.D. in hydroelectric engineering. They were married in 1949. No children. Three months ago, the Soviets invaded Hungary. Uri was killed in the demonstrations. Your sister was rescued and placed in a refugee camp. Those refugees who had advanced degrees and who were fluent in English were put on the top of the list for international placement. Senator Porter's office received a copy of the list for possible interest. The Senator noticed in your sister's bio data that she has a brother, Helmut Sommerfield and that he had been taken as a prisoner of war. Senator Porter called me in and asked me to look into the matter. I reminded the Senator that Sommerfield had been killed and given a hero's funeral as a result of his actions. The Senator has asked me to ask you if the people of this community would like to sponsor this girl and bring her here."

Adam, still looking deep into Wolf's eyes, said in a whisper, "Yes! Of course! She is my sister."

Wolf shook his head, "No, she was Helmut Sommerfield's sister. If anyone finds out that Helmut Sommerfield is still alive, you will be deported. Everything you have built here will end. Not even Senator Porter could get you out of this situation. If you agree to have her come here, you will have to find a way to keep the truth from the community and the authorities."

Adam continued to stare into Wolf's eyes and nodded.

Taking a deep breath and wiping his nose with a handkerchief, Adam agreed, "We will find a way. Bring her here."

Wolf whispered, "I have already talked with Dr. Hogan over at the tech school. He would be delighted to have another Ph.D. on staff. Somehow, we will arrange for her to teach something or another until we can make some long term arrangements. Actually, Senator Porter was hoping that he would be able to boast that he found a sanctuary for a Hungarian refugee. He sees it as a vote getter."

Adam's head began to spin. What would he tell her? How would he keep the secret from those in the community? Where would she live? What would Laurel say? "I will be right back," Adam said to Wolf.

At that point Adam jumped up and ran toward the school. Finding Laurel on the playground, watching a tetherball match, he pulled here aside and gave her the news. Laurel's shock was almost as great as Adam's. She was delighted. "Of course we will bring her here. She can live with us or we can build her a new house, whatever she wants." Adam kissed Laurel as all the kids on the playground cheered and whistled. Adam ran back to the service station. "Let's do it," Adam beamed. "Let's do it!" Wolf responded as he banged his fist on the table. Wolf handed Becker a handful of papers and a ball point pen. "Here, sign these and I will take it from there," Wolf said with a broad toothy smile. Becker scribbled his name across a dozen or so lines.

The next twenty-seven days were spent getting the guest bedroom ready in the Becker house. Excitement was electric throughout both the Becker and the Schmidt household. There was almost a sense of panic over how the event would be handled. How could the secret be kept from the community and especially the authorities. It would be impossible to keep the truth from Adam's sister. She would certainly find the truth or perhaps even recognize Adam as her brother at the first meeting. She must be told. But then how will the community see the relationship between Adam and this woman? The answer came while Harriett was sitting on the yard swing pealing apples for an apple pie. Her eyes lit up as she ran for the telephone. "Laurel, come over quick. I can't talk on the phone." Within seconds, Laurel was roaring down the road and into the front yard. "What's the matter Momma?"

"I have figured out how we can deal with this problem. We will tell everyone that Adam's sister is a distant relative of Adam's mother and that the authorities in Washington made the connection through some Mormon genealogy project. She can be a long lost cousin. That's not too far off the truth." Laurel thought for a minute. "That's the best answer yet, Momma. A long lost cousin she is."

Roland Wolf had made special arrangements for Senator Porter to present a plaque to one of the buildings at the tech school. This and several other minor functions were set in motion and would include as many local personalities as possible. A lunch with the head of the school, local VIPs, and, of course, all the clergy in the realm was planned for noon. Several side trips to see 4-H projects and to visit wounded veterans were scheduled prior to the big baseball game. Originally, Wolf wanted to have some sort of a dinner for Porter; but the Senator had a better idea. He would buy hot dogs and cokes for all those attending the baseball game. What could be more American than that?

By three o'clock the two ball teams had arrived on the field and were practicing their respective skills. At four, Mac McCloud arrived as did over a hundred others. Porter immediately spotted McCloud and whistled loudly. "Get over here you old coot. We have a baseball game to play." Everyone within earshot exploded in laughter. The wooden bleachers immediately filled and people were standing along both the first base line and the third base line. Rod had arranged for a microphone to be placed on the pitcher's mound. Wolf beckoned Adam, Mac and Sy and asked them to follow him to the center of the McCloud. As the four men stood on the pitchers mound, Sy in his army uniform, Wolf asked a color guard to present the colors. Four local VFW members, all in uniform, walked to the center of the field, in front of the microphone. Sy led the assembly in the Pledge of Allegiance. Roland Wolf followed with a brief invocation and a blessing on all those who made this place and this event possible. Then Wolf began to introduce Senator Porter. After a few words of introduction, Porter grabbed the microphone away from Wolf. "You all know who I am. We don't need any long winded introductions here." Turning to Mac the Senator barked, "Mac, if you can still see, get yourself behind home plate. We need an umpire." Turning to Adam and pulling a baseball from out of a paper bag, he said, "Mr. Becker, I would be honored if you would throw the first ball." Senator Porter handed the ball to Adam. Adam looked at the ball in his hand. Written on the ball in black ink were the words "Camp Alexis, Thanksgiving Day, 1945." Porter knew! Adam's mouth went dry and he froze.

"Well, Mr. Becker, are you going to stand there all day looking at that thing or are we going to play baseball?" the Senator growled into the microphone. Adam swallowed and tossed the ball to the catcher standing behind the plate. The Senator put his arm around Adam as the two walked toward the bleachers.

He knows!

42

ADAM WAS JOLTED BY the sound of a bell ringing a few feet from him. He blinked back a few tears as he looked toward the sound. It was Luther the stationmaster announcing the arrival of the train from the east. "Just got the word, the train is about five minutes down the track. Won't be long now," Luther uttered.

The locomotive passed where Adam was standing and slowed to a halt. A uniformed conductor got down from one of the passenger cars and placed a metal step on the platform. A small, frail woman, carrying a single leather suitcase moved slowly down from the train. Adam recognized her immediately. She looked around at this strange place before seeing Adam standing there. Adam moved toward her as she dropped her suitcase on the cement. The conductor signaled the engineer to move the train on toward its final destination. The two stood on the platform, simply looking at each other. Finally the young woman spoke. "Helmut?"

CPSIA information can be obtained at www.ICGtesting.com
Printed in the USA
LVOW071415150312

273246LV00005B/7/P